ROSIE MEDDON

A Wife's War

CANELO

First published in the United Kingdom in 2019 by Canelo

This edition published in the United Kingdom in 2020 by

Canelo Digital Publishing Limited
Third Floor, 20 Mortimer Street
London W1T 3JW
United Kingdom

Print ISBN 978 1 78863 391 8
Ebook ISBN 978 1 78863 080 1

Look for more great books at www.canelo.co

Printed and bound in Great Britain by Clays Ltd, Elcograf S.p.A.

April 1915

Chapter One

Amends

'I'm sick of this war.' Squeezing another couple of books into the top of the wooden packing crate, Kate Channer shook her head in frustration. 'I loathe it. No, I don't loathe it, I *hate* it. I hate it with a… with a *passion*.'

From the other side of the desk, Naomi Colborne leant across and patted her hand. 'My dearest Kate,' she said, 'so do I. Indeed, I can't imagine there's a soldier's wife in the land who doesn't feel the same way.'

While probably true, Kate was in no mood to be consoled. Her husband was away at war and she missed him. She wanted him back.

'No sooner were the rings on our fingers,' she continued, standing back to gauge the remaining space in the crate, 'than our husbands were sent off Lord-knows-where to do heaven-only-knows-what. And them few days of leave aside, we ain't seen hide nor hair of them since. Is it too much to ask the powers-that-be to let them come home from time to time? Or even to send word of their well-being now and again? Do we wives count for nothing?' Reaching for another book, she pressed it on top of the others and, not waiting for Naomi to reply, went on, 'I don't blame our menfolk for volunteering,

2

ma'am, truly I don't, but honest to goodness, I do surely rue the day they did.'

'I know,' Naomi agreed, 'the longer they're gone, the harder it becomes. But we must bear our burden without complaint. Our husbands did a brave thing, and the least we can do is bear their absence with grace.'

Grace. Hm. *Not* one of her fortes at the best of times. 'It *is* terrible brave of them, 'course it is,' she conceded, 'doing what they did without a moment's thought as to the perils of it, but at least they *chose* to do it. You an' me, on the other hand, had no say in the matter. *You an' me* are just left to wait and wonder and worry. But do the army care one jot for our nerves?'

'It would seem not, no.'

'Worse than that,' she pressed on, Naomi's words of agreement barely registering as she tried to wedge a particularly weighty tome onto the topmost layer of books, 'but it's doing shameful things to good folk – good folk like poor Mr Latimer.'

'I know. That it should come to this is so terribly sad.'

Heaving a lengthy sigh, Kate stepped back from the crate and surveyed the remaining books. When she had first learnt from Naomi that they were to travel back down to Woodicombe, she had struggled to hide her dismay. Having settled quite happily into her new life in Hartland Street, Devon had come to feel a world away, events at Woodicombe – such as they were – having long since become of no consequence to her. Indeed, being back there now, she felt out of place: no longer properly one thing nor the other – neither family nor staff.

Staff, huh. There was another thing; apart from poor old Mr Channer – doing his best to see to everything

3

outdoors all by himself – the only people now left below stairs were Edith and Mabel. According to the latter, in their rush to take on the jobs vacated by their enlisting menfolk, the dozen or so day girls and kitchen maids had left without so much as a backward glance: a couple of them going to take over the milking of the cows on Abe Pardey's farm; a couple more going to learn the ropes in their uncle's bakery; others choosing to risk life and limb fishing from dayboats whose crews had been left short-handed by departing brothers and cousins. Reflecting upon it all now, she shook her head. Not *so* long ago, she would have admired them for their courage and envied them their escape. Thankfully, she no longer needed to; she had a new life of her own now. Mercifully, it no longer mattered to *her* that with the loss of those girls – and the disappearance of their good-natured gossip and cheery chatter – below stairs had come to resemble a museum, a forlorn collection of lifeless rooms and echoing corridors.

Lost in her ruminations, she sighed. Throughout the seemingly endless railway journey down from London, she had sat hoping that, once back in her former home, she wouldn't be overcome by regret at having left. As it had turned out, she needn't have worried, the sheer soullessness of the place meaning that no sooner had they set foot in the porch than she was itching to be back in Hartland Street.

The wooden crate in front of her now packed to the point where not a single further book could be accommodated within, she heaved a vexed sigh. It was a sad state of affairs when a nice man had to sell a house that had been in his family for hundreds of years. Maybe even *hundreds and hundreds* of years. But then just about everything to do with this war was turning out to be unfair. If nothing else, the government had promised them it would be over and done with by now, the enemy defeated, the country jubilant, their menfolk safely back where they belonged.

'I still don't see why us being at war with the Germans means Mr Sidney has to sell *this* place,' she said, casting her eyes over the row of book-filled crates.

'Well, as I explained to you the other day, it came about because—'

Listening to Naomi once again explaining the reason for the sale of the house did nothing to change her mind; they were still having to pack up all of Mr Latimer's possessions, and he was still losing his family's home.

'Shouldn't nobody be made to sell up their house and all their belongings just because some mazed war has made their... their *whatever-they-ares*... worthless.'

'Their stockholdings.'

'Aye, them things. Poor Mr Sidney.' She glanced to the rows of empty shelves, the only evidence now that several generations of Latimers had once collected books being the rectangular shapes left behind in the dust. 'Still, fortunate for *him*, I suppose,' she conceded wearily, 'that your father had the means to buy it from him—'

'*Our* father – that *our* father had the means.'

'—sparing him the embarrassment of a full-blown sale – half the county traipsing in, picking over his knick-knacks, eyeing up the paintings and criticising the curtains.'

'Yes,' Naomi agreed, 'I suppose that *would* have been worse.'

'What'll he do with it anyway?' she asked, watching Naomi move away to look out through the window.

'Do with it? I'm afraid I don't understand you. What will who do with what?'

'Mr Russell,' she said, staring back down at the packed crate. 'What is he minded to do with the place? Only, last time he was here, seemed to me he couldn't wait to get away from it and back to London.'

Across the room from her, Naomi looked thoughtful. 'To be honest, I don't know,' she said. 'He didn't say – at least, not to me he didn't. Other than wanting to help Uncle Sidney, I'm not sure he gave it much thought.'

'Hm.'

'It will be nice to have it in the family, though, don't you think?'

She frowned. 'Not sure I follow you, ma'am.'

'Well, one day, we will be able to bring our children and spend the summer here. There's so much space for playing games and running around. And then there's the cove where they'll be able to learn to swim. Lawrence will love teaching them. He's a terribly good swimmer.'

Arching her back against the onset of stiffness, she tried to picture what Naomi was describing. She couldn't recall there ever being children at Woodicombe – certainly not young ones. 'I won't deny it,' she said, picturing chubby-legged infants toddling about in the hallways, 'a family *would* bring the place alive. But, to my mind, with the way *we're* both fixed, the coming about of children is a long way off. Won't neither of *us* be finding ourselves in the family way any time soon – least, not while our husbands are away fighting this war, we won't. In any event, I can't say as I feel ready for such things. I scarce feel like a wife yet, let alone a mother.' It was true, too; the longer the war ground on, the less and less she felt like a married woman.

And it was beginning to make her resentful. 'And I don't know who to blame for it most – the blessed Germans or all those doddery old men in our own government.'

'But you are looking forward to starting a family, aren't you?'

She shrugged her shoulders. With Luke away, the question struck her as moot. 'S'pose,' she said flatly. 'Once I've had the chance to be a proper wife for a bit first.'

With Naomi making no move to comment, she glanced across the vast walnut desk to see her studying the cover of one of the few remaining books yet to be packed.

'*Great Expectations*,' Naomi announced. 'By the look of it, a first edition. I remember reading this story at school. It's the one about the orphaned child.'

Without stopping to think, Kate scoffed. 'An orphaned child? Not much fun to be had from a tale about an orphan, I shouldn't think.'

Carefully, Naomi closed the book. 'Oh, I don't know, an abandoned child and a tale of rags-to-riches always holds a certain appeal, does it not?'

She shook her head. Where was the attraction of reading about hardships? Stories were supposed to tell of heroic adventures, or the search for true love, not the woes of orphans. Honestly, the whole world really did seem to be turning upside-down. 'If you say so, ma'am.'

'Kate, my dear Kate, I did ask that when it's just the two of us together, you call me Naomi.'

'I know you did, ma'am. *Naomi*. But, like I said to you at the time, I do fear that once it became a habit, I should slip up in front of company.' That, she reflected, and the fact that she just didn't seem able to do it; *Naomi* didn't roll off the tongue without forethought in the same way that *ma'am* did.

'Well, I shan't insist either way. The last thing I want is for you to feel uncomfortable.'

'No, I know that… ma'am. It just seems to me easier if I stick with the one thing.'

'As you wish.'

'Anyhow,' she picked up again, 'later on, I'll fetch Mr Channer down to nail the lids onto these crates. Then, once you've written out the labels, they'll be all set for fetching by the porter.'

Naomi nodded. 'I'll attend to it straight after luncheon. Thank you for seeing to it all.'

'Just doing what had to be done,' she replied, at the same time drawn to examining her fingertips. Heavens, they were going to need a good long scrub with carbolic. 'But now, if we're done here, I'd best go and wash my hands.'

Not *so* long ago, being able to pack up every trace of her past and forget about it was something she had craved. So why, now that she was dismantling what felt like the last little bits of it, did she feel overcome by such a deep sadness? Surely, given all that had happened within and around these four walls in the last year, things were turning out for the best, weren't they? She had a new home and new employment. She could put Woodicombe behind her, couldn't she?

Beside her, Naomi stood examining her own hands. 'Mine smell musty, too,' she said. 'But, before we go, there's something I've been wanting to tell you.'

Detecting a change to Naomi's tone, Kate settled for wiping her hands down her apron. 'Yes, ma'am?'

8

'Although, once I have, you cannot repeat it to anyone.'

Intrigued, she straightened up. What was this then? 'Swear I won't breathe a word.'

'I know you won't,' Naomi remarked, 'which is why I feel able to tell you that… I think I'm expecting a baby.'

In that split of a second, Kate felt as though her breath had become stuck somewhere in her chest. Naomi was going to have a baby? *That's* what all the talk of children and holidays had been in aid of?

Momentarily too muddled to know how to reply, she frowned deeply. 'N–not sure I understand,' she stammered. Then, feeling her face reddening, she hastened to add, 'What with Mr Lawrence so long gone, I mean.'

Opening her mouth to reply, Naomi cast her eyes towards the partly open door to the hallway. Then, very softly, she said, 'Well, you see, I do believe I'm already quite far along. When it comes to keeping track of my dates, I've always been quite the scatterbrain – an embarrassing thing to have to admit, I know. That said, I'm certain I've missed three months.'

Three months. Now it made sense.

'The menfolk had those few days of leave in January…'

'Precisely. Which is why I don't believe I'm mistaken.'

Goodness. Naomi was going to start a family. When she'd mentioned having something to tell her, she hadn't been expecting it to be *that* – hadn't been expecting it to be *joyous* news. *Joyous*. Hm. If it was so joyous, why wasn't she rushing to offer congratulations? Why did she feel as though she'd lost the use of her tongue? Yes, it was something of a shock, but that alone couldn't account for why she was feeling so… but so *what*? What *was* she feeling? Unsettled? Disturbed? Panicked? Panicked. Yes, among other things she could definitely feel panic. But there was also relief; after all, it could have been *her* finding out that *she* was expecting a child. And the thought of that was nothing short of alarming. As she'd said only moments earlier, she barely felt married, let alone broody. It was true that she'd been Luke's wife for more than seven months now but, in all of that time, they had spent less than ten days together. *And less than ten nights.* Indeed, only the other day, Naomi had joked that some women spent longer than that on their honeymoon. So how any husband and wife could welcome starting a family when they'd spent so little time together, she didn't know. *She* certainly didn't feel ready. And she didn't think Luke would, either. Or would he? He'd made no secret of wanting children – four or five by his last reckoning. But that had been last summer – before he had sworn an oath and gone to war. Who knew what he thought now? She certainly didn't.

Realizing with a jolt that she had drifted off into her thoughts, she looked back up. Naomi was staring at her, her expression one of curiosity. And so, despite feeling deeply unsettled, and forcing herself to smile, she sidestepped the wooden packing-crates and reached to take Naomi's hands.

'But, ma'am, that's tremendous!' she said, giving them a quick squeeze and then letting them go. 'Why wouldn't you want no one knowing such a fine bit of news as that?'

'I suppose because it feels only right that Lawrence should be the first to hear of it.'

'Will you be writing to him, then?' she asked. 'Or will you be a-wanting to see the doctor first? Ma says there's a new man hereabouts – a Doctor Huntleigh. Apparently, he's a sight more purposeful than old Doctor Brinsworthy ever was – a good deal younger, too. You could telephone for him to come out. Ma says he goes about his house calls in a new motorcar.'

To her suggestion, she was surprised to see Naomi shake her head.

'No, I think I'd prefer to wait until we're back in Hartland Street. After all, whether I am expecting or whether I'm not won't change just because I delay finding out, will it? No, I'll make it my first task once we get home. And *then* I shall write to Lawrence.'

'He'll be proper thrilled, won't he?' she said. *Astonished* was the actual word that had come to mind.

'I suppose he will be, yes. Although perhaps somewhat astounded, too,' Naomi agreed. 'I mean, they were home barely four days. Almost half of their week's leave was taken up with travelling.'

Casting her mind back, she smiled. Their poor husbands had arrived home in a state of utter exhaustion. 'Weren't best pleased by that, were they?' she said, recalling how the first thing Luke had done was sleep for more than twelve hours straight.

'They were not,' Naomi agreed. 'But better a few brief days than none at all.'

'Most surely.'

'Anyway,' Naomi continued, folding back her cuff to peer at her wristwatch, 'to more mundane matters. With everything on Uncle Sidney's list now taken care of, tomorrow morning I shall check the railway timetable and see about booking our tickets for the Paddington train. And, since that will mean making a trip into the village, why don't we call in to that nice tea room afterwards and have a little treat?'

She smiled. It was a nice idea. 'I'd like that,' she said.

'In the meantime,' Naomi added as she started to turn away, 'don't forget what you said to me about wanting to have a proper chat with Mrs Bratton and Edith. *Clear the air*, was how I think you put it.'

In dismay, she shook her head. That old chestnut again. 'To be fair, ma'am,' she said, choosing her words carefully, 'I think *clear the air* was how *you* put it.'

'Well, irrespective of who said what, you know my view – one should never leave bad feelings to fester. And so, since we unexpectedly find ourselves back here, you have the perfect opportunity to make the first move – to be the better woman. Proffer the olive branch and bring about a reconciliation.'

Proffer the olive branch. That was all very well for Naomi to say; *she* didn't have to face Edith. Annoyingly, though, it didn't change the fact that she was right. Matters between her and Edith and Mabel *had* been left somewhat unresolved and did continue to sit uneasily with her – did still gnaw away at her conscience even from a distance of two-hundred-odd miles. So, yes, she really ought to go down and have a proper chat with them. *Reconcile.* But not right now, though. No, she'd make time for that later. She'd need to get herself into the right sort of mood before taking on *that* task.

Following Naomi out of the study, she pulled the door closed, her thoughts returning to news of the baby. She was happy for her, of course she was. But piercing her happiness was still that odd little prickle of what could only really be envy. Why? By her own admission, she was relieved not to find herself in the same position. Perhaps, then, it had more to do with how thrilled Naomi seemed. That could be it: perhaps what she envied wasn't so much that Naomi was going to start a family, but that she was so delighted by the prospect.

Realizing that yet again she had become lost in her thoughts, she straightened up and looked about the hallway. With Naomi gone to freshen up, she might as well make the effort to go down and see Edith and Mabel – get it over and done with.

The decision made, she set off with a purpose but, when she reached the service corridor, she faltered, her mind still on the matter of marriage and families. She wished everything between her and Luke didn't feel so *up in the air*. She wished she felt more married. For years Luke had kept pressing her to wed, and throughout those same years her response had been to shilly-shally. But then, when they *had* finally tied the knot, it had been with unimaginable haste – the recently declared war leaving them little choice but to get on with it. And, although it was something to which she would never admit, she had *still* been beleaguered by doubts as to whether she was doing the right thing even while she had been delivering her vows. In the end, she'd simply reminded herself that the chance to get out of Woodicombe was too good an opportunity to let slip.

Now, though, her doubts long gone, the only regret she still harboured was that it *had* all happened in such a rush, the brevity of events leaving her struggling to recall her own wedding day. Even their wedding night – something she would have expected to recall in great detail – was difficult to bring to mind with any clarity. Through a generous and surprising gesture from Mr Lawrence – a wedding gift, he had said – she and Luke had spent their first night as husband and wife in a room at The Ship at Anchor in Westward Quay. When Luke had broken the news to her a couple of days beforehand, the prospect of such a luxury had left her giddy with excitement. But, once in that lofty room, with its sloping floor and vast four-poster bed, their time together had been overshadowed by the knowledge that, within days, they would be heading in different directions – Luke destined for a place in Wiltshire neither of them had ever heard of; herself, for the time being, back to Woodicombe House. Looking back on it now, the whole thing had been a blur, the speed with which it had been over and done with making it easy to see why she scarcely felt married at all.

Mercifully, within days of Luke departing, Naomi had written to say that Mr Lawrence had found a house to rent. It was at number twelve, Hartland Street, in an area of London called Marylebone. Enclosed with the letter had been money for her train fare and instructions to help her find the address. Her new life in London beckoned. Finally, and despite at the last minute feeling woefully underprepared, she was on her way out of Woodicombe!

She shook her head ruefully. Dear old Woodicombe. Having been gone these last months, the whole place now struck her as so very antiquated. She supposed it was only to be expected. Since leaving, she had become a housekeeper in her own right – in a modern home in a smart street in a vast and vibrant city. Her longed-for life of meaning and purpose had finally come about. The only thing left to wish for now was that Luke would hurry up and return from this godforsaken war and that together, they could finally get on with making a proper married life.

Sadly, if reports from the front were to be believed, it was going to be some while yet before that particular wish was granted.

–

'I see London suits you, then.'

Having finally mustered her courage, Kate had arrived in the kitchen to talk to Mabel and Edith. But being greeted by such a snide remark now put her in two minds about turning around, walking away, and forgetting the whole idea. The only thing preventing her from doing so was picturing the disappointment that would come across Naomi's face; Naomi hated things left unresolved. Besides which, she needed to do this; she needed to clear her conscience and lay the matter to rest, once and for all.

And so, looking at the two women sitting across the table from one another, she told herself to ignore the uncalled-for tone of Edith's greeting and get on with it.

'Aye,' she replied, 'I'll own to having grown used to the place.'

'Wouldn't do for me,' Edith was quick to respond, 'all them folk living cheek-by-jowl. All that dirt and noise and commotion.'

There it was again: the disparagement; the derision. Well, she would ignore it. She had come to mend fences.

''Course,' she began, holding her voice as level as she could to disguise how rattled she felt, 'a good deal of what goes on up there – and the ways of some of the folk – still strikes me as foreign. That said, for the most part, I'm coming to learn what's what.'

'Bought you a whole new wardrobe, I see,' Edith remarked next, her eyes not lifting from her knitting. To Kate, it appeared she was close to completing a pair of shapeless grey bedsocks. What a spinster-like thing to be doing! Not helping the picture was that with her mousy-brown hair pulled tightly back into a knot at the nape of her neck, and a deep frown of either displeasure or concentration on her forehead, the poor woman looked well beyond two-score years, rather than still the right side of it. 'Didn't want you seeming too *Devon* in front of her London friends?' Edith interrupted her thoughts. 'Was that it?'

'You have to understand,' she said, brought back to the present by the scathing tone of Edith's observation, 'it's different in town. In town, *everyone's* smart. So, yes, since I had nothing to suit, she most generously bought me a couple of frocks for going about in. Rest of the day I'm in livery and an apron same as yourself.'

'And another thing,' Edith continued regardless, 'what do *he* want with buying *this* place? Can't intend any good by it, that's for sure.'

'Edith, love——' When Mabel Bratton made to inter-vene, Kate looked across the table at her. '——for certain he means no harm by it, either.'

'Be-as-t'will, you'd think he'd done enough damage for one lifetime.'

Damage? If Naomi's supposition was true, then for once in his life, the man had actually been trying to do some good. 'If by *he* you mean Mr Russell,' she said, keeping a tight check on her frustration with Edith's manner, 'then I think you'll find he meant it as a favour to Mr Sidney.'

'Huh.'

'I don't suppose you'd happen to know, love,' Mabel apparently saw this as her chance to ask, 'just what Mr Russell's plans for the place are? Only, since this war's been on, we've lost all of the staff. And if he was thinking to use the place again, in particular for entertaining, well, I can't see how we would cope...'

At least *her* concern was reasonable, Kate thought.

'Can't say as I've heard of his plans,' she said. 'Only this morning I asked Mrs Colborne that very thing. But she doesn't know either. So, strikes me that for now at least, nothing has changed. Besides—'

'*Nothing has changed?* Maybe not for you it hasn't.'

Her feet still itching to turn about and carry her away, Kate forced herself to draw a long breath. If Naomi was right about one thing, it was that she had to see this through – and that meant despite Edith being a cantankerous old shrew. In a way, the woman's continued crabbiness ought to make it easier for her to be the bigger person. She might not be able to do anything about the facts of her birth, but she *could* make peace with them. If nothing else, she owed it to herself to lay them to rest and get on with her new life.

'Anyways,' she said to that end, forcing herself to adopt a lightness of manner she didn't feel, 'strikes me what's called for here is a clearing of the air.' Ha! That had got their attention. They hadn't been expecting to hear *that* from her. Edith, for sure, had been expecting her to gloat. Reminded of Naomi's thoughts on the matter, she went on, 'I never did like how things got left between us and so, this would seem a good time for the extending of an olive branch.'

Unable to bring herself to look at Edith, she instead directed her attention to Mabel. Were her eyes paler than she remembered them? For certain her hair was thinner. Somehow, she looked shorter, too. She supposed it was simply that she was growing old.

'An olive branch, love?'

'Yes,' she replied, '…an olive branch.' But, as quickly as she had started, she faltered. Where, all of a sudden, were all those words that, only moments ago, had been bursting from her head? Well, having started, she had little choice but to go on as best she could and so, to that end, she cleared her throat, looked at Mabel, and said, 'See, that day when things about me and the… circumstances of my birth… *came to light*… it was you who said that despite how things had turned out, nothing need change. At the time I couldn't see it – 'though happen I didn't want to. Any rate, over these last few months, I've come to realize that you were right. You, Mabel, are still the woman who raised me. And you, Edith, are still the sister I grew up with. More than that, though, being away from here has helped me see that what the pair of you did back then, you did with the best of intentions.' From Mabel's direction there came a little sob but, already grappling to keep her own shakiness in check, she hurried on. 'Edith, it must have been dreadful hard on you. Like you said to us that day, you had a daughter, and yet you didn't. Well, I don't need to have had a babe of my own to know just how sorely you must have wished that otherwise. On the other hand, I can quite see how it could never have been.' Briefly, she stopped to draw a proper breath. *Nearly there*. 'Nonetheless, it would be untruthful of me to let you think I could ever look upon you as anything other than

18

my sister – for I couldn't. What *has* changed, though, is that I no longer bear you malice. You were wronged – by *my* reckoning, twice over. Maybe even more than twice over. But, if you're truly honest with yourself, you'll see how, at this point in my life, I couldn't possibly take easy to calling you *Ma.*'

'Love—'

At Mabel Bratton's interjection, Kate looked across at her and, fixing her gaze, determined to keep going. 'But *you,*' she said, 'you *were* my Ma – leastways, the only Ma I ever knew. No matter the circumstances of my coming into this world, from a sense of love and duty, you raised me for your own. And so, seems only right and proper that I keep referring to you as such. So, that's how I should like us to go on – if that sits right with the pair of you.'

When she finally paused, it was to see that both women had started to cry.

'Yes, love,' Mabel Bratton said, hurrying towards her and reaching for her hand. 'Though I can only speak for myself, I should like that greatly. For certain it would make the seeing-out of the rest of my days that much easier to bear.'

When Mabel then moved to put her arms around her, the familiar aroma of lily-of-the-valley soap and the feel of woollen-worsted against her cheek finally brought tears to her own eyes, too. Easing herself from Mabel's embrace, she wiped at them with the back of her hand.

Behind her, Edith was also now getting to her feet. 'If you've made your peace with the truth,' she said, speaking properly for the first time, 'then I've no right to ask anything more of you. When all's said and done, I'd rather we got along as sisters than not at all.'

'Well, then,' she said, giving Edith's shoulder a quick squeeze, 'from here on, that's how it'll be. And needn't nobody 'cept the three of us be concerned with it.'

'And, once you're back up there in London,' Mabel Bratton picked up again, dabbing at her cheeks with her handkerchief, 'happen you'll write to us from time to time – you know, let us know how you're going along.'

'Tell of all the sights for those of us as shall never see them with our own eyes,' Edith joined in, her eagerness seemingly genuine. 'For I should like most dearly to hear of Buckingham Palace and the King, should you ever see him abroad in his carriage.'

Somehow, despite brimming with all manner of feelings, Kate managed to raise a smile. 'I shall see if I can't buy a postcard of the palace to send you – a tinted one, no expense spared.' In the circumstances, it felt the least she could do for the woman she had spent her entire childhood taunting and despising, and then casting aside with little more than a perfunctory wave from the window of a departing railway carriage.

Surprised to feel her limbs softening with the relief of being done with it, she smiled warmly. Naomi, it seemed, had been right: it really was never too late to make amends.

–

'Oh, good, it's from Ned. I've been hoping he would write.'

It was the following morning and, lifting the empty toast rack onto her tray, Kate nodded. Although interested in Ned's well-being, she nevertheless tried not to get drawn into talking about him, the events of last summer still having the power to make her feel all hot and sticky with embarrassment. And worryingly sad sometimes, too.

That being the case, she stuck, as she usually did when his name was mentioned, to giving only the most general of replies. 'That's nice.'

She had been about to clear away Naomi's breakfast things when, hearing the rattle of the letterbox, she had gone through to the porch and retrieved the single envelope that had dropped onto the doormat.

Recognising the handwriting, Naomi had wasted no time slitting it open and extracting the single sheet of notepaper from inside.

Watching her now scanning the length of the page, Kate pushed her hand down into the pocket of her uniform until her fingers touched the corner of the battered envelope containing Luke's last letter to her. In the absence of anything since, she had taken to carrying it about with her, just to feel a little less abandoned. She knew its contents by heart. Even so, seeing Naomi reading news from Ned, she felt a sudden need to be comforted by it.

Slipping out into the hallway, she pulled it from her pocket, slid out the single sheet of paper and, skipping the line that began, *Dear Kate*, started to read.

Sorry I haven't written in a while but we are miles from anywhere and real busy. Thank you for sending all your news from Marylebone. Receiving word from you keeps me going.

My duties, driving in these bad conditions, are tiring but at least I usually only do it during the daytime and then get to sleep in a bunk in a barn

> *at night. Some lads can't do that, being on duty*
> *at all hours. Despite us being promised it, the food*
> *has got no better than when I last wrote but the*
> *lads I am with here are like brothers to me now.*

Although reading of it for the umpteenth time, she nevertheless felt her lips curl into a smile. It helped her to know that at least he had good company.

When she looked back down, and his words blurred in front of her, she hastened to wipe at the corner of her eyes. Then, with an unexpected little sob, she tried to concentrate on reading all the way to the end.

> *Thank you for the socks. They are just right. And*
> *thank you for the photograph. Please thank Mrs*
> *Colborne for thinking to take you to get one done*
> *for me. You look so pretty I can't believe you are*
> *finally my wife. I look at it first thing each and*
> *every morning and again last thing every night.*
> *Rest of the day it's tucked safe and sound inside*
> *my breast pocket.*

Feeling tears coming more quickly now, she hastily folded the letter along its original crease and slid it into its envelope. Then, withdrawing from her apron pocket a handkerchief, she blew her nose. She didn't need to read the ending, anyway; she knew it word-perfect.

> *Do not worry for me. I am as safe as I can be here.*
> *I do hope this war ends soon and I can be back*
> *with you before much longer.*
> *All my love,*
> *Luke*

Sniffing a couple of times, she crept back towards the door and peered into the dining room. Seeing Naomi still reading, she went back in.

'He writes that he was in town on weekend leave and is disappointed to have missed me,' Naomi glanced up to say.

'I suppose that would be disappointing, yes.'

'He goes on to say that by the time I read this—' With that, she saw Naomi turn over the envelope and examine the franking mark on the stamp before continuing, '—he will have reported to Farnborough, where he is to join No. 2 Squadron and fly a BE2 – at least, I think that's what it says – that awaits delivery to France. He says he's hopeful of getting one of the new-type aeroplanes because they have – goodness, his handwriting is *dreadful* – well, it looks as though it says *wormless*, no wait, wireless... sending... apparatus. Not that I'm any the wiser. He writes that he has now flown twenty solo hours and is very much looking forward to crossing the English Channel. Apparently, being able to go along at a speed of seventy miles an hour and look down upon everything from above is exhilarating. He also writes that once up there, it is freezing cold. Goodness, you'd think, wouldn't you, that being closer to the sun would make it warmer, not colder.'

Crossing to the table, Kate reached for the silver cruet and put it on her tray. She didn't know what to think about it. She did know that the idea of anyone flying over the sea smacked of recklessness. With nowhere to land if things went wrong, it had to be madness. And that was without trying to imagine what a speed of seventy miles an hour might feel like. It had to be faster than even the worst of the winter gales that tore in from the Atlantic with no regard to neither man nor beast.

Deciding not to burden Naomi with her concerns, she opted instead to say, 'France. That's where Luke and Mr Lawrence are.'

'It is, yes.'

'Perhaps Mr Edwin will see them there.'

Judging by the depth of Naomi's frown, she realized it was probably a daft thing to suppose; if France was as big as England, they could be hundreds of miles apart.

'It's always possible,' Naomi nonetheless agreed. 'Although, realistically, I should imagine the chances of that happening to be quite low. Judging by the maps one sees drawn in the *Telegraph*, our army appears to be spread far and wide.'

'Do you think they might be due some more leave soon?' she asked, talk of Ned leaving her once again longing to have Luke back. She did so long to be a proper wife. Sadly, the more time that passed without him, the less she seemed able to picture what that would even be like. She supposed the same must be true for him, too.

Across the table from her, Naomi refolded the sheet of paper and slipped it back into the envelope. 'One can only hope. Although, if we're getting anywhere close to winning this war, I'd rather they stayed there, saw it through to the end, and *then* came home. I want Lawrence back for good – as I'm sure you do Luke – so that we can get on with our lives, especially now, with a baby coming. I do so heartily detest existing in this peculiar state of limbo.'

Idly, Kate refolded a spare napkin. She hated it more than almost anything. What wife wouldn't? She'd heard recently that the newspapers had coined a phrase for women like her and Naomi. *War wives*, they'd taken to calling them – patriotic women who had seen their husbands off to fight without a moment's complaint nor thought for their own hardship. There was even that song by Ivor Novello that everyone kept singing, *Till the Boys Come Home* which exhorted wives to 'keep the home fires burning'. If only that was all there was to it.

Her thoughts returning to Naomi's remark, she looked across the table. 'Back before Christmas, that's what they said when they left.'

Naomi sighed. 'They did. Although I suppose the best I can hope *now*, is that Lawrence arrives back before this baby comes.'

What? 'You think they might be away for another *six months*?'

Lifting her napkin from her lap, Naomi crumpled it onto her plate. 'No, what I'm saying is that they had better not be.'

For a woman with a husband fighting in France and a baby on the way, she thought Naomi Colborne looked remarkably calm – certainly calmer than she thought *she* would feel in the same situation.

Watching her pick up Ned's letter and then put it down again, she said, 'Does Mr Edwin say anything else?'

'What? Oh, no, not really. I think he just wanted to let me know where he's being sent. Since he didn't see fit to cross through the Clarence Square address at the top of the page, I can only imagine he doesn't expect to be away for very long. Anyway, once we're back at home, I shall call upon Mamma and see when he's due to return so that *next* time he is in town, we don't miss each other.'

'That's a good idea.'

'And, upon the matter of *home*, I suppose we had best get on and make our arrangements to return there. We'll go to the railway station, make our booking, and then pop along to that little tea room.'

'And after that, I'd best go up and say goodbye to Mrs Channer,' she said. 'Poor old soul, it must be hard on her, too, hearing nothing from Luke from one month to the next.'

'It must indeed,' Naomi agreed, rising to her feet. 'The longer this war goes on without a victory, the harder it becomes for all of us. Do you know, it said in the newspaper yesterday that over one and a half million men have now volunteered, which made me realize that there must be a similar number of women left behind to fear for them – not just wives, but mothers, sisters… daughters. Makes me feel mean about moaning,' she observed, 'if there's so many of us in the same boat.'

'Me too.'

'We *did* say, ma'am, that we would try to find a way to volunteer,' she remarked as she cleared the remaining few items from the table to her tray.

'We did, yes. And we shall. Once we're settled back at home I shall telephone cousin Elizabeth and ask her advice. She's bound to know of something we might do to help.'

Cousin Elizabeth. Ned. 'Yes, ma'am,' she said. 'That'll take our minds off things.' *All sorts of things.*

'And before we know it, the baby will be here. And no doubt *then*, we'll rue having ever moaned about struggling to fill our days.'

Unable to help but laugh in agreement, Kate lifted her tray from the table. 'I daresay we shan't know ourselves, ma'am, no.'

Perhaps, then, she reflected as she went along the hall and negotiated the door at the top of the stairs, a baby would be just the thing to bring some purpose into their lives. With precious little else to occupy their days, it might also stop them from dwelling quite so much on the continual lack of news from their husbands. As for how she was going to quell that nagging pang of envy, though, she had no idea. Perhaps being back in London would see it off.

She sighed heavily. London. The truth was, she couldn't wait to be back there. More than anything, though, she longed to be able to get on with making a proper life – a life that didn't involve all this waiting about and hoping for an end to the war, just so that she might have Luke back by her side, where he should have been all along.

Chapter Two

The Visitor

'I'm sorry to disturb you, Mrs Colborne, ma'am, but you've a gentleman caller asking to see you.'

It was mid-afternoon and Kate was in the drawing room, seated across from where Naomi was reclined upon the chaise longue.

'A visitor, Mrs Bratton? For me?' At such unexpected news, Naomi swung her legs smartly down to the floor. When she then pushed her feet into her shoes, Kate quickly arose from her own seat and bent to fasten them for her.

'Ordinary times, ma'am, I wouldn't have admitted anyone,' Mabel Bratton went on, 'but it's Lieutenant Colborne – Lieutenant *Aubrey* Colborne, perhaps I ought more properly say.'

At the mention of Aubrey, Kate felt her pulse quicken, a glance to Naomi's face suggesting that she was similarly astonished.

'Aubrey? Good heavens. What on earth is *he* doing all the way down *here*?'

Yes, Kate thought, raising herself back to her feet, what on earth could have brought *him* back to Woodicombe? Hopefully it wouldn't turn out to be distressing news from the front.

'He didn't say, ma'am,' Mabel Bratton replied. 'He just announced himself and asked whether you would receive him.'

Without meaning to, Kate frowned. What an odd thing.

'Goodness,' Naomi remarked. 'Does he look… well, does he look at all upset?'

She held her breath. *Please say no*, she willed.

'No, ma'am, I wouldn't rightly say that he does.'

She exhaled. God be praised for small mercies at least.

'One might safely presume, then,' Naomi remarked, 'that he isn't bearing bad news.'

'From the look of him, I wouldn't say that he is, ma'am, no.'

'Very well. Thank you, Mrs Bratton. Show him in to… well, actually, no, ask him to wait where he is for a moment and I'll send Kate for him when I'm ready. Kate, pass me my wrap, would you? And tell me, do I look presentable – fit to receive a guest? Or ought I to go and freshen up?'

Reaching for Naomi's angora shawl, Kate shook her head. 'No, ma'am, you look just fine.'

'You don't think I need a touch of rouge, or a little more colour to my lips? Or to run a comb through the front of my hair?'

Again, she shook her head. 'For Mr Aubrey, ma'am? No, I wouldn't say so.'

'Only, when I dressed this morning, it wasn't on the expectation that I would be receiving anyone.'

In the knowledge that Naomi wouldn't be satisfied otherwise, she affected an examination of her appearance: her glossy dark tresses sat where she had pinned them earlier into a pile of soft loose curls, low at the back of her head; her ivory complexion gave no evidence of having developed even the hint of a shine; her lips still exhibited a light coat of her favourite *Parisian Pink*. In other words, she looked nothing other than entirely acceptable. 'Truly, ma'am,' she said, her supposed inspection complete, 'you look just fine.'

'Hm. Well, if you think I look all right…'

Oh, do come on, she longed to chide, her patience wearing thin. *Surely you must be as desperate as I am to learn what brings your brother-in-law all the way down here!* When Naomi still didn't seem convinced, though, rather than let her impatience show, she distracted herself by tidying up. She closed the copy of *Tatler* Naomi had abandoned on the sofa and slipped it onto the shelf beneath the side table; she plumped the cushions where she had been sitting. Then, with a quick glance about the room and unable to bear it any longer, she asked, 'Shall I go and fetch him in then?'

Seemingly still uncertain, Naomi ran a hand over her hair. 'I suppose you had better. And then, if you would, pop down and see whether Edith can rustle up some cake and a pot of tea. And Kate…'

Having started towards the door, Kate turned back. 'Yes, ma'am?'

'When you've done *that*, I should like you to go and sit over there by the window – to start with, at least. While I've no reason to expect any unpleasantness from him, I should prefer not to be left alone in his company until it's clear why he's here.'

She nodded her understanding. 'Yes, ma'am.'

'And needless to say, not a word in front of him about the baby.'

'Of course not, ma'am.'

In the hallway, Kate found Aubrey Colborne standing looking out through the porch, a kitbag at his feet. *Please don't let him be bearing bad news*, she pleaded yet again, taking in the back of his military uniform. *And please don't let him have come to cause trouble, either*, she willed, conscious that this time, they would have no easy way to summon help, should it prove necessary.

Steeling herself against what felt to be all possible eventualities, she went towards him. But when, evidently hearing her approach, he turned to face her, she stopped dead. Around his neck was a sling. And in it was his left arm. Oh, dear God, Mr Aubrey was wounded!

'Ah, good afternoon,' he greeted her. 'Kate, isn't it?'

Still reeling from discovering that he was injured, she drew a breath and tried to smile back at him. 'Yes, sir,' she said, thrown further by the unexpectedly cheery nature of his address. 'Good afternoon to you. Mrs Colborne is… um… in the drawing room. Please, won't you come through?'

When she gestured across the hallway, he went on ahead of her, his long stride necessitating that she scurry to keep up. The very instant he was through the door, though, she slipped away, her heart thudding. If Mr Aubrey – an officer no less – could become injured, then what chance was there for… No! She wouldn't think such things. That Mr Aubrey had been wounded was no reason for her to fear for Luke. After all, who knew what the man had been doing to get hurt? He always had struck her as hot-headed and so, it was altogether possible that through sheer recklessness he had brought the misfortune upon himself. More than possible. Luke, on the other hand, was seldom reckless – certainly not where matters of a serious nature were concerned. But, if that was so, then why was her heart racing? And why did she feel so beset by fear? Because she was being foolish, that was why. There was no call for panic. None whatsoever.

Nevertheless, when she arrived in the kitchen, she still felt uncomfortably hot and flustered, a situation not helped by the fact that Mabel had obviously already imparted the news to Edith, since, when she looked up from slicing the remains of the Dundee cake, her expression was doom-laden.

'So Mr Aubrey's been wounded.' Goodness, how lurid, the woman's fascination with all things morbid! 'Lord, there's a worry an' *no* mistake. Must have set you to fearing for what might have happened to—'

'That Lieutenant Colborne has been injured is of no concern to me,' she said quickly, cutting short Edith's doom-mongering. For heaven's sake, why did the woman always have to be so quick to pick over someone else's misfortune and fan the flames of their fear? Well, this afternoon, she was in no mood for it: she would pay her no heed. Better still, she would put the woman straight. 'Mr Aubrey's being wounded has no bearing on Luke and *his* well-being.'

'Happen not,' Edith did at least concede, starting to arrange the slices of cake on a serving plate. 'But it must have set you to wondering – you know, whether the same fate mightn't befall him…'

From across the kitchen, Mabel Bratton came to place a hand on her daughter's arm. 'Edith, dear,' she said, 'I'm sure there's no need to go spreading alarm. Just because Mr Aubrey has been injured needn't make us fear for her Luke.'

With her hands clenched tightly, Kate nodded. 'Precisely,' she said. 'For a start, Luke's not on the front line. He's a driver. He ferries supplies and despatches. In fact, when he was home on leave, January past, he took great pains to explain to me that rarely is he dreckly in harm's way.'

'Only saying how it must have seemed,' Edith said. 'That's all.'

Gritting her teeth, Kate snatched up the tea tray. 'Well, *don't* say how it must have seemed,' she said. 'In fact, when it comes to Luke, don't say anything at all, especially since, *as usual*, you're speaking of summat you know nothing about.' *And making me think thoughts I'd rather not have!*

Turning stiffly towards the door, she caught sight of Mabel, the look on her face one that seemed to urge her to take no notice. Well, that was precisely what she intended. Exasperating though Edith's behaviour was, she would ignore her. Her own conscience was clear – she had done as Naomi had suggested and extended an olive branch. That Edith had now chosen to trample all over it was down to her.

Resolving to try not to let it get to her, she made her way back upstairs to the drawing room, arriving at the door to overhear a conversation going on within. Adjusting the weight of the tray on her arm, she paused to listen. Aubrey was speaking.

'Actually, I should say I was *annoyed* more than anything,' she heard him remark. 'Taken by surprise. Fine one moment, felled the next. Won't let it keep me out of action for long, though. Not a chance. No, it's going to need rather more than one lousy bullet from the Hun to keep *me* from doing *my* duty.'

Hearing him apparently able to make light of having been wounded, she felt the tension in her shoulders begin to ease. If he could speak so easily of what had happened, then surely it couldn't have been anything truly awful, could it?

'Ah, Kate, thank you,' Naomi greeted her as she tapped on the door and went into the room. 'Set it down here, if you will.' Turning back to Aubrey, she went on, 'I assumed you wouldn't decline refreshments.'

'Much appreciated. Utterly gasping as it happens.'

The tray safely on the table, Kate did as Naomi had instructed earlier and went to sit by the window; if Mr Aubrey thought it odd, he didn't comment. And then, with the sound of tea being poured into cups, she directed her eyes out to the gardens. It was a pleasant spring afternoon, the lawn refreshed to a dazzling emerald by the morning's showers, the pale-pink tulips in the border bejewelled by the very rain responsible for their state of dishevelment. In the mulch beneath their fleshy leaves, she spotted a male blackbird poking about, the fat worm trailing from its bill no doubt destined as sustenance for its mate. Somewhere in the shrubbery, she would be hatching a clutch of glossy blue-green eggs.

'Called at Hartland Street first, of course,' she overheard Aubrey continue. 'Couldn't have been more surprised to find that you were back down *here*. Knew nothing of your father buying the place until Aunt Pamela mentioned it. Didn't even know Sidney Latimer was selling up.'

'You saw Mamma?'

'Went straight there when I found Hartland Street empty.'

'And she told you about Uncle Sidney?'

'Hinted at straitened circumstances, that's all. Said you had come down to see to the packing up and what-not. Gave me to understand that your father hadn't been well.'

She heard Naomi sigh. 'Sadly, no. About a month ago, he simply collapsed to the floor. His physician attributed it to apoplexy and, much to Papa's displeasure, prescribed bed rest and a plain diet. Needless to say, complying with both made him unbearably grouchy. He continues to improve by the day, though, I'm glad to say.'

'Relieved to hear it.'

When the conversation paused, Kate looked across to see the two of them sipping their tea.

'Tell me,' Naomi began again a moment later, lowering her cup to its saucer and placing it back on the table, 'have you seen Lawrence? Or heard from him at all?'

From her position at the far side of the room, Kate held her breath. If Mr Aubrey had seen Mr Lawrence, he might also have news of Luke. After all, if he had no news of either of them, why was he here?

'Not in a while, no. But don't look at me like that. Just because there's been no word from him in a while is no reason for you to be concerned. Fighting a war requires that men and machinery be continually on the move. At little more than a moment's notice, a platoon can be reassigned, a whole battalion relocated. Indeed, it's not unheard of for entire divisions to either be joined together or split apart. Arrive somewhere new and the first thing one gets asked is whether one has seen so-and-so, or knows the whereabouts of such and such fellow. Almost to a man, every soldier over there is trying to find out news of a brother or a pal or a cousin.'

On the window seat, Kate held back a sigh of disappointment; seemingly then, there was to be no news of Luke. The picture of him she carried in her mind – and to which she clung dearly – had him looking sharp and handsome in his uniform, his slightly crooked front teeth bared as he stood laughing and joking with Mr Lawrence, his cap under his arm and his newly cut sandy hair glinting in the sunshine. From Mr Aubrey's telling of events though, the war sounded a very different business to the one in her head, pictures now forming of men on endless marches and soldiers desperate for news of relatives. In a bid to banish them – after all, it did no good to dwell – she stared back out through the window. Keeping low to the lawn, the blackbird was now heading towards the shrubbery, the staccato beating of its wings seeming barely sufficient to keep it aloft. To her dismay, though, the images of the distressed soldiers persisted. In a bid to will them away, she reminded herself of what Pa Channer had said to her only the other day, which was that no news was good news; the time for worry – and the *only* time for worry – was when the telegram boy came cycling up the lane.

Across the room from her, Naomi seemed equally disappointed by the lack of any word. 'When Mrs Bratton said that you were here, I hoped to learn that you'd seen him.'

''Fraid not. Although it is partly on Lawrence's account that I've come.'

Continuing to stare out through the window but listening keenly, Kate heard Naomi shift her position on the sofa.

'Oh? Do explain.'

'Well, you see, I feel I owe you an apology.'

'An apology?'

Carefully, she, too, sat more upright; this sounded interesting.

'That night last summer – the night of your mother's party, I behaved... well, I behaved appallingly—'

'Yes, but Aubrey, you've already apologized for that—'

'I did offer you an apology, yes – although in truth only because Mamma was standing over me, demanding that I do so. Since then however, being so far away from... *loved ones...* being over there at the sharp end, so to speak, well, let us just say that it has the effect of magnifying one's regrets and focusing one's thoughts upon matters left unresolved. And so, if for no other reason than to put my mind at rest, I should like to apologize, sincerely this time, for the way I behaved. I should also like to say, somewhat belatedly I do concede, how delighted I am that you married Lawrence.'

Waiting to hear how Naomi would reply, Kate frowned. Mr Aubrey's apology *sounded* genuinely made, so, why the niggle of doubt? Was it because, in her experience, men like Aubrey Colborne rarely did anything unless they somehow stood to gain by it? Although, quite how coming all the way down to Woodicombe could be of benefit to him, she couldn't imagine. In which case, it had to be much as he'd said: being away from home had led him to regret his behaviour, and now he was making amends. Well, good for him.

'Thank you, Aubrey,' she heard Naomi reply. 'Let us now consider the matter laid to rest.'

'Most gracious.'

'So, tell me,' Naomi picked up again a little while later, 'what plans do you have going forward? How long are you on leave? Of course, tonight—' In the corner of the room, Kate knew what Naomi was going to say next. '—you shall stay here with us. I'm afraid there are few comforts to be had and very little to drink. But there will be a bed and a hot bath.'

'Then I accept your kind offer.'

'Kate—'

Kate, though, was already on her feet. 'Yes, ma'am.'

'Would you please make up a guest room? And, while I appreciate that this is rather short notice, please go down and ask Edith to stretch supper to another serving.'

'Yes, ma'am.'

'And it goes without saying that this evening, we shall dine up here.' Turning back to Aubrey, and by way of explanation, Naomi went on, 'Whilst I have been here on my own, I have taken to dining with Kate in the staff parlour – much cosier than sitting alone at that vast dining table. Although please, I beg you, not a word to Mamma. No point sending *her* apoplectic as well.' Returning her attention to Kate, she continued, 'Do apologize to Edith for the lack of notice and tell her not to fret too much. We don't need a banquet. I'm sure Aubrey will be grateful for anything hot and wholesome.'

'*Ra-ther.*'

'Good. Then that's settled. You shall sing for your supper though—'

'Oh yes?'

'—by telling me what it's like in France. And by describing your heroics.'

'I don't know about heroics. Merely a case of doing one's duty.'

'Well, you must have been doing *something* brave to have got shot in the arm!'

'If you say so, my dear lady. If you say so.'

Slipping from the room, Kate smiled. Unless it was all a very clever act, Mr Aubrey really did seem a reformed character. Perhaps, then, *some* good had come from this wretched war after all.

—

Laughter? Goodness, something was making Naomi laugh; that was a pleasing thing to hear. Of late, her manner had been rather subdued – what with Mr Russell being unwell and then having to traipse all the way down here to sort out the purchase of the house for him. Odd, nevertheless, that the thing to lift her spirits should be the surprise arrival of Mr Aubrey – who still hadn't actually said why he had come.

It was after breakfast the following morning and, although she had cleared the table around them, Naomi and Aubrey had yet to stir from it.

'If only that was how it worked,' she overheard Aubrey remarking. 'The rather sorrier truth of the matter is that *we* take a few hundred yards of countryside from *them*, whereupon *they* launch a raid and recover some of it. *We* dig in and defend; *they* take their eye off things; *we* attack their positions and recover what we lost. Meanwhile, back at HQ, the generals pronounce it a great success, even though all either side has to show for their effort is the ground they started out with.'

'You make it sound like a game of chess,' Naomi remarked with another light laugh. 'A rather trying one at that.'

'I'd say that's about the measure of it – a game of strategy waged in the mud.'

'By the way,' Naomi said, 'you still haven't told me exactly how you came to be shot.'

Out of their sight, Kate kept quite still. It was something she, too, had been wondering about, it being gratifying to think of there being a hero in the family.

'I haven't, no,' Aubrey replied. 'And I'm afraid I'm not truly at liberty to do so, either. All I *can* say, is that under orders one day, we were out reconnoitring a position when one of my men heard a noise. Naturally, I went forward to investigate, signalling the men to remain where they were. Next thing I know, there's a sharp sound like a *crack* and then a sensation I can only liken to having my lower arm engulfed by flames. Of course, by the time I'd got my wits together, the blighter who'd shot me had fled.'

'Was it a German spy, do you think,' Naomi asked, 'creeping about to see what you were up to?'

'My dear lady,' Aubrey replied, his tone filled with the sort of indulgence one would more normally reserve for a child, 'you make it all sound so terribly daring, whereas the reality is rather different. But yes, I believe it was indeed a German scout. Coming upon our party, no doubt quite by chance, he probably let off his weapon – more through fear than anything else – before hot-footing it back from whence he came.'

Unexpectedly, Kate shivered. How awful to think of Germans creeping about, spying upon brave British soldiers. It was an underhand way to carry on. And sly.

'Fortunate, I suppose, that he only caught you in the hand—'

'Just missed my wrist, actually, but yes, those were my very words when they carted me off to the field hospital. Let me do my job, I said. It's no more than a scratch. But no, when they saw the scale of the wound, they insisted upon sending me back to Blighty. Go home and get yourself fighting fit again, was the order.'

'And does it hurt? Are you still in pain?' she heard Naomi ask.

'Now and again. But one tries not to grumble. Others suffer far worse. *Far* worse.'

Purposely trying not to think about Mr Aubrey's injury, Kate nevertheless found her mind picturing a bloody wound. What a nasty thing for a man to have happen to him. She could only pray that nothing similar would ever befall Luke. Luke. Oh, how she missed him!

Across the room, the conversation continued.

'I must remember to tell Lawrence when I next write to him—'

'Well...'

'He'll be so relieved to learn that you are all right.'

'...actually, I'd really rather you didn't mention it,' Aubrey said. 'If word gets out that I've been talking about operations, even just to you, a rather dim view might be taken.'

Then she, too, Kate found herself thinking, must guard against letting slip what she had just overheard; it would be all too easy to relay such a conversation without thinking of the consequences.

'Oh. Yes. I suppose so,' Naomi agreed.

'In fact, it's probably safest for now that you don't mention having seen me at all,' Aubrey went on.

'If you think that would be for the best.'

'I'm afraid I do. Shame and all that – having to keep it a secret – not that I was ever one to brag.'

'I do understand,' Naomi assured him.

'You know, it's rather good fortune you were down here,' Aubrey remarked a moment later. 'I couldn't have wished for a finer place to rest up for a day or two.'

'Aubrey, I'm glad to have been able to help out. After all, we're family now, with all that entails.'

'With all that entails, yes.'

'Besides, I suppose you will be back out there soon – maybe even see Lawrence for yourself,' Naomi continued.

Kate listened with interest. Despite the cheering effect Mr Aubrey seemed to be having upon Naomi, she did hope he wouldn't be staying *too* long; up until his arrival, she had been looking forward to returning to London.

'Possibly. Although I shan't know much until I'm called before an assessment board,' Aubrey replied. 'Ought to be quite soon now, I should think, which is just as well because this whole business of being on leave has turned into something of a shambles. One finds oneself sent home to recuperate only to discover that an almighty bungle somewhere along the line has left one without pay.'

Trying to digest what Mr Aubrey had just said, Kate frowned.

'They haven't paid you?' she heard Naomi remark. 'But that's extraordinary.'

Unwittingly – and unseen – she nodded her agreement. What a disgraceful thing to have happened.

'It would seem they have temporarily lost track of me,' Aubrey explained.

'Goodness. Can you not speak to someone?'

'I have. Thus far it has brought no remedy.'

'Then how are you managing for money?'

'Well… that's just it. I find myself in a bit of a bind.'

'How unforgivable of the army to put you in such a position!' Naomi remarked.

'I couldn't agree more.'

'No, truly. It is unforgivable.'

Equally enraged, Kate held still and continued to listen.

'Look, Naomi, one doesn't like to ask – Lawrence being away and all that – but I don't suppose you could find your way to helping a fellow out, could you? One doesn't need a vast sum – just enough to get one back on one's feet. I shall of course repay you the moment it's all sorted. In fact, if you have a telephone—'

'Yes, but of course,' Naomi was quick to reply. 'Uncle Sidney only recently had one installed in the study. Telephone from there. And of course I shall help you out. Lawrence would never forgive me if I left you to go penniless. What a dreadful embarrassment for you. Once we're done here, I'll go upstairs and fetch my handbag.'

'That's terribly decent of you. Then I shall telephone forthwith.'

'And perhaps, once you have, you might like to accompany me on a little stroll around the gardens. Considering Mr Channer has been left to cope all on his own, he seems to be doing a splendid job. They're looking quite lovely.'

'I should be delighted to. And so, if you will excuse me, I shall see if I can place that call.'

Having sat silently in the corner of the room throughout their exchange, Kate now let out a sigh – in part from relief but also from frustration. How terrible for Mr Aubrey to find himself without money, especially with him having been shot and wounded in the service of king and empire. And how fortunate that, after the events of last summer, Naomi bore him no ill will and was prepared to help him out.

Perhaps she shouldn't have been so quick to suspect his motives for turning up after all. She was often told that she was too quick to judge a person. Well, she would think badly of him no more. From now on, given all the poor man had been through, she would go out of her way to be nice to him.

–

'Do you know, Naomi, I do believe the air down here agrees with you.'

It was the following afternoon – a fresh and blowy one – and, having spotted Naomi and Aubrey returning from taking a stroll, Kate had gone to wait in the hallway in readiness to relieve Naomi of her outdoor jacket and hat.

'You could be right,' she heard Naomi reply as the couple came in through the porch. 'The air here is certainly a good deal less filthy than it is in town.'

'Difficult to imagine it being any worse,' Aubrey remarked, smoothing a hand over his oiled hair. To Kate's mind, the shorter styling of it suited him. 'But I rather meant – and please, forgive me if I'm speaking out of turn here – that it appears to be lending you a fetching *bloom*, a radiance, if you will. And *that*, I can only attribute to the sea air.'

When Naomi gave an embarrassed little laugh, Kate guessed she hoped to lead Aubrey away from the more likely reason behind the bloom to her cheeks.

'Did you hear that, Kate? Apparently, I look very well; the sea air suits me.'

She smiled. 'For certain it does, ma'am. Mr Aubrey's not wrong there.'

'Indeed,' Aubrey Colborne picked up again, 'is it possible that next time I am on leave, I shall find that you have decamped down here permanently?'

Accepting Naomi's hat from her, Kate sincerely hoped not. The more she saw of Woodicombe, the less she wanted to be there any longer than was absolutely necessary. Already she missed the liveliness of London – and the way that no one there knew your business or criticized you for it.

'I think it unlikely,' Naomi replied to Aubrey's question, and Kate exhaled with relief. 'I *do* like it here; it's quite lovely. When Papa said he thought he might do Uncle Sidney a favour and buy the place from him, I must confess to being delighted. That said, I don't believe I'm cut out for a life so far from town. I fear I should miss Selfridges and Liberty's rather too much.'

When Aubrey laughed, it was a deep and spontaneous sound that seemed to rumble up from inside of him. 'Never say never,' he replied.

Having divested herself of her outer garments, Naomi met Kate's grin with raised eyebrows. 'Shall we take some tea?' she turned back to Aubrey to enquire.

'Tea would be delightful.'

'Kate, would you—'

'I'll see to it, ma'am.'

From then on, Kate noticed that Naomi and Aubrey seemed to adopt a sort of routine. Depending upon the time of day, she would come upon them engaged in some or other pastime, Naomi either concentrating deeply or, just as often, laughing helplessly.

'My dear lady,' she discovered Mr Aubrey explaining one evening, a game of chess underway in front of them, 'please desist from calling it *the horse*. Those pieces are your knights.'

'I know,' Naomi replied. 'But to my mind, a horse with no rider is simply a horse. Besides which, what sort of knight would ride his mount this way and that in such indecisive fashion – especially into a battle?'

'A useful one. Remember what I told you?'

'Um...'

'A knight's unique way of moving means that he is at his most useful when near the centre of the board: *a knight on the rim is dim*. Yes?'

'If you say so.'

Then there was the afternoon when she came across the two of them on the terrace, seated together on the bench under the window, Mr Aubrey holding out a book from which they appeared to be reading alternating parts.

'*Methinks, mistress, you should have little reason for that. And yet, to say the truth, reason and love keep little company together nowadays.*' For a while, she had remained where she was, able to make next-to-no sense of whatever it was they were reading. 'Tell me again why I'm playing the part of *Bottom*,' Mr Aubrey had broken off to ask.

46

'Because *I* am *Titania*, of course,' Naomi had replied with a giggle.

'Not because I am the ass…?'

In an altogether more sombre mood, there was also their daily study of progress on the front line, as reported in the *Telegraph*. Indeed, it was through overhearing their discussions in this regard that she came to understand how battles were raging far more widely than just Flanders and France, as she had come to suppose.

'So, Mesopotamia,' Naomi commented on this particular morning, bending over the newspaper laid out on the table, 'is *where* on this map?'

'Here,' Aubrey pointed out. 'And this is the Tigris Valley, with Baghdad… there.'

Witnessing the respect and patience with which Mr Aubrey answered Naomi's questions, Kate thought him precisely the sort of company for which, in the absence of Mr Lawrence, Naomi had begun to have need.

After dinner that evening, though, when she peered into the drawing room, it was to find Naomi standing alone, her eyes cast out through the opened-back French doors.

'Kate, come here,' she greeted her, her voice little more than a whisper. 'Come and listen.'

At that moment, from across the lawn floated a refrain of rich and melodious birdsong. Hearing it, she smiled. 'It's a nightingale, ma'am.'

'I thought as much. We used to hear them sometimes in the grounds at school. Such a wistful song, isn't it?'

'It's wistful because he sings to woo a lady nightingale,' she replied to Naomi's observation. 'The cock birds return from overseas before the hens so as to compete with each other for the best nesting places. Then, when the females do return, the cock birds must sing their hearts out in the hope of winning one of them as a mate.'

Briefly they remained motionless, each hoping for the singing to resume, their patience rewarded when into the stillness came another rapid succession of notes: some reminiscent of a man's whistle, some more suggestive of a flute; some vigorous, some soft, some almost pleading. Gradually, the lament built to a crescendo before, without warning, coming abruptly to a halt.

'Bravo,' Naomi whispered into the velvety silence that followed, her hands clasped in front of her. 'How I wish Lawrence could have been here to hear it.'

'Happen he will be soon, ma'am,' she replied. 'Happen they both will be.'

'You know, I'm sure Aubrey suspects something is afoot.'

Deducing that Naomi must be referring to the baby, she turned to examine her expression. 'Truly? I wouldn't have thought a man capable of noticing such things. Certainly not with you being so early along.'

'Before *this*, *I* wouldn't have thought so, either,' Naomi agreed. 'But there have been a couple of times when I've caught him looking at me as though trying to decide what it is that's different.'

Staring at Naomi was something she, too, had noticed Mr Aubrey doing. At the time, she'd wondered whether perhaps he rued having fumbled his chance with her. It wasn't really something she could tell Naomi, though. Instead, she said, 'But he was right to say you look well. Unlike some women in your condition, you haven't even been sick of a morning.'

For a moment, Naomi looked thoughtful. 'I haven't, have I?' she replied. 'How fortuitous. But, how very *not* fortuitous that when the time comes to tell Lawrence, I shall be unable to do so in person. I should love to be able to see his expression.'

She smiled. She could understand that. 'For certain he'll be thrilled,' she said.

'Just remember though, not a word in front of Aubrey.'

She shook her head. But then, with Aubrey once again in her thoughts, she asked, 'By the way, ma'am, where *is* Mr Aubrey this evening?'

'He said earlier that he was going to follow the cliff path into Westward Quay. He said it was such a fine evening that he felt moved to take a stroll.'

The discovery made her want to laugh out loud. Never for a single moment had Mr Aubrey put her in mind of someone inclined to walk for the sake of it. But who knew how being at war might alter a man's appreciation of the simple things? Indeed, who knew how, at this very moment, it might be altering Luke – and *his* feelings and views of life and the world? Who knew how different he might be when he came back?

''Tis a treacherous old walk back after sundown,' she said, preferring not to dwell on the possibility of Luke coming back to her a changed man. Sometimes, she had enough trouble just conjuring the details of his face, let alone his ways. 'I do hope he doesn't leave it *too* late to return,' she added, 'especially since 'tis a dark moon tonight.'

'I said that very same thing to him – well, obviously, not about the moon. To that end, we agreed that once there, he would go to the station and procure the cab. And to make certain of it, I gave him the fare.'

Turning away, she frowned even harder. Mr Aubrey didn't even have the fare for a cab? Then he *was* in dire straits. 'Oh. Well, then,' she said, 'he should be all right.'

'Of course he will be. Any man who's led other men into battle and been shot in the process ought surely to be able to find his way home without incident.'

That much did seem true. 'I suppose so, yes.'

'You know, I do feel mean deceiving him.'

Turning again to study Naomi's expression, she noticed that her forehead was set with deep lines. 'Deceiving him? Not telling him about the baby, is that what you mean?'

'He seems so *changed* – not at all the same man who came to stay last summer. But then I suppose it's as he said – being away at war has made him see things differently. Since he *is* so altered though, I feel mean not telling him. He *is* Lawrence's brother, after all.'

To her mind, Naomi seemed to be confusing many things; her loyalty, in this instance, wildly misplaced. 'He is, ma'am, yes,' she ventured. 'But Mr Lawrence is your *husband*. Don't *he* deserve to be first to learn of the news?' Picturing herself in the same situation, she felt certain Luke would be mortally upset to find out she'd told someone else first – even just Mabel or Edith. Or Naomi, come to that.

'You're right. He does.'

'And happen Mr Lawrence would welcome the chance to tell his brother the news for himself.'

For a moment, Naomi looked taken aback. 'Gosh, how right you are. I hadn't thought of that.'

'Besides, not long now and we'll be back at home. Then, once you've seen the doctor, it need be a secret no more.'

'No.'

Home. Since Mr Aubrey's arrival, Naomi's plans in that regard seemed to have fallen by the wayside. It was something she'd been meaning to raise with her. 'On that note, ma'am,' she said carefully, 'before Mr Aubrey arrived, we were all but ready to depart. Since then, though, you've made no further mention of it. And so, I was wondering… well, wondering about your plans.'

'My plans,' Naomi repeated thoughtfully. 'Yes, Aubrey's arrival *has* rather thrown them, hasn't it? The thing is, I do believe all this fresh air and calm is doing him good. That being the case, I feel obliged to remain here a while longer, you know, do my little bit to help him.'

Not the answer she had been hoping for, it was, nonetheless, the one she had been expecting – not that it helped her to sound any less dejected. 'Yes, I see that.'

'The poor man was wounded in battle,' Naomi went on, as though to justify her point. 'And I find myself hoping that were Lawrence in the same boat, Aubrey would do the same for him.'

'I should hope for that too, ma'am.'

'In any event, apart from delaying my seeing the doctor, I don't see that our remaining down here is causing any real disruption, is it?'

She withheld a sigh. She'd been hoping to learn they were about to make fresh arrangements to leave. With no real purpose there now, her days felt long and empty. Rather than admit to that, though, she decided to try another tack. 'Has Mr Aubrey not mentioned when he will be returning to his regiment?'

'Not directly,' Naomi said. 'He did mention having to go before a board to be passed as fit. Why do you ask? Are you really so anxious to return to Hartland Street?'

Feeling unable to press her point any further, she buried her feelings. 'Not especially, ma'am. But, if we're to be here a while longer, perhaps I ought to speak to Edith, you know, so she's prepared.'

'You do make a fair point. Look, I doubt I shall see Aubrey again tonight since shortly, now, I intend to retire. But, at breakfast, I shall enquire of his plans. Once we know those, you can advise Edith accordingly.'

'Very well, ma'am.'

'And do go on up to bed. I shan't need anything else tonight.'

'All right, thank you. I'll do that. Good night, ma'am.'

'Good night, Kate.'

Making her way slowly up to her old bedroom on the second floor, Kate reflected upon how quickly everything seemed to change these days. No sooner had she become a wife than she had been left without a husband. No sooner had she settled into Hartland Street than she had unexpectedly been brought back to Woodicombe, the upshot being that during these last few days, London had started to feel like little more than a distant dream. In truth, it was how her marriage was beginning to feel, too.

Still, she thought, wearily unbuttoning the bodice of her uniform, it was unlikely that Naomi would want to remain in Devon too much longer. With a baby on the way, she would soon become anxious to return home. And then it would be Woodicombe that felt to be little more than a dream. And thank goodness for that.

Chapter Three

Absence

'So, child, why don't you come on in and tell me what's ailing you?'

To Ma Channer's greeting, Kate laughed. She hadn't heard anyone call her *child* in years.

'Oh, 'tis just the usual,' she replied, stepping inside and glancing about. Where Luke's mother was concerned, there was no point pretending everything was all right because the woman could read faces more easily than most people could read a book. 'Just this 'n that, you know how it is.'

It was an afternoon a few days later and, with Naomi and Mr Aubrey gone for a walk around the cove, she'd been struck by the idea to wander up the lane and see Mrs Channer, especially since it was something she'd been meaning to do anyway.

'I know it. Tell you what, lover, since you've come all the way up here, why don't you an' me rest up awhile and set the world to rights over a nice brew?'

Smiling back at the suggestion, Kate nodded. 'Thank you, yes, I'd like that.'

For as long as she could remember, Loveday Channer had seemed to be an old lady. Her simple little knot of grey hair and sparrow-like frame had always made her look more like someone's granny than their ma. She supposed that with Luke being the youngest of seven children, she'd already been that good bit older when he'd come into the world. She was certainly now more Mabel's age than Edith's.

'You heard from that boy of mine lately?'

Watching as her bony arm reached to the dresser for two cups, Kate shook her head; if only she *had* heard from him. Maybe then she wouldn't be in such a fret. 'Not in a while. But those in the know would say that's no cause for concern.'

Lifting the teapot, Ma Channer gave a sharp nod. 'True enough. There you are then,' she said, placing a brimming tea cup on the table, 'let 'un cool off a bit first, though. Don't want to go a-scalding your tongue.'

'No,' she replied. 'Thank you.' From the fragrant smell rising up with the steam, she realized then that this wasn't, as she had been expecting, a brew of plain old tea but rather a steeping of fresh elderflower. The smell of it was lemony. Grassy. Summery. A scent that in London would seem out of place, to Kate, it was a smell that conjured all the hopefulness and expectancy of the first warm days of summer.

'So, what be a-vexing you then, girl? That fancy piece up yonder proving a tricky madam to please?'

Out of respect for Naomi, she stifled the urge to laugh. That was something else she remembered about Ma Channer: she always told it how she saw it.

Trying to decide how best to answer her, she bent to blow across the top of her cup, watching as the steam coiled away from the steady stream of her breath. 'No, not at all,' she sat back up to say. 'Mrs Colborne is very kind to me.'

Loveday Channer nodded her approval. 'My mother always used to say you could tell the quality of a lady by the way she treated her staff. And I'd have it no different. I saw three Mrs Latimers pass through this place, and won't hear a word said agin' any of them.'

Raising her cup carefully to her lips, Kate took a sip of her drink. As a child, she had detested the taste of elderflower – had thought it akin to swallowing the smell of old ladies' perfumes. Now, though, she was surprised to find it not nearly as floral as she remembered but instead, light and crisp and very slightly sweet. 'Isn't it a bit early in the year for elder blossom?' she asked, setting her cup back on the table.

Across from her, Mrs Channer tapped the side of her nose. 'Know of a favoured spot to look for 'un, see. Couple of bushes quite sheltered in a little hollow. Never fail to blossom weeks before any other. But I'm minded you didn't come a-traipsing all the way up the lane to enquire about elderflower now, did you? You came because you've summat on your mind.'

Pressing her lips together, Kate paused to think for a moment before replying. The truth was that any number of things had brought her there, that she had been bored and looking for a way to fill some time being one of them. That it had struck her as a pleasant stroll to take on a sunny afternoon was another. But Ma Channer was right to remark that she was preoccupied. The trouble was, so far, she'd been unable to boil down her preoccupation to just the one thing. Lately, so *many* things seemed amiss that she struggled to know where to begin.

'Happen I just don't feel settled,' she ventured, her answer feeling like a suitable catch-all. 'Just lately, I seem all at sea.'

'Not settled with life and the ways of the world in general,' Mrs Channer immediately wanted to know, 'or just in your own bones?'

She stared down at the surface of the table. Scarred from decades of use, the wood nevertheless still bore a deep lustre – no doubt the result of liberal and frequent applications of Mrs Channer's own concoction of beeswax and linseed oil.

Spotting a particularly swirly knot in the grain, she traced around it with the tip of her forefinger. *Elm wood*, she decided, remembering back to one evening when Luke had tried to explain to her about the uses of the different timbers on the Latimers' estate. Picking out one from another came naturally to him; with no hesitation whatsoever, he could identify any piece of wood you cared to put in front of him.

'I suppose I just wish Luke would hurry up and come home,' she eventually said. 'And that we could get on with our lives.' But then, deciding there to be no point telling only half the truth, she went on, 'Though even that's not the worst of it.'

'No?'

Slowly, she shook her head. 'No. See, Luke went off so quick that most of the time, it don't seem like I'm wed at all. I long for him to be back so as to be a wife, yet in truth, I don't even really know what that means. And that leaves me feeling cross at him for having gone away. And angry at the government for taking him. And sad for all these months we're wasting while he's not here.

Sometimes, I'm even taken to wishing we'd waited to get wed until after he came back – you know, so I'd never have been left feeling like I do now.'

From the other side of the table, Ma Channer reached out to pat her hand, the skin of the back of her own marbled with purple-grey veins and dotted with freckles. ''Course you feel that way, love. Poor thing, there you are, weddin' band on your finger but your husband neither home at your hearth nor in your bed of a night-time. Course you're cross with the way things have turned out. You miss him. 'Tis only natural. Had you wanted the life of one of those bloomin' *sufferingette* women, you wouldn't have got yourself wed in the first place, would you? No. But here you are anyway, all on your own, the two of you leading your lives as though the other didn't exist.'

Leading your lives as though the other didn't exist. That was about the size of it. And no, it wasn't natural. As usual, Ma Channer had hit the nail on the head.

'It's not *just* that he's not here,' she said, doing nothing more, really, than thinking aloud, 'it's not knowing when he'll be back… or… or even…'

'It's all right, love, you can say what's in your heart. I won't judge you for owning to it. Happen it's no bad thing to give voice to your worst fears. Show a fear the light of day and as often as not, he'll lose some of his bluster and his menace.'

When she glanced up, it was to see Ma Channer looking back at her, her expression kindly. Was it possible she could read her thoughts? It certainly felt that way.

'…or even whether he'll be back at all,' she forced herself to finish. 'I mean, don't get me wrong, I've not such a dread of it that it fills my every waking hour to leave me good for nothing else. But, all the same, it does lurk at the back of my mind.'

'For certain it does, maid. Like I said, 'tis only natural.'

'So,' she began again, hoping Ma Channer would have some words of wisdom to offer, 'that being the case, what do I do? How do I stop feeling so… so *all up in the air*?'

'Well, when faced with a thing that won't be bent to your will, as often as not, you're best served casting it from your mind altogether. Best thing, of course, would be if you had a child to chivvy about after. But, since you've not yet had the chance to fall, you'd be best finding summat else to fill your days. And in that regard, each and every one of us is different. Some women might take to working till they're fit to drop, the exhaustion of it bringing them the sleep of the dead come nightfall. Some would fill their time helping out folk in need. Others I can think of would most likely take to knitting scarves and mittens for sending to soldiers. Others still would go to evensong, or take to reading the words of the Bible for the comfort it would bring to them.'

'Hm.' Sadly, none of those suggestions felt to offer the sort of reassurance and respite she was seeking – certainly not the knitting part; that was more up Edith's street. Not that *she* had worries to be distracted from.

'Take your mind from it,' Ma Channer picked up again, 'that would be my advice to you. If nothing else, few folk regret a day spent all a-bustle. A day *wasted* on the other hand, well, we all know what the devil does upon sighting a pair of idle hands. And what husband wants to come home from fighting a war to find his wife taken by the devil, eh?'

When Ma Channer laughed, she made a chortling sound so filled with mischief that Kate found herself grinning back. 'I do understand what you're telling me,' she said. 'Truly I do. I just wish I didn't have to wait about, constantly wondering what's happening to Luke. I wish I didn't feel as though I have no control over my own life – of my own destiny, if you will.'

Loveday Channer released her hand. 'Can any one of us truly claim to be in control of anything?' she asked. 'Even were we all blessed with the power to see what was waiting for us around the corner – a year from now, a score years from now – would we want to know? No, trust me, girl, keeping busy is what *you* need. That way, before you know it, young Luke will be back here. And, once he is, and you've a family constantly getting under your feet, I'll warrant you'll give anything for even a pinch of the peace and quiet you rue as being so irksome right this very moment.'

Reflecting on her mother-in-law's words, Kate swallowed the last mouthful of her tea. 'I'm sure you're right,' she said, replacing her cup on the table.

'And don't overlook the good to be had from putting it all down in a letter to him, either – let him know how you feel and how you're looking forward to getting settled. Take it from me, it'll please the poor lad no end to hear it from you.'

'Yes,' she said, struck by the suggestion and wondering why she hadn't thought of that for herself. 'I think I'll do that. Thank you. That's good advice. I'm glad I came.'

'Aye. Well, maybe don't leave it so long to drop by another time. And when you *do* next write to him, happen you'd let him know how me an' his pa are going along just fine. I'm minded my shaky hand don't put it down on paper so clear these days.'

'Yes, I'll do that too,' she said. 'And thank you again for the tea. I really enjoyed it.'

Walking back along the lane a short while later, she reflected upon what Ma Channer had just advised. *Fill your days*, she had said. Well, there was sense to that. Doing something – especially something worthwhile, if it could be found – ought to overcome the feeling that she was merely waiting for something to happen – for good or for bad. For certain, keeping busy couldn't make matters any worse! So, yes, as soon as a suitable opportunity arose, she would remind Naomi about their plan to volunteer in support of the war. If she filled her mind and her days with new and worthy things, then perhaps there would be less chance for it to dwell on other, more distressing, thoughts. And, in the meantime, she would do as Ma Channer had suggested and use some of her tediously empty hours to write a nice long letter to Luke. With a bit of luck, it would prove to be of comfort to both of them.

–

'Good God!'

On her way to clear the breakfast things the following morning, Kate stopped in her tracks. Concerned as to the reason for Mr Aubrey's sudden alarm, she then edged closer to the door.

'What is it?' she heard Naomi ask him, her question followed by the sound of the pages of the *Telegraph* being given a vigorous shake.

'Here, under *Prisoners of War*,' she heard Aubrey begin, 'I've just spotted the name *Ryland, W. A., Wiltshire*

Regiment. That's William Ryland. I was at school with him. Quite by chance, he even enlisted the same week I did. We went through officer school together. Good Lord. I knew I was right to... well, no matter.'

Hearing nothing more for a moment, Kate peered into the room. Naomi had risen from her chair and was looking over Aubrey's shoulder at the newspaper.

'Is this a list of all the men taken prisoner?'

Alarmed to realize what lay behind Naomi's enquiry, Kate shivered: both of their husbands were in the Wiltshire Regiment – the same as the man reported as captured by the enemy. The thought that either of them could be taken prisoner made her feel sick. Ordinarily, her concern was that he would get injured but now, here was something new for her to worry about.

Trying to calm the rate at which she was suddenly breathing, she took a step away from the door but continued to listen intently.

'In theory, it is a complete account, yes. But I'm afraid that in practice, that's rarely how it works. You see, if a man is unaccounted for, then initially, he will be listed by his battalion as 'missing' or 'died', or possibly even as 'wounded,' it being presumed that any one of those fates could have befallen the poor chap. What you wouldn't understand, you see, is that when a platoon comes under attack, things can quickly become confused, it being hard to keep good account of what has happened to whom. Both sides – ourselves and the Germans alike – are supposed to issue lists of any men they take prisoner, which, from time to time, they do. Look, it says here, for instance, that the German Government has provided the names of five hundred and seventeen men captured, many of whom had previously been reported by their regiment as 'killed', 'wounded' or 'missing.' But, by the time these lists were exchanged, these numbers and these names would already have been out of date.'

Edging forward and risking another peek into the room, Kate saw Naomi sink onto the chair next to Mr Aubrey. Reaching to the doorframe for support, she wished that she, too, had somewhere to sit down. This was all just too distressing.

'I see. So—'

'Look, my dear lady, you have no reason to fear for Lawrence – none whatsoever. Were he listed as 'missing', then clearly, having been taken prisoner would be a possibility. But, on the rare occasion when an officer *does* go missing, his family is always notified. As his next of kin, you would learn of it quite promptly. That you haven't heard from him in a while is more likely down to him being somewhere remote, where getting word out is difficult... or even inadvisable. In this war, as in any other, it is very much the case that no news is good news.'

Standing in the hallway, Kate slowly shook her head. Oh, how she wished she could believe that!

'I'm so glad you are here to explain these things to me,' she overheard Naomi reply. 'Most of the time I don't even look at the newspaper for fear of what I might read. But then, as a result, I feel so terribly ignorant. As it is, I spend most of my time wavering between feeling either helpless or just plain useless.'

Yes, she, too, knew how that felt.

'I'm sure you must do. It's only natural. But, if I know my brother, he'll be doing his darnedest to keep himself and his men out of harm's way. He's sharp-witted... and thorough. He won't be taking foolish risks – it's simply not who he is.'

'No. I know that,' she heard Naomi reply. 'And I'm sure you're right. It's just that seeing these lists – I mean, look at them, there's hundreds of names here – you realize that they were all... *are* all... somebody's husband or father, or son or brother. They're not just names, are they? They're men. Brave men like yourself and Lawrence.'

'Indeed.'

Out in the hallway, Kate decided it time to creep away. No sense getting caught eavesdropping. And anyway, despite spending much of her time desperate to learn of anything that might help her to picture where Luke was – and what he was doing – when she *did* happen to read or hear of something, she quickly wished she hadn't. Mr Aubrey's tale, for instance, had painted an even starker picture than those that often haunted her dreams. Where *he* had been, men were routinely shot or taken captive and yet, despite the horror, he was still able to speak of it quite calmly.

Having moved away from the door, she paused. What she would do was draw on Mr Aubrey's calmness to still her own concerns for Luke. Having heard him reassure Naomi that no news really was good news, she would choose to believe him. He had been there; he knew these things. In any event, other than worry herself silly, she had little choice but to trust that he was telling the truth.

–

Good grief, what a mess she'd made! Now she'd have to start all over again; she couldn't send it with a blob of ink at the top!

Grateful to be alone, Kate growled with frustration and, ripping the top sheet of paper from her writing pad, screwed it into a ball. *Another* page wasted, another attempt destined only for the waste bin. Why was it, she wondered, that the words in her mind sounded so completely wrong once put down on paper?

In despair, she shook her head and stared down at the fresh page of her notepad. Coming across it in her old chest of drawers had been a stroke of good fortune since otherwise, she would have been forced to wait until she could go into Westward Quay to buy another. Her patience couldn't have borne that. Since her chat with Ma Channer yesterday, she had been desperate for a quiet moment to sit and write to Luke. If nothing else, she was hoping that setting down her thoughts to him would do as his mother had suggested and help to calm her mind. Irritatingly, though, while it appeared a straightforward enough thing to do – write to Luke and tell him that she missed him – finding the words to convey those thoughts was proving unexpectedly tricky.

Dipping the nib of her pen into the bottle of ink, she started over. Since she was hoping not to be at Wood-icombe for much longer, she had decided to put her address as Hartland Street. With that once again written out neatly, she paused to recall the date and then wrote that underneath. So far, so good. Next, she moved across to the other side of the page and wrote *Dear Luke*. Holding aside her pen, she sat back and stared down at her effort thus far. Her handwriting was tidy enough, but she wasn't so enamoured with the way those last two words seemed to stare back at her. Did they sound too cold and wooden? Should she have chosen something warmer, such as *Dearest Luke*? Or even, *My Dearest Luke*? No, both of those were too soppy. Better, surely, just to be plain-spoken. After all, neither of them were people for flowery words.

So, what next? What did she say now? With her hand hovering in readiness to write, she wracked her brains, dismayed to find herself once again lost for a way to start. Oh, but this was ridiculous! This was Luke she was writing to – the person she had known all of her life and then chosen to wed – not some stranger she was beseeching for a position of employment. So why wouldn't the words come to her? *Because, though you might have known him all of your life, you don't properly know him as a husband*, a little voice in her mind rather unhelpfully chipped in. The little voice spoke the truth.

Then she had a thought. She would tell him how she came to be back in Woodicombe again. Yes, the sale of the house would be a proper piece of news for him. He would be staggered to learn that Hugh Russell had bought it. Well, assuming he didn't already know as much – assuming he hadn't already been told by Mr Lawrence, himself having already been told by Naomi. Either way, for sheer want of a better way to start, she would tell him.

For a while after that she got along just fine, writing of Edith's wariness at the discovery of what Hugh Russell had done, and, determining to be charitable, describing her reaction as *understandable*. Unfortunately, once she finally finished committing that piece of news to paper, she found herself once again stuck for something to say. What she *wanted* to do was convey to him some of her turmoil – to say that with him having been gone so long now, at times, she struggled to recall the details of his face and that, the harder she tried to do so, the more the finer details of it seemed to evade her. She wanted to tell him that when she tried to picture his features, in the places where his eyes and his mouth and his nose should be was just a blank and fuzzy flesh-coloured oval. She wanted to admit to him that while she knew that his hair was coarse to the touch, she could no longer remember the actual feel of it between her fingers. Most of all, she longed to confess that, most of the time, she didn't even feel as though she was married. Of course, she couldn't do that. Despite what Ma Channer had suggested, she couldn't write a single word of it. It couldn't possibly be the sort of thing he spent his days longing to hear. *Longing to hear.* That was it! She would tell him what he would surely be longing to hear.

Once again dipping her nib into the ink, she started to write.

> *I do miss you so. I do miss that we don't share a home. I do miss that I don't make you your breakfast or cook you your suppers. And though I do surely hate the job, I do miss that I don't iron your collars. Or even darn your socks. I miss that we don't never have a chance to sit down together come evening time and tell each other of our days. Naomi is forever reminding me to be brave and I do try my best not to complain. After all, I am well in myself and I have both a home and work with no worries on either score. But I do wish we were together in the way of proper married folk.*

With the words seeming to have poured from her pen – her only fear being that she might not capture them all – she finally paused to draw breath. Well, how much better did she feel for that! How badly must she have needed to admit to those feelings of missing him? Being brave was all well and good but, if these last few minutes of scribbling were anything to go by, there was still a place in this time of war for honesty – and for sentimentality, too – as well as for stiffness and brave faces. It was never helpful to bottle things up anyway – even Naomi, who always urged bravery in the face of adversity, held that speaking one's mind was the best policy.

When she read back what she had written, though, she was left wondering whether she had now been *too* honest, and whether Luke would think her letter either too soppy or too maudlin. Just in case he did, she would end by writing something cheering. She couldn't tell him Naomi's news – nor that they had seen Mr Aubrey. But then it came to her, and once again she started to write.

> *The other afternoon, I went to visit with your ma.*
> *She brewed me some elderflower tea, what I didn't*
> *know I liked. She is very well and busy as always.*
> *Your pa is fine too. Although on his own and*
> *without help, he keeps the gardens looking nice.*
> *His sweet peas are racing to the top of the poles,*
> *even though mostly he now gives his time over to*
> *the vegetables.*

She sat back in her chair. Yes, that was good. But now, what did she say to end with? To her surprise, she suddenly had no doubt.

> *My dear husband, I do miss you so much. Every*
> *day I do think of you and do long sorely for this*

war to be over with. Meantime, please take every
care to stay safe. I hope you can write to me soon
with news of what it is like there.
     Your loving wife,
     Kate.

Noticing that her hand had begun to tremble, she carefully
set down her pen. And then, unexpectedly, and from out
of nowhere, she felt tears racing down her cheeks and
found herself sobbing as though she would never stop.

–

'Kate, there you are. Won't you come and sit with me a
while?'

It was after supper the following day and going to check
on Naomi's whereabouts had brought Kate to the terrace,
where she had found her sitting on one of the ornamentals
benches, swathed against the evening chill in one of her
shawls. Her face looked serene, not a fold to her forehead
nor a crease to the corners of her eyes.

'Ma'am?'

With a smile, Naomi patted the space beside her. 'Fetch
a cushion and sit next to me, won't you? It seems we've
barely had a chance to speak to each other today.'

The reason they'd barely spoken, Kate thought,
returning indoors for a cushion, was down to their house
guest. When he wasn't teaching Naomi the rules of a new
card game or playing a piece on the piano for her, he was
explaining the finer points of the various battle campaigns
being waged by the army. Not that she was complaining;
Mr Aubrey was good for Naomi in ways she knew she
could never be.

Noticing Naomi eyeing her expectantly, she tried to recall what she had said. 'No, well, ma'am,' she replied, Naomi's earlier remark coming back to her, 'your time has been taken up with Mr Aubrey. Rightly so, of course, given what he's been through.'

'It does sound as though he's been through rather a lot, doesn't it?'

'Though you wouldn't know it to hear him talk,' she agreed. Then, realizing how much of what she knew had been learnt from eavesdropping, she carefully qualified her remark. 'Well, from the little I've heard him speak of it, it would seem so, yes.'

'I must say,' Naomi began afresh, 'he looks remarkably well on it. The loss of a little weight suits him – sharpens his features. Makes him look more like Lawrence.'

It was something she, too, had noticed. 'Yes, ma'am.'

'Being in the army has smartened him up as well – has made him appear far tidier generally.'

'Quite changed him,' she felt it safe to agree.

'Makes one wonder...'

Assuming that Naomi would finish her thought, she waited. When she didn't seem in any rush to do so, though, she ventured to enquire, 'Makes one wonder what, ma'am?'

'Oh, nothing, really.' Again, she waited, hoping that if she kept quiet for long enough Naomi would eventually elaborate. In this instance, her patience was rewarded. 'I was just thinking that had Aubrey been like he is now – last summer, I mean – I wonder whether I might have married him after all. I wonder whether I might now have been at Avingham Park, just as Mamma wanted.'

Feeling disloyal to Mr Lawrence to be even considering the possibility, Kate decided to confine herself to only the airiest of replies. 'I couldn't possibly say, ma'am.'

'No, nor I, I suppose.'

Then, feeling that even her woolliness was a betrayal of Mr Lawrence, she added, 'I still think Mr Lawrence far nicer. If it were me, even taking account of a fancy home, Mr Aubrey wouldn't hold a candle to your Mr Lawrence.'

Beside her, Naomi smiled warmly. 'Well said! It's just that one can't help but wonder, can one? Especially when one is, to all intents and purposes, still so newly married.'

'Um… well…' With a better understanding now of just how much she missed Luke, she could quite see how Naomi's own thoughts might be similarly muddled, especially given that Mr Aubrey was Mr Lawrence's brother – and that the two of them shared more than passing similarities.

'And I never thought I would say this about Aubrey, but I've been glad of his company. At first, I resented that he should be the one to come home while Lawrence had to remain in France – and yes, I do know that he is only here by virtue of being wounded. Today in particular, though, I've realized that his presence has made me feel closer to Lawrence.'

'That's good, ma'am,' she said, grateful that they now appeared to be on safer ground.

'It's difficult to explain but, through his stories of being at the front, I feel as though I have a better understanding of what Lawrence must be going through. Does that make any sense to you?'

She nodded. 'It does. I've learned from him, too. Though I can't profess to understand the half of it.'

Glancing about the garden, she asked, 'Is he not about tonight – Mr Aubrey?'

'Gone for another walk.'

'Oh.' That Mr Aubrey should have developed a fondnes for rambling still struck her as odd – out of character, to say the very least. But then many things about him seemed to have changed. For a start, his general manner was far less harrying. 'Gone to explore in the other direction, has he?' she enquired, largely in the name of conversation.

'I didn't ask. He just happened to mention that his previous outing had proved most rewarding and that he wished to see whether he might repeat the experience.'

'If he's gone tramping up over the headland,' she said, trying to picture him puffing his way up the steep rise, 'then he'll need to have a care to turn back well before dusk. There can be no ferrying him home in the cab from out there. The only way back from *that* direction is the same as your manner of getting there – on foot.'

'I did warn him to be careful. And he assured me that he would take no risks – his words, not mine.'

'That's all right then.' What she really wanted to ask Naomi was how much longer Mr Aubrey intended to remain with them. From what she had gathered by eavesdropping upon several conversations, he had yet to make mention of returning to his regiment. And if they were ever to return to London and get stuck into some meaningful voluntary work, they first had to get shot of Mr Aubrey. Uncertain how to proceed for the best, she glanced at Naomi's face and, finding it calm and untroubled, asked, 'Has he discussed with you yet when he plans to leave?'

Naomi, though, found her question amusing. 'Kate, really! How terribly direct you can be at times. If I didn't know better, I'd say you were anxious to be rid of the poor man. Pining for London and its myriad delights, are you?'

Seeing Naomi's sly smile, she grinned back. 'It *is* terrible quiet here. With my days all but empty not only do I grow... listless... but I'm starting to feel a bit of a fraud. Most everywhere else, women like me are working their fingers to the bone to bring in a wage and keep the family together while their menfolk are away. Somehow, it don't feel right, being here like this, almost as though we're on a spree.' There, that should do it; that should shepherd Naomi's thoughts where she wanted them to go.

'A spree?'

'You know – a jolly jaunt. A holiday.'

'Ah. Yes. I suppose that's not an unfair observation,' Naomi replied. 'We did say we would volunteer, didn't we? I had intended speaking to cousin Elizabeth on the matter.'

At last! 'You had, yes. But we can't volunteer our labour all the while we remain down here.'

'Kate, were it just the two of us to consider, I assure you we would have been back there last week. But I can't just ask Aubrey to *leave*. He said himself that this has turned out to be the ideal place for him to convalesce. And his mood does seem so very much brighter for being here.'

Inwardly, she sighed. There could be no disputing that. 'He does, ma'am, yes.' No sense seeming hostile towards Mr Aubrey – not if it risked having Naomi dig in her heels. She did tend towards stubborn at times.

'You're not wrong, though,' Naomi relented. 'We *should* have a plan. What I will do, is talk to him in the morning and see how he fared with regard to the matter of his salary.'

'Yes, ma'am.'

'And perhaps, in anticipation of our return home, I shall also write to cousin Elizabeth and ask her advice about volunteering.'

'Yes, ma'am.' This time when she sighed, it was with a mixture of satisfaction and relief. Not only would she shortly get to fill her days with activity, she had begun to think it might be better were there to be some distance between Naomi and her brother-in-law. Rising from the bench, she bent to pick up the cushion. 'That sounds like a good idea.'

'You know, Kate, I still can't believe how fortunate I am that you came into my life. And, once this baby comes, I'm sure I shall be more grateful still.'

Surprised to feel tears welling, Kate started to turn away. 'Come on, then,' she said, only half-turning back. 'You can't stop out in this night air. It grows damp about you. Sit here much longer and you'll start to glisten with dew.'

Getting to her feet and reaching to pick up her own cushion, Naomi slipped her free arm through Kate's. 'See what I mean? Without you to look after me, heaven only knows what sort of harm I should come to.'

'Very amusing, ma'am,' she said. 'But kind of you to say so, nevertheless.'

–

'It grieves me greatly to report that my difficulties continue.'

As good as her word, over breakfast the next morning, Naomi raised with Aubrey the matter of his situation.

'Oh dear. That is bad news,' she replied to his report.

'But I am assured that by the time I go to be assessed for readiness to return to the front, the matter will have been resolved.'

'It's unforgivable.'

'Dammed inconvenient. Begging your pardon.'

'And have they said when that will be?'

Away from the table, Kate listened carefully, her spirits sinking. This wasn't what she had been hoping to hear.

'Soon, I'm led to believe,' Aubrey replied to Naomi's enquiry. 'No more than a further week or so, I shouldn't imagine.'

'That's good.'

'I say,' he said, straightening himself up. 'Am I holding up your return to town? Only, if I'm disrupting your plans, I beg you, do say.'

'We do need to return before *too* much longer,' Naomi answered him, and to which Kate glanced across to study his reaction. Over the last twenty-four hours, she had begun to feel wary of his behaviour – although other than detecting a new shiftiness from him, she couldn't pinpoint why. Perhaps Naomi's peculiar thoughts about him had her on alert. 'But, not knowing when you—'

'Then I shall detain you here no longer,' he said. 'You have been gracious and understanding in the extreme, but I have no wish to outstay my welcome. Indeed, it might serve me to return to Regimental HQ sooner rather than later anyway and demand that the matter of my salary be resolved forthwith.' As the thought seemed to occur to him, he then added, 'I shall spend a night or two at Avingham on the way. Mamma will be delighted to see me, I'm sure. Yes, this afternoon, I shall go to the railway station and enquire of the trains. Timetables permitting, within a day or two I should be out of your way. You know, Naomi, I do wish you had said something sooner. Outstaying one's welcome shows a lack of consideration worthy only of a rotter or a cad.'

'Nonsense, Aubrey,' Naomi responded evenly. 'You have been no trouble whatsoever, has he, Kate?'

From where she had been stacking unused china back into the sideboard, Kate got to her feet. With a smile, she shook her head. 'Not at all, ma'am, no.'

'Quite to the contrary. I was saying to Kate only last night how your company has been most enjoyable.'

'You are so very gracious. Nevertheless, there *are* things to which I ought to attend.'

'Of course.'

'I *shall* have to request, though, that you bear with me a little longer for repayment of your kind loan.'

In the corner of the room, Kate frowned. This morning, despite appearances, something about Mr Aubrey's mood definitely seemed a little *off*; if nothing else, he struck her as displeased – agitated, even.

'Of course,' Naomi replied, clearly oblivious to any of that. 'The money is yours for as long as you need it. It's hardly a fortune. And you're not likely to disappear without trace.'

'I think the army would be rather displeased if I did.'

To his response, Naomi laughed. 'Yes,' she said, 'I should imagine they would be.'

'Well, I shall go and make my arrangements.'

With Aubrey taking his leave of them, Kate crossed quickly to the table. In a deliberately quiet tone, she asked, 'Is Mr Aubrey all right this morning?'

Her question met with a frown.

'I have no reason to suppose otherwise,' Naomi replied. 'Why do you ask? Does something about him seem amiss?'

Uncertain as to how much of her observation she should share, Kate shrugged her shoulders. After all, she might very well be imagining it. 'It's just that he seems more... more *tense* than usual.'

Stretching her arms above her head and then stifling a yawn, Naomi pulled a face. To Kate, her actions suggested that she was about to disagree. 'If he *was* more tense, as you put it, I didn't notice. Perhaps the prospect of returning to the front is unsettling him. I imagine it would be enough to make even the bravest of men feel somewhat apprehensive.'

'Yes,' she hurried to agree. 'More than likely that would be it.' Inside, though, she remained unconvinced. In general, she found Mr Aubrey's attitude to the whole business of war surprisingly nonchalant. And yet, in this instance, he had appeared mildly irked by the ease with which Naomi seemed happy to let him depart. And his displeasure had only seemed to abate when Naomi had been unruffled by his inability to repay her loan. Perhaps that was it: perhaps he was embarrassed by the prospect of having to depart without being able to settle his debt.

'Fortunate for him you trust he will repay your money,' she said, convinced she wasn't wrong.

'Kate, really! Of course I trust him. Aubrey is family. I don't doubt him for one moment. And nor should you.'

'Sorry, ma'am.' Blushing fiercely, she once again busied herself at the sideboard. 'Forgive me,' she said. 'I spoke out of turn. I… don't know what came over me.' And nor did she – other than that she had come to feel a certain protectiveness towards Naomi. *Please keep an eye out for her*, Mr Lawrence had whispered as he and Luke had prepared to return to their regiment at the end of their brief spell of leave. *I fear that at times, she can be rather too trusting of people.*

The following morning, though, his kitbag deposited in the porch while he awaited the arrival of the station cab, Aubrey's subsequent act left her feeling regretful in the extreme.

'Thank you,' he said, leaning to kiss Naomi's cheek, 'for being my salvation. This short spell of rest and fresh air, and your generosity with the loan, have been true lifesavers. And, although I indicated yesterday that I might not be able to repay you, I find now that I can.' With that, into Naomi's hand he pressed what appeared to be several bank notes, neatly folded. 'I shan't forget how, in my hour of need, you have been so kind. And, if I *should* see Lawrence, I shall make sure to tell him as much. I shall also remind him what a damned fortunate fellow he is to have married you.'

Standing a few feet behind Naomi, Kate squirmed. She might be guilty of misjudging his intentions regarding Naomi's loan, but those last few words had just provided a flash of the oily-mannered Aubrey Colborne she remembered from last summer. So, she wondered, which had been the act: his apparent new-found agree-ableness, or this belated flicker of someone rather less genuine? Hopefully, it would be a long while before she was faced with having to try to work it out.

When, a few moments later, the station cab finally scrunched away over the gravel and, from within, Aubrey had given them a mock salute, Naomi turned to her. 'So?' she said, 'do you still believe my trust in him to have been misplaced?'

But, before Kate could muster a suitably contrite response, beside her, Naomi doubled over, clutching at her abdomen and sinking slowly to her knees, a long groan of pain escaping her lips and a blood-red stain appearing on her skirt.

Chapter Four

Loss

'Forgive me, Doctor, but I don't understand. She seemed perfectly well.'

Standing in the hallway, still scarcely able to believe what had happened, Kate watched Dr Huntleigh set his bag on the hall table.

'Often the case, Mrs Channer,' the doctor replied. Pausing to slip his arms into the sleeves of his mackintosh, he went on, 'Unfortunately, on occasion, the workings of the female body still baffle us – even in these enlightened times. And, while it will be of no comfort to Mrs Colborne to know it, this is just one such occasion. What she must do now – and this is where you, yourself, must assist her – is get plenty of rest and lots of wholesome food. Ox-bone broth, in particular, is most nourishing.'

'Ox-bone broth, yes, sir. I'll see to it that she gets some.'

'And plenty of red meat for the iron.'

'Red meat, yes, sir.'

His mackintosh belted about him, Dr Huntleigh lifted his bag from the table. 'I'm given to understand her husband is away.'

She nodded. 'With the Wiltshire Regiment in France.'

'No need to trouble him with this, then. He'll have his hands full already. No sense him receiving a maudlin letter from a tearful woman. Poor man needs his mind on his men, not on his wife and affairs at home.'

'Yes, sir.' Goodness, the man had to be utterly without heart. *Maudlin*, indeed. Naomi had just lost her unborn child; surely there was nothing more natural than to want to share her grief with her husband and have him console her?

Going ahead of Dr Huntleigh to open the door to the porch, she turned back to see him halt alongside the packing crates. 'Coming or going?' he asked, inclining his head towards them.

She frowned, but then, realizing what he was asking, said, 'Oh, that lot's to be sent on to the previous owner, sir. Then, once it's gone, Mrs Colborne and I will be returning to London.'

'Not for a while yet, you won't,' he said stiffly. 'Mrs Colborne is in no fit state to undertake a journey of that nature. She needs bed rest, not exhaustion. Please see to it that she gets it, at least until I call again next week.'

'Next week, yes, sir.'

'Now, I've left my account on her side table. Please do me the service of bringing it to her attention.'

Behind Dr Huntleigh's departing back, Kate raised her eyebrows. What an objectionable man! 'Yes, Dr Huntleigh. Thank you, I will.'

'Well, good day to you, Mrs Channer.'

As soon as he had stepped out into the squally rain and closed the door to the porch behind him, Kate swivelled about and sped across the hall, hastening on up the stairs to Naomi's room. But, outside of her door, she drew to a halt. What on earth was she going to say to her? It would be pointless to enquire how she was feeling because clearly, she was grief-stricken. And it was all very well Dr Huntleigh instructing that repeated floods of tears would do nothing to help but what did *he* know of these things? How many babies had *he* lost?

Reaching towards the door handle, she drew a long breath. Then, she carefully opened the door and peered into the room. Propped up by several pillows, Naomi was staring across to the rain-splashed window, her ivory complexion blotched with pink.

Easing the door quietly back into its frame she turned about, with still no idea, even as she crossed the rug towards the bed, of what she was going to say to her.

In the event, it was Naomi who spoke first.

'*He* was rather a cold man, wasn't he?'

She nodded in agreement. 'A mite… brisk, yes.'

'But I suppose, when you spend every day alongside other people's suffering, you must become hardened to it.'

So far, so good; for the moment at least, Naomi seemed calm and accepting.

'Are you comfortable?' she asked, largely for want of knowing what else to say. 'Are you warm enough? It's turned into a rotten old morning out there.' When Naomi didn't respond, though, she had no clue what to do next. Did she make mention of what had happened and offer sympathy? Did she ignore what had come about and say nothing? Or did she report what the doctor had just said? None of those things felt in the least appropriate. Nor particularly helpful.

In the end, she chose to say nothing. Instead, she stood, her eyes drawn to contemplating the rust-coloured scrolls around the border of the Chinese rug beneath her feet; she would let Naomi speak when she was ready.

'He asked me to describe the bleeding.'

Puzzled by what Naomi indeed had chosen to say, she frowned. 'He asked you to *describe* it?' Surely, bleeding was bleeding.

Fearful of putting a foot wrong, she glanced about the room. Spotting the stool at the dressing table, she went to fetch it, returning to place it alongside the bed and sit down. She would wait for Naomi to explain.

'Apparently, if a doctor is present when it happens, the nature of the bleeding can tell them... certain things. I don't know what things, he didn't really say. He asked me whether I'd had any cramping or any unusual pain in the last few days and how much morning sickness I'd suffered.'

'Oh.'

'When I told him that I hadn't had *any* sickness, he said that for a woman to suffer none at all was highly unusual.'

'Oh.' *Highly unusual.* That didn't sound encouraging. Neither did the way Naomi was recounting all of this – relaying the details as though discussing something as ordinary and everyday as railway timetables or the price of coal. Perhaps the shock of it had left her numb. Or perhaps the only way she could find to speak of it was to distance herself from what had happened.

She sighed. Thus far in her life, she been spared the loss of anyone close to her, and what little she knew of losing a baby before its time was very much by way of third-hand account. The upshot was that she had next-to-no experience of grief upon which to draw. While she could just about conceive of the devastation of losing an infant, she imagined this to be different. But *how* was it different?

Was the grief less because the child had no form? Or did that make it worse – more difficult to grasp?

'He asked how long it was since my doctor confirmed the pregnancy.' Hearing Naomi start speaking again, she looked back at her. 'When I told him that I hadn't seen him yet, he shook his head as though quite irritated. And then he said...'

When she saw tears brimming over Naomi's lashes, she reached to clasp her hand. It felt limp and clammy, her action in taking it seeming only to make Naomi cry even harder. 'You don't have to tell me if you don't want to,' she said, feeling unable now to release her hand back to the eiderdown.

But Naomi shook her head, the tears spilling down her cheeks flying from her face as she did so. 'No. I *do* have to tell you. I must.' But, despite her determination, when her sobbing gave way only to a series of heaving and shuddering breaths, she was unable to continue.

At a loss, Kate simply sat and waited. Deep within her, something jagged felt to be tearing at her insides, and she knew that soon, no amount of willing her own eyes to remain dry would do any good. In anticipation of that moment, she bit hard on the side of her tongue. She knew of old that sometimes it helped to hold off tears.

For a moment or two, she simply sat holding Naomi's hand and listening to the rain clattering at the window. But eventually, with Naomi continuing to weep, she felt she had to say something – anything feeling better than nothing. 'Naomi—'

Unexpectedly, it prompted Naomi to continue. 'He said...' she picked up again, and to which Kate presumed her to still be referring to Dr Huntleigh, 'he said... maybe there hadn't been a baby at all—' Feeling Naomi tighten her grip on her fingers, she swallowed hard. '—but that if there *had* been, it might have been lost quite a while back.' Despite the tears coursing down her cheeks and into the corner of her lips, and the sobs that kept catching in her throat and leaving her struggling to speak, this time Naomi seemed determined to finish. 'He said it happens that way sometimes. The baby dies – the *foetus*, he called it – but that it takes a while for the body to… to *expel* it. He said… it would account for why I'd had no sickness – because the baby had been dead for some time.' When Naomi then turned to look straight at her, strands of her long hair stuck to the sides of her face and her lashes clumped by tears, Kate once again bit hard on the side of her tongue. She must not cry. She *must not*. No matter how harrowing this was to hear, in front of Naomi she must not shed tears. Her insides might be twisted as tight as a rope, but she had to remain strong. 'But there *was* a baby, wasn't there?'

Despite trying to swallow down the lump constricting her throat, in that moment, all she could do was nod. 'Yes,' she eventually managed to whisper. 'There *was* a baby. And one day there will be another one. I just know it.'

Hollow. And empty. To Kate, that was how the next few days felt. With Naomi confined to bed rest and Aubrey gone, her days felt even more endless than previously, the lifelessness of the near-empty house serving only to magnify the general melancholy.

'The poor lamb,' Mabel Bratton compounded the gloom by lamenting at every opportunity. 'Though I hadn't known she was expecting, I do feel her loss as surely as though she was one of my own. The Lord saw me safely through the birthing of my own babes and I'd wish no less than that for any woman.'

Edith, too, seemed surprisingly affected. 'I've made sure to boil all the goodness out of those bones for her. She can sip at this broth like she would a cup of tea. Then, come luncheon, I've got in a nice piece of porterhouse, and Mr Channer has fetched a few new potatoes out of the ground, special. Fresh as can be, they are. They'll be just right with a dab of butter, a sprig of mint, and some of that nice spring cabbage. Feed her up a treat, that will.'

For Kate, though, it wasn't Naomi's body that concerned her, but her mind, Dr Huntleigh's insistence upon bed rest seeming only to increase the opportunities for her to dwell upon what had happened.

Taking a glass of warmed milk up to her later that evening, she had barely sat down on the stool when Naomi said, 'I shouldn't have delayed, should I?'

Trying to think what she might mean, she frowned. 'Delayed? Delayed what, ma'am?'

'Delayed seeing the doctor. *You* wanted me to see Dr Huntleigh. But *I* wanted to wait until we were back in town. *Why* did I? Why didn't I take your advice? He might have spotted that something was amiss and done… something… to avoid it.'

'All due respect, ma'am,' she ventured, wary of worsening the situation, 'but I can't think it would have made any difference. Dr Huntleigh said himself that more often than not, there's no rhyme nor reason as to why these things happen.'

Naomi, though, was insistent, shaking her head as she said, 'No, this was *my* fault. This was something *I did*. Or something I *didn't* do. I know it was.'

Sensing she was going to have an uphill task to convince Naomi otherwise, she nevertheless felt it behoved her to try. 'You can't know that,' she said carefully. 'It's not as though you went galloping about the countryside on horseback or... or decided to move all of the furniture about and spring-clean the place single-handed.'

'But I did help you pack all those books.'

In her dismay, she sighed yet again. The truth of the matter was that Naomi had barely lifted a finger, let alone a crate of books.

'Some women do work a lot heavier than that and fare just fine,' she said. Telling it like it was felt mean but, on the other hand, allowing Naomi to blame herself wouldn't help either. 'If you don't believe me, ask Dr Huntleigh when he returns. Truly, ma'am, I'm sure he'll tell you the same thing – this wasn't your fault. Not that I can't see why you might believe it so.'

Naomi continued to shake her head. 'I keep thinking how devastated Lawrence will be when he hears of it.'

Recalling the doctor's words about not bothering Mr Lawrence, Kate hesitated; just how far should she intervene? When it came to marriage, ten days' experience of having a husband hardly qualified her as an expert. Even so, she could see the sense in what Dr Huntleigh had advised. 'Perhaps he needn't know just yet,' she ventured. 'Tedn't as though he knew you were expecting. Happen it might be best not to give him something of such sadness to fret over.'

Seemingly digesting her words, Naomi continued to stare towards the window. 'You might be right,' she said wearily. 'Perhaps it *is* selfish of me to want him to share my grief.'

'Not selfish, ma'am,' she said. 'Were he not away at the front, then it would be only natural to want him to know... and to have him console you.'

'Mm.'

'I'm not suggesting you keep it from him altogether – just until he comes back.'

'But what if he doesn't *come* back?'

She stiffened. Why was Naomi even thinking such a thing? Thoughts like that would do her no good at all. But what was she to do? The poor woman had just lost a baby – she couldn't very well tell her to stop being so gloomy and pull herself together. Not helping was the fact that outside, it was *still* raining, the flatness of the grey light making the room feel cold and dismal.

'Ma'am... *Naomi...*'

'If Lawrence doesn't come back, I will have lost my only chance to have his child. *I* will have lost it. *Me.*'

While there could be no disputing the first part of Naomi's observation, in the overall scheme of things, she didn't think that the worst of it. In fact, the longer she reflected upon Naomi's words, the more she realized that *she* saw things quite differently. If *she* had been the one to find herself expecting, and *Luke* didn't come back from the war, would she really want to be faced with trying to raise a child on her own? Or to be otherwise left hoping that another returning soldier might be looking for a wife and be prepared to take on not only a widow but her child as well? Having grown up without a father herself, wouldn't she want her own child to have one? Wouldn't that in itself leave her with no choice *but* to marry again? On the other hand, faced with the tragedy of losing Luke *and* having to find a way to make a different life, how would she feel about being left with his child in the first place? Wouldn't she feel unable to make a fresh start? Wouldn't things just be twice as difficult? Twice as painful? Twice the burden?

When Naomi chose that moment to regard her, presumably in the expectation of some sort of a response, she thought she looked utterly defeated: pale and drawn and small. The problem was, to Naomi, her concerns about Mr Lawrence's well-being – or lack thereof – were very real. They just weren't the sort of thing upon which she should be dwelling.

'But Mr Lawrence is fine,' she said calmly. 'He and Luke both are. They'll be back. Mark my words, they will.' Among the folds of her skirt, her fingers were so tightly crossed against the possibility that she was lying that they started to cramp.

'How can you be so sure?' Naomi wanted to know. 'It's weeks since we've heard from them.'

Unwinding her fingers, Kate sat for a moment in reflection. Naomi's questions weren't unreasonable; it *was* a long time. But then she remembered a conversation from a few days earlier and so, pulling herself upright, she said, 'It *is* a long while now, yes. But Mr Aubrey – Lieutenant Colborne – said we weren't to let that worry us. He said it's a perfectly normal state of affairs for it to be hard to get letters out, and for mail to be held up.'

'*Aubrey* was shot.'

Don't get cross with her, she told herself. There but for the grace of God and all that. 'He was, ma'am, yes. But that's no reason to fear the same fate will befall Mr Lawrence.'

'They're in the same regiment.'

Oh, this was getting them nowhere. Seemingly, Naomi was hell-bent on rejecting every helpful observation she tried to make.

In her head, she scrabbled about yet again for something that might be of comfort, all the time aware that Naomi was stirring her own barely controlled fears. 'They are in the same regiment, yes,' she said, going quickly on to add, 'which should make everything Mr Aubrey said to you even more reassuring. He's been there. He's seen what it's like. We can trust what he said to us as being the truth. After all, he has no reason to lie to you, none whatsoever.'

'I should *like* to think you're right… but I still can't bring myself to believe you.'

Before she could answer this time, she had to unclench her jaw. That she was both out of her depth *and* running out of patience was undeniable. 'We have to stay strong for them, ma'am,' she said. 'As we said only the other day, there are thousands and thousands of us women, all in the same boat. Besides which, Mr Aubrey said that with Mr Lawrence being an officer, if he were to… *suffer a mishap*… then you would get to hear of it real quick.' *If only the same was true of Luke*, she found herself thinking. From what she had been able to gather, with enlisted men there wasn't necessarily quite the same rush to inform their nearest and dearest.

Naomi gave a resigned sigh. 'I know. I do wish Aubrey hadn't left us. I wish he were here now.'

For a moment, Kate simply sat where she was, trying to decide whether or not that *would* be a good thing. That he had lifted Naomi's spirits was clear. But was he the right man for her to come to rely upon – to use as a prop? Of that she felt less certain. Besides, in her current grief, she wasn't sure Naomi might not confuse him with Mr Lawrence. She did seem to have latched onto him in a way that perhaps wasn't altogether healthy. Moreover, for her own part, she still couldn't decide what it was about him that hadn't seemed entirely right.

Yet again, she sighed. This really was quite hopeless.

'He had to go back to the front, ma'am.'

'I know. But it could be that when he went for his medical – or whatever he called it – he might not have been passed as fit to *go* back. For all we know, he's still in Wiltshire. How would we know? More to the point, how would one find out?' With that, Naomi sat bolt upright. 'Oh, I know! They have a telephone now at Avingham Park – Lawrence mentioned it. You could speak to Cicely Colborne. Aubrey was going to go and stay there, wasn't he? So, she would know whether he has returned to France yet. Just think, Kate, we could be sitting here, missing his company and imagining him back in France when he might still be quite close by.'

Despite the way that Naomi had raised herself up, and regardless of the changed look that had come over her face, Kate remained wary. To her mind, the best thing might be to get Naomi back to Hartland Street, not undertake a fool's errand by trying to track down Mr Aubrey. At home, she would have the company of her mother and Aunt Diana. *Aunt Diana.* She would be just the person to help – far more so even than Mrs Russell.

'Let's get you a little better first,' she said cautiously. 'I've attended you long enough to know that you wouldn't want Mr Aubrey to see you looking like this—'

Once again, Naomi straightened herself up. This time, she pressed a hand to her hair. 'Do I look a fright?' she asked. 'I suppose I must do. Pass me my hand-mirror, would you?'

With no intention of letting Naomi see how gaunt and dishevelled she looked, she got up and went to the dressing table. But, instead of reaching for the mirror, she picked up Naomi's hairbrush.

'Let me tidy your hair, a little,' she said, returning to sit on the side of the bed. 'I'll just brush it through for now, and then, in a day or two, we'll get you all nice and cleaned up.'

Briefly, Naomi looked doubtful. But then, to Kate's relief, she consented. 'All right. I don't feel like undressing for a bath at the moment anyway.'

'No, of course you don't,' she said softly, starting to stroke the brush lightly through Naomi's dark curls. 'Then, when I'm done here, I'll go down and fetch you a little something to eat. What do you have a fancy for? Boiled egg and toast perhaps?'

To her surprise, the attention seemed to soothe Naomi.

'Perhaps I could eat a little something, yes. But runny yolks.'

'And firm whites, yes, I know,' she said. When Naomi then settled back against her pillows, she added, 'You rest there then, and I'll be back just as quick as I can with a little tray for you.'

'Thank you, Kate. I have no idea what I would do without you, truly, I don't.'

'Oh, but this is dreadful.'

It was the following day and, having partaken of a modest breakfast in bed, Naomi, dressed in her robe, was now occupying the window seat in her room, shafts of pale sunlight falling onto the newspaper she was reading.

'What's dreadful?' Kate asked. It was encouraging to see her out of bed and showing an interest in something.

'Poisonous gas.'

In the act of crossing to the window, she felt her feet hesitate beneath her. 'Poisonous gas?'

'In France, somewhere close to Ypres, the Germans are using it against our soldiers.' Feeling suddenly wobbly, Kate reached a hand to the easy chair. How could anyone think up such an evil thing? Poisonous gas? It was barbaric. 'It makes for harrowing reading, truly,' Naomi went on. 'There's a report here from a young soldier who was with his platoon when they saw German bombs bursting overhead and releasing clouds of greenish-yellow. The report says they thought it a smokescreen to hide a German attack and started to prepare accordingly. But, when the mist fell to the ground and began to drift about them, they report there being a dreadful smell and how it became difficult to breathe, their throats and noses and eyes burning.'

Gripping the back of the chair harder still, Kate watched her fingernails darkening to an ever-deeper shade of pink. 'Ma'am, does it do any good to read of this? Would it perhaps be better not to know of such things?'

Naomi merely leant closer to the page. 'It says here that the War Office is appealing for respirators, which can be bought from Dickins & Jones and then donated, or otherwise assembled from gauze, wadding and elastic, all of which the store also sells.'

Unable to picture anything useful that could be made from such flimsy materials, she moved a step closer and repeated her plea. 'Ma'am, I don't like to see you troubled by these reports. I don't think Dr Huntleigh would think it wise, either.'

'Pah! Does Dr Huntleigh have a husband fighting in France?'

'No, ma'am, for certain he doesn't. But he might have a son... or a son-in-law.'

'Hm. I do concede that's possible.' Lowering the news-paper, Naomi turned towards her. 'I do understand your concern, you know. And I thank you for it. But I feel I owe it to Lawrence to know the facts – to know what he faces, even though the details of it might make for distressing reading.' Returning her eyes to the page of the newspaper, Naomi shook her head, seemingly in despair. 'Gas. What evil mind could even dream up such a thing? It is wicked. Poisoning men doing nothing more than following orders and defending their country is unforgiv-able. What makes it worse is that our soldiers aren't even supposed to still be over there. This war was supposed to be won by Christmas. The government assured us of it. It's why so many of our young men were so quick in volunteering to go.'

Despite sharing Naomi's views, Kate knew she had to find a way to distract her. The problem was, with their days so empty, it was difficult to think of anything they could discuss that didn't involve either Naomi's health or something to do with the war. Surely, there had to be *something* they could talk about?

'Edith is going to make you steak and kidney puddin' for luncheon today,' she said as the thought sprang into her head, the idea of discussing food when men were being gassed feeling inappropriate even as the words left her mouth. But, she reasoned with herself, while she could do nothing about the cruelty of the enemy, she *could* see to it that Naomi gave herself the best chance of recovering. After all, Mr Lawrence could suddenly be granted leave, in which case Naomi would want to be at her best. 'She said that Mr Channer has pulled some early carrots,' she persisted. 'Small they are, but for certain they'll have the loveliest of flavours.'

When she looked to Naomi for a response, it was to see tears running down her cheeks. With a sigh of despair, she pulled a handkerchief from her pocket and bent to dab them away.

'Oh, Kate, I don't know what to do. I feel so utterly wretched. At this very moment, somewhere in France, Lawrence could be engulfed in a cloud of this deadly gas, struggling to breathe but thinking only of his men. Meanwhile, here is his wife, surrounded by every comfort and yet not even capable of looking after his unborn child. I'm a disgrace. I'm not worthy of him. If he knew what I'd allowed to happen, he'd be so...' With this, her sobbing became so violent and choking that she couldn't continue.

'Shush,' she said, bending lower and putting her arms about her. 'That's not true and you know it isn't. Mr Lawrence is a fine man, a kind and caring man. He'll know you did nothing to lose the baby. He won't blame you, not for one minute. The thought won't even enter his mind. His only concern will be for you and your well-being.'

'He'll be disappointed in me.'

Stopping herself from shaking her head in despair, she said, 'No, he won't. And I say that not to mollify you but because I know it for the truth. Were he here, he would seek only to comfort you and assure you that everything will be all right.'

'I must admit,' Naomi replied, 'that does sound like Lawrence.'

'Of course it does. I wouldn't say it otherwise.' Feeling as though Naomi had cried herself out for the moment, she gently released her grasp and, unseen, wiped a hand across her own cheeks. 'Now, why don't you get back into bed for a little while. I'm going to take your breakfast tray downstairs but then, when I come back up, we'll see whether you feel like getting dressed or whether you'd prefer to stop where you are for now. How about I fetch over that book you started reading a while back?'

Accepting Kate's help to get to her feet, Naomi nodded. And then, letting out a long and weary sigh, she said, 'All right. I do feel rather tired again. Perhaps leave the book and draw the curtains back across. I'll do as you suggest and stay here and rest.'

Thank goodness: common sense at last. 'Good idea, ma'am. I'll pop back up in a bit and look in on you.'

With the pillows freshly plumped, the eiderdown tidied and Naomi back in bed, she went to close the curtains.

When she then headed towards the door, Naomi called across to her. 'Kate?'

'Yes, ma'am?'

'Thank you for taking care of me.'

With a weak smile, she nodded. 'Think nothing of it, ma'am.'

Arriving in the scullery moments later, she set down her tray and turned on the tap, staring absently into the sink as it started to fill with water.

'Everything all right, love?'

Over her shoulder, she offered Mabel Bratton the limpest of smiles. 'Not really, no.'

'She's taking it hard, poor mite.'

Tucking a loose strand of hair behind her ear, Kate gave a long and weary sigh. 'That she is.'

'Hardly surprising,' Mabel Bratton surmised, moving to turn off the tap and scrape the waste from the plates into the slops pail. 'What young woman wouldn't, in particular with it being her first? And with her husband away fighting a war.'

She nodded her agreement. 'So terrible sad, all of it.'

'And what about you, love? How are you faring?'

Her tentative grasp on her feelings finally slipping away, when tears began to well she gave in to them. 'Oh, Ma,' she mumbled, feeling Mabel's arms close about her shoulders. ''Tis such a pitiful carry on. And I don't know what to do about it.'

'What you'll do,' Mabel Bratton said softly, her arms closing tighter still about Kate's heaving shoulders, 'is have a good cry while you're down here with me. Then, when you've splashed your face and gone out and drawn a few breaths of air, you'll go back up there and get on with doing your best to help her. Seems to me, your Miss Naomi has led a sheltered sort of a life. Most likely she's not had a single day of hardship in her entire two-and-twenty years. Not that I blame her for it, of course I don't, nor do I think any the less of her for her good fortune. The way I see it, you, me, Edith, old Mrs Channer even, we're all sprung from tough Devon stock. Your Miss Naomi, on the other hand, well, seems to me she's more of a hothouse flower. Happen it's why the two of you get along as you do. You might have some of the same London blood running through your veins, but trust me, girl, it's your Devon half that gives you your strength – that'll see you through this. You've got it in you to be strong for everyone; you see if I'm not wrong.'

When Mabel Bratton lowered her arms, Kate met her look. And then she thought for a moment. 'Do you truly believe that about me?' she asked.

'I've believed it since the day you were born, love. Proper wilful little scrap you were. And that refusal to give in has never left you. Life might have knocked you sideways recent times, but you haven't let it alter who you are nor sway you from doing the right thing.'

'Hm.' At that moment, she wished she shared Mabel's conviction.

'Now, why don't you go an' give your face a quick splash and then take yourself off outside for a breath or two of air while I see to these dishes?'

Sniffing loudly, and then turning to where Mabel Bratton had begun to busy herself at the sink, she nodded. 'Thank you… Ma.'

'No trouble, girl. I might not be able to right the world's wrongs, but I'll always make time to listen to your woes. After all, as the saying goes, a problem shared is a problem halved.'

Yes, she reflected, halving any problem was always a good start. But, as ever, it still left the matter of what to do with the other half – which, in her experience of these things, was more often than not the thorniest part of all.

There. Success. Granted, it was a bit of an underhand thing to do but, if Naomi was ever to find her way out of her gloom, she had to stop reading of things that would only add to her woes.

It had been the newsagent's boy, delivering the *Telegraph* to the back door, who had put the idea into her head.

'Mornin', miss,' he had greeted her brightly. 'Copy of the *Telegraph* for the lady. You know, I said to me Pa only last eve, strikes me they should print two newspapers these days, one with word of the war for the menfolk to read, and another for those as don't want to know of it, like the ladies. That's what I said to 'im. Anyways, there you go, miss. Good day to you.'

And so, with the seed sown, Kate had taken the newspaper to the scullery and spread it out on the bench. Then, she had flicked through the pages, past the stocks and financial reports, on past the Court pages and the reviews of the latest theatrical productions, until her eyes had settled upon a headline at the top of a page that read, 'No Change on the Western Front, Germans Hold Fast.' With a quick scan of its length and a cursory glimpse at its reverse, she had taken the fabric scissors from the haberdashery closet and set about removing the page. Pleased with her inventiveness, she then refolded the entire paper along its original creases. All she could do next was hope Naomi wouldn't notice that a page had gone missing. But if she did, she did; at least she had tried.

As it turned out, her good intentions were thwarted by her failure to spot tragedy elsewhere in that particular day's newspaper, her oversight only becoming evident when

Naomi had finished reading the section headed 'Musical Concerts of the Coming Week' and turned the page to be greeted by heavy typeset proclaiming:

LUSITANIA TORPEDOED: 1,400 LIVES
LOST

'They've sunk the *Lusitania*,' she announced upon seeing it, her voice unsteady. 'Oh, dear Lord, Kate. Look.' Similarly unsettled, Kate turned away. But Naomi continued reading. 'It says here that in the middle of the afternoon, with no warning whatsoever, German submarine pirates fired two torpedoes and sank the Cunard Liner *Lusitania* with its fourteen hundred passengers, many of them women and children, and its crew of seven hundred and fifty. Good God. Is there nothing to which our enemy won't stoop? Are we none of us safe? What will they do next? Send one of these submarine things up the Thames and then march up The Mall to murder everyone in Buckingham Palace? I wouldn't put it past them.'

Listening to Naomi talking, Kate felt overcome by such despair that she couldn't even attempt a response. On the one hand, Naomi was right: to do such a thing, the enemy had to be cowards. And if they were capable of murdering people on a ship out at sea, then it was only natural to fear what else might they do. At the same time, she cursed her own oversight. So preoccupied had she been with removing the reports of British casualties at the front, she had somehow missed the most mortal news of all. Still, it was marginally better that Naomi be enraged rather than distressed, even though what she *needed* her to be was calm.

'Ma'am, do you think perhaps that today—'

'Oh, no.'

Slowly, she turned to see Naomi straightening the page. At the sight of her craning to read the small print, she felt her own shoulders slump. 'Ma'am?'

'Oh, no, this is dreadful. It says here, "among the passengers was the pitiful sight of five women, each with a baby in her arms." Can you imagine it? Can you imagine the fear of being out at sea, with the ship going down and nothing to be done? Oh, my heart breaks for them. This is evil of the very worst kind. Those little babies. Those poor women. Something must be done. Something...' When Naomi once again started to sob, and Kate moved to comfort her, this time it was in mechanical fashion, her mind and body beyond knowing what to do. The sinking of this ship would have been bad enough; the mention of babies, the final straw. 'Oh, my poor lost baby,' Naomi wailed. 'I did so want it, you know that, don't you?'

Damn the newspaper, and damn her oversight! Now look what had happened. 'Of course you did,' she said gently. 'I wouldn't never have thought otherwise.'

'I know... I might... have seemed...'

'There, there,' she soothed, deciding there was nothing for it but to just let Naomi cry it out all over again.

'...unmoved. But once I'd... got over... the shock, I felt pleased. Truly happy. I was going... to start... a family. I was going... to have... a baby. It was going to be a girl. I knew it. And I wanted her... so much.'

Moving to sit closer on the bed, Kate put her arms about Naomi's heaving shoulders and held her close. There had to be something she could do to help her recover. But what? This wasn't an everyday illness with an ordinary sort of a cure. There was no clear remedy.

But wait a minute: *remedy*. Ma Channer and her herbal remedies. It was worth a try – even if all it did was bring Naomi some calm and help her to rest.

And so, later that morning, having peered into Naomi's room and found her sleeping, she put on her jacket, pressed her hat onto her head and set off up the drive. Reaching the lane for the second time in as many days, she turned in the direction of Woodicombe Cross and the lodge at the entrance to the old manor.

The showers of rain having petered out, the sun was surprisingly warm – peeking as it was through the unfurling foliage – the breeze barely sufficient to worry the emerald canopy of newly emerged oak leaves. Some-where nearby, the simple refrain of a great tit betrayed its presence. *Tea-cher, tea-cher, tea-cher.* Stepping from the rutted track onto the verge in order to avoid a puddle, the sound of its singing made her realize that she didn't hear many birds in London, even on the occasions when she accompanied Naomi on a stroll through Regent's Park. Even so, she still pined to be back there.

At the little lodge house, Loveday Channer was delighted to see her again so soon and listened carefully while she explained – taking care to mention neither Naomi nor her recent loss – that she hoped to avail herself of something to calm a person whose nerves had become frayed by distress and lack of sleep. Even though Ma Channer clearly knew to whom she alluded, she was discreet enough not to say.

'I'm minded a brew of herbal tea is called for,' Mrs Channer remarked. 'I'd prefer it be a tincture, but there are those who will have nothing to do with them. Don't trust 'em. Fear their power, some do. A tea, though, well, 'most anyone can be got to sip a nice brew. Nerviness, you say, and not viddy all round?'

Kate nodded. 'She's easy distressed by news from the front and prone to weepiness at the least thing. She's frail of disposition and given to such sleeplessness that each morning, she wakes listless and unrested.'

'Not with child, is she, this maid?'

Hearing Naomi described as a 'maid' brought a smile. 'No,' she said. 'I know for a fact she's not.'

'I ask only since some herbs mustn't be gi'd to a woman in the family way. Nor when she be a-nursin'.'

'She's neither of those things.'

'Then I'll make you up a screw.' When Ma Channer moved across to the dresser and pulled open a drawer, she watched her fetch out a slip of paper, place it on the table and then smooth it flat with her hand. Then she stood for a moment, her eyes cast up to the row of little tins on the top shelf. 'Six parts lemon balm,' she said, lifting down the one at the end, removing its lid, and spooning some of the dried leaves from within, 'to calm her thoughts.' Replacing the tin on the shelf, she reached for another. 'Four parts hop flowers, to bring her to drowsiness and help her to fall asleep.' She reached for the next tin. 'Two parts lavender to make that sleep restful. And lastly, I'm minded to add two parts valerian to soothe her listlessness and quell her anxiety. How do that sound, my dear?'

Kate pulled what she hoped was an appreciative face. It sounded just the thing: a miracle – if it worked. 'How do I use it?'

Using her fingers as though rubbing fat into flour to make pastry, Loveday Channer blended together the little pile of ingredients on the square of paper and then, drawing up the corners, twisted them securely closed.

'My, my, as impatient as ever,' she said, straightening her back. 'Still all a-fidget, I see.' Under Ma Channer's direct gaze, she smiled; there was precious little point mounting a denial. 'Now, listen up good an' proper. Two teaspoons into a teapot. Don't go adding more – there's no gain to be had from brewing it stronger and thinking it'll work the better for it. Pour over boiling water, put back your lid, cover over the pot and leave it ten minutes. Then, strain the tea into the cup, same as you would any other. If you happen to think she'll take to it easier, add a scant teaspoon of honey. No more than that, mind. We don't want her flitting about the place like a flutterby, unable to settle.'

Despite thinking it would be an improvement on Naomi's current lethargy, she tried not to laugh at the picture that came to mind. 'No, Ma Channer.'

'Now, there be enough here to brew a half-dozen pots. 'Less she's proper distressed, best give it to her once a day, around a half-hour before she retires of a night being perfect. The mending of the mind starts with the getting of a good night's sleep.'

'Thank you, Ma Channer.'

'Now be off with you, maid. But just make good an' sure to come up and see me before you leave.'

'I will. Thank you again for this, and bye for now.'

Once back in the privacy of her room at Woodi-combe House, Kate opened the little packet and sniffed the contents. The fragrance was complex: lavender and lemon, obviously; a beery scent from the hops, and some-thing that reminded her of either damp wool or the coat of a wet animal. Thankfully, the last smell was the hardest to detect, and hopefully wouldn't be evident in the taste.

Later that evening, with Naomi having only picked at her supper, but nevertheless managing to keep up a ceaseless invective about the ghastliness of civilians being harmed by the enemy, she cleared away her tray, carried it downstairs, and set about brewing the herbal tea. Leaning against the edge of the table while she waited for it to steep, she tried to think of ways to convince Naomi to drink it. *It will calm you.* No, that would be no good: Naomi wouldn't accept that she wasn't calm in the first place. *It will help you to sleep*, seemed a better way to encourage her. The problem with *that* was that Naomi might suspect her of lacing the tea with a sleeping draft, the likes of which she had repeatedly refused.

With that, she had an idea. Reaching to the dresser, she set two cups and two saucers on the tray alongside the teapot. Then she set off back to Naomi's room, where, without comment, she put the tray on the side table, dragged the easy chair alongside Naomi's bed, and sat down.

Eventually, Naomi having made no observation at all, she said, 'I've made us some herbal tea. It's been that sort of a day I could do with calming my thoughts before retiring to bed – no point even trying to sleep while I'm in such a frazzle.' When Naomi still didn't reply, she added, 'Happen you might like a cup as well.'

Having prepared for what she thought to be every possible reaction, she was astonished to see Naomi simply reach for the cup, offer it to her lips, and take a sip.

'Lovely smell,' she remarked absently. 'Most soothing.'

Hiding her surprise, Kate simply sat, her eyes fixed upon the wavy patterns in the walnut wood of the head-board, her shoulders gradually softening and her breathing slowing. Silence: none of the bustle and noise from the traffic that formed the background to her life in London; none of the heart-wrenching sobbing of the last few days – truly, a much-needed moment of calm.

Eventually, her cup empty, she replaced it on her saucer and relieved Naomi of hers.

'I'll leave you to go to sleep, then,' she said softly, reaching to extinguish the lamp and then feeling about in the near darkness for her tray.

'Yes, all right,' Naomi said. 'Goodnight, Kate. I hope the tea helps you to sleep.'

In the darkness, Kate smiled. 'You, too, ma'am.'

'Is it too early, do you think, to ask you to draw me a bath?'

Naomi's request, first thing the following morning, caught Kate by surprise. Despite having slept unexpectedly well herself, it was with some trepidation that she had opened the door to Naomi's room, astonished and relieved to find that not only was she wide awake but also sitting up in bed, stretching.

'No, ma'am. 'Course it isn't,' she said, going across to fasten back the curtains.

'Only, I don't feel very clean.'

'Understandable.'

'And I don't know what was in that tea you gave me last night but this morning I feel far more rested.'

'Me, too, ma'am.'

'Perhaps we should partake of another cup this evening – if you have any more of it.'

Barely able to conceal her relief, she smiled warmly. 'I'll see to it, yes. But for now, I'll pop along and draw you a bath. And then, while you're having a lovely soak, I'll change the bedlinens.' Reaching to pull aside the blankets for her, she watched with delight as Naomi tentatively lowered her feet to the rug. 'But, while I'm along the way, drawing the water, please don't go wandering about the place. If you were to feel faint, I might not hear you call out.'

Naomi gave a tiny nod. 'Very well. I've no wish to be even more of a nuisance.'

'You're not a nuisance, ma'am, truly you're not. We just need to take every care.'

To Kate's mind, Naomi's new mood augured well. But better was to come. Once bathed and back in her room, rather than climbing back into bed, Naomi asked for help to get dressed.

'I know Dr Huntleigh prescribed bed rest,' she said, sitting at the dressing table for Kate to brush her hair, 'but I don't think it's doing me any good. In fact, I do believe it's serving only to make me dwell. If I am to recover, I'm going to need something to look at, or to listen to. Staring at the wallpaper is starting to drive me to distraction. And I know every crack in the ceiling by heart.'

And when, the morning after that, Naomi wanted to do the same again, Kate felt justified in assuming that she was now on the mend. Awaiting the arrival of Dr Huntleigh later that same afternoon, she was even minded to ask him whether Naomi might travel home, certain that once there, her progress would be even stronger.

Dr Huntleigh, though, was aghast that she should even be considering it; in response to her carefully worded enquiry, he almost exploded. 'My dear Mrs Channer,' he bellowed, 'the patient is far too frail. No, it is out of the question so soon after her episode. As it is, finding Mrs Colborne neither in bed nor in nightclothes, I have reason to suspect that she has not been following my instructions.'

'Remaining in bed wasn't helping me to feel any better,' Naomi rose to her own defence. 'I am out of bed at my own insistence. But I have not been out of doors, nor have I undertaken anything evenly remotely strenuous—'

'I sincerely hope *not*. At some point in the coming weeks, you will ask me how things stand with regard to you trying again—'

'My dear Dr Huntleigh,' Naomi interrupted the doctor, 'my husband is away at war. Sadly, the question of *trying again* doesn't arise.'

'You will ask me nevertheless. Ladies always do. Gallivanting about as though nothing has happened—'

'Dr Huntleigh, I do not gallivant.'

'—simply will not do. You are not one of those fish-wives down at the harbour, with no choice but to return to work or else face destitution. Nor do you have a dozen or more offspring for whom you must care single-handedly. Thus, it will neither harm nor inconvenience you to follow my advice. Now, since you are already out of bed and dressed – and, since all being well, today, I had been going to suggest it anyway – I will permit you to continue to rise each morning. But *only* if you agree to retire to sleep for an hour each afternoon.'

'Doctor, I agree.'

'Very well. Mrs Channer, I shall rely upon you to see that she keeps her word. And put from your minds, both of you, all thoughts of making the wearying railway journey back to London.'

'Yes, sir.'

'Very well. Incidentally, *were* your husband at home,' Dr Huntleigh went on, 'I should say to you, as a married couple, that trying for another child is inadvisable for at least six months, twelve being preferable. And only *then* if your poor husband is able to rein in your headstrong ways.' Slipping a paper chit onto the corner of Naomi's dressing table, he went on, 'I shall call again one week from today. In the meantime, here is my account.'

When, having shown Dr Huntleigh out, Kate returned upstairs, without saying anything to each other the two women burst into laughter.

'I thought you said he was a better doctor than his predecessor,' Naomi remarked.

'Trust me, he is,' she replied, a picture of the frail – and, by some people's reckoning, senile – Dr Brinsworthy coming to mind.

'Well, I give you my word that *should* I feel weary, I shall take a nap,' Naomi said. 'Apart from that, I should like to return to normal. Just because I don't have *a dozen offspring*—'

'Or a basket of mackerel to gut—'

'Quite! Oh dear, his remarks were so comical it was as much as I could do not to whinny with laughter. No, but to be serious for a moment, I see no reason to behave like an invalid. I won't deny that for much of the time I feel overwhelmed by a deep and terrible sadness. And, no matter how hard you try to reassure me, I still can't rid myself of the feeling that I must have done something to bring about the loss—'

In dismay, Kate shook her head. This again! She thought they'd got past this. 'You didn't, ma'am, I assure you.'

'So you maintain. My point is that, where my body is concerned, I feel fine. Anyway, now that Dr Huntleigh isn't here to know, I should quite like to take a stroll around the gardens. From what I can see of it, the afternoon looks most pleasant. And I do believe that by taking some air, I might feel even better. So, Nurse Channer, will my light jacket suffice? Or shall I need something warmer?'

After having for so long read from Naomi's face only blankness or pain, Kate smiled broadly and, lest Naomi change her mind, quickly helped her to don her outdoor jacket and walking shoes.

Having made their way slowly down the stairs and out onto the terrace, they stood for a moment to survey the gardens before descending the short flight of steps onto the lawn.

'Not too cold?' she enquired, examining the expression on Naomi's face.

Naomi shook her head. 'Not in the least. This is glorious. Fancy a medical man instructing a convalescent to remain in bed when they could be recovering their spirits out here.'

And there, suddenly, was the old Naomi again. There was that bullheadedness.

'I daresay,' she said, smiling, 'that were you a man, he would have told you to pull yourself together and to get up and get on with it. But, because you are a woman, well, seems to me it's a way to keep you in your place – like you haven't a brain in your head to think for yourself and know how to get better. No doubt giving you orders makes him feel important.' *And justifies his bills*, she thought but stopped short of adding.

Taking Kate's arm, Naomi raised her face towards the sun. 'You might be right. Nevertheless, I suppose we should do as he insists and at least remain down here for a further week. Of course, while he might have forbidden me to *travel*, he said nothing to prevent us from *making ready* to do so.'

Yes, there was the wiliness.

'He didn't, no,' she agreed, heartened by the thought of returning to Marylebone at last.

'In which case, we shall do just that. And then, immediately after his next visit, we shall return home.'

'Yes, ma'am.'

'And try to put all of this behind us.'

'Yes, ma'am.'

'Despite this awful war, we'll go home and get on with our lives as best we can.'

'Yes, ma'am,' she agreed. 'That's just what we'll do.'

Chapter Five

The Volunteers

'It's from cousin Elizabeth. She's replying to my enquiry about voluntary work.'

Seated opposite Naomi at the table in the kitchen of the house in Hartland Street, Kate replaced her teacup on its saucer. This was an encouraging thing to hear; they might only have been back in London for a week but, already, she had found herself itching to do something – anything, really, to take her mind from the continuing silence from Luke. And to take Naomi's from seemingly just about everything.

'That was quick,' she said, hoping to draw her into reading something of interest from her letter. ''Tis but a few days since you wrote to her.'

Turning the page to continue reading down the reverse of the single sheet of notepaper, Naomi nodded. 'Earlier this week, yes. And I have to say, there would seem to be plenty of opportunities for us to do something useful with our time.'

This sounded promising. 'Does she write of anything in particular?' she asked.

When Naomi placed the letter on the tablecloth, she was able to see just how many rows of tiny writing cousin

Elizabeth had managed to fit onto the page. Surely, among so many words, there had to be *something* that would prove helpful.

'She starts by saying that what the VAD needs most – that's the Voluntary Aid Detachment—'

'Yes, I remember.'

'—is women willing to train as nurses.'

Having been leaning expectantly forwards, her chin resting in her cupped hands, Kate sat back in her chair and sighed. They'd already discounted nursing as being too bloody. 'But we're not keen on that.'

'No. They must be desperate for nurses, though, because she writes in some detail about how one is taught by trained medical staff in the matters of first aid, home caring, and hygiene, and how, at the end of it, one has to pass an examination.'

She shook her head. If the blood and the gore wasn't already enough to deter her, the prospect of having to sit an examination definitely was. Other than taking spelling tests at school, she'd never sat an examination in her life and didn't feel inclined to start now. 'Does she mention anything that doesn't involve needing to pass a test?'

Naomi scanned the page. 'She goes on to mention something called Red Cross working parties. Apparently, these are groups of women volunteers who organize everything from supplies of bandages and swabs for field hospitals to blankets and clothing for men arriving back injured from the front line. She says there are a couple of depots close to us here in Marylebone, and that she can give us the addresses if we're interested.'

'That sounds better.'

'Ah, unfortunately,' Naomi continued, 'she goes on to advise that while not *always* the case, what these working parties need most are volunteers fit enough to lift and move supplies, and to load vehicles.'

Across the table, Kate's heart sank; that excluded Naomi, then. 'Not what Dr Huntleigh had in mind when he reluctantly conceded you were well enough to return home.'

'No. And, although I didn't like the man, it might be prudent not to disregard *all* of his advice – certainly not for a while yet.'

'No.' Naomi was right. Bother. Working parties had sounded interesting.

'Well, reading on, then, she writes next about something called *rest stations*.'

She sat upright. This sounded interesting, too. But, when Naomi continued to read without offering up further details, she asked, 'What do *rest stations* do, then?'

'Have patience, Kate. That's what I'm trying to establish. I saw it here somewhere. Oh, yes, here we are. I'll read to you what she writes.

> *Rest stations have been set up at some of the London railway termini to provide food and other essential supplies, such as clothing, to soldiers arriving back by ambulance train.*

She says that irrespective of where the returning soldiers are waiting to go next, be that their ultimate destination or simply to a nearby hospital, they must be fed, watered, and generally tended to.'

Definitely interesting. 'That might not be so bad,' she said, staring towards the window, and noticing that it was splashed with rain. Typical – just when they might want to go out – *strike while the iron was hot*, and all that.

Naomi read on. 'She says that troop trains arrive into Victoria from Dover and into Waterloo from Southampton.' Glancing up, she went on, 'Waterloo is rather a way from here, being south of the river. But Victoria is no more than a few minutes by cab.'

'Could we go and look, do you think? Once this rain lets up, I mean.'

Naomi's response was to give a thoughtful nod. 'I suppose it couldn't harm to go and see what's involved. Victoria wouldn't be *too* far to go a couple of days a week.'

Hm, clearly, Naomi wasn't entirely convinced. And yet, from the sound of it, it appeared just the sort of opportunity they were seeking – too good, in fact, to let slip through their fingers. So, she would sound encouraging. Sometimes, all Naomi needed was just a little coaxing in the right direction. 'If we *don't* go,' she ventured, 'we won't know whether they need anyone at all, let alone the two of *us.*'

'You're quite right, of course,' Naomi agreed. 'And in which case I had better go up and dress. Something smart and cheerful for the weary soldiers to look at but nothing too showy.'

Surprised by Naomi's sudden decisiveness, Kate got to her feet; this was more like it. 'Once I've cleared away these few things, I'll go up and do the same,' she replied. 'Then, as soon as this rain stops, we'll go along and see what it's all about.'

–

'You may set us down here, driver.'

'Right-o, ma'am.'

It was an hour or so later that morning and Kate and Naomi were on their way to Victoria.

'It's quite ridiculous,' Naomi turned to explain. 'We've moved less than five yards in five minutes. We'll get down here and walk through Grosvenor Gardens. I'm sure it will be quicker.'

While Naomi settled the fare with the cabbie, Kate stood on the pavement and looked around. To her, it seemed as though every motorised vehicle in London – and most of the horse-drawn ones, too – had chosen that very moment to converge upon Victoria Street, the result being raised voices and frayed tempers but absolutely no forward movement whatsoever. She thought of Mabel and Edith, and how they bemoaned the holidaymakers crowding the pavements and packing the quayside every summer in Westward Quay, and wondered what they would make of this.

Leaving behind the mayhem of the street and strolling through the relative calm of Grosvenor Gardens, she suddenly felt nervy. It was all very well talking about volunteering but what if, after all those weeks of pinning her hopes upon it as a way to occupy her mind, no one would have her? Or what if someone was willing to take her on but she proved to be no good at it? What if, after all of this hoping to be useful, it wasn't to be? What would she do then? *Better to have tried and failed* were not words she wanted to hear Naomi offer up in consolation.

'I'm glad you were persuaded to choose the pale peach striped fabric that day.'

Startled from her reverie, she glanced to Naomi's face. 'I'm sorry, ma'am?'

Naomi gestured to her outfit. 'I said I'm glad you chose the peach colour for that dress rather than the blue. The colour is most cheerful on you. And the ribbon you picked to trim your hat tones nicely.'

Drawing her thoughts back from the matter of volunteering, Kate looked down at the front of her dress. That the garments Naomi had bought her from Dickins & Jones' rather pricey array of ready-mades were far nicer than anything she had ever worn was beyond dispute. For a while afterwards, she had even felt out of place in them, as though she had borrowed them from another – smarter – woman. The experience had caused her to think about Edith and how, had she been able to see her trying on all of those new things, she would have been unable to resist making a comment about silk purses and sows' ears. She'd been a *bit* snide as it was. Although this particular dress wasn't one she would have chosen for herself, Naomi was right: in comparison to the safer blue colour she had picked out to begin with, it *was* cheerful, seeming to brighten her complexion and lift the rather ordinary brown of her hair. And, presumably, returning soldiers, especially wounded ones, could have their mood lifted by the sight of something bright and cheerful.

She smiled. 'Yes, amid all these smartly dressed folk, I find it don't stand out as much as I'd first feared. I shouldn't care to wear it in Woodicombe, though. Such bold fabric would attract no end of unwanted comment.'

'Bold? Nonsense. It's elegant and restrained – far more so than some of those floral prints I saw on a number of the young women in Westward Quay last summer.'

'Hm.' To her mind, dresses worn by holidaymakers didn't have to meet the same criteria as garments worn every day by the ordinary inhabitants. On holidays, a certain *taking leave of one's senses* could be overlooked, indulged, even. In any event, in any given summer, there were generally fewer than a dozen days when such light and flimsy fabrics were truly appropriate.

'Look, there's the railway station ahead of us,' Naomi observed. 'Cousin Elizabeth said we should make our way to the very farthest platform, which, if I remember correctly, she described as being *set back and almost hidden from ordinary view.*'

Coming to a halt at the kerb and looking up at the vast building in front of them, she directed her thoughts back to their reason for being there. 'Sounds proper furtive.'

'It does sound a bit cloak-and-dagger, doesn't it?'

She wasn't alone in feeling apprehensive, then; from the tone of Naomi's voice, she could tell that she was wary, too. Daft to be nervy, though – they had been looking forward to this.

Having negotiated the crossing of Buckingham Palace Road – picking their way in front of a slow-moving omnibus, its billboard extolling the virtues of Colman's Mustard Powder – the two women made their way towards the station's main entrance and then, looking in both directions along the concourse, spotted activity away to their left.

'I expect that will be it,' Naomi said, gesturing with her gloved hand. 'No doubt they use that far exit to take soldiers out to ambulances waiting on that side street.'

For a moment, neither woman moved. But when they did make their approach, it was to find everything beyond the entrance to the platform screened from view.

'Does your cousin say who we should report to?' she asked, trying to catch a glimpse between the screens.

'She didn't mention a particular name, no. But look, those two nurses over there are bound to know. Wait here and I'll go and ask them.'

Doing as instructed, she watched Naomi approach the two women in nurses' uniform and observed the conversation that followed. 'What did they say?' she greeted her return.

'They said they report to a nursing sister but that she's not in charge of the volunteers. They suggested we just go through the barrier and find someone once we're inside.'

'Oh.' Frustratingly, the venture seemed to be getting off to a less-than-promising start. But she would try not to let that put her off. She'd been wanting to do this for ages. 'Then I suppose we'd best do as they say.'

Despite the purposefulness with which the two of them then slipped between the screens, once on the other side, they stopped in their tracks. The actual platform was hidden beneath a mass of khaki, which was broken only here and there by the occasional flash of white apron and red cross.

'Good Lord,' Naomi breathed, her fingers flying to her lips. 'Do you think we have the wrong place? Only, this is not what I was expecting.'

Beside her, Kate exhaled a long breath. 'Me neither.'

Everywhere they looked were soldiers: some, cigarettes between their lips, leaning against the wall; some sitting, propped up against it; others apparently asleep on the floor. From more distant platforms came the everyday sounds of a busy railway station – the hissing of steam engines as they prepared to depart, the tooting of their whistles echoing about the cathedral-like space. From this particular platform, though, there was just a monotonous hum, broken only in tone or volume when a lone voice cried out as though from the throes of a ghastly nightmare. And there was a nauseous smell, too. If pressed, she would have to describe it as the worst mixture of dirt and damp, sweat and vomit. But there was something else, too: something familiar and yet not – something metallic and slightly sweet. *Blood*.

Needing to be convinced that the scene before her was real, and yet not wanting to take in too many of the details, she looked randomly about. Then she realized that some of the soldiers from a nearby group – all of them around about Luke's age – had noticed them, and were staring and commenting in a manner that turned her cheeks scarlet. When her blushing brought an appreciative cheer, she felt her cheeks turn even darker. Mortified, she bowed her head.

Barely an hour earlier, when they had been getting ready to leave Hartland Street, they had agreed to dress brightly so as to appear cheerful. Standing there now, she thought they must look as though they had wandered onto the wrong platform, their intended destination more properly the eleven fifteen to Hastings. Feeling herself breathing rather too quickly, she spun about. This was all wrong; they could do no good somewhere like this. She turned to Naomi, not even sure how to say what she was thinking, which was, in essence, that she felt foolish.

At that moment, a woman's voice called loudly towards them. 'I say there.' Together, they turned towards it. From the direction of the screens, a dour-looking middle-aged woman was coming towards them. 'Didn't you see the notices?' she demanded. 'For heaven's sake, go back out onto the concourse and follow the signs for your train. Ask a station official if you're not sure.'

Having barely recovered her composure from her last bout of embarrassment, Kate felt herself flushing all over again.

Beside her, though, Naomi seemed more composed. 'Oh, no, thank you for your concern but we're here for the rest station. We've come to find out about volunteering and were just looking about for where to go.'

The woman, stocky and humourless of expression, raised her hands to her hips and looked Naomi up and down. Then, with a shake of her head, she bellowed, 'Have you volunteered before?'

'No, we haven't.'

'*Anywhere?*'

Still Naomi didn't lose her composure. 'No, this is our first time. The rest station was recommended to us by a cousin I have at the VAD. She wrote to inform me that it can always use more hands.'

Caught off guard by Naomi's sudden purposeful manner, Kate was surprised to feel dismay. A mix-up with the platforms would have provided them with the perfect excuse to save face and leave.

The woman, meanwhile, raised her eyebrows. 'Well, it's nurses we need most. That said, your cousin is right. We rarely turn away willing hands.'

'Well, good,' Naomi replied. 'Then we fit the bill on two counts at least. We have hands and we're willing. So perhaps you would point us to the person in charge.'

'As luck would have it, you're talking to her. This next shift is mine. I'm Dorothea Hill. If it's volunteering you're after, you'd best come and see what it is we do here. You will have noticed, I'm sure, that a troop train has just arrived.'

When Dorothea started towards the throng, for so many reasons, Kate's instinct was to hang back. Naomi, though, motioned that they should follow.

Trailing in her wake, and narrowly managing to sidestep two porters bearing an empty stretcher, she strained to hear what Dorothea was saying. *Casualties. Injuries. Wounds.* Already, she felt out of her depth. When they then drew level with the hospital train, its dark-green livery painted at intervals with emblems of red crosses on white backgrounds, morbid curiosity compelled her to peer inside. Through its opened-back doors she glimpsed tiers of bunks three-high, made up like beds in an ordinary hospital ward. On a side table was even a small vase of flowers. At the next doorway, though, an elderly porter appeared. With a wink at her, he tossed a bundle of sheets into a waiting trolley. The sight of the stains on them made her look away.

Skipping a pace to match Dorothea's manly stride, she glanced about. From what she could see, the term 'rest station' was a misnomer. It certainly wasn't the sort of set-up she had been expecting when Naomi had read the details from cousin Elizabeth's letter. For a start, the only soldiers doing anything even close to 'resting' were those unable to move anyway – those laid out on stretchers, some of their injuries causing her to put her hand to her mouth and look away. One man, his image instantly burnt into the back of her eyelids, was missing the lower half of both of his legs, his uniform and face so bloodied that it was impossible to tell anything about his former appearance, let alone his age. Another needed the help of two orderlies to settle into a wheelchair, his eyes completely obscured by field dressings.

'Gas,' Dorothea said over her shoulder, evidently deeming no further explanation necessary. 'This train met one of the boats coming from Calais. It has bunks for 384 wounded but brought closer to 600. Most of these men are destined to be taken by train to receiving hospitals elsewhere in the country. Those who are to remain in London must wait here for an ambulance. I say, I don't suppose either of you know how to drive?' The shaking of their heads met with a shrug. 'Shame. We've a dozen new ambulances arriving next week but we need more drivers. Anyway, see that staircase?' Coming to a halt behind her, both women followed the line of her finger. 'Up there, in that first room, is Fee McAllister. She organizes the shifts for the volunteers. Tell her I sent you up. If anyone knows what we need most and where you might best be put to work, it'll be her.' With Dorothea whirling about to take her leave of them, Naomi and Kate exchanged glances. 'Oh, and don't be put off by her dour manner,' she called back over her shoulder. 'She can't help being a Scot.'

Kate sighed heavily. How on earth would she be able to make a difference *here*? How would either of them? She felt utterly out of place. Pretty much all she knew how to do without supervision was wash up dishes, dust furniture and mop floors. Oh, and repair torn clothing. But how would any of that be of use here? She glanced across the sea of heads to the metal staircase that led to an open door in the side of the building.

'I suppose we had better go up then,' Naomi remarked, clutching her handbag tightly to the front of her lavender-coloured jacket.

Her doubtful expression doing little to give her confidence, Kate nodded. 'I suppose so.'

As they made their way up the staircase, the wrought iron clanking beneath their shoes and the scene below spreading out like a field of bloodstained khaki, she wrapped her fingers tightly around the handrail and cast her eyes further afield. In stark contrast, the distant platforms were a scene of calm and order, passengers – dressed in spring apparel, their items of luggage small and neat and clean – making their way to trains that would whisk them out of the grime of the city and into the fresh air of the countryside: to their homes, their relatives, their boarding-house holidays on the south coast. They have no idea, she thought, eyeing their carefree progress along the wide and empty platforms. They have no idea of the chaos and the carnage just yards away from them. How many of *them*, she wondered, spotting two young women apparently examining their tickets and then peering in through the window of a carriage, their hats trimmed with spring blossom, would, if they knew what was happening here, cancel their trips to come and lend a hand?

At the top of the staircase, Naomi turned to look back down at her. 'All right?'

Despite longing to answer to the contrary, she nodded her agreement. 'Yes, ma'am.'

'Then let's see if we can't find this McAllister woman.'

Stretching away beyond a door wedged open by a metal box, was a long and dimly lit corridor. Painted green up to the height of the dado rail and a grubby cream colour above it, at regular intervals were green-painted doors, most of them standing open.

In front of her, Naomi poked her head through the first doorway. 'Excuse me, but I'm told this is where I might find Fee McAllister.'

From out in the corridor, Kate heard chair legs scraping across the floor. Was it too late to change her mind? Only, this sort of volunteering wasn't going to distract her from what might be happening to Luke – quite the contrary.

'I am she. And you are?'

Naomi went in through the doorway. 'I am Mrs Colborne. And this,' she said, gesturing behind her, 'is Mrs Channer. A lady downstairs told us you are the person to see regarding volunteering our services.'

Seeing no option but to follow Naomi in, Kate took in the woman's appearance. Tall, with square shoulders and wide hips, she was wearing a serviceable suit of grey wool, her auburn hair drawn tightly back into a knot at the nape of her neck.

'Are either of you nurses?'

Naomi shook her head. 'We're not, no. But my cousin, Elizabeth Newsome, who runs the VAD in Knightsbridge, told me that rest stations like this one can always use assistance. You see, our husbands are in France with the Wiltshire Regiment and so we've time to spare. And we'd really like to do something to help.'

'Well, your cousin is right to say we've need of more hands,' the woman answered her. 'We've *always* need of more hands. But, as you will no doubt have seen on your way up here, to be of any use, you need a strong stomach. The work is hard and the shifts long. And, while I'm not one to turn away any pair of hands, I'll say this to you: if it's an hour or two a week you're minded to offer us, then no matter how well intentioned, you'll not be of much use—'

'Oh, well, we'd want to do more than that,' Naomi rose to their defence.

Yes, Kate thought, they should most definitely have walked away while they had the chance. And surely Naomi could see that.

'I don't doubt you *think* you'd want to, aye,' Fee McAllister replied. Bringing her hands to her hips, she went on, 'Look, lassie, don't take exception to this, but it strikes me your labours might be better directed elsewhere. So, I'll make ye this suggestion. There's more to our operation than just the arrivals area. Down below us are the recovery rooms, along with a rec room and a canteen. Why don't the two of you go and take a look? If any of the chores down there are more up your alley, then by all means you come straight back up and let me know. I could have you in pinafores before dinnertime. If you find it not to your liking, I'll not disrespect ye for it.' Slowly, the two women nodded. This, then, was to be their escape: Naomi would want no part in kitchen chores; even *she* didn't want any more of those. Glancing between them, Fee McAllister then seemed struck by something. 'On second thoughts, I've a friend who runs a place for the widows of young Tommies. It's called St. Ursula's and she runs it from a building close to the station in Paddington. There's no wounded – no blood – just young women and their children, sometimes orphans, too, all of them in need of help with things like applying for relief or finding somewhere to live.'

When Naomi turned to look at her, her expression one of interest, Kate returned her look with a nod of relief. This latest suggestion offered them a worthy escape from what had quickly turned out to be a tricky dilemma.

'I *should* like to help these men,' she said once Naomi had accepted the slip of paper upon which Fee McAllister had written the address of St. Ursula's and they were carefully making their way back down to the confusion of the arrivals platform. 'After all's said and done, most of them are little more than youngsters.' *Much like Luke.* 'But I don't think I'd know where to start. I don't think I'd be of the least use. In fact, for certain I'd be a hindrance.' She stopped short of adding that, in any event, when she'd pictured volunteering, she hadn't seen herself somewhere like that. The point was to give her something to think about and to look forward to doing – not to make her worry even more for Luke's well-being.

'No, I shouldn't imagine I would be of much use either,' Naomi agreed. 'And, to her credit, the formidable Fee McAllister could see that, couldn't she? Very kindly, she's given us a way out.'

When Naomi held out the slip of paper containing the address, she took it from her and read it. 'Do you know this Wharf Street?' she asked.

Naomi shook her head. 'Apart from recognising the way home from the station in a cab, I know nothing of Paddington at all. But I can't imagine it will be hard to find. With a name like that, one imagines it to be near the canal. What do you say, then? Do you *want* to go and see these other rooms downstairs – the canteen and what-not?'

Standing close to the wall, out of the path of stretchers being carried towards two newly arrived ambulances, she shook her head. *Definitely not*, was her immediate reaction. 'I think perhaps we should try this St. Ursula's instead,' she said carefully. 'At the very least we should go and see the place. And if *that's* not to our liking, well, then we'll just have to wait until we find something that is. At least we will have tried.'

'Then that's what we'll do,' Naomi agreed. 'But, wherever we do go next, I shall make certain to wear something more suitable than lavender silk. I feel thoroughly mortified by my stupidity.'

Passing between the screens at the barrier to arrive back out amid the bustle of the station concourse, Kate felt the tension flooding from her limbs. 'I shouldn't think we've need to feel mortified,' she replied to Naomi's observation. 'We weren't to know.'

'You're right. We weren't, were we?'

No, surely, she thought, matching her pace to Naomi's, of greatest importance was that their hearts had been in the right place. After all, not everyone was cut out to tend the wounded. That, she decided, recalling the terrible wounds on some of those poor soldiers, must take a woman whose fortitude was nothing short of extraordinary – certainly it required someone whose own feelings weren't constantly quite so close to the surface, as hers and Naomi's seemed to be of late.

Once out in the sunshine, she drew a couple of deeper breaths. While the air wasn't exactly fresh, it did make her feel more settled. Whenever she had cause to look back to this morning, she would try to see it merely as a setback and nothing more. If anything, seeing what some women were capable of made her even more determined to find a way to give up some of her time and volunteer her labours. What she would have to do now, though, was hope that this next place – this St. Ursula's – would turn out to be better suited to someone whose talents were rather less extraordinary and rather more everyday. In other words, someone more like her.

—

'Tell me, Aunt, is it me, or is Mamma in a bad mood?'

When Naomi had announced that Mrs Russell and Mrs Lloyd were to come to Hartland Street to take afternoon tea, Kate had been left in a quandary – not because of the entertaining that lay ahead of her, but because she worried that Naomi would feel bound to confess to having lost her baby. That she might want to confide in her mother was understandable. The trouble was that by doing so, she would probably undo all they had achieved so far and jeopardise her continuing return to her normal self. More than once, she had made to voice that concern, only to fail at each attempt for want of courage, thus leaving her thoughts on the matter unsaid. It didn't make her any less watchful, though.

Having taken their tea, and ostensibly so that Aunt Diana might see the garden, Naomi and her aunt were now standing just beyond the open window to the kitchen, thus enabling Kate to follow their conversation.

'I wish I could say that you *were* imagining it,' Diana Lloyd replied to her niece's earlier observation, 'and that you were wrong about her mood. But I fear you are not. Just lately, your mother seems perpetually disgruntled.'

'Disgruntled?'

'At best unhappy; at worst, positively seething.'

'Has it to do with Papa?' she heard Naomi go on to ask, a degree of concern entering her voice.

'When *hasn't* it, my dear?'

Concealed from their view, Kate shook her head in dismay. In a way, she felt sorry for Hugh Russell: even had he not fathered two illegitimate children, Pamela Russell seemed the sort of woman who would still have it in for him. In her opinion, there was no man on earth capable of making *her* happy.

'Is she cross with him for being unwell, do you think?'

From Aunt Diana, she heard a long sigh. 'She does seem to have taken his being incapacitated as a personal affront, yes. But, if you want my true opinion, this time, it would seem to owe rather more to him having bought the house in Devon.'

At the mention of Devon, Kate carefully set down the stack of plates she was about to put on the dresser and listened more intently.

'Woodicombe? Really? Why?'

'To use her own words, she considers it *a slap in the face* – which I take to mean that it serves to remind her of Hugh's past misdemeanour there.'

'But he bought it to bail Uncle Sidney out of a mess. He told me so himself. What went on there more than two decades ago had no bearing on it.'

In the kitchen, Kate glanced over her shoulder. While it was *unlikely* that Mrs Russell would bother to come downstairs, it wasn't beyond the bounds of possibilities. She *could* come through the door at any moment. She didn't think she would: when Naomi had mentioned showing Aunt Diana the garden, Pamela Russell had made a scoffing noise. *That patch of scrub*, she had said. And anyway, even Mrs Russell couldn't hold her responsible for the volume at which Naomi and her aunt were choosing to discuss the matter. Nor could she be censured for being in the kitchen in the first place.

'In part, I'm sure it *was* his intention to help Sidney,' Aunt Diana carried on. 'Indeed, a while back, I overheard a discussion between the two of them to that very effect. However, in that same conversation, I also heard him disclose that by buying Woodicombe, he would be doing *himself* a favour, too.'

'Oh?'

'Assuaging his conscience, was how he actually put it. At the time I thought nothing of it. But then, a week or so later, I called to see your mother only to find her having one of her rants. It was when she said something about having *got rid of one reminder of the past only to gain another* that I realized she was referring to Kate. Or perhaps more correctly, to the girl's poor mother, Edith, and Woodicombe House.'

Resting her hands on the dresser, Kate froze. Now it did feel wrong to be listening. They did say that eavesdroppers never heard good of themselves.

'You think he went to all of that palaver and expense just to make amends – just so that Kate's mother might continue to have... well, employment? And a home?'

'That is the inference *I* drew from his remarks.'

'Goodness,' she heard Naomi say. 'Then my father has just gone up in my estimation.'

It was how Kate unexpectedly felt, too. Indeed, she wished that Edith and Mabel could learn of this new reason behind what he'd done.

'And the *reminder* Mamma referred to having *got rid of* – I presume she meant that *other* woman?'

'One assumes so.'

'But surely she can't still have been stewing about *her*? *She* was *got rid of* at the time, wasn't she?'

'She was, yes. Paid off. Handsomely, according to your mother. I was never privy to the actual details. At the time when it was all going on, I was newly married to Kingsley and, since he lived for his stables and his horses, we spent most of the year out at his house in Berkshire. Much of what was happening between your mother and father – the finer points of it, at least – passed me by. The only thing I know with any certainty is that more recently, the woman with whom he was involved has died. I read of it in the newspaper. I daresay your mother did, too.'

'Hence *getting rid of one reminder...*'

'That's right.'

For a moment after that, Kate could hear nothing but birdsong and then the distant whistle of a train.

'Well, you've seen all there supposedly is to see out here,' she eventually heard Naomi say. 'I suppose we had better go back in and rejoin Mamma.'

Indoors, Kate still hadn't moved but, when she heard the two women coming up the steps to the back door, she hastened through to the scullery.

'For what it's worth, my dear,' Diana Lloyd remarked as they arrived back inside, 'I still say this is a very pleasant little house – just perfect for you while Lawrence is away. When your mother disparages it, I suggest you take no notice.'

'Easier said than done, Aunt.'

'Wave aside her opinion. How she chooses to feel about it is immaterial. I think you'll find she's still smarting over missing out on Avingham Park.'

When Naomi laughed, Kate thought it a sound laden with irony.

'Another personal affront?'

When the two women started up the stairs, she felt it safe to openly follow them, arriving in the hallway to catch the glint in Diana Lloyd's eye as she said, 'Precisely, my dear. But that's *her* problem. No need to let it become yours. You did as you wished and married Lawrence. Who knows where the two of you will live going forward, once this war is over. Nice as it is – and terribly convenient – there's no reason to think this house will be your home for evermore.'

Eventually, with Naomi's two guests having left in a cab, and with the clearing up finished, Kate came across her in the drawing room, standing at the window, her expression suggesting that she was far away in her thoughts.

'Penny for 'em, ma'am,' she said, hoping not to discover that in the act of departing, Mrs Russell had said something to leave her daughter in tears.

When Naomi turned towards her, though, her eyes were dry. 'Keep your penny, Kate. My thoughts aren't worth even a farthing. I was only thinking about Mamma.'

Time to affect ignorance. 'Yes, ma'am?'

'You see, according to my aunt, Mamma has been acting disgruntled of late. And, despite Aunt Diana's reas-surances, I can't help but think I'm partly to blame – you know, for marrying the *wrong* brother.'

Exasperated that Naomi should be thinking about this again, *and* knowing for a fact that she was wrong, she didn't even trouble to withhold a sigh. 'You're *not* to blame,' she said. 'And, deep down, for certain you know that.'

'I had thought to tell them about the baby—'

In despair, she shook her head. They had been through this – more than once in the preceding days. 'We agreed that Mr Lawrence should be the first to know.'

'Yes. And that was what caused me to hesitate. Although, in the *end*, the reason I didn't tell her was because I couldn't bear to be the cause of even greater disappointment for her.'

Slowly, Kate approached the window. Clearly, Naomi wasn't as well in her mind as she had supposed; to keep going over and over the same thoughts, she couldn't be. Perhaps she should suggest that she see a doctor. Better still might be to find a way to distract her – give her something else to think about and to occupy her days. Later, then, she would suggest that tomorrow, they go and see this St. Ursula's place. With a bit of luck, it would prove to be precisely the diversion they both so badly needed.

–

'I did *want* to help those soldiers at the rest station.'

It was the day after the visit to Hartland Street by Pamela Russell and Diana Lloyd, and Kate had been surprised by the ease with which she had been able to persuade Naomi to take a cab to Paddington, where they were now walking along a narrow side street in search of St. Ursula's.

'So did I,' Naomi replied. 'But I'm not sure that was the sort of voluntary work one can just step into – not without some sort of training or preparation beforehand. And yes, I know that helping out in the kitchen or wherever would still have been a valuable contribution, but it wasn't... well, it wasn't...'

'It wasn't quite what you had in mind when you thought to volunteer.'

Naomi smiled. 'Nicely put.'

She cast her mind back to the sight of all of those soldiers on the platform at Victoria station. To be there in the first place, each and every one of them had suffered some sort of injury. It was a chilling thing to realize – all those young men, fighting fit when they had left for war, each of them now in need of nursing and care, some of them forced to accept that the lives they were expecting to come back to were now gone forever. With their eyesight lost or their hearing shot to pieces, they might never again be able to earn a wage to support their wives and little ones. With broken or missing limbs, their sweethearts might move on to another man. They had gone to war without looking back, only to return with no proper life ahead of them. Her heart broke for them, it really did. She was just so grateful, every minute of the day, that nothing similar had happened to Luke. Although, on the other hand, if something awful like that *had* befallen him – if he had suffered a gunshot like Mr Aubrey – at least she would know where he was; at least she wouldn't be faced with waking up every morning and wondering whether he was still all right. In truth, the constant wondering and worrying was the worst part of all.

In her distractedness, she turned an ankle on the uneven cobbles. Wincing, she hobbled a few more steps before coming to a halt and looking about at their surroundings. For certain it wasn't the nicest of streets.

Beside her, Naomi too came to a halt, examining the slip of paper she had been clutching as she did so.

'Wharf Street,' she said. 'Well, this is Wharf Street. So I suppose all we can do is keep walking until we see some sort of a sign on one of these doorways.'

'Hard to imagine it being in any of these places,' Kate said, craning her neck to look up at the narrow strip of sky between the towering brick buildings on either side of the narrow street. 'They look like warehouses… or them what'll-you-call-'ems—'

'Depositories.'

'That's them.' Her neck beginning to crick, she looked back down just in time to avoid stepping into a puddle. She had to start paying more attention to what she was doing and stop wandering off quite so much into her thoughts. 'For certain I shouldn't want to be along here after dark.'

'No,' Naomi agreed. 'But then there are any number of places I shouldn't want to be after dark. I say, look, the shutters on this next entrance are open. Perhaps there is someone inside we might ask.'

She nodded. She also decided that if anyone was going to walk into one of these unwelcoming buildings, it would be her. To that end, she quickened her pace. 'Hello,' she called, her voice echoing in the dark and cavernous space beyond the opened-back shutters. 'Hello? Is anyone there?'

Eventually, she heard footsteps and into the light from the doorway came a man in his fifties wearing the leather apron of a storeman.

'And how might I be of 'elp to *you*, young lady?'

At least he didn't look sinister, she thought, even if he did have more gaps in his mouth than actual teeth. 'Forgive me for bringing you from your business, sir,' she began, 'but my friend and I are looking for St. Ursula's. We were led to believe we'd find it on Wharf Street.'

The man gestured away to his left. 'You're up the wrong end, love. Come at it back to front, you 'ave. Keep going on down 'ere, all the way to the bridge, and you'll see it on the right-hand side. Last building before the canal, pretty much.'

She smiled back at him. 'Thank you. And good day to you, sir.'

With more purpose now, the two women set off again.

'I was rather hoping it wasn't going to be in one of *these* brooding buildings,' Naomi said, picking her way along the cobbles.

'Me too. Oh, look, there's the bridge over the canal. Then it can't be much further.' Where the warehouses eventually came to an end, there stood a squat flat-fronted building and, as they continued to draw nearer, she was able to make out that central to its frontage was a black-painted door with windows to either side, the glass in which was so dirty that it might as well have been of the obscured variety. More hesitantly now, she said, 'I think this must be it.'

Arriving alongside her, Naomi glanced about. 'I don't see a bell to press.'

'Me neither. I'll try the latch.' When she pressed down on the thumb plate and it clicked open, she wasn't altogether surprised. When she then tentatively eased back the door, it was to hear sounds of activity and the wailing of a small child. Surely this, then, had to be the right place.

By unspoken agreement, the two women stepped inside to find themselves in a square vestibule with a black and white tiled floor and an overpowering smell of disinfectant. From pegs on the walls to either side hung an assortment of jackets, mainly well-worn in appearance and drab in colour. Ahead of them was a pair of double doors.

'Look at it this way,' Naomi whispered. 'It can't be any worse than the platform at the rest station the other day.'

A picture of blood-soaked khaki returning to her mind, she slowly shook her head in the hope of dislodging the memory. 'Never was there a sight more likely to cause a person distress,' she said. But, having felt unable to help there, she now had a chance to do so here instead. Hopefully. And so, looping the handle of her handbag over her forearm and straightening her collar, without further reference to Naomi she pushed open one of the doors.

On the other side, in a large room that reminded her of a school hall, the hum of conversation stilled. Blinking to acclimatize her eyes to the dim light, she glanced about. But, before she had got much beyond taking in the scuffed wooden floor and the hissing gas lamps hanging from the iron ceiling-beams, a voice away to her left said, 'Can I 'elp you there, Missus?'

She turned sharply. The girl addressing her couldn't be more than fifteen years old. Startlingly pale of complexion, her large eyes were the palest of blues, her hair, worn loose, thin and long and unremarkably brown.

She cleared her throat to reply. 'Could you tell me, please, is this St. Ursula's?'

'It is.'

From behind, Naomi stepped forward. 'Then would you mind showing us to the person in charge, please?'

'You from the work 'ouse?'

'I beg your pardon?'

With a weary sigh, the girl rephrased her question. 'Come from the parish, 'ave you?'

Quickly, Kate shook her head. 'Oh, no. No, we're not here from the parish. No, we've come because we've been told the person in charge could use some volunteers.'

'You what?'

Kate frowned. More than once, recently, a shopkeeper or stallholder had remarked upon her manner of speaking and asked her where she was from, but, on this occasion, she didn't think that she could have spoken any more plainly. 'We're told she needs some helpers.'

Jadedly, the girl shook her head. 'You ain't wrong there, Missus. But she's gone along to Trick's Dairy for the milk. They give it her for nothing, see.'

Naomi stepped further forward. 'And what's the name of this person who's gone for the milk?'

The girl eyed her suspiciously. 'We ain't supposed to speak to strangers.'

She noticed Naomi soften her expression.

'No. And, ordinarily, that's good advice. Very good advice.'

'You can wait for her, though, if you want to.' Her offer made, the girl gestured towards a row of wooden chairs arranged along the far wall.

'I think we should,' Kate said. 'We should at least find out what this place is all about.'

'I agree. We'll wait.'

Once the two women had crossed to the chairs and sat down, interest in them from the room seemed to fade, conversations slowly resuming.

'Some of the littl'uns look mortal thin,' she whispered, trying to appear as though she wasn't staring at them.

Beside her, Naomi looked into her lap. 'Alarmingly so. You don't suppose they *live* here, do you?'

Discreetly, she shook her head. 'I shouldn't think so. But it wouldn't surprise me to find that they come here daytimes because they've nowhere else to go.' Careful not to look at any of the women in particular, she allowed her gaze to wander over the group. A number of them had arranged some of the chairs into a loose circle, where they sat, for the most part slumped forward, their chins resting on their fists, their elbows on their knees. When they conversed – something they did only sporadically – it was in a desultory fashion, as though anything of any importance had long since been said. At the feet of one of them sat two small children, scarcely a year apart in age, the larger no more than two years old at most. Barefoot and sandy-haired, they were dressed tidily enough but, to Kate's eyes, in need of a good meal. Of more striking interest, though, was the fact that they rarely moved. Unusually, for infants of their age, they made no effort to crawl about or even to make a noise. Perhaps they were unwell, she found herself thinking.

On the opposite side of the room, occupying some of the chairs against the far wall, sat another half-dozen women. They looked older than the first group – perhaps in their late twenties or thirties. One of them had a young boy, who, sprawled at her feet, was repeatedly setting up and then knocking down a dozen or so tin soldiers. Each time he flicked them to the floor, he exclaimed 'boom' and then rocked with laughter. A few feet away sat a little girl who Kate imagined to be his sister, chewing at the hand of a cloth doll.

As she was about to remark upon them to Naomi, the door swung open and a woman entered. In her hands was a jug of striped blue-and-white Cornishware.

'That must be her,' Naomi whispered, getting to her feet and smoothing down the front of her pale grey mackintosh. 'We should go and introduce ourselves.'

Kate, too, got to her feet. And then, giggling apprehensively, she whispered, 'What was it that gave her away?'

From a separate room at the back of the hall, the girl who had greeted them earlier reappeared. Slamming the door behind her, she scampered the length of the room, lifted the milk jug from the newcomer's hands, whispered something into her ear, and then made her way back from whence she had come.

The newly arrived woman turned to look across at them. She was tall and plainly but expensively dressed. Around her neck was a single strand of pearls that hung from the rather severe shelf of her bosom to swing in time with her footsteps as she came towards them.

'My dear ladies, good day to you. Nell tells me you've been waiting to see me, although I'm afraid she was unable to say why.'

In that moment, Kate felt the stiffness leaving her shoulders, something about the woman's manner telling her that this was going to be all right.

'We were given this address by Fee McAllister at the army rest station in Victoria.' While Naomi then went on to explain their purpose and the woman listened, Kate tried to determine her age. Her appearance gave surprisingly few clues. Her dark hair, pinned elegantly high upon her head, did have a few flecks of grey. But her complexion was smooth and unlined. On her lips was the merest touch of pale pink lipstick. Her eyes – a warm brown – showed a keenness and intelligence.

'My dear ladies, what excellent news! St. Ursula's welcomes you. Please, do come through with me to the back. There's a little room I use as an office where we can sit down and I can tell you what we try to do here.' But then, as suddenly as she started to walk, she stopped, turned back towards them and, extending a hand, said, 'Goodness, but where are my manners? My name is Marjorie Randolph. My brother is the Reverend Randolph of the parish of St. Mary's and this little hall belongs to his church. Since it would otherwise stand empty, we make use of it with his blessing.'

While they were settling into Marjorie's office, the girl they now knew as Nell reappeared. She was bearing a tray upon which rattled three pottery cups and saucers, each of them already filled with a steaming and muddy brew. Her tray relieved of its contents, she left the room without having uttered a single word or met a single look.

And so, seated upon rickety chairs at a heavily scarred wooden table, Naomi and Kate found themselves being introduced into the little world of St Ursula's Advisory for the Widows and Orphans of Fallen Soldiers.

Finally, Kate thought, raising the cup to her lips and listening to what the kindly Marjorie Randolph was saying, they might get to be of some use and do some good. And take their minds from the fates of their husbands whilst they were about it.

Chapter Six

St. Ursula's

'You know, I find this morning that I'm quite excited.'

It was after breakfast the following morning and, in the hallway of the house in Hartland Street, peering into the little mirror behind the coat stand, Naomi was adjusting the angle of her hat.

Beside her, Kate was thrusting her arms into her light jacket. 'Me too,' she said, slipping the end of her belt through its buckle and tightening it about her waist. 'Though I do still fear I know nothing to be of any real help—'

Evidently satisfied with her appearance, Naomi stood back. 'I suppose we shall learn.'

Pressing her straw hat onto her head, she nodded. 'I do hope you're right. Since seeing the suffering of those soldiers at Victoria, I am determined to do some good, howsoever I can.'

'I've been thinking much the same,' Naomi said. 'Ready to do just that, then?'

In a sudden fit of nervousness, Kate giggled. 'I suppose so, 'though I do feel mightily ill prepared. We'll just have to hope that Miss Randolph meant it when she said she would be on hand to guide us.'

144

Turning to lock the door behind them, Naomi smiled. 'I expect we'll soon get the hang of it. After all, we can read and write letters as well as anyone. And she did say that's mostly what it involves – helping the women to apply for assistance from that fund she spoke of, or for the payments from the army to which they're entitled.'

This morning, careful to have the cab take them to the correct end of Wharf Street, the women arrived at St. Ursula's to find it busier than it had been the day before, Marjorie Randolph moving between groups of women, scribbling notes on a reporter's notepad as she went.

'Ah, my good ladies, you're here,' she welcomed them. With a warm and wide smile, she strode across to greet them. 'Nell, come and take the ladies' jackets, please. We mustn't waste a moment of their precious time. We must get them straight down to business. Do you know,' she said, lowering her voice and bringing her fingers to her lips as though to apologize for her foolishness, 'last night, I offered up a prayer asking our Lord to see to it that this morning, you didn't wake up and change your minds about coming to help us.'

While Kate was shaking her head in surprise, Naomi answered for both of them. 'It didn't occur to us for one minute, Miss Randolph. Since leaving here yesterday, we've talked of little else but helping out.'

'Please, both of you, do call me Marjorie. And no, it was but a momentary fear. *Marjorie,* I said to myself, *did you not remark to Crispin that they looked like ladies of their word?*'

Pleasantries exchanged, Marjorie showed the women to the far corner of the room, where a couple of wooden tables had been set up with chairs, ink pens, pencils and notepaper. On one of them stood an open cardboard box. Peering into it, Kate discovered it to be filled with sheaves of printed documents, from between which protruded dog-eared corners of carbon paper. She pulled a face; now that they were here, it all felt rather daunting. But, she reminded herself, looking up and glancing about the room, these women needed help, and the least she could do was try to give it to them. If she came unstuck while trying, well, so be it.

'What would you like us to do?' Naomi asked, setting her handbag on the corner of one of the tables.

'I thought I'd start you off with someone whose enquiry is straightforward, someone I know we can help – ease you in, as it were. That way, I hope you will find your feet. So, today, we have a young woman called Elsie Goode. Her husband responded to the call and enlisted into the Essex Regiment with two of his brothers. What he couldn't have known at the time was that Elsie was expecting their first child. Sadly, early last month, Elsie received notification that he had been killed by a German shell.'

Discreetly, Kate reached for the edge of the table.

'Oh dear,' Naomi commented, flicking her a glance.

Marjorie Randolph, though, clearly seasoned to such losses, pressed on with her tale. 'Now, despite Prime Minister Asquith stating last year that a widow's pension of five shillings per week would be payable to the wives of fallen volunteers as it is to regulars, such payments have proven not only difficult to claim but harder still to actually receive. The whole system, I'm afraid, is mired in paperwork. Even when the poor widow succeeds in having her claim agreed, the payments can take months to materialise. And even when they do, as you might imagine, five shillings is a wholly inadequate sum. Twice that amount would be bad enough.'

'So what on earth do they do?' Naomi enquired. 'How do they pay for their rent or buy their food?'

'Mostly, they don't. Mostly, they are left having to cadge help from family members – if they have any. If they don't, then it's not unusual for them to be evicted from their homes.'

'That's terrible,' Kate remarked, glancing about the room. It was no wonder so few of the women could muster a smile.

'It is a tragedy of the worst kind. As I make a point of telling anyone who will listen to me, it's not only brave men on battlefields fighting this war, it's their wives and children as well. However, you haven't given up your morning and come all this way to listen to me go on. Much better I show you what we do to help a woman who finds herself in such straits.'

'Yes, do,' Naomi encouraged her.

By her side, Kate couldn't help but smile. That Naomi shared her own enthusiasm was such a relief!

'Well, firstly, we apply to the War Office for her pension. By now, I have come to know several of the officials there, which does help a little. Then we apply to the Patriotic Fund – that's a charitable organization – for any assistance they can give in the meantime. Both of those bodies send people to assess the women's situations. Sadly, the people they send sometimes try harder to find reason *not* to make payment than they do to provide actual help. So, that's where we come in *again*, acting as a sort of advocate for women who would otherwise be bullied by these officials and their tactics.'

'It all sounds quite dreadful,' Naomi observed, 'given that they've lost their husbands in the service of their country.'

'It *is* dreadful. The treatment of some of these women is appalling. Now you can see why, as often as not, we are their last hope.'

Kate nodded in agreement. 'Shouldn't no one have to beg for help.'

'Indeed. However, all is not entirely lost,' Marjorie Randolph went on. 'Last month, the government agreed in principle that the war widow's pension should be increased to the sum of ten shillings per week. Unfortunately, they were less able to agree where the money should come from to pay for it, nor were they able to decide which department should oversee its provision. That, I'm afraid I can do nothing about. What I can do, though, is see that these women are given every assistance to claim the pension due to them, along with anything else to which I believe they have a right – moral or otherwise.'

When Marjorie Randolph smiled at her, she once again nodded. Already, she liked this woman. At Victoria Station, Fee McAllister had struck her as purposeful but, in addition to tenacity, Marjorie Randolph seemed to have compassion. 'And that's where *we* can help?' she asked.

'That's right. So, back to Elsie Goode. We must help her to apply for her widow's pension. At the same time – bearing in mind there will be a lengthy wait to receive even an acknowledgment of her application – I have suggested to her that she seeks assistance from the Patriotic

Fund to tide her over. If they agree that she has a case, they will probably refer her to another charity, the Soldiers' and Sailors' Families Association. Get that far, and help is at hand – they understand what these families need.'

'Does anyone *ever* get what they're entitled to?' Naomi asked.

Marjorie Randolph smiled. 'If they come to *me* for help they do. I make sure of it. So, Mrs Colborne—'

'Please, do call me Naomi.'

'Naomi, if I bring Elsie across to you, would you fill in the form of application for her? You'll find several of them in the box there. Once you've done that, I'll show you what must happen to it next.'

Although Marjorie's instructions didn't sound overly complicated, Kate nevertheless felt as though her head was spinning. These poor women! Here they were, newly widowed, having to go through all of this just to get what was due to them. Besides sympathy, though, she felt excitement; at last, she would be directly helping someone.

Watching Naomi pull the chair from under the table and sit down, Kate turned to await her own instructions.

'Kate, you, my dear, might like to come with me.' With Marjorie then setting off across the room, Kate scurried to keep up; the woman was certainly enthusiastic. At the second of the two doors on the far wall, Marjorie came to a halt and began to hunt in her pockets for the key. 'In this storeroom are a couple of boxes of clothing that has been donated to us,' she explained. Lowering her voice, she went on, 'I confess to finding it necessary to keep them locked away and out of sight so that they end up with only the neediest of cases. I'm sure you understand.' Kate nodded. Seeing the plight of some of these women, she could imagine all too well what Miss Randolph meant. 'I bring you here, since it would appear that Elise's child has no proper clothing. The things it is wearing are little more than rags. So, dear, have a sort through these boxes and see whether you can find anything suitable for a newborn.'

Relieved to be put to something that didn't involve filling in documents, Kate took a step into the room. 'A newborn. Yes.'

'Two or three garments should suffice for now.'

'Yes, ma'am.'

The smell in the storeroom, as she stood looking about, made her wrinkle her nose; it was a mixture of mothballs, old cloth, and damp cardboard. She glanced towards the windows in the far wall; although they were too high for her to reach, in the corner was a window pole. With Marjorie having left her to it, she crossed to fetch it and then reached to unlatch each of the windows. Then she turned back to the trestle. Heaped upon it were what appeared to be blankets, rugs, and an assortment of garments. On the floor beneath the table stood a couple of trunks, similar to – but smaller and much older than – those Naomi used for travelling. Warily, she bent to lift back one of the lids: more clothing, most of it appearing to be women's, most of it folded surprisingly neatly. The items on the table, on the other hand, looked to have been subjected to a good rummaging.

Her instinct being to sort and tidy it, she withdrew her hand and reminded herself why she was there: not to tidy up as she would do at home, but to find Elsie Goode's baby some clothes. Tidying up could wait.

In her search, she lifted aside skirts, petticoats, and nightgowns. Mostly, they seemed old but serviceable. She also found blouses and chemises. Unexpectedly, her eyes then fell upon several smaller garments. She separated them out: a couple of long muslin slips; a baby's linen undershirt, badly creased; an infant's nightgown edged with yellowing lace. The latter, she held up. Was it the right size for a newborn? A bit on the big side, possibly, but it might be made to do.

Opening back the door, she looked across to where, behind the table, Naomi was getting to her feet, the young woman on the other side of it looking as though she was thanking her. In her arms was her child. She glanced quickly to the garments: they seemed about right. In any event, she was sure that Elsie would find a way to make use of them.

When she approached and explained what she'd found, the expression on the young woman's face altered beyond all recognition. Gone was the down-turned mouth and the mistrustful stare and in their place was a smile that radiated with gratitude. With those few hand-me-down garments, Elsie Goode's demeanour had transformed from careworn drudge into the sort of young woman for whom Kate imagined her husband must once have fallen.

'Cor, thanks ever so, miss,' she said. 'Me sister give us this thing to tide me over but look, over his arse here, it's worn right through.'

When Elsie held up her pink-faced baby in his ragged slip, Kate forced her lips into a smile of delight. 'Well, hopefully these will at least see you through for now,' she remarked.

'Have no fear on that score, miss. I'll see to it they do just that. Thanks again, the both of you. I shall hope to have no need of troubling you again.'

'Well, if you do,' Naomi said, reaching to touch the tiny fingers curled into a fist, 'you'll know where we are.'

For Kate and Naomi, the rest of the morning brought more of the same, Kate quickly coming to realize that the official-looking forms of application appeared more daunting than they actually were. Really, she told herself later on, they were just questions requiring answers. Invariably, addressing the first questions served to break the ice with the woman in front of her. And, once she got talking to them – and, in some cases, to their children – they seemed to open up to her, to trust that she wasn't there to report them to the parish or cast an opinion as to the length of their skirts, the state of their fingernails, or the fact that, from the colour of their teeth, they evidently enjoyed tobacco.

Back at home that afternoon, over a late luncheon in the kitchen, Kate and Naomi discussed their first morning of volunteering.

'Seems a bit daft now to have got so nervy about going there,' she remarked.

Sat across the table from her, Naomi nodded. 'It does seem silly to have felt so apprehensive, yes. Seeing the plight of those women, it makes one grateful for the things one so often takes for granted.'

'Like a home,' she replied, thinking back to one particular woman. 'This girl called May had been told by a busybody from the Patriotic Fund to sell all of her late husband's possessions before asking for help. But when that little bit of money ran out, the landlord turned her out anyway because she still had no pension. Now she has nothing at all.'

'Heartbreaking. And *I* had a young widow who had been sleeping on the floor in the rooms her sister rented, until the sister's husband was discharged from the army after being severely wounded himself and then they were *all* thrown out. You would think there could be a little leeway, a little compassion for these people, wouldn't you?'

Kate chewed thoughtfully on the last mouthful of her meal. That the wives and families of brave soldiers should be reduced to homelessness was shameful. 'I can't imagine finding myself without a home,' she said, unsettled to be even contemplating such a thing.

'I found myself thinking the same,' Naomi replied. 'Until this morning I hadn't given it a moment's thought – well, why would I? – but then I realized that even the lease on this very house is in Lawrence's name. Should anything happen to *him*, there would be no obligation on the part of the landlord to allow me to remain here. Not that I could afford to anyway. In that eventuality, I suppose I should have to pack up my belongings and go back to Clarence Square.'

Reflecting upon what Naomi had just said, Kate felt a wave of panic. At least Naomi had Clarence Square to go back *to*. Where did *she* have? Woodicombe? If circumstances ever meant that Naomi *did* have to return to live with her parents – because Mr Lawrence didn't come back, or because he was too badly injured to work and pay the rent – then she would no longer have need for a housekeeper. And she, Kate, would have no other choice *but* to go back to Devon, even had no mishap befallen Luke.

Disturbed by the realization of just how precarious her situation was, she got to her feet and began to clear the table. She carried their plates and cutlery through to the scullery and then returned for their glasses and napkins. Standing at the sink, she turned on the tap and watched distractedly as the sink began to fill with water. She couldn't go back to Devon. Not now – not having finally achieved her dream of living in London.

When she glanced up, it was to see Naomi still seated at the table. Wiping her hands, she went to stand in the doorway. 'It won't come to that, though, will it?' she said.

'What won't come to what?' Naomi looked back at her to ask.

But, on the verge of explaining what was troubling her, she changed her mind. Where was the good in seeking reassurance that Naomi couldn't possibly give? Why cause herself yet more worry? She had enough things whirling about in her head as it was. Yes, better perhaps to simply cast the whole thing from her mind.

'No matter,' she replied. 'Weren't nothin' important.'

Unfortunately, even to her own ears she sounded far from convincing.

'Hm.' Faced with Naomi's enquiring look, she bowed her head. 'Why don't I believe that? You know my views on keeping things bottled up. If something's worrying you, you should talk about it.'

Hearing the water still trickling into the sink, she wished she'd just kept quiet. Now, even though no good would come from discussing matters that were beyond anyone's power to control, she would have to do so anyway.

'I was only thinking,' she began, the resignation in her tone unmissable, 'about what we'd do if Luke or Mr Lawrence came home with such fearful injuries – like those poor soldiers we saw at the rest station – that they couldn't work another day for as long as they lived.'

Across the table, Naomi leant back in her chair. Drawing a long breath, she said, 'Oh my dear Kate, while I can quite see why that would be of concern to you, I can but assure you that one way or another, we would find a way to cope. Although at this precise moment I can't tell you how, I do know that we would find a way to manage. And, although I should prefer to tell you there's no need to even contemplate the possibility, I realize that would be disingenuous. Instead, all I can tell you is that every night I pray, most fervently, as I am sure you do too, for the safe return of all of them – of Lawrence and Luke and Ned—'

'I do pray for it, ma'am.'

'—though of late, I must admit to wondering whether God is listening. After all, no doubt Elsie Goode prayed for the same thing for *her* husband, as I expect did all of those other poor women widowed at such young ages. And what good did it do them?'

What good indeed. It was seeing *their* plight that had brought her to considering her own position in the first place. 'I wonder that too, ma'am.'

'Even so, we must *not* abandon hope. Tonight, I shall still pray that tomorrow morning, we awake to find that this despicable war has been won, and all of the ghastly bloodshed that goes with it is over. And that all of our brave men are on their way home.'

'I shall pray for that too.' Leaning against the door-frame, she exhaled heavily. 'Sometimes, ma'am,' she began wearily, 'I wish Luke had never gone. I know I've said it before, and yes, I know the War Office keeps harping on about such thoughts being unpatriotic, but that don't change how I feel in my heart. I miss him so much. And I fear for him even more.'

'Of course you do. I wish now that Lawrence hadn't gone, either. At first, it seemed terribly brave of him to have volunteered with such speed. He looked so dashing in his uniform, with his hair sharply cut and his moustache all trimmed just so. Even his having to depart so soon after our wedding seemed romantic at the time. But now, well… what I'd give to be able to urge him not to leave me!'

On the verge of replying to Naomi's admission, Kate froze. Was that…? Oh, dear Lord, she had left the water running! Spinning about, she fled to the sink and yanked out the plug. Then, realizing how narrowly she had avoided flooding the scullery, she turned off the tap.

Heaving a sigh of relief and watching the water gurgling slowly down into the drain, she realized that Naomi's sudden bout of gloomy introspection had been *her* doing. What carelessness – especially when it was precisely what she spent most of her time trying to avoid.

'Anyway,' she said, returning to stand in the doorway to the kitchen and lean against the frame. 'Isn't this why we've volunteered? Because not only do we want to do something helpful, we want our minds taken off what might be happening to our brave menfolk. So don't we owe it to them to throw ourselves into the chance of doing good and be of as much help as we possibly can?'

'You're right. From now on, we won't sit here feeling sorry for ourselves, we will remember the plight of the young women like Elsie Goode and do something to help.'

Turning back into the scullery, she pushed the plug down into the now partly emptied sink. 'Tomorrow,' she said, recalling the pile of clothing on the trestle in the storeroom, 'do you think we might get there a bit earlier? Only, all that donated clothing would benefit from a real good sort out.' Picturing some of the garments, she went on, 'There's a lot of clothing there, nearly all of it serviceable in one way or another. But, with it all in one great mound, there's no way of telling what's what. So, if I sort through it and put like with like, it ought to be easier to find things.'

'That would seem a good idea,' Naomi agreed. 'Very well, then, let's get there earlier tomorrow morning. And, while you sort out the storeroom, I'll try to make a start helping someone with their forms. Even if Marjorie isn't there, I'm sure I can have a go. In the meantime,' she said, getting to her feet, 'there's something else that needs addressing – sorting out, if you will.'

Having been about to turn back to the sink, Kate instead studied Naomi's expression. 'Oh?' No doubt whatever it turned out to be would mean more work.

'Well, for me, going to help at St. Ursula's simply occupies time that might otherwise be idle. But for you, it means time taken away from your work here. At the moment, you do everything single-handedly – and, I might add, make a very thorough job of it, too. But, I do feel that from now on, I ought perhaps to lend you a hand.'

Feeling her eyes widen, she tried not to laugh. Lend a hand? What on earth did Naomi have in mind to do?

'Ma'am...'

'Yes. Take now, for instance, and all of these luncheon things that need seeing to. Why don't I help you with them? Hm?'

Now what did she say? Although clearly well meant, Naomi's suggestion struck her as faintly ridiculous. 'That's a very kind offer, ma'am,' she said carefully. 'But I really do think you should go on upstairs and do something else, if for no other reason than having you help me out down here wouldn't be... seemly.'

'Not seemly? Nonsense. Who is there to care for such stuffiness? Not I.'

'Well, there's—'

'You see, spending this morning at St. Ursula's has made me appreciate just how fortunate I am – how different my life is to that of most women. And it's a privilege I shouldn't take for granted. So, while you wouldn't want me to go so far as to offer to cook you luncheon, or to take the flat iron to your best blouse, I ought surely to be able to wield a drying up cloth without mishap.'

Where was the point in arguing with that, Kate wondered? She might toil for her living, but she wasn't a martyr. And anyway, if they *were* to become more involved with St Ursula's, Naomi was right to say there would be less time at home in which to get things done.

'Very well,' she said, reaching to hand Naomi a tea towel. 'But just have a care. Wet plates can be real slippery. And we don't want to have to account to Mr Lawrence for a new dinner service.'

'No,' Naomi agreed, raising her eyebrows. 'Things are already going to be different enough for him when he gets home. We don't need to give him apoplexy over his account at Selfridges as well!'

With a light laugh, Kate plunged her hands into the soapy water. St. Ursula's, it seemed, might be about to do good for more than just the young women who went there for help. Very possibly, it was going to be of benefit to the helpers, too.

—

'I can't believe they should both arrive on the same morning.'

It was after breakfast a couple of days later, and the postman had just delivered two envelopes. One, addressed in a very elegant hand, was for Naomi; the other, upon which the writing was altogether more schoolboyish, bore Kate's name.

'Quite fortuitous,' Naomi agreed, accepting the envelope Kate was holding towards her. 'I shall take mine up to the drawing room. That way, we may both read in private.'

Grateful for the suggestion, Kate nodded. And then, forcing herself to wait until she had heard the heels of Naomi's shoes tap their way right to the very top of the stairs, she reached for the nearest knife, wiped it quickly across one of the discarded napkins to remove the butter, and then slit along the top of the envelope.

That done, she simply stared down at it. At last, Luke had written to her. He had written! Her fingers suddenly feeling as large as her thumbs, she carefully separated the single sheet of paper from the envelope and pulled it out.

My Dearest Kate, her eyes read as she unfolded it. *I trust this letter will find you well. I am altogether fine.* Reading those first few words, she felt her whole body begin to relax: thank goodness, he was all right. Waiting for her heart to slow a little, she glanced the length of the letter. Then, with her fingers trembling a little less, she read on. *My moustache is coming in real good now.* It was a piece of news that made her grin. When he had come home on leave in January, she had been shocked to discover that he had grown a moustache; to her mind, it made him look older. *Army rules,* he had responded to her wariness: all men had to grow a moustache. When she'd later confessed to not liking it, he'd promised that as soon as the war was over, he would shave it off.

Looking back down, she read on.

> *My only wish is that it was dark in colour like our captain's and not sort of sandy brown. Still, better than Corporal Plummer, who do not seem able to grow one at all!*

Hm. She wasn't so sure that *was* better.

> *Thank you for your letters. Your last one arrived real quick this time. You say that you and Mrs Colborne are trying to find work as volunteers. That makes me feel real proud of you and I hope you find something to fit in with all your other duties. Though you might find this hard to credit, not every minute here is taken up with fighting the Germans. We do get the odd moment of peace. Being billeted on a farm, we think we are the lucky ones. Geordie says it reminds him of when he once*

> went on a Boy Scouts' camping holiday. He has
> a football, which we kick about in the yard or, if
> there are officers about, in one of the farmer's fields.
> If the weather is not so good, we play cards instead.
> He has taught me quite a few new games.

She smiled. She liked to know that he had friends.
Somehow, it made it all seem more bearable for him.
Looking back down, she read on.

> Sometimes, in the evening, we go into the town to
> the estaminet. It is a bit like a public house, though
> to me, it seems more like someone's front room with
> a bar in it than one of the inns you would think of
> in Westward Quay. There are tables and chairs and
> a piano. Sometimes we have a bit of a sing-song.
> 'Pack Up Your Troubles' is a favourite. Another
> one is called 'Mademoiselle from Armentieres' but
> some of the words in that one would make you
> blush.

She blushed anyway, even just reading about it. One of
the downsides of him having these new friends was that
not all of them seemed as clean-living as him. As it was,
she knew he had taken to smoking cigarettes. *They all do
it*, he had told her. She read on.

> The estaminet is run by the Voisey family and
> quite a few of the lads have a crush on Madame's
> daughter, Marie-Josephine.

Yes, there! That was just what she meant – not that Luke
would be interested in a girl who worked in a bar, even

if she was French. And glamorous. If Naomi's magazines were anything to go by, all Frenchwomen were elegant and beautiful and knew how to use all manner of cosmetic preparations to attract men. *Marie-Josephine*. Her name by itself was enough to lure a lonely soldier a long way from home. Straightening the page, she determined not to think of such things and read on.

We don't seem to get so much fresh meat now.

She scanned back a couple of lines. Had she missed something? Apparently not. Perhaps he had been interrupted at that point and lost his thread.

> *Mainly it is bully in tins. Otherwise and all things considered, I do not have too many complaints. Please write again soon.*
>   *All my love,*
>   *Luke*

From his words, he seemed so assured and so confident that she wondered whether if he turned up unannounced, right this minute, she would even recognize him. He certainly no longer sounded like the wide-eyed and eager young lad from Woodicombe she had grown up with. She stared down at the erratic slant of his handwriting. Somehow, although long awaited and intended to bring them closer, his letter had only succeeded in making her feel disquieted. It was also making her doubt her standing as a wife.

Distractedly, she extended a finger towards the flimsy page. If nothing else, that Luke's hands had been the last to touch it was of comfort. But then, remembering something Mr Aubrey had told them, she reached for the envelope and turned it over. On the front was stamped *PASSED BY CENSOR*. So, no, his hands *wouldn't* have been the last to touch it. Back in Woodicombe, Mr Aubrey had explained that once a man had written his letter home, it had to be read by one of his regimental officers to check that he hadn't written anything that could be of use to the enemy. At first, she had thought him to be joking. Quickly, though, it had become apparent that he wasn't. She remembered being aghast at the discovery and recalled Naomi claiming to be affronted by such flagrant disrespecting of their privacy. Mr Aubrey had tried to reassure them by explaining that it wasn't the invasion of privacy they imagined. Being one of those officers charged with reading his men's letters, he had said that after a while, they all looked the same and that, once read, the details were quickly forgotten. Even so, she had felt unsettled and, for a while afterwards, had been more circumspect about what she wrote, fearing how it might lead Luke to reply.

'May I come in?'

Startled from her thoughts, she turned to look over her shoulder. That Naomi should be asking permission to enter her own kitchen struck her as upside down – respectful, but upside down just the same. Scraping back her chair, she tucked the letter into its envelope and put it in her pocket.

''Course,' she said, getting to her feet and brushing a hand across her cheeks.

'Luke writes that he is well, I hope.'

'He does. He writes of the things he gets up to with the other lads. They seem to have fun at times.'

'That must be of comfort for you to know. I suppose, no matter how terrible the circumstances of their being there, among so many young men, a sort of camaraderie must develop.'

She nodded. 'It would seem to, yes.' And then, to distract from the sudden wateriness of her eyes, she said, 'I trust Mr Lawrence writes that he too is well?'

Naomi smiled warmly. 'He does. And, although for my peace of mind I suppose he *would* do, the tone of his letter leads me to believe that he is genuinely all right.'

She smiled back. 'That's good to hear.'

'Of course, he knows nothing of the baby – and yes, I know, it is a state of affairs that is precisely as it should be. Reading his letter, I realized that you were right. You said it was selfish of me to want to tell him. From the little he is able to tell me of what he is doing, I can tell that he has his hands full. And full of the sort of matters I can't even begin to comprehend. So thank you for insisting that I shouldn't mention it to him. There will be time enough for me to tell him once he is back at home.'

Embarrassed and yet pleased in equal measure, Kate bowed her head, mumbling a sort of thanks as she did so. Goodness, sometimes Naomi *did* listen to what she said!

Mainly, though, she was just relieved that both Luke and Mr Lawrence were all right. And reassured that her worst fears for their safety seemed without foundation.

–

'Now, you've haven't forgotten, have you?'

Unbuttoning her jacket, Kate frowned. And then, hanging her hat on one of the coat pegs in the vestibule, had no choice but to ask, 'Forgotten what?'

It was the following afternoon and, having spent another morning at St. Ursula's, the two women had just arrived back at Hartland Street.

'That I'm going to Clarence Square later to take tea with Mamma.'

Forgotten? Not a chance! All the way home in the cab she had been relishing the prospect; she even had a plan for how she was going to spend her time. Once Naomi had left, she would scurry about and complete her chores before her remaining stamina could desert her. Then, she would sit down and put her feet up with a cup of tea and a slice of treacle cake. No one, but no one, could say she hadn't earned it.

'No, ma'am,' she said. 'I remember well enough. You warned me you might not want supper.'

'I doubt I shall. And, since luncheon is now somewhat delayed, I suppose I shouldn't eat too much of that, either. Although I must say, I am quite famished.'

Hanging up her jacket, Kate nodded. 'Me too. Who would have thought that talking to people and filling out forms of application could make a person feel so hungry?'

'One of the women I saw,' Naomi said, trailing behind her as she made her way downstairs, 'was already a widow but has now also lost her eldest son.'

Listening to what Naomi was saying, she unlocked the back door and glanced down the garden. Although suffering dreadful neglect – Mr Lawrence having had no time to organize a gardener – it looked peaceful and lush.

'Uh-huh,' she agreed as Naomi continued her tale.

'She was beside herself, sobbing and saying that without his wage, she didn't know how she was going to feed herself and the rest of her children. It was so heartbreaking I wanted to get out my purse and give her some of my own money.'

In alarm, she swivelled towards her. 'You didn't, though, did you? Please tell me you didn't?'

'No, I didn't. I remembered Marjorie warning us about setting a precedent. I did feel mean, though. Even the smallest coins from my purse would have made a real difference to her.'

'You've *made* a difference to her,' she said. 'You've helped her to apply for support, something she wouldn't have been able to do by herself.'

Naomi sighed. 'I know that's true. But my effort in that regard feels so very little.'

'It isn't.'

'I know.'

'Shall you tell Mrs Russell about St. Ursula's?' she enquired, slicing through the remainder of the chicken and ham pie from the day before and glancing across to the new potatoes boiling in the saucepan. Overcome by a weariness she felt more in her heart and mind than in her limbs, she was thankful for having had the presence of mind to scrub and prepare vegetables for their luncheon before they had gone out.

'Of course I shall tell her. I'm proud of what we're doing. Why? Is it your contention that I shouldn't?'

'Oh, no, that weren't why I asked,' she replied, stabbing a potato with the tip of a paring knife: a couple more minutes of boiling needed yet. 'No, I should imagine she'll be delighted to learn you've found something rewarding to do with your time.' In her heart, though, she wasn't so sure. Mrs Russell could be snippy about *getting too close to the labouring classes*, as she had once heard her put it.

Later, though, when Naomi returned from her visit to Clarence Square, Kate found that not only had she lost the colour from her cheeks but that her manner seemed distracted. Was it her place to enquire what had happened to bring that about? Given Mr Russell's recent state of health, she decided it was only polite.

'Did you have a pleasant afternoon, ma'am?' she asked.

'What? Oh, no, not especially. Well, no, that's not fair. It was perfectly agreeable until… Oh dear. This really isn't a conversation one should be having in the hallway. Do you think you might make a pot of tea? And do you think you might bring it up to the drawing room and sit with me a while?'

Kate did her best not to look alarmed. Clearly, something was amiss. Best do as she was asked and wait for Naomi to confide what it was. 'Of course, ma'am,' she said. 'You go on in and make yourself comfortable. I'll be back in two ticks.'

Once downstairs, she hared about the kitchen, her mind working at twice the speed of her limbs. Whatever could have happened? Had there been bad news? Had some misfortune befallen Ned? She knew for a fact he had given Clarence Square as his home address, meaning that in the event of a *mishap*, Mrs Russell would be the first to learn of it. *Oh, dear Lord*, she willed, scooting about to make the tea, as an afterthought adding the barrel of biscuits to the tray, *please don't let there be bad news*; Naomi could do without more upset.

Forcing herself to slow down, she made her way back up the stairs. 'There,' she made a point of announcing as she set the tray on the table. 'I took the liberty of making a pot of your chamomile. Only, forgive me for saying so, ma'am, but you look to me like you've had a shock.'

'In a way, I have,' Naomi replied, fingering the single strand of pearls at her throat, her expression troubled. 'You see, this is the first chance I've had to see Mamma properly since we've been back from Devon – to see her on her own, I mean.' Apparently unaware that she was doing so, Naomi sank onto one of the sofas. 'When I first arrived, Aunt Diana was there. But, once she had left, although not really having intended to, I felt moved to tell Mamma about... well, about the baby. These last few days, seeing those women at St. Ursula's with their infants, I've found my mind returning more and more to what happened. Well, of course, the thoughts have never really left me. So, when I was sat there with Mamma, just the two of us, I thought that to talk about it might help me to... well, lay the matter to rest, so to speak – bring some perspective to bear. You see, when I reflect upon the hardships and the woes of the women we see at St. Ursula's, I feel I shouldn't still be dwelling upon my own misfortune. By comparison, my own loss seems very little.'

Going to sit beside Naomi on the sofa, she reached for her hand. 'Naomi, I don't think it *is* very little. Nor do I think—'

'Anyway, I told her what had happened, quite plainly and without becoming upset, for which I felt quite pleased. *I can talk about it matter-of-factly now*, I thought to myself. *That is a good sign*. But, when I looked across at Mamma for her response, it was to see that every last drop of colour had gone from her face. She was completely white.'

'Was she all right?'

'I made her draw a breath from my smelling salts and yes, after a while, she seemed to recover a little. She asked me to describe precisely what had happened and what Dr Huntleigh had said, to which I answered her as best I could. Then, she excused herself, went upstairs, and returned a moment or two later with a card – you know, a gentleman's business card. I have it here somewhere.' When Naomi opened the clasp of her handbag and fished about inside, Kate waited. 'Here. This is it.'

Reaching to accept the card, she wasn't sure what to expect. Turning it the right way up, she could see that on it was printed the name *Dr Angus Fitzwilliam*, followed by a row of letters and, underneath, an address in Harley Street. Reading it again, she frowned and handed it back.

'Not sure I understand, ma'am.'

'I learned from Mamma that this Dr Fitzwilliam attended to her after Ned and I were born. He's a—' Despite there being no one else in the house, Naomi lowered her voice. '—a *woman's doctor.*'

To disguise that she was blushing, Kate frowned. 'I see...'

'And she gave me this card because she wants me to go and see him.'

Her frown didn't lift. There was something here that Naomi wasn't telling her – there had to be. Finding out what it was, though, was going to require patience. 'So, is she of the mind that you need a medical treatment of some sort?'

Beside her, Naomi sat shaking her head.

'I feel a dunce, I really do. But, until now, it had never occurred to me to wonder – not even once.'

What hadn't, she wanted to scream back at Naomi. *What?* Instead, she forced herself to swallow. Clearly, whatever this was all about was proving hard for Naomi to speak of. And yet she had intimated that she wanted to do just that.

Discreetly, she drew a deep breath. 'What never occurred to you, ma'am?'

'That after Ned and I were born, Mamma never had any more children – that we didn't have siblings. I never, ever thought of it. I suppose, because I wasn't an only child, it never occurred to me to think our situation odd. What I didn't know until this afternoon was that not only were Ned and I born several weeks early, but that after she'd had us, her next baby was miscarried. And so was the one after that.'

Unable to help it, she let out a little gasp. Then, in a whisper, she said, 'Goodness.'

'All told, she went on to lose four babies, nearly all of them at around the same number of months along as I was.'

There was something about Naomi's careful choice of words that made Kate think there was yet more to this tale. Her reference to the number of months seemed hardly coincidental. 'What a terrible sad thing to learn,' she said.

Naomi seemed not to notice, continuing with her account. 'Once she had confessed to that, a number of things suddenly made sense to me – her constant protectiveness towards us, her concerted and repeated efforts to get Ned to enlist somewhere other than the Royal Flying Corps, her general watchfulness and tendency to interfere in everything we ever did. Don't you see? Being unable to have more children explains not only why she was always so overly protective of us, but her constant worrying and her drive to see us not make mistakes. She'd lost four babies. She wasn't going to lose us, too. To her, we were... we *are*... irreplaceable.' With no idea what to say, Kate sat quite still. 'Anyway,' Naomi eventually went on, 'when I tried to express my sympathy and tell her that I understood, her response frightened me.'

Desperate that Naomi shouldn't stop recounting the conversation and leave her guessing, she asked, 'Why? What did she say?'

'She said that I didn't understand – that I couldn't yet – but that I would do.'

With that, she saw Naomi's eyes start to fill with tears. Without hesitation, she put an arm around her shoulders. 'Naomi—'

'Wait. What I mean is, *please*, wait a moment, I must tell you the rest. I need you to know why all of this is so important.'

Withdrawing her arm, Kate returned her hands to her lap.

'Mamma *then* told me that Aunt Diana had suffered the same fate, except that in *her* case, she never succeeded in carrying even one child. Apparently, in the beginning, with her first husband, the doctors attributed her miscarriages to her fondness for horse-riding and drinking and socialising. By all accounts, she led quite the life. But, when Kingsley died, and she married again, her misfortune continued, despite a rather more sober existence. And she never did have a child.'

While Naomi sobbed, Kate reached into Naomi's handbag and pulled out a neatly folded handkerchief. To her way of looking at it, it had been selfish of Mrs

Russell to sadden her daughter with such news, especially knowing just how recently she had suffered a loss of her own. Having been through such a thing herself, she ought to have known better. Where was the point in making Naomi feel worse – just when she had been recovering her former self? Now, it was once again going to fall into *her* lap to try to restore Naomi's mood.

'Naomi,' she said gently. 'While all of that is very sad, you shouldn't think it means—'

'But that's just the point. That's why Mamma gave me the card for her physician. According to her, it is the view of this Dr Fitzwilliam – something of a specialist in this particular field, apparently – that the women in our family have an unfortunate tendency to lose babies before they're born. There is, if you will, a family trait.'

'But that still doesn't mean—'

'But it does, though, doesn't it?' Naomi said bitterly. 'It means I might *never* have a child. Even if Lawrence somehow manages to return unscathed from this appalling war, because of *me*, we might never have a family. And with all of the other terrible things happening at the moment, *that* is a prospect I find just too awful for words.'

–

'I'm afraid, Mrs Colborne, it is not something we fully understand.'

Seated on a chair in the corner of Dr Fitzwilliam's plush office, Kate was in two minds about getting up and going over to comfort Naomi. Looking across at her, seated by herself in front of the enormous desk, the chair beside her empty, she looked lost and small and alone. And if there was one thing that Naomi Colborne rarely looked, it was lost.

Thinking such a move might be frowned upon, she instead turned her attention to the doctor himself. Before their arrival at his office, his name had conjured a dour and elderly Scotsman, whereas, although he had to be in his sixties, his rounded face and receding hairline gave him a look of kindliness.

'So there is nothing I can do? Is that what you're telling me, Doctor? There is nothing to be done?'

'Mrs Colborne, when it comes to childbearing, there is very little *any* of us can do. Clearly, certain factors give cause for concern – such as malnutrition in the mother or insanitary living conditions. But, for an otherwise healthy young woman with your station in life, repeated miscarrying of foetuses can only be attributed to a familial tendency to such an outcome. Certainly, your own family history would support such a theory. Medicine may have made incredible advances – even during my own years in the profession – but we still don't have all of the answers. Mother Nature keeps a firm hold on the secrets of her mysterious ways.'

From her distant seat, Kate barely avoided snorting. *Mysterious ways*, indeed.

'So, what do I do?'

At least Naomi wasn't crying, she noticed as she studied her partly turned face. If she started crying, then she would *have* to go and comfort her, doctor's office or not.

'Continue to live a clean and honest life is the best advice I can offer to you. Curb any fondness you may have for tipples such as gin, take gentle regular exercise in fresh air – if you can find it – and adhere to a diet of red meat, fresh fruit and vegetables, and plenty of milk. Avoiding becoming overly excited or overly anxious will help, too. A balanced and wholesome life is what you should be striving for. Moderation in all things. And, next time, the moment you believe you might be expecting, telephone my office for an appointment. Do not delay. Once I have examined you, I will provide you with a list of instructions and precautions that, while not necessarily removing altogether the possibility of failure, will certainly do you no harm.'

The consultation with Dr Fitzwilliam seemingly at an end, Kate shifted on her seat. When she then heard Naomi sigh, unwittingly, she did the same. It wasn't until the two women had taken a cab for the short ride back to Hartland Street that any words passed between them.

'Whatever will Lawrence say?' Naomi wanted to know.

'I should imagine,' she said, helping Naomi out of her jacket, 'he will suggest that you try not to worry.'

'But what if he's appalled by it all and no longer wants to be married to me? Indeed, what if he thinks I knew about this all along and duped him into marrying me in the first place?'

Folding Naomi's jacket over her arm and waiting to take her hat, Kate shook her head. Knowing the little she did of Mr Lawrence, she thought it the last thing that would occur to him – the last thing that would occur to any man in his shoes. Even Luke – who had often talked of one day starting a family – would still be concerned, first and foremost, for her well-being. 'I can't think that will even enter his head,' she said. 'Rather, I think he will be concerned that you are all right.'

'At first he might be, yes. He is, by nature, a considerate man. But what about later on?'

Puzzled, she took Naomi's hat. 'Later on?'

'Later on. In the years to come. When time and again, I fail? When, like Mamma or Aunt Diana, I've lost four or five babies. Do you think that by then, his only thought will still be for my well-being? Because *I* don't. *I* think he will find himself looking around at friends and acquaintances – people on the street, even – and come to see how, through having no children of his own, he's missing out. Through no fault of *his*, he will be doomed never to have a son—'

'You don't know that,' she said, weighed down by her dismay. 'Dr Fitzwilliam said that women miscarry all the time, most of them going on to have at least one child, sometimes as many as a dozen or more. It's more than possible you might never lose another baby.'

Naomi shook her head. 'To borrow an expression from Ned,' she replied, '*I don't much fancy my odds.* And, although I thank you for your optimism, you should know that I don't share it.'

Share it or not, she was *not* going to give up. 'You have to remain hopeful, ma'am,' she persisted, watching as Naomi wandered absently through to the drawing room. 'While Mr Lawrence is away, we must concentrate on feeding you well, building up your strength, and not letting you suffer any undue distress.' *Undue distress*. St. Ursula's. Oh dear. Just when they had started to do some good there.

'Distress. Hm. The thing is distress enough by itself, without all the other upsetting matters this war has foisted upon us.'

Deciding there was little she could do to lift Naomi's spirits – at least, for now – she decided it better to say nothing more. She would be patient, take a gentle approach, use subterfuge if necessary. But, one way or another, she would try to lead Naomi's thoughts away from the subject.

The following morning, though, arriving to check whether Naomi had awoken, she found her sitting up in bed, grasping at her eiderdown. In despair, she crossed to the deep sash window, drew aside the curtains, and stood back to marvel at the light that came flooding in. 'Shame 'tis too far for us to walk,' she said, determining to carry on as any other morning. 'For the sun is shining its heart out and the sky is as clear as can be.'

When she turned back into the room, it was to see Naomi bring a hand to her brow and shy away from the light. 'Too far to walk where?'

Lifting her ruby-red silk robe from the stool at the dressing table and carrying it across to the bed, her manner intentionally purposeful, she smiled. Holding out the robe, she said, 'To St. Ursula's, of course. We told Miss Randolph we would attend three days this week. Then, tomorrow, you have that invitation to Selfridges for the showing of their latest collection.'

Smiling fixedly, she continued to hold out the robe.

Naomi, though, sank back into her pillows. 'I shan't go.'

She lowered her arms. 'To Selfridges?'

'To either. The thought of new outfits leaves me cold. The thought of facing distraught widows, even more so. The very prospect brings on a sensation of panic. How can I possibly help *them* when my mind is on my own matter? No, I shall be of no use to them.'

'Ma'am, *Naomi*, forgive me for speaking plainly, but happen it's just what you need—'

'Dr Fitzwilliam said not to become overly anxious.'

Folding the robe over her arm and trying not to sigh with dismay, Kate tried a different tack. 'That's true enough. He did. But I think *that* piece of advice was intended more for once you're expecting again. I think that in the meantime, he intended you to... well, to try to get on with your days.'

'No, I have no appetite for it. You may go. Indeed, you *should* go. I shall write a note to Marjorie Randolph, explaining that I am currently indisposed.'

She stared down at the floor. Perhaps, on this particular occasion, she should relent. Although convinced that Naomi would benefit from being out of the house and doing something useful, it wasn't her place to force her into doing anything she didn't want to – quite the contrary.

'Very well,' she said. 'Since you don't feel like rising, I shall bring you some breakfast, see you bathed and dressed, and then I shall go on alone.'

'Good. I shall give you the cab fare.'

'Thank you, ma'am.'

'And Kate—'

On the point of walking away, she turned back. 'Ma'am?'

'Please, don't think harshly of me. I'm not as resilient as you are.'

She sighed. 'I think you are, ma'am. I also think that once you've had time to come to terms with what you've learnt, you'll see that where Mr Lawrence is concerned, you have nothing to fear. Nothing at all. He's a fine man.'

For the first time that morning, she found Naomi looking back at her. 'He is, isn't he?'

It was, at least, a glimmer of hope. 'He's the sort of man, who, if ever the worst came to the worst, would manage to find *some* goodness in the situation, no matter how small.'

'I'm sure you're right,' Naomi agreed. 'But I struggle to see how he will find the good to be had from us never having a family. But anyway, don't let me detain you. If you're going to St. Ursula's, you won't want to get behind.'

Her thoughts turning from Naomi's problem to those of the women at St. Ursula's, she sighed. How cruel life could be. Lawrence and Naomi, with the means to provide a child with a good start in life, were, it now seemed, going to struggle to have a baby. By contrast, the widows at St. Ursula's were blessed with children but lacked the means with which to raise them up. Worse still, there were the orphans – babies and children with no parents at all – for whom Marjorie Randolph did her best to find homes, but could not always succeed.

Under the weight of her despair, she sighed heavily. Sometimes, just lately, not only did the world appear topsy-turvy, it seemed cruel, as well. And all the hope in the land felt unlikely to change it.

Chapter Seven

The Gala

It had been a long day. Her head ached, her feet ached, and her eyes were so tired that she couldn't see to thread the needle.

Sitting by the drawing-room window, Kate was sewing a button back onto one of Naomi's jackets; or at least, she was trying to. But, with the last vestiges of natural light fading and her mind elsewhere, she was inclined to give up and try again tomorrow. The problem was that in the last few days, she had begun to find it difficult to make time for everything there was to be done and, if she didn't make use of odd moments like these, she would *never* keep on top of her chores.

Failing yet again to thread the cotton through the needle, she gave a long sigh.

Behind her, on the sofa, Naomi stirred. 'There's no need for you to do that *now*, you know. If you want to wait until the morning for better light, I shan't mind. It isn't as though I have urgent need of that particular garment.'

Carefully placing the needle and thread on the top of her sewing basket, Kate got to her feet and, stretching her arms above her head, arched her back. 'I know,' she said. 'But it has to be done sometime.'

'I *would* offer to do it myself,' Naomi went on, wriggling her stockinged toes as she lay reclined upon the sofa, 'but you would almost certainly despair of my efforts and decide to do it all over again.'

Turning towards the window, Kate looked down into the street. The electrical street lamps were now alight, their incandescent bulbs picking out the railings and casting yellows pools over the damp pavements. Coupled with a glow from some of the windows of the houses opposite, it was a sign that another day was over. Another four-and-twenty hours had sped past, Naomi barely stirring from the sofa let alone from the house. Since visiting Dr Fitzwilliam earlier in the week, she appeared to have become consumed by a mixture of grief and apathy, a state from which, seemingly, nothing would rouse her.

She turned back into the room. Should she go and make them both a cup of Ovaltine? It aided sleep – or so the advertisements on the sides of the omnibuses would have it. And she knew for a fact that it was given to people who were convalescing from illness. Naomi might not have been ill, but she had the fragility of someone who had been. So, yes, she would go down and make some. It couldn't do any harm.

Returning upstairs a few minutes later, her tray bearing two cups and saucers and a plate of Marie biscuits, she was unsurprised to find that Naomi hadn't moved.

Depositing her tray on the side table, she sat down heavily in the adjacent armchair. 'I've brought you a cup of Ovaltine,' she announced, setting down a coaster and then placing one of the drinks upon it. 'I thought it might help you sleep.' Still Naomi didn't move. 'We could both do with a good night.'

Eventually, Naomi swung her feet down to the floor and slipped her feet into her shoes.

'I suppose it *might* help. Although generally, nothing does.'

'Another thing that might help,' she went on, desperate that Naomi should take an interest in something, 'would be if you could find it in yourself to get out and about a bit.'

'Hm.'

Despite Naomi's stony response, she resolved not to give up. 'With tomorrow being Saturday, we could go to St. James's Park.' But then, remembering that the lake there had been drained to make way for yet more buildings for the War Office – in much the same way that Regent's Park had become the site of a giant wooden depot for the Royal Mail – she quickly went on, 'No, not St. James's Park. I meant Hyde Park. We could go there. You said last time that you like the boating lake.' But *then*, remembering how they had stood watching two charming little boys with their pond yachts, and thinking such a sight unlikely to help Naomi's mood, she backtracked yet again. 'Although, it doesn't have to be *there*. We could go anywhere. You did say that one day you would take me to see St. Paul's Cathedral. Or, if that's too far away, we could go for tea at Fortnum & Mason. We haven't been *there* in quite a while.'

Without otherwise moving, Naomi gave a long yawn. 'Hm. We'll see.'

Exhausted with trying, she lowered her head. This was getting her nowhere and she felt like saying as much. 'It just strikes me that—'

What she had intended as one final attempt to draw Naomi into committing to doing something was halted by the sound of someone rapping the door knocker, the business-like double tap echoing around the hallway and causing both of them to start.

'Whoever could that be?' Naomi asked, staring out through the doorway into the reception hall. 'And at this late hour?'

Getting to her feet, Kate went to the window and eased aside the curtain. At the top of the steps stood a man in uniform. It being too dark for her to make out much more, she slipped past the sofa and, with her heart racing, hastened to the front door. Opening it back, she gave a little gasp.

'Lieutenant Colborne, Mr Aubrey, sir.' Astounded, but relieved to find it wasn't someone bearing bad news, she quickly stood aside. 'Please, do come in.'

'Awfully sorry to trouble you so late. But, what with one thing and another, my journey into town became terribly delayed.'

'Aubrey?' Coming through from the drawing room, Naomi's manner was livelier than it had been in ages. 'Is it you? It is! Aubrey! What on earth are *you* doing here?'

'Naomi, my dear. How lovely.'

'*Mwah.*'

'I'm so dreadfully sorry to turn up unannounced—'

'You haven't rejoined your regiment? They didn't pass you as fit? But no, of course they didn't – your arm is still in a sling.'

Stepping further aside, Kate looked Aubrey up and down. In contrast to the last time she had seen him, his face had more colour and he looked considerably less drawn.

'Alas, no. Had a medical, then went before the board. Buffoons ruled me unfit – said I must regain more movement in my wrist and hand. Doc tore me off a strip for not resting it enough. Said if I insist on hurrying it, I risk hindering a full recovery. Damned disappointing.'

'I imagine it must have been.'

'So, I'm afraid it's back in the sling. Doc's orders.'

'Look, do come through,' Naomi said, gesturing towards the drawing room. 'What will you have? Tea? Coffee? Cognac?'

As Aubrey followed Naomi across the hall, Kate awaited his response.

'Don't suppose there would be a bite to eat, would there? Frightful imposition, I know, but the train was delayed so badly that the station buffet had been eaten bare. Not a morsel to be had on the train itself, either.'

Kate turned for the door. Although it was late, she could rustle up *something* for the poor man – a bowl of soup or a round of sandwiches, at least.

'Where have you travelled from?'

'Wiltshire.'

'Of course. Well, Kate, what can we manage by way of supper for our hungry lieutenant?'

She smiled. 'I could heat up a portion of the chicken and leek soup, ma'am. Or make a round of sandwiches with some of the cold beef.'

Settling himself into one of the armchairs, Aubrey turned to look over his shoulder. 'I say, soup and sandwiches would go down a treat. Thanks awfully.'

Soup *and* sandwiches. With a nod, she turned to head away, hearing Naomi go on to say, 'And at this hour, I should imagine you would welcome a bed for the night, too.'

'Terribly kind of you to offer. That would be an absolute lifesaver.'

Trotting downstairs to the kitchen, Kate sighed. Fancy Mr Aubrey arriving, just like that. Fortunate timing, really, because if his presence lifted Naomi's spirits as it had done back in Woodicombe, it would ease her own burden in that regard no end. And, if that *was* the case, then he was welcome to all the soup and sandwiches he could eat.

–

'Naomi tells me that you volunteer.'

In response to Mr Aubrey's remark, Kate nodded. 'That's right, sir.'

It was Monday morning and, at Mr Aubrey's insistence, she had served breakfast at the kitchen table, the debris from which she was now clearing away.

'I have no desire to cause you more work,' he had said the previous evening, Naomi having mentioned something to her about laying the table in the dining room. 'If eating in the kitchen is good enough for you, Naomi, then it's perfectly fine for me, too. When one has stood knee-deep in mud, fighting off rats and devouring one's rations from a tin mug with enemy shells sailing over one's head, a proper plate at a kitchen table is the height of luxury, I can tell you. So please, Mrs Channer, do proceed as you would on any other day of the week. Pay not the least heed to my being here.'

And so, despite the peculiar sight of an army lieutenant eating in her kitchen, she had done just that.

'I volunteer at St. Ursula's in Paddington,' she replied now to his earlier observation. It had been on her tongue to say, '*we* volunteer', but she'd thought Naomi could probably do without having to explain to him why she had given it up.

'And what happens at St. Ursula's?'

Continuing to clear the table, she explained to him about Marjorie Randolph, and about the wives and the widows of the Tommies who went there for help. 'In fact, sir, not knowing that you were a-coming,' she said, glancing to Naomi and anticipating a problem, 'I *had* volunteered to go there this morning. But perhaps that won't now be possible...'

By way of response, Aubrey Colborne raised an eyebrow. 'No? Why ever not?'

'On account of needing to prepare a luncheon for you, sir – a proper sort of a luncheon, I mean.'

'And is the preparation of my luncheon the only impediment to your going there and doing good?'

Warily, she nodded. 'As things stand at present, sir, yes.'

'Then that is most easily remedied,' Aubrey said, bringing his hand smartly down upon the table and causing the single remaining coffee cup to rattle upon its saucer. 'I shall take Mrs Colborne out to luncheon. I ought to, anyway, as a thank you for putting me up – for the *second* time in a matter of weeks. Yes, we shall go to the Albemarle. I shall make a reservation. Do you have a telephone?'

Naomi shook her head. 'Lawrence didn't have time to organize for one to be connected up.'

'No matter. I shall go there myself, first thing, and make a reservation. Would one o'clock suit?'

Clearly, Kate mused, to treat Naomi to luncheon, Mr Aubrey must have resolved the matter of his outstanding pay. But then she chided herself for such a mean-spirited thought; he was making a generous gesture, in no small part so that *she* might spend the morning at St. Ursula's. In addition to which, it would do Naomi good – proper company and a nice luncheon being just what she needed.

And so it was that a while later, with the arrangement settled upon and the kitchen cleaned and tidied, she set off to St. Ursula's. Estimating the distance to be no more than two miles at most, she decided to dispense with a cab and go on foot.

As May mornings went, this particular one was overcast and still, the walk quickly proving sticky rather than refreshing. But, when she arrived without incident, she felt a sense of satisfaction; she had proved to herself that this was something she could do on her own – something she could do without even needing the cab fare from Naomi. In terms of achievements, although modest, it felt liberating – reminding her of how she had felt on the day she had travelled from Woodicombe to join Naomi in Hartland Street. Momentous, that was how she now recalled it feeling. *Uplifting.*

Pushing open the door to the gloomy-looking little building of St. Ursula's, she went straight through the vestibule and into the main hall.

'On your own again today, miss?' Nell was quick to greet her arrival. 'Your Mrs Colborne still poorly?'

Unpinning her straw hat, she shook her head. 'No, she's better than she was, thank you for asking. But a member of her family has just arrived, and she has decided he should stay a while. He's on sick leave, you see, having been injured at the front – shot in the arm by a German spy. So, for the moment, I can't rightly say when she'll be back here.'

'Soon, I 'opes,' Nell said, taking her hat and waiting while she unbuttoned her jacket. 'I likes Mrs Colborne. She ain't like most of her sort.'

She smiled; *her sort*. She knew well enough what Nell meant, though. 'No, she isn't, is she?'

'Cuppa? Should be nice an' stewed by now.'

'Please,' she answered, glancing about the hall. As usual, there were one or two familiar faces in the circle of chairs, the women in question seeming to come, day after day, solely for the company. The two standing separately against the far wall, though, were new. 'Which one of those two came in first?' she lowered her voice to ask.

''Er with the 'at. Says she's 'ad her seven shillins from the Patriotic Fund stopped on account of being up before the beak for drunkenness.'

'Can they do that?' she asked. 'Stop her payments?'

Pursing her lips Nell nodded and then, lowering her voice, went on, 'Swears blind she weren't drunk – not then nor since. Wants to see what can be done about it. Says it ain't fair.'

Unwittingly, Kate raised her eyebrows. 'Sadly, I wouldn't have the least idea of how to go about dealing with that sort of thing. Happen she'd best wait to see Miss Randolph. Is she not here yet?'

'Should be along in a tick. Someone abandoned a baby at the church last night and she's been trying to find people to take it in.'

'Someone abandoned their baby?' She blinked rapidly. Women still did that? In this day and age?

Apparently unmoved by such an event, Nell replied with several slow nods of her head. 'Happens more often than you'd think. 'Specially since women have started losing their fellas to this war.'

'What about the other woman?' she asked. 'What does *she* want?'

'Went on some long story about a couple of busybodies from the Soldiers' and Sailors' turnin' up to see whether she should get an allowance. When they saw how she rents *two* rooms, they told her to give up the smaller one and just live in the other. Told her to sell the extra furniture, too. But see, she looks after her 'usband's mum, and *she* ain't well. Says it ain't right and wants to know what can be done about it. Couple of posh sorts, she said they were, pryin' and pokin' their noses into everyfink.'

Kate sighed. It wasn't the best of starts to the day. 'Oh dear. I don't know how to go about helping *her*, either.' Beginning to despair of her uselessness, she looked about the room. 'Does no one this morning need something more straightforward?'

Turning about, Nell stood surveying the scene. 'Maggie's had word from her sister there's a kitchen-maid's job going at the Midland Grand. 'Er sister's been there a while now and reckons she can get her in. Trouble is, she ain't got nothing to wear to go and see about the getting of it.'

'She's after an outfit to go for a job interview?'

'Ain't the cheek you might think it is.'

To Kate's mind, it didn't sound cheeky at all; it sounded like a perfectly sensible use of some of the donated clothing. 'Then Maggie's needs,' she said, brightening up, 'are something I *can* help with.'

–

'Did you have a good morning at the orphanage, Mrs Channer?'

It was much later that afternoon and Kate was back in the kitchen at Hartland Street, running the smoothing iron over one of Naomi's linen blouses. It was one with pin-tucks down the front and always a real trial to make look presentable.

Setting the iron on its stand, she wiped a hand across her brow. 'Not so much today, sir, no,' she replied to Mr Aubrey's enquiry. 'Though I do thank you for asking.'

'It isn't an orphanage,' Naomi pointed out, coming in and glancing about. 'It's a place where the widows of soldiers can go to get help.'

'Forgive me my ignorance,' Aubrey replied. Bringing his hands to rest on the back of one of the kitchen chairs, he went on, 'But why was it not a good morning? Do explain.'

Hanging Naomi's blouse on a clothes hanger and buttoning the front, she heaved a vexed sigh. 'Because I'm new at it, sir. And because, as often as not, sorting out some of the women's problems needs more than the little bit I've learned how to do. I have to rely on Miss Randolph to point me in the right direction. And, since there's only the two of us now, if she's already busy with another woman, I have to wait to speak to her. And then, because I'm waiting on *her*, I can't get on and help as many women as I'd like to.' Realizing she must have sounded as though she was whining, she shot him an embarrassed look. 'Forgive me, sir. When you asked after my morning, you weren't after hearing a long tale of woe.'

Aubrey, though, seemed untroubled. 'I see why you would find that frustrating,' he said. 'And I know from experience that hot on the heels of frustration can come despair.'

Raising a smile of agreement, she nodded. 'Despair. I suffer that, too, sir. I despair that some days, there's easily enough work for three or four of Miss Randolph.'

'But you've just the one.'

She smiled more warmly. 'Yes, sir. We've just the one. One of her and one of me. I'm told there *is* another lady sometimes, but that she's there just the occasional afternoon, when she can fit it in.'

To Kate's eyes, Aubrey looked thoughtful. Turning to regard Naomi, he then asked, 'Are *you* not moved to lend a hand? Strikes me you'd make a decent job of something like that – helping the needy.'

Flushing red, Kate ducked her head. Bother! Now Naomi would have to explain something that was none of Aubrey's business. And *that* had been *her* doing.

'Actually, I *have* been along and *lent a hand*, as you put it. But, for reasons I shan't bother you with now, more recently I haven't felt up to it.'

Slowly, she relaxed. Embarrassment averted – although no thanks to her.

'To have become involved at all, you must consider the work worthwhile.'

Watching Mr Aubrey continue to regard Naomi, she frowned. Why this sudden interest from him? Though she would never admit to it, she still didn't *entirely* trust him.

'Oh, it is worthwhile,' Naomi replied. 'Hugely so.'

Feeling obliged to spare Naomi further discomfort, she decided to step in. 'It's worthwhile because the women who end up there only do so because there's no help to be had from anyone else. Encouraged by Mr Kitchener, they gave up their husbands to the service of their country – like *we* both did – but now, made widowed, they're left without two farthings to rub together. The poor souls sell everything they own and yet *still* they can't afford to keep a roof over their heads. The army… and the government… are worse than useless. Half the time, because their husbands were volunteers and not regulars, that lot don't even recognize the poor women's existence, let alone offer help.' Forced to pause for breath, she was mortified to realize she had been preaching – not that she could help it; the more she saw at St. Ursula's, the more she understood what a pitiful state of affairs the whole business was. 'Miss Randolph,' she picked up again, this time taking care to measure her tone, 'has been told that the situation is about to change – that *one* day, there will be widows' pensions for all, as of right. But, though the decision has been made, no one can tell her when this pension will come about. She says it could be *years*. So, fine talk though it is, it don't help the women who've already lost their homes, or whose children are bare-arsed and starving, begging your pardon for my language, sir.'

Her tirade over, she stood, breathless, her face burning, while across the table from her Naomi bowed her head.

'Kate's right,' she said. 'The way these women and their children are ignored is unforgivable. I just wish I didn't find it so distressing to be among them…'

'I'm sorry, ma'am,' she said, regretting that her outburst had cast Naomi in a poor light. 'I didn't mean to imply anything.'

'No, of course you didn't. Every word you say is true. It's not your fault I find it hard to go there. I just wish there was another way we could help. Getting one or two women and a half-dozen children the assistance they need is all well and good, but only if it comes in time to keep them from losing their homes... or from becoming sickly and perishing for want of a decent meal.'

'What you would appear to be saying,' Aubrey chipped in, 'is that you need more than just your Miss Randolph.'

With a sigh of resignation, Kate nodded her head. 'We do, sir. Dozens more.'

'Naomi, my dear, why don't you accompany me up to the drawing room? An idea occurs and, were you to fix me a drink, I might be persuaded to share it with you.'

'Having piqued my interest,' Naomi replied, 'you leave me little choice.'

When Naomi left the kitchen with Mr Aubrey in tow, Kate gathered up the garments she had been pressing. What was this idea of Mr Aubrey's? Did it have to do with St. Ursula's? If it did, she thought, as she climbed the stairs, her feet aching beneath her, then perhaps eventually they would share it with her.

It wasn't until after supper, though – taken that evening in the dining room – that she discovered what they had subsequently gone on to discuss.

'Aubrey has an idea,' Naomi greeted her when, at the end of the meal, she arrived to clear the cheeseboard – a helping of her strawberry tart having been declined.

Wearily, she raised a smile. How she was going to remain on her feet long enough to do the clearing up, she didn't know. 'Found a way to magic up more helpers, has he?' Mortified by the lack of respect she'd just shown, she stiffened: exhaustion was never an excuse for scorn.

Fortunately, on this occasion, her disrespect went unremarked upon.

'In a way, he has, yes. Certainly, it would raise funds, which, in turn, could be put to obtaining help – perhaps even of the professional variety.'

The debris of the meal cleared to the side table, she set out coffee cups and saucers. She did have to admit that his idea sounded intriguing. 'Oh yes?'

'You explain it to her, Aubrey. You were the one who thought of it.'

'All I said,' Aubrey began, his tone striking her as overly modest, 'was that Naomi could do worse than invite people from Aunt Pamela's address book to buy tickets to a gala, or a dinner or a ball of some sort, the proceeds going to your St. Ursula's.'

Carefully, Kate placed a coffee spoon in each of the two saucers. It wasn't just an interesting idea, it was a brilliant one. If Miss Randolph had some money, she might be able to pay for some proper help. Or she could give out small sums of it to tide over some of the women in more desperate need.

'Would people do that, do you think? Pay money for something like that?'

'Make it sound grand enough and worthwhile enough,' Aubrey replied, 'and I'm certain a good number would *do their bit*, as it were. Aunt Pamela certainly knows how to throw a party. And if I've seen anything since I've been back here, it's that those not at the front do shoulder a certain guilt. And guilt, you should know, opens wallets. So, given the chance to assuage their consciences *and* be seen to be contributing to a worthy cause, well, as ideas go, I don't see how it could fail.'

'It's true,' Naomi agreed, absently fingering the cross and chain at her throat. 'And, thinking about it further, holding it in aid of charity ought to overcome any reservations from Papa about the upheaval and the amount of work involved. In fact, it would be the chance for Mamma to hold a grand event with a clear conscience.'

'And your St. Ursula's would be the beneficiary.'

'Black tie, of course,' Naomi remarked.

'Or themed.'

'Ooh, yes, Mamma adores a theme.'

'Nothing too ostentatious, though. After all, there *is* a war on.'

'Yes, of course. Oh! How about a masked ball?'

With the suggestions continuing back and forth, unnoticed, Kate picked up her tray and withdrew. Mr Aubrey's idea did seem like a good one. And, if anyone could pull off something like that, it was Pamela Russell. That being the case, she would do whatever she could to nudge Naomi towards seeing it through, not only because of the benefit to St. Ursula's, but because it would also give Naomi something to do, hopefully improving her mood in the process. Yes, all told, Mr Aubrey's unexpected arrival could turn out to be fortuitous all round.

–

The following morning, when Kate arrived at St. Ursula's, it was with a spring in her step. Sworn by Naomi to keep Aubrey's idea secret – just in case she was unable to persuade her mother to go along with it – she nevertheless felt a renewed sense of purpose.

'You look bright and cheerful this morning,' Marjorie Randolph greeted her as she went in through the doors. 'Another letter from your husband, perhaps?'

She shook her head. In fact, these last few days, Luke seemed to have slipped clean from her thoughts. 'No, not since...' Goodness, how long *was* it? 'Not since the last one,' she said, uneasy at the sudden fuzziness of her recollection. 'But it's a nice morning and... well, I always look forward to coming here, truth be told.'

Marjorie Randolph's face lit up. 'What a lovely thing to hear, my dear. I suppose you'll quite miss this – once your husband returns from the war, I mean.'

Looking back at her, Kate frowned. Miss it? Why would Luke coming back from the war mean that she missed it? Presumably, even once the war was eventually over and done with, there would still be women who needed help – women whose husbands *weren't* coming home. 'Um...'

'When your days of gadding about town in the manner of a single young woman come to an end, and you must keep house for him. I suppose I *could* beseech that he let you out on the odd afternoon now and again so that you might still lend us the occasional hand. Well, until you start your family, of course.' Evidently reading Kate's puzzlement, Marjorie Randolph seemed suddenly flustered. 'Forgive me. I've overstepped the mark, haven't I? I'm often told that in my desire to do good I do that sometimes. Anyway, on the subject of families, the first person I'd like you to help this morning is that young lady over there, the one in the brown skirt.' Still puzzled, Kate turned to look. 'She tells me her name is Vi, that she's fourteen years old, and that the children with her are her brothers and sisters. Her father was a regular before the war, meaning that once he was sent to the front, her mother became eligible to receive separation allowance. Sadly, her mother passed away just this last month, so I'm minded to see whether his allowance can now be paid to Vi instead. After all, it *has* now fallen to her to run the home and care for the little ones. As to my chances of success, I have no idea. But it has to be worth a try. In the meantime, I should like you to apply to the Patriotic Fund for some form of temporary relief for them. Since you seem to have an aptitude for writing that sort of letter, I have no qualms about leaving you to get on with it.' Then, turning around, she said, 'Nell, please keep Kate supplied with tea. I intend keeping her very busy today.'

Nothing new there, then. Just lately, no matter her where-abouts, there always seemed to be someone with some-thing for her to do. Still, it was in her nature to keep busy, drifting about aimlessly her very idea of torture. *Gadding about town*, indeed. What *was* Miss Randolph on about? Well, whatever it was, she didn't have time to concern herself with it now.

Attributing Marjorie Randolph's riddles to the consid-erable strain she must be under, she slid her jacket from her shoulders. Coming towards her was Nell, grinning broadly.

'You'd best give me that,' the young girl said, gesturing with her head towards Kate's jacket. And then, nodding towards the two dozen or so women in the hall, she went on, 'Just look at this lot this morning – more of them than ever. I reckon word's got about – get yourself down to St. Ursula's; when no one else gives a damn, you can wager your last farthin' *they* will.'

This morning, where once she would have winced, Kate found that Nell's fondness for cursing made her grin. 'Then you'd best keep that tea coming,' she remarked before setting off across the hall to look over the stationery supplies on the table already set up for her. One day, she mused, examining the nib of the pen and checking the well for ink, she must ask Miss Randolph about Nell; something about her eager ways always put her in mind of a rescued puppy. Then, smiling at the fierceness of the points on the pencils – Nell's doing, for certain – she tweaked the fabric of her skirt, straightened her shoulders, and set off back across the room to introduce herself to the young girl Miss Randolph had referred to as Vi.

When, some time later – her three hours at St. Ursula's crammed with enough activity to ordinarily fill six – she arrived back at Hartland Street and called out to announce her return, she was surprised to find there was no reply. Naomi had gone out? That would be welcome news.

Removing her jacket and hanging it from one of the coat pegs, she called again. It was only then that she spotted a slip of notepaper on the hall table.

Gone to Mamma's for luncheon. Aubrey out for the day. See you for supper this evening. N.

On two counts, she gave a little sigh of relief. Clearly, Naomi had brightened up enough to go out – albeit only to Clarence Square – which meant that she herself could look forward to a few moments with her feet up. Before then, though, she would go and heat up a bowl of leek and potato soup and cut herself a chunk of crusty bread.

Before Naomi had ceased volunteering, it had become their custom over luncheon each day to discuss the women they had met, comparing their stories of misfortune and hardship. Although she hadn't realized it at the time, doing so had eased what could sometimes feel like quite a burden. But, now that Naomi no longer volunteered, she had no one with whom to share the load. Naomi still thought to enquire after her morning, of course, but it was in a perfunctory fashion and with no real care to hear the sometimes harrowing details. She wondered whether it was the same for Marjorie Randolph: did *she* go home to the rectory and talk to her brother about her day? Or did she simply shoulder the weight alone? If so, how did she manage it? Perhaps, over the months, she had become used to it. She never *looked* worn down by any of it; she looked purposeful and fulfilled.

Setting down her soup spoon, she gave a little sigh. Volunteering by herself might leave her feeling weighed down at times but she knew that it was also doing her good. For a start, she seemed to have stopped worrying about Luke – something she had only just come to realize. But that was a good thing, since it also meant that she had stopped constantly fearing that awful things might be happening to him.

St. Ursula's was of benefit to her in other ways, too. At first, she had been petrified of travelling about London on her own – of having no one whose lead she could follow. But, quite quickly, she had begun to feel more assured. Each time she ventured to tackle something on her own, her confidence grew. Whenever she was out and about with Naomi, she always felt like second fiddle: hardly surprising – she *was* second fiddle; Naomi had breeding, while she herself was nothing more than a Devon house-maid. That they shared the same father was moot: they could scarcely be more different. Naomi was educated and confident. She had poise. When they stood side by side, people always addressed Naomi first, looked to her for instruction or direction. Again, it was hardly surprising. One glance at Naomi told anyone with even only one good eye that, of the two of them, *she* was the lady. The mistress. But, for all of that, being out without Naomi had shown her that she could hold her own – that she was nobody's shadow. Deep down, she might be an illegiti-mate housemaid born to an unwed sixteen-year-old girl, but there was no need for anyone to know that. It wasn't as though, just from looking at her, anyone could tell it.

She sighed. No, in so many respects, living in London was turning out to be everything she had once hoped for – a place where, with a mind to, she could live a life filled with promise and colour and reward. And that was without Mrs Russell's forthcoming gala dinner. When *that* eventually came around, she would have to try to remember every minute of it in order to be able to put it all in a letter to Mabel and Edith. They would struggle to believe it. *Her*, at a fancy do with Naomi and Mr Aubrey!

In her contentment, she smiled. She had always known that London would be an exciting place to live. Turned out she had been right. That day she had accepted Naomi's offer to be her housekeeper, a whole new world had opened up to her. And, now that she was part of it, nothing and no one was going to take it away from her.

Not even Luke, when he came back – no matter what dear old Marjorie Randolph had, in her rather muddled fashion, been appearing to suggest.

–

'Well, you will be pleased to learn that Mamma has agreed to host an event.'

Later that day, pouring boiling water into the teapot, Kate turned to Naomi and gave her a smile of delight. 'She has? Well, that's fine news.'

Naomi smiled back. 'It is, yes. She didn't hesitate, not even for one moment. "Yes," she said to me, "of course I shall help your cause."'

Your cause? Naomi had let Pamela Russell think that it was *her* cause? That was a bit much. On the other hand, why get steamed up over it? If believing it was a cause dear to her daughter's heart got Mrs Russell to agree to holding the gala, what did it matter? This wasn't about glory or praise, it was about the women and children whose husbands and fathers had been taken from them by this awful war.

'So, when will it be?' she asked.

'Finding a date proved tricky – as you might imagine – but her diary is free in the days immediately after Whitsun, so she has pencilled in Saturday the twenty-ninth. It's short notice, I know, but if anyone can manage it, Mamma can.'

'And what's it to be?' she enquired, stirring the tea in the pot and watching the way that the leaves swirled in the water. One day, she would go next door with her teacup and ask May Davis to read her leaves for her; she had suggested doing so often enough.

Drawing her thoughts back to Naomi's news, she hoped to learn that the event was going to be a dance. She would love to hear beautiful music and watch ladies and gentlemen whirling about in their finery.

'She thinks a gala dinner would be best,' Naomi replied to her question. 'She's concerned that to host something that could be construed as too frivolous or too extravagant would be wrong. And she does make a good point. It *will* be a formal affair, though, probably at either the Cleveland or the Faulkner, depending upon numbers. She said she will make sure to invite some names from the War Office so that we will be able to buttonhole them about how they're failing these families.'

Reaching for two cups and saucers from the dresser, Kate poured the tea. 'Having the chance to bend someone's ears will please Miss Randolph,' she said, watching as the steam spiralled up from the cups.

'Marjorie Randolph? You think I should invite *her*? Goodness. Would she even accept, do you think?'

Kate frowned. Was there some question as to her inclusion, then? Was she not to be there by rights – as the person behind St. Ursula's?

'I can't rightly say whether she would *choose* to go,' she said carefully, 'but, if you want folk to know first-hand about the plight of these women, strikes me she's best placed to tell how they come to be in such dire predicaments. And about how badly they're being let down.'

Her comments caused Naomi to reflect for a moment. 'You don't think she's too dreary?'

Dreary? What did it matter if the woman was dreary? She was a saint on earth.

Controlling an urge to sigh with despair, she instead shook her head; she could always tell when Naomi had been to visit her mother. Living in Hartland Street just about kept Naomi's feet on the ground, whereas visiting Clarence Square pulled her head straight back up into the clouds. In Hartland Street, she was happy to drink tea at the kitchen table, her shoes kicked off for comfort. In Clarence Square, she only ever took refreshments from cups of almost-translucent porcelain presented in the drawing room by a liveried butler. And, as she moved between the two, she inadvertently brought her Clarence Square ways home with her.

Forcing herself to relax her shoulders, she looked back up, only to realize that she had completely forgotten what Naomi had just said. She cast her mind back. Oh, yes, the dreariness of Marjorie Randolph – what nonsense. 'I wouldn't have thought her appearance mattered.'

'No? You don't think she might feel out of place at such a formal affair? I'll ask Mamma what *she* thinks. I told her I will call again the day after tomorrow, by which time she should have a better idea of the arrangements.'

'Quite exciting, isn't it?' she observed, sitting down at the table and trying to shrug off growing concerns. 'To be able to do some proper good, I mean.'

'Exciting,' Naomi agreed absently. 'Yes.'

From that afternoon onwards, Kate noticed how Aubrey's idea, and Naomi's planning for it, seemed to bring a new pattern to the routine in Hartland Street. While she spent her own mornings at St. Ursula's, Naomi passed her afternoons at Clarence Square, returning home each evening to relay details of how the arrangements were coming along.

'We've agreed the guest list,' she came home one particular afternoon to announce. 'Mamma has narrowed it down to one hundred of her finest.'

From where she was watering the pelargoniums in the window box outside of the kitchen, Kate turned to look back. Wearing her pale-grey Lanvin shift dress, Naomi was standing in the doorway, her hand shading her eyes against the early-evening sunshine. Fleetingly, she looked just like her old self. 'Her finest whats?'

'Names, you ninny. The top one hundred names in her address book.'

'*One hundred?*'

'Yes, I know it's a modest number but, at such short notice, many people will already have commitments. She's holding another thirty in reserve.'

Modest? To Kate, it seemed incredible. 'One hundred people for a dinner to raise money for St. Ursula's?'

'You think it too few? You think I should ask her to invite more?'

Unable to help it, Kate scoffed. 'More?' she said, ceasing her task and bringing her free hand to her hip. 'I'm staggered it should be *that* many.'

'No point doing a thing by halves,' Naomi remarked.

Not if you're Pamela Russell, she thought. But then, becoming aware of the scornfulness in that thought, she reminded herself how this was for St. Ursula's. 'You're right,' she said. 'The more, the merrier.'

'Quite.'

Idly trying to picture one hundred guests, she plucked a couple of shrivelled leaves from one of the plants and stuffed them into the pocket of her apron. While it was almost beyond belief that one woman could know so many people, on this occasion, Pamela Russell and her cronies might actually do some good. 'So it could raise quite a lot of money, then?' she observed.

'I should hope so. No point doing it if it doesn't.'

'That's good then.'

'The next task will be to work out how much to charge for the tickets. Mamma's hoping to convince the Royal Gardens Hotel to make their ballroom available gratis, in exchange for which she will invite the editor from the *Telegraph* and ensure that his report mentions their generosity. She's done it successfully with other events.'

It's a different life, Kate thought, emptying the dregs from her watering can into the flower border: a completely different life that some people led; the people they knew; the things they did.

Following Naomi back indoors, she glanced at the clock. 'Did Mr Aubrey happen to mention whether he will be returning for supper?' she asked, her mind moving from gala dinners to lamb cutlets and new potatoes.

'Oh, did I not tell you earlier?' Naomi answered her airily. 'He said not to go to any effort on his account. Apparently, the other day, he bumped into someone he knows of old and tonight, they're going to dine at this fellow's club.'

'That will be nice for him,' she said. She was pleased that Mr Aubrey had some company. It was the same for Naomi; she had begun to look so much better these last few days. People, it seemed, needed company and friendship. Thankfully, while she herself didn't have any real friends of her own, she did have St. Ursula's. And Naomi. And she now had Mrs Russell's gala dinner to look forward to. She would need a gown, of course. There was a thing: she'd never had an evening gown before – had never needed one. Would the expense of it be a problem? If it was, there had to be a dress that Naomi was unlikely to wear again and that she could alter to fit. They weren't terribly different in size; hemming it up an inch or two would be easy enough. And, if it needed taking in a little over the bust, well, she could probably manage that, too. And then there was her hair; although quite adept at pinning it up, she would need to practice a couple of times beforehand – just to be sure. And, afterwards, she would buy a copy of the newspaper and cut out the report to send to Edith and Ma. They would scarcely believe it otherwise. Oh, and while she was at it, she would send one to Luke, too.

Grinning with delight, she hugged herself. How glorious to have such a fine thing to look forward to!

–

Not a moment to stand and think; to Kate, trying to juggle her waking hours between St. Ursula's and Hartland Street, that was how it often felt. With Naomi coming and going from and to her meetings with her mother at Clarence Square, and Aubrey seeming to vanish and reappear without warning, at times the house felt like Paddington Station. Already, breakfast had become a fragmented affair that stretched over several hours to accommodate varying timetables and commitments. Luncheon had also taken on the nature of a moveable feast, and supper – well, there was no telling what would be required there until she returned from St. Ursula's to read the notes left for her by Naomi:

Supper at 7pm, please, N.

Or sometimes:

Dining with Mamma and Papa tonight. See you in the morning, N.

Occasionally, Aubrey would think to leave something similar:

Shan't be back until late. Won't need feeding, AC.

But she didn't mind; she enjoyed the sense of busyness – the feeling of being a part of something so grown-up and full of life. It was just how she had hoped life in London would be – and precisely the thing Luke had once chided her for craving. Well, right now, he wasn't there to pour scorn over the things she had come to enjoy. And, when he did return, her routine would already be well established and quite normal. He shouldn't find it *too* hard to fit in.

'Now,' she arrived in the dining-room doorway to hear Mr Aubrey saying to Naomi. It was an evening a few days before the night of the gala dinner and she was bearing the cheese board he had requested. 'These notes are purely an *aide-memoire*. It is not my intention that you read from them verbatim. Far better to use them as a prompt and speak from the heart. It's clearly a cause about which you are passionate, and so you should have no trouble talking as though you were simply relaying details to a friend.'

'Easy for you to say,' Naomi replied.

On the table between the two of them, Kate could see a series of small cards, upon each of them a couple of lines of handwriting. Trying not to appear as though she was prying, she strained to read the one closest to her. Unfortunately, from her angle of approach, it was upside down.

'Forgive me disturbing you,' she said, setting down the cheese board. 'I'll just fetch some glasses for the port and then I'll be out of your way.'

'Actually,' Aubrey looked across at her to say, 'stay for a moment, if you will. You can serve as the audience.' When she looked back at him blankly, he went on, 'Naomi needs to practice her after-dinner speech.'

Across the table, Naomi was shaking her head. 'Aubrey! For pity's sake, do give me a chance. I'm some way off needing an audience yet!'

'Tomorrow evening, then,' Aubrey looked back at her to say. 'Tomorrow evening, whether I am here for supper or not, insist that she delivers her speech.'

She smiled. 'I'll do just that, sir.'

'And don't hold back. If she's no good, tell her so. There's no need for her to sound polished so much as passionate – moved by the plights of these women. Jerk the odd tear from the wealthy bastards, speak to their consciences and loosen their wallets.'

'Aubrey, really!'

'Sorry. But that *is* what all this is in aid of, isn't it? Getting at some of their money?'

'Well, yes. But I don't want to sound as though I'm threatening them, surely?'

'You won't. And I'm sorry, Mrs Channer, I know I asked you for some cheese, but I've just seen the time and I have somewhere to be. I give you my word that I will lock up when I come in. And I'll fend for myself at breakfast – if that's all right with you.'

'Of course, Lieutenant Colborne – if you don't mind making do.'

'Don't mind in the least.'

And so, over the next few days, Aubrey continued to come and go as he pleased, rarely seen by either woman and leaving few signs of his presence.

'Where do you think he goes?' she asked Naomi a few days later. She had been watching her flick along her rail of evening gowns, trying to choose one to wear for the gala dinner.

'I really don't know. I assume this friend of his must have a place somewhere in town. I don't see it as my business to ask.' Then, with a long sigh, she said, 'Of more interest is what to wear to Mamma's dinner. Courtesy of this war, this will be the second season running I haven't been to Paris for new outfits.'

'No, ma'am.'

'Not that my little trust would enable me to go to Monsieur Henri now anyway – nor Lawrence's salary, for that matter. I fear that's going to be beyond me from now on. Such a lovely little *atelier* he has on Place Vendôme.'

Mumbling her agreement, Kate watched Naomi finger the skirt of the pale blue silk gown from last summer, a garment she had admired in Devon. 'I do like you in that one,' she remarked.

'I like it too,' Naomi agreed. 'But the colour feels all wrong for London, even though we *are* almost in June.'

'The midnight-blue velvet with the lace overlay on the bodice might be suitable,' she ventured.

'The House of Worth gown? Yes, I suppose it might be. I do like it, but I've worn it at least a half a dozen times. Honestly, men have it easy by comparison, don't they? Evening dress for them requires no thought whatsoever. It's a stroke of luck to have Aubrey as an escort, though – very fortunate timing. Shall we get this one out and have a look then?'

With Naomi gesturing to the blue velvet, Kate stepped forward and carefully unhooked the hanger from the rail before helping Naomi to hold the gown in front of her. 'We could always dress it up with something nice from your jewellery box,' she suggested.

'I suppose so. You know,' Naomi said, staring at her reflection in the cheval mirror and shaking her head ruefully, 'I realize now just how much I took Papa's generosity for granted. Whenever I said that I needed a new outfit for this event or a new gown for the so-and-so ball, he would simply nod and tell me to go ahead and see to it. Poor Papa. Poor *me!*'

Poor me. After all the sympathy Naomi purported to show for the women at St. Ursula's, did she really believe *she* was hard done by? Sometimes it was difficult to tell.

Watching Naomi considering her reflection, she wondered whether this would be a good time to ask about a dress for herself. Perhaps, yes – although she mustn't catch her unawares, she must build up to it.

'Have you practised your speech today, ma'am?' she asked as the thought came into her head.

'I've got as far as deciding what I shall say. But I do feel daft, standing in front of the mirror, speaking the words aloud. I shall just have to trust that it will be fine. Aubrey said to try to sound natural. Incidentally, not only has he helped to write my speech, he has also offered to get talking to people on the night so as to solicit additional donations from them. He has even offered to take charge of all matters financial, which will be a tremendous help. And of course, he will be my chaperone. Honestly, the things one can't do without one's husband! And how much easier things will be once Lawrence is back. Anyway, I could stare into this wardrobe until Christmas, I'm not going to find anything I haven't worn before. So, let's settle upon this one, shall we? As you say, we can dress it up. I trust you will have time to make the skirt and all of this trim on the bodice look less crumpled.'

"Course,' she replied, accepting the gown back from Naomi and trying not to sigh. At least, she thought, turning away to lay the dress over the easy chair, she would if she burned the midnight oil; she thought she might just have one last jar of it left somewhere. Now, though, to raise the matter of her own outfit, something she ought really to have done several days ago. Thankfully, there was still just enough time to sort something out.

'Ma'am – *Naomi*,' she began, 'about a gown for me. I was wondering, to save the expense, is there one of yours that might—'

Naomi swivelled about. 'A gown? For you? I'm afraid I don't understand. Why do *you* need a gown?'

Feeling her cheeks redden, Kate bowed her head. Oh, dear Lord – she wasn't invited. It was the only possible explanation for Naomi's reaction.

With that, Naomi, too, seemed suddenly to understand. 'Oh, Kate. Oh, my dear Kate.' Quickly she reached to take her hand. 'I'm so sorry. A formal dinner with stuffy old men and their snooty wives? It didn't for one moment occur to me that you would want any part of such a tedious thing. I'm so sorry. I should have thought to ask you. I shouldn't have presumed, should I? I see now that you would have liked to come.'

Biting the side of her tongue to hold back tears, Kate shook her head. 'No, no,' she said, staring determinedly down at the floor. 'You're quite right. I would be out of place. I don't know what I was thinking.'

Feeling Naomi's hand move to her arm, she forced herself not to shrug it off. How had she got it so wrong? Clearly, she had, as Mrs Russell would call it, taken to having ideas above her station. But truthfully, how had she not seen it for herself?

'Truly, Kate, it was wrong of me to assume you would want no part in it. But I assure you, you won't be missing anything enjoyable. As it happens, I rather think you'll be sparing yourself a good deal of boredom.'

'Yes, I'm sure you're right,' she rushed to agree. 'Like I said, I would be out of place.'

'But I shall mention you in my speech. I shall make sure everyone knows how tirelessly you volunteer and how—'

'No, ma'am,' she interrupted. 'Please don't do that.' Slowly, she raised her head and met Naomi's look. She did appear truly sorrowful. 'It wouldn't be right, drawing attention to me like that. I don't do in a week even one-tenth of what Marjorie Randolph does in a *day*. Tell them what *she* does instead. It's she who should get the admiration and the praise – all of it. It's her doings that'll get folk to donate their money.'

'Well, I'll see. But you have my word that I will make it up to you – make up for wrongly presuming, I mean.'

'No need, ma'am,' she said. 'Truly, the mistake was mine. You and Mr Aubrey raising money for St. Ursula's will be reward enough.'

'Well, I disagree. But, for now, we'll say no more of it. Although I should just tell you that tomorrow evening—'

'Yes, ma'am?'

'—I shall need to be there in plenty of time to go over all of the arrangements before our guests arrive. To that end, Aubrey has arranged for the cab to collect us at six. It is a dreadfully early hour for you to have me ready, I know, but, once we're gone, you'll have the entire evening to yourself. Just think what a luxury that will be!'

Not wanting to seem churlish, she raised a smile. 'Yes, ma'am. A real luxury.'

With Naomi then muttering something about having left her wristwatch somewhere and turning to go downstairs, Kate simply stood, her shock and incredulity rooting her to the spot. How could this have happened? How could she have so completely misunderstood? She cast her mind back over the days of planning and the myriad discussions that had taken place. How, given everything Naomi had told her about the evening, had she got it so wrong? How had she failed to notice there being no mention of an invitation for *her*? How?

Her eyes falling once again upon the midnight-blue gown draped over the chair, she sank onto the end of Naomi's bed. She wasn't sure what she felt most – saddened, embarrassed, or just plain peeved. Considering she was the only one who still volunteered at St. Ursula's, her omission from the guest list was – to borrow an expression from Mr Aubrey – *a bit rich*. On the other hand, what had she been expecting? Hugh Russell might be her father, but she would never be *one of them*. She wasn't even really *half* one of them, despite having his blood in her veins.

Recalling how, on more than one occasion, Luke had said that the Russells had *risen above themselves*, she vowed to let no one – not Mabel nor Edith, nor especially Luke himself – know of her silly mistake. She could do without them gloating and talking about how pride came before a fall. No, whatever it took, she wouldn't let them see just how hard done by she felt. In any event, the last thing she wanted to appear was ungrateful for the effort Mr Aubrey and Naomi were going to in order to raise money for women in *genuine* despair.

Genuine despair. Yes. Who cared that, for whatever reasons, she didn't warrant an invite? What mattered most was that the right people benefitted. Oh, and that she, herself, didn't let the disappointment turn her sour. While too polite to say it plainly, Naomi had been right: how on earth would *she* have conducted herself without mishap at such a grand do? And why on earth would she even have wanted to try? She had no desire to pretend to be something she wasn't. All told, for a housemaid from Devon, she didn't think she was faring too badly at all. She might still be someone of no account, but she was beginning to discover what mattered to her and had begun to make something of a life for herself – and in London, no less.

London. Hm. For the most part, she really did enjoy being here. The busyness of it made her feel grown-up and independent. What would Luke make of it? Deep down, she had a feeling he wouldn't share her keenness for it at all. Well, how he felt about it was up to him. She wouldn't let him spoil it for her. And no, the irony wasn't lost on her: as recently as just this last month or so, she had wanted nothing more than to have him back so as to become a proper wife to him. But now, with him so long gone, and with her just beginning to find her feet as a woman in her own right, she was starting to wonder whether there weren't other things she would prefer rather more than being just Mrs Luke Channer, wife and mother.

Chapter Eight

Ada

'Cor, did you 'ear 'em, love?'

From where she was sweeping the front doorstep, Kate got to her feet to see May Davis, the charwoman at number fourteen, leaning across from the neighbouring porch. 'Hear what?' she asked, straightening herself up.

'Love a duck, girl! The Zeppelin! The bombs.'

Bombs? Her hand reached to the railings. She hadn't heard a thing – not that she would know what a Zeppelin sounded like anyway. A couple of months back she'd seen a picture of one in the newspaper, but that was all. She remembered hoping she would never have occasion to see one in real life.

'A Zeppelin?' she said.

'Dropped ever so many bombs over at Dalston, love,' May Davis replied. '*Incendiaries*, my nipper Albie says they were. You know Albie. Well, he's just started on the railways over at Kings Cross. On a late shift, he was – any road, one of the cleaners over there, on 'is way in to start the same shift, told him 'e heard this sort of throbbing sound coming from the sky. Loud enough to get people out of their 'ouses, 'e said it was. Panicked, they all were. Couldn't nobody pick it out from the darkness, you see.

Not a sign of it to be had anywhere, just this God-awful din. Rumbled right through yer ribs, this other lad reckoned.'

Staring back at May Davis's unusually animated features, Kate shivered. 'And it dropped a bomb out of the sky?' In the time she had been at number twelve, she had learned to take some of the things May Davis said with a pinch of salt – a three-fingered pinch of salt – but surely even *she* wouldn't make up something as grim as this? Surely such lurid tales were even beyond the imagination of that lump of a son of hers, too.

'A sight more than *one*, love. Set fire to 'ouses with folk still sound asleep in their beds, didn't they? Dearie me, I dunno, something to do with it all, ain't it?'

'In Dalston, you say?' Although she didn't know precisely where that was, she had a feeling it was close by.

'*And* further over – Hoxton and Spitalfields. Shoreditch and Whitechapel copped it, too. Here, take a gander at this if you don't believe me.' With that, May Davis bent to retrieve something from inside the front door, which she then poked through the railings to her. It was a newspaper. 'They've run a late one,' she added, 'the war edition, they're calling it. Picked it up in the High Street on me way over. Keep it an' have a good read, love. Only 'eading into the grate otherwise.'

Uncertainly, she took it, ZEPPELIN RAID OVER OUTER LONDON stark and unmissable at the top of the front page. *Many fires reported*, it said underneath.

'Dear Lord,' she muttered, scanning down the page to a picture of a cylindrical balloon-type craft apparently hovering above a field, and beneath which was printed the caption *German Zeppelin in Flight*.

'Nuffink we can do though, love, is there? 'Cept maybe pray to the Almighty – if you're that way inclined.'

Somehow, Kate didn't think that praying was going to keep them safe – not if their enemy had *these* monstrous machines.

Stepping back inside, she reached to lean her broom in the corner of the hallway. Before she'd had the chance to examine the newspaper further, though, she heard someone coming up the steps and a man's voice calling in through the open door.

'Mornin', love.'

She turned about. It was the postman. 'Morning,' she replied.

'Terrible business,' he said, nodding towards the newspaper. 'Don't know what the world's coming to.'

Distractedly, she took the piece of post he was holding towards her; buff-coloured and slightly dog-eared, she saw that it wasn't an envelope but a field postcard. Noticing that the address on the front was written in Luke's messy hand, her heart gathered speed. In that moment, she would have given anything not to have to turn it over and read the message on the other side. After all, he'd never resorted to sending these postcards before, denouncing them as impersonal, and claiming she was worth the time it took him to write her a proper letter.

Despite staring down at his handwriting, she still didn't turn it over.

Designed to enable a soldier serving at the front to send a quick message home, field postcards were printed on the reverse with an assortment of broad and all-purpose statements, the sender simply crossing through those that didn't apply. She knew from seeing them at St. Ursula's that a section at the top warned of the draconian penalty for breaching the rules for their use:

> NOTHING to be written on this side except the date and signature of the sender. Sentences not required may be erased. If anything else is added the postcard will be destroyed.

The one most women dreaded receiving was where all of the lines had been crossed through except the one that stated *I have been admitted to hospital wounded.*

This morning, already running behind with her chores, she was grateful for the simplicity of the card's design; in the fix that she was, she wouldn't have been able to stop to read a letter anyway. Finally forcing herself to turn it over, she quickly ran her eyes down its length to see which statements Luke had left for her to read. *I am quite well* leapt out at her. Well, praise be for that, at least. She scanned the rest of it, the only other sentence not thoroughly obliterated by Luke's black ink was, *I have received no letter from you lately.*

Prickling with a mixture of irritation and guilt, she stuffed it into the pocket of her apron. No, well, there was a reason for that. She was rushed off her feet. She was kept occupied all morning and afternoon, and then, come day's end, as often as not, she was too dog-tired to even direct her thoughts to what to tell him, let alone sit by the lamp and put pen neatly to paper. And anyway, it couldn't be *that* long since she'd written to him – could it? She knew her last letter hadn't gone astray because he'd already responded to it. Well, she would write to him just as soon as she got the chance. And, while she was at it, she would ask him – politely of course – to desist from chivvying her up. It wouldn't get a letter to him any quicker – not unless the government started printing field postcards for use by busy wives. Ha! There was an idea. They could print them with statements like *Laundry covered in coal smuts again. Youngest has measles. Price of butter up. Too busy making ends meet to stop to write.* Rather than *Field Postcards*, they could call them *Home Postcards*. And they could advertise them as *A Boon to the Busy Wife!* A statement that said *Failed to keep the home fires burning* might come in handy for some women, too.

'Ah, Kate, there you are.' Tutting under her breath at yet another intrusion to her time, she turned to see Naomi coming along the hallway. Dressed in a pale-blue skirt and floral blouse, she looked like a proper lady of leisure. 'I was just thinking about the best way to hand over the donations to St. Ursula's, you know, whether we should have a proper little – goodness, are you all right? You look quite… odd. Ought you to come in and sit down?'

Trying desperately hard not to shake her head in despair, she nevertheless did just that. 'Me, ma'am? No, I'm just fine.' *Hardly convincing.*

'Oh, did the boy deliver two *Telegraphs* again this morning?'

Realizing she was still clutching the newspaper May Davis had given her, she held it out, minded that this latest news might be just the thing to distract Naomi from continuing to enquire after her well-being. 'No,' she said, 'it's the *Daily News*. May Davis – you know, the char next door – gave it to me to read about the Zeppelin.'

A while back, she would have gone out of her way to keep such harrowing news from Naomi's sight but now – certainly while Aubrey continued to reside with them – there seemed little point. If the *Telegraph* hadn't already reported upon it today, they almost certainly would tomorrow. And, even if Naomi did somehow manage to miss the details of it *there*, sooner or later, Mr Aubrey was bound to tell her all about it. Sometimes, it was as though he *wanted* her to fret.

'Don't tell me they've been dropping bombs on poor old Norfolk again—' Watching Naomi unfold the paper, Kate saw her eyes widen in alarm. '*London*? There were Zeppelins over *London*? But—'

'Apparently, folk as close by as Kings Cross heard the commotion.' Now she was being just as ghoulish as May Davis.

'But this is awful – destroying people's homes. It was bad enough that time they reached East Anglia. But *London*? I know it says it was only the *outlying districts*, but how long before they come back and bomb *us*, right here in town? My goodness. It's a terrible day when one doesn't feel safe in one's home.'

'No doubt that's how they want us to feel,' she replied, managing to sound rather more pragmatic than she felt. 'No doubt they want us to live in dread—'

'Well, we'll do no such thing.'

In her puzzlement, she shook her head. Whatever did Naomi have in mind to do – arm herself with a rifle and shoot down the next Zeppelin that came throbbing its way towards them? If those few guns in Whitehall – and even those newer ones that had recently been placed in the parks – had been unable to bring down the beastly things, then as far as she could see, dread was going to continue to be the order of the day.

'We'll go about our business as normal, is that what you mean?' she asked. If so, while defiant, it didn't seem like much of a plan.

'Well, no. I was thinking more along the lines of decamping to Devon.'

'Woodicombe? Go back *there*?' She despaired, she really did. How was *that* continuing as normal? How was *that* defying the enemy? It wasn't. Not only that, but no sooner would they get there than Naomi would be bored and itching to return.

'We would certainly be safer.'

No, she had to put a stop to this. But she would have to be furtive about it. Naomi could be quite obstinate once she'd got an idea into her head. 'All the while we were down there last time,' she said, 'you couldn't wait to leave.'

'As I recall, neither could you,' Naomi observed drily. 'Who was it who kept asking me when I thought Aubrey would be on his way?'

She blushed. 'Well, yes. But that was so as to get *you* back *here*. You needed something to—'

'I know. It's all right. I'm rather teasing you. The place does indeed have the capacity to drive me to distraction. But I suppose what it boils down to is that I'd rather be bored out of my mind than burnt in my bed. And I'm sure Lawrence would rather that, too. Luke as well.'

'But we've Mr Aubrey staying,' she said. Despite her objection to Naomi's suggestion, she could see her point. Bombs or boredom did indeed seem to be the gist of it. But just how real *was* the risk? Now that the Germans had come here and frightened everyone, perhaps they wouldn't come back again; perhaps they would fear the army being ready for them next time. Perhaps they had done enough to make their point. And anyway, going to Devon felt like giving in to them. And if everyone did that, the Germans would soon have won.

'The same consideration applies to Aubrey as it did last time,' Naomi answered her question. 'Any day now, he will be rejoining his regiment. He's obviously recovering because he's hardly ever here. He's nearly always out – which, of course, is pleasing to see.'

She could hardly argue with that. Soon, Mr Aubrey would be gone. And then there would be nothing to keep them in Hartland Street.

'But there's St. Ursula's,' she said. If being subtle had failed, then she was going to have to resort to honesty. 'Folk there have come to rely on me and I shouldn't want to let them down.'

Moving through to the drawing room, Naomi sighed. 'No, and I appreciate that, truly I do. You are a great help to Marjorie Randolph. But, once we give her the money we raised, she might be able to put the whole place on less of a makeshift footing for a while. It's not as though we will be gone forever – just while there's this threat to our well-being.'

The problem for Kate was that the time she spent at St. Ursula's had quickly become the most meaningful part of her days. Everything else filling her hours was little different to being a housewife in her own home. Granted, the effort involved at St. Ursula's was tiring her out, and it was also true that at Woodicombe, she wouldn't have the cooking of their meals to see to – or indeed, most of the cleaning. On the other hand, there would be very little else to occupy her. What it seemed to come down to, then, was that she could either be run ragged but feel fulfilled in London, or else she could be less tired but bored rigid in Devon.

'Was it a good sum you collected?' she asked, realizing that neither Naomi nor Mr Aubrey had thought to tell her how much had been raised by the gala dinner.

'Come and see,' Naomi said, her face brightening. 'Aubrey very kindly arranged for a banker's cheque to be drawn.'

Nearing the dining table, Kate's eyes fell upon a rectangular chit of paper, the figure written upon it sufficiently large to make her gasp. 'Heavens,' she said, studying the words written alongside the numbers to check that she had read it correctly. 'Folk must have been real generous.'

'They were. Aubrey wasn't wrong to say that guilt opens wallets. Not only do we have the sum raised from the sale of the tickets, but he pressed every man present into giving a little bit more besides. Although, from the look of satisfaction in his eyes on the night, I had actually been expecting the final total to be even higher than this. Still, the sum is quite magnificent, don't you think?'

Magnificent? It beggared belief. 'Miss Randolph will be speechless,' she said.

'Do you think so?'

'I do.'

'Then there must be no delay in getting it to her. You and I will go along to see her and make a little presentation. At the dinner, I promised to invite the reporter from the *Telegraph*, who said he would like to bring along a photographer.'

'And Mrs Russell?' she asked, noticing that Naomi had made no mention of her mother.

'I can't see *her* in Wharf Street, can you? No, I shall act as her representative. Tell me, were you planning to go there tomorrow?'

'Yes, ma'am, all being well, I was.'

'Then not a word until I've made the necessary arrangements. No point spoiling the surprise at this late stage.'

'No, ma'am.'

Goodness. She was going to have her photograph in the newspaper; that was something to look forward to. It might even make up for the disappointment of not being part of the dinner itself. Yes, she would watch out for the article being printed and then buy up several copies in order to send cuttings to Woodicombe – and one to Luke, of course, when she got around to it. Best of all, though, she couldn't wait to see Marjorie Randolph's face when they presented her with the cheque.

–

'My dears, I hardly know what to say.'

'Say that it will make a difference,' Naomi replied to Marjorie Randolph's breathy admission when, a couple of days later, they presented her with the donation.

'Oh, Mrs Colborne, Mrs Channer, it will! It will! I can think of so many ways in which this can be put to good use. There's the making of grants for clothing so that some of the older children might stay in school. There's emergency awards to pay rents where a family is about to become homeless, or legal opinion on some of our thornier relief cases… to name just a few. And the sum is so generous. So incredibly generous!'

'Marjorie,' Naomi began, 'that such essential work should fall to a charitable organization, especially in this day and age, is lamentable. That St. Ursula's exists at all is down to you. You deserve the help.'

'Thank you, thank you, my dears. Tonight, my brother and I will remember you in our prayers – *and* all of the donors, of course. Oh, and on the subject of donors, Kate, you will be pleased to learn that very late yesterday, a young woman arrived at the vicarage with a bundle of women's clothing. She wouldn't give me her name, wanting to say only that she had been turning out her late aunt's belongings. I've brought them in and put them to one side in the storeroom for you to have a look at. I was rather wary of upsetting your careful arrangement of it all.'

She smiled. Miss Randolph was right: this *was* good news. 'I'll just pop an' take a look, then – seeing as the man from the newspaper isn't here yet.'

'Newspaper?'

'Oh, yes,' she heard Naomi say as she headed away across the hall. 'We thought it would be a nice idea to…'

In the storeroom, she let out a gasp of delight. There at one end of the trestle was a mound of clothing. Quickly, she reached to the uppermost item. It was a plain skirt of navy-blue bombazine, old fashioned but well made and seemingly little-worn. Perfectly serviceable, it would help some poor woman out of difficulties. Beneath that were several blouses, largely of lightweight cotton; rather prim, but again, in good condition. Beneath those were a couple of nightshirts and two more skirts, similar in style to the first. She separated out the garments by type and then, lifting each one in turn, held them up, examining the seams, the hems, and their general condition. What luck! These would do nicely, especially for a slightly older and larger lady.

Folding each of them neatly, she bent to place them in the trunk beneath the trestle. She wouldn't give them out willy-nilly; she would wait until she recognized a suitable recipient. She would know her when she saw her.

Several minutes later, stepping back out into the main hall, she noticed that Miss Randolph and Naomi were now standing by the door to the vestibule. As she crossed towards them, both women looked in her direction.

'Well, what did you think?' Marjorie asked, smiling brightly.

'Very good quality. Real useful,' she replied, sensing that in her absence, something had happened.

'Well, then,' Naomi said, straightening the front of her jacket, 'Marjorie, I'm afraid we must away.'

'Yes, you must have so much to do. And thank you again, both of you.'

Warily, she flicked a look to Naomi. Much to do? Much to do about what?

'Come along, Kate. The cab is waiting.'

'Enjoy your break, my dear,' Marjorie Randolph chose that moment to say, leaning across and patting her arm. 'And we'll hope to see you once you return.'

Return? Return from where? What was going on? Skipping a step to keep up with Naomi as she pressed open the door and began to make her way across the vestibule, she asked, 'Are we not waiting for the man from the newspaper? And the photographer?'

'He's been,' Naomi replied matter-of-factly, stepping through the far doors and out onto the street. 'He and his assistant took two photographs, noted down our names, and said that the article will probably be printed in a day or two.'

The photographer had *been*? She had *missed* him? Arriving alongside Naomi on the pavement, she frowned. How? Why had no one thought to come and get her – for a photograph to be included in the *Telegraph*?

Unsure where to start with her questions, she followed Naomi into the cab and slammed the door shut behind her.

'Back to Hartland Street, please, driver.'

'Yes, ma'am.'

And what had Miss Randolph meant when she had said, 'enjoy your break'? What break?

'The moment we arrive home, I shall make a list for you of the outfits I shall require. It will be difficult – not knowing how long we shall be away – but it isn't as though you won't be able to see to any laundry while we are there. Then, while you are attending to the packing, I shall send a telegram to Woodicombe and let Mrs Bratton know when to expect us—'

Woodicombe. Naomi had decided – without further reference to her – that they *were* to decamp to Devon? By her sides, and of their own accord, her hands curled into fists while, in her chest, something felt to be sinking like a stone.

'Oh,' she said quietly. 'Well, I wish I'd known. I would have said to Miss Randolph about—'

'Fear not. I explained to Marjorie that, in addition to this recent Zeppelin attack unsettling us, you have become exhausted and are in need of a rest.'

'Exhausted? Me? No, I'm just—'

'My dear Kate, you can't see it for yourself but trust me, you've become very pale and drawn-looking. Not only have you been volunteering four mornings a week instead of the original three but, since we've had Aubrey staying, your workload at home has become rather greater.'

'Mr Aubrey's been no trouble, ma'am,' she said. Of all the things adding to her workload, Mr Aubrey's presence wasn't one of them. For a start, he was hardly ever there. It had become rare for him to even want a meal.

'Perhaps not directly, no. Before his arrival though, I was helping out with the chores.' Helping out with the chores? Drying up dishes now and again counted as helping out with the chores? 'But, more recently, I haven't been able to do so. Trust me, Kate, you need a break.'

A break. Wasn't that for *her* to decide – or at least to be consulted about?

'But ma'am—'

'No, I shall hear no *buts*. We are going to spend some time at Woodicombe. I've already spoken to Papa and he's quite happy for us to stay there for as long as we want.'

'And Mr Aubrey?' she asked. 'What's to happen to him?' When it had come to considering him last time, Naomi had been most unwilling to upset him.

'I shall explain to him that he will need to find somewhere else to stay. If he is not yet fit enough to return to his regiment, and if he is unable to lodge with this friend of his, he can always go to Avingham.'

Well, there was a turnabout. 'I see.'

'And yes, you may trust that the irony isn't lost on me – having said that you need a break, I am now landing you with more than ever to do. But it will be worth it.'

'If you say so, ma'am.'

'I do.'

Looking out through the window of the cab, Kate felt close to tears. Curse the Germans and their stupid Zeppelins. They had only just got settled back into Hartland Street. She hadn't even minded that Mr Aubrey had arrived. She'd been busy, yes, and dog-tired at times, too – she wouldn't deny any of that. But she had been enjoying her mornings at St. Ursula's. She looked forward to going there. Nell was good fun and Marjorie Randolph was truly inspiring. Quite possibly, she was the happiest she could remember being. Quite by chance she'd found a purpose – one that didn't involve getting down on her hands and knees and scrubbing. Or standing over a range or a kitchen sink. Of late, she awoke every morning feeling glad to be alive. And proud. But now, just like that, Naomi was making them go back to Woodicombe. And, to rub salt into the wound, she was using *her* well-being as the excuse. But what could she do? She could hardly challenge her. Naomi might be her half-sister – after a fashion – but she was also her employer. And there couldn't be many employers who would let their housekeeper spend four mornings a week away from their duties to help out elsewhere.

Nevertheless, making no effort to disguise it, she let out a long and weary sigh. Not so long ago, it had been her greatest hope that this war would come to a swift end, that Luke would come home unscathed, and that she could settle down to a normal sort of existence as a wife. And, in due course, she supposed, as a mother. Now, though, faced with having the thing she enjoyed doing most taken away from her, that once-longed-for normality felt to have lost some of its appeal. In fact, the prospect of having to knuckle down to such a boring existence made her feel very disgruntled indeed.

—

Under her breath, Kate growled. Although several hours since Naomi had broken the news about returning to Woodicombe, her frustration hadn't subsided. In fact, she felt more cross than ever! Not only was she seething about having to return to Woodicombe, she was still smarting from what had happened at St. Ursula's. Granted, Naomi had been instrumental in organizing the charity dinner and should therefore accept the bigger part of the praise. She would even concede that the whole thing had been Aubrey's idea; it had never been her intention to try to take credit for *that*. But, having been led to believe that she was to be part of the presentation of the money to Miss Randolph, she had naturally assumed that she would also be captured in the photograph. *Mrs Lawrence Colborne and charity helper Mrs Luke Channer presenting the donated funds to St. Ursula's supervisor, Miss Marjorie Randolph.* That was the sort of thing she had been expecting. Well, it was a good job she hadn't told anyone beforehand, otherwise, now, she would have been left with egg on her face. Again. And she could do without *more* snide remarks from Edith when she saw her.

Kneeling alongside one of Naomi's travelling trunks, her jaw clamped tightly with displeasure, she briskly folded a half-dozen of Naomi's underslips, wrapped the resulting pile in tissue paper, and placed them into the bottom. Next, she set about coiling pairs of stockings, pushing them into their linen bag, ready to be used to pad out the top of one of her foundation garments. Then, looking around her at the various outfits Naomi had selected, she sighed. It was her own fault. How many times before had this happened to her? How many times previously had she misread Naomi's intentions? Enough, surely, that any sane person would expect her to know better by now. As far as Naomi was concerned, the day she had offered her the position of housekeeper, her conscience had been appeased. With that single act, any sisterly guilt had been assuaged. But, if it was that obvious to her, why did it always prove so hard to remember? Why did she persist in expecting the relationship between them to amount to something more than merely employer and domestic?

'Everything all right in here?'

In response to Naomi's question, posed as she peered around the doorway from the landing, Kate bristled.

'Fine,' she answered.

'Still annoyed to be packing for Devon again?'

Bother the woman! She could read her moods too well.

From where she was kneeling on the floor, she reluctantly turned towards the door. 'To be truthful, ma'am, yes, I am.' Deciding this was the sort of conversation for which she ought really to look Naomi in the eye, she got slowly to her feet. 'But it wasn't my decision to make. If *you* believe we will be safer in Devon, for certain it's not my place to argue with you.'

For the briefest of moments, she thought she saw a look of discomfort flicker across Naomi's face.

'Perhaps not,' Naomi said, turning more fully into the room. 'But equally, perhaps it wouldn't harm me to consider your feelings rather more than I sometimes do. After all, for the foreseeable future – however long that might turn out to be – it is just the two of us in this household. And, while you might be my housekeeper, you are also part of my family. In addition to which, given what has happened over these last few months, if you were to become fed up with me and leave, I should be truly lost. So, next time it comes to a decision of this magnitude, I shall try to remember to consult you first. In any event, you are by far and away the more level-headed of the two of us. I could do far worse than seek your counsel anyway.'

She swallowed hard. Oddly, she now felt ashamed – not unlike someone who angled for a compliment only to find that when it came, it didn't mean as much as they had hoped it would.

'I wouldn't never presume to tell you what to do,' she ventured.

Her pronouncement made Naomi laugh. 'Well, actually, Nurse Channer, sometimes you tell me *precisely* what to do, and in no uncertain terms, either. To be fair to you, though, often is the time I need to be made to see sense.'

'And you needn't fear. I shouldn't leave you,' she hastened to add. 'At least, not over some petty nonsense like this.'

'The petty nonsense on this occasion being the small matter of where we reside, do you mean?'

Seeing the smile on Naomi's lips, she grinned. 'Nothing as unimportant as that, no.'

'Look, why don't you leave that for now? Why don't we go down to the kitchen, make ourselves a drink, take it up to the drawing room and relax for a moment or two before we retire for the night? Perhaps you could think of some things we might do together while we're down in Devon – you know, some sightseeing, or some walks we might take. I never have taken the chance to explore the place.'

She knew what Naomi was doing; she was trying to appease her conscience again. But what did it matter why she was doing it? If she had been shamed into showing a little more consideration, all well and good. Day to day, the two of them got along surprisingly well. And since she wasn't about to suddenly gain any other company, she needed to make the best of what she had.

'Then you've been missing out,' she said, determining to be less grudging. 'And yes, I shouldn't mind putting my feet up for a while.'

'Come on, then. Let's go and make a drink. And if, through being inconsiderate, I ever make you this cross again, you are not to stew over it, you are to tell me. I've said this to you before, about the perils of resentment, and of letting it fester.'

Smiling ruefully, she shook her head. 'Very well, ma'am—'

'*Naomi*.'

'Next time I get in a fret, *Naomi*, I'll try 'n remember to do just that.'

–

'Well then, it seems we're all set.' Getting to her feet, Kate wiped the palms of her hands down her apron. 'I shan't lock this one just yet though,' she said, gesturing to one of the two trunks in front of her, 'in case you think of anything else at the last minute.'

'Good idea. And well done,' Naomi said, reaching out to squeeze her arm. 'I do know this has made a lot of work for you. Have you packed your own things yet?'

Kate arched her back. It was early evening the following day and, having spent the entire afternoon readying and packing Naomi's wardrobe, her neck felt stiff and her knees were aching; the last thing she wanted to think about now was sorting out her own belongings. And anyway, there wasn't much to see to: pretty much everything she owned would be going with her. 'Not yet,' she said. 'I'll see to them tomorrow.'

'Yes, of course. Well, I've made all of the arrangements. On Friday morning, the porter will call at eight thirty, leaving plenty of time once we get up to remember anything we might have overlooked. Our cab is booked for nine o'clock. I know that sounds a little early for the ten fifteen train, but I would prefer that we didn't have to make a mad dash to Waterloo. You know how frightfully busy the roads can be at that time of day.'

'Yes, ma'am. I'll make sure we're good an' ready.'

'Do you know,' Naomi began thoughtfully, 'I'm quite looking forward to it now.'

Beside her, Kate grimaced. For her own part, she wasn't so sure, the matter bothering her most being the apparently open-ended nature of the arrangement. As things currently stood, she could be stuck in Devon for months.

'Have you spoken to Aubrey yet?' she enquired, it seeming a clever way to avoid having to admit to her feelings. 'Does he have somewhere to go?'

'I slipped a note under his door. That way, if he comes back when we we're out, at least he'll know of our plans. If he can't arrange to stay in town, one imagines he can always go back to Avingham. It will put him close to *Regimental HQ*, as he refers to it.'

'Yes, I suppose—'

'Perhaps that's him now,' Naomi remarked of a knocking at the front door.

Going down the stairs to find out, Kate conceded that it would be just like him to have misplaced his key. These last few days in particular, his manner seemed to have become quite distracted.

At the front door, though, Kate was greeted by the sight of a young woman, the likes of which she was more accustomed to helping at St. Ursula's. The fabric of her dark skirt and jacket sported the sort of sheen suggesting they had seen better days, her head was bare, her hair undressed, and her eyes had the puffiness of someone who had recently been crying. Instinctively, her mind went to the cache of donated clothing in the storeroom, and how it probably contained a couple of garments of broadly the right size. There were even a few baby slips left, she thought, noting that the child in the girl's arms looked to be little more than a few days old.

'This the 'ouse of Mrs Lawrence Colborne?' the girl asked while Kate was still sizing her up.

Not meaning to, she frowned. 'Did Miss Randolph send you?' she asked. While on the one hand it seemed unlikely, on the other, it felt to be the only explanation.

'Who?'

'Miss Marjorie Randolph, from St. Ursula's?'

The girl shrugged her shoulders. 'Ain't never heard of no Marjorie Randolph. I'm 'ere to see Mrs Colborne. This *is* where she lives, ain't it?'

Again, Kate frowned. 'What is your business with her?' she asked, the girl hardly having the appearance of someone she should just randomly admit.

'Look, it's important, all right? Why else would I have come all this way?'

'You'd best come in, then,' she said, taking a quick glance in both directions along the street, largely to satisfy herself that the girl was alone. 'I'll go and see whether she is able to come down. But stay right there,' she added as an afterthought. 'Don't step off the mat.'

Looking back over her shoulder, she watched the girl stare down to the floor and then adjust her feet so as to stand precisely in the centre of the doormat. Reaching the half-landing, she glanced back again. Although the girl hadn't moved, she was looking around in a manner that suggested she would rather not be there. What on earth could she want? She *looked* harmless, but should she have let her in?

'Who is it?' Naomi asked, arriving on the landing to peer over the bannister.

'I'm not sure,' she admitted, realizing she had forgotten to ask the girl's name. 'But, by the look of her, I'd say she's no older than seventeen or eighteen. And the baby just a few days. She asked for you by name. Mrs Lawrence Colborne, she said.'

'*The baby*, did you say? She has a baby?'

She nodded. 'Tiny little mite. Newborn if I'm not mistaken.'

'Well, I suppose I had better go down and see what she wants. But come and stand next to me while I talk to her, will you? Faced with the two of us together, she might be dissuaded from trying anything foolhardy. You can't trust anyone these days.'

'Yes, ma'am.'

Arriving back at the bottom of the staircase, Kate did as she had been asked.

'Good evening,' Naomi greeted the girl. 'I am Mrs Lawrence Colborne. And you are?'

'Ada, ma'am. Me name is Ada.'

'I see. Well, Ada, how may I help you?'

'I've come to find you on account of a promise I made to me friend, Bertha, God rest her soul.'

Standing behind Naomi, Kate studied the girl's expression. She looked pale and tired, the awkward way she was holding the baby suggesting that perhaps it wasn't her own. Certainly, *something* was amiss. She also noticed how she pronounced her friend's name as *Berfa*.

'I see. But what does that have to do with me? And how do you know my name? And where I live?'

'Look, Missus, I'm not 'ere to make trouble. This,' the girl said, proffering the bundle containing the baby towards them, 'is Bertha's daughter. She were born a bit too soon. Though, as it turns out, that weren't no bad thing. See, Bertha was sickly a long while. And then last night, the delivering of this one finished her off. If you ask me, it were only luck the poor thing made it into this world at all. Delirious with fever, poor Bertha was. Already knew she weren't going to make it, though, 'cos the day before, she made me swear that if anyfink should 'appen to her, I'd bring the baby here to you.'

'To *me*?'

Equally startled, Kate frowned. Something about all of this definitely wasn't what it seemed.

At that point, Ada began sobbing loudly, once again holding the baby towards Naomi. Behind her, ready to intervene, Kate stepped forward. To her surprise, Naomi accepted the child. 'Kate, I think perhaps we should all go down to the kitchen. There's clearly something here that we don't understand but, if we're to have any chance of getting at the truth, we need to help Ada calm down.'

Stuck for any particular reason to object, she could see no way to avoid agreeing. 'Yes, ma'am.'

'Come, Ada,' Naomi said softly, reaching towards the girl with her free arm as she did so. 'Would you like a hot drink? Or something to eat? Then perhaps you can explain to me why your friend wanted you to bring her baby *here*, to *me*.'

When Ada gave a single nod, the three women traipsed down to the kitchen where Kate pulled back a chair from the table and gestured to Ada that she should sit down. Naomi, she noticed, still had the baby, cradling it quite naturally. If it weren't for the ragged state of its shawl, the two of them might have looked as though they belonged together. Shivering unexpectedly, she reminded herself not to be so fanciful. It had been a long day and she knew from experience that when she was tired, her judgement was, at best, prone to failing her. She would still be watchful, though.

'Would you like a cup of tea?' she asked, directing her question to Ada, now huddled uneasily at the far side of the table. The girl nodded. 'Will you be all right if I go through and draw the water?' she turned to ask Naomi, gesturing with the kettle towards the scullery.

'Of course, yes. Make the big pot. I shouldn't mind one myself. You might want one too.'

'Yes, ma'am.'

'So, Ada,' Naomi said a while later when they were all seated at the table, cups of tea in front of them and the baby still asleep in her arms. 'Tell me about your friend Bertha. Who was she and how did she come to know of *me*?'

Ada gripped her teacup. 'Bertha,' she eventually began, 'was me best friend. When we was growing up, our grans was friends and our 'ouses shared the same pump. Then, last spring, Bertha went and got wed to Ernie – Ernest Ward, that is. Before that, she was Bertha Jones.' When Ada paused for breath, neither Kate nor Naomi spoke. 'Not long after 'e joined up with his pals from the depot,' the girl picked up again, 'Bertha says to me she thinks she's got a babe on the way. So, I 'elps her write to Ernie. Next thing we know, a letter comes. Ernie's been killed. Dead, it says he is.'

Across the table, Kate tried to swallow a gasp, a look to Naomi telling her that she was trying to do something similar.

'And Bertha has also now died,' Naomi checked.

Ada nodded. 'Like I said, last eve.'

'The baby has no parents.'

Somewhere inside of her, Kate felt a deep unease. The arrival of this apparently orphaned baby couldn't possibly be a coincidence. So what was going on? Who could be fashioning some sort of scheme against Naomi? And why?

'That's right, Missus. None.'

'Well, while that's all terribly sad, what I don't under-stand is why Bertha would ask you to bring the baby *here*, to *me*?'

It was the thing troubling Kate, too. 'Did you ever know of a family by the name of Jones?' she asked Naomi. 'Or… Ward, was it?'

Ada nodded. 'That's right, Ward.'

'No,' Naomi replied. 'Not to my knowledge.' And then, turning to Ada, she said, 'And what of the child's grandparents? Where are they?'

Ada shrugged. 'Ernie were a runaway, miss. He left his folks when he weren't much more than a nipper and made his way to London. Never said more than that they were a bad lot who could rot in hell as far as he was concerned.'

'And Bertha's parents,' Naomi coaxed. 'Where are *they*?'

Without warning, Ada shot up from her chair and began to fumble about in her pockets. 'Christ almighty!' she said. 'I'd forget me 'ed if it weren't screwed on. Here,' she went on, handing a cutting from a newspaper across the table, 'this'll tell you. She give me this a couple of days back and begged me hang on to it. Said it would 'elp.'

With Naomi holding the baby – by some miracle still sound asleep – it was Kate who took the slip of paper and laid it on the table, smoothing her hand across it in an attempt to flatten the wrinkles and render it legible. The print was tiny but the word that jumped out at her, as though illuminated by electric light, was *Russell*. Hastily, she read from the top:

On Saturday, at St. George's church, Lawrence Hector Colborne, younger son of

Mr and Mrs Ralph Colborne of Avingham Park, Avingham Ducis, to Naomi Florentina Russell, only daughter of Mr and Mrs Hugh Russell of Clarence Square, Kensington. After a wedding breakfast at the Royal Hotel, the groom left to join his regiment (Wiltshires), the bride to take up residence at the couple's new home in Hartland Street, Marylebone.

Fascinated by details of the wedding until then unknown to her – and by Naomi's curious middle name – she slid the scrap of paper across to Naomi, noticing the surprise in her eyes as she scanned its length. 'Why on earth did your friend Bertha keep this?' she asked.

Wondering the same thing, Kate swivelled her attention to Ada.

'She said somefink about that Hugh Russell fella being fam'ly – and about how he should have done better by her mam. Then she said that through you – *this Naomi woman*, were her words, beggin' your pardon, ma'am – a grave wrong could be righted.'

A grave wrong could be righted? Feeling her throat tighten, Kate looked across at Naomi, only mildly surprised to see that she had turned pale.

'So—'

'An' now it makes sense,' Ada continued. 'See, Bertha lived with her gran because her mam worked up west. On the stage, she were. A dancer. I seen her once or twice when she came to visit. Beautiful, she was. Tall, with shiny hair and lovely frocks. And furs. Bertha used to say that every man in the world was in love with her mam and that rich men were always giving her things. It was a rich man what give her Bertha, if you believe what she said. And a lot of money to keep quiet about it.'

Unexpectedly, Kate felt dizzy. 'Ma'am—' she ventured.

'Are you thinking what I'm thinking?' Naomi turned to her to ask.

'That this is a cruel joke, concocted by someone who knows what happened once upon a time? It has been going through my mind, yes.'

'No!' Naomi said, surprising her with her sharpness. 'That wasn't at all what I was thinking. Ada,' she said, rising awkwardly to her feet, 'please would you excuse us for a moment? I need to talk to Kate in private. Please, do stay where you are. We will be back in a moment.'

When Naomi then got to her feet and left the room, Kate followed. *Please*, she willed, *please don't let Naomi be taken in by this sham of a story.*

At the top of the stairs, Naomi turned to face her.

'What is it, ma'am?' she asked, bracing herself for what she guessed she was about to hear.

'Kate, remember back in the summer, when it came to light about us having the same father?'

Slowly, she nodded. She was hardly likely to have forgotten. ''Course I do.'

'Well, do you also remember how I told you that Papa had another child – from an affair he had with someone not long after he married Mamma?' Again, she nodded. 'Well, I recall now an occasion when they were having an argument and I overheard Mamma refer to – and forgive me – *your little dancer whore*. Since then, in a quite separate conversation with Aunt Diana, she mentioned something about the woman in question being paid off.

242

And now, this evening, Ada tells us that Bertha's mother was a dancer, and her father a wealthy man who paid her to keep the child a secret. Well, I do believe now that Bertha is... *was*... Papa's other child. In fact, I'm certain of it.'

'Ma'am,' she began uneasily.

'Think about it,' Naomi rushed on, her eyes wide and her manner agitated. 'With all of the secrecy that surrounded it, how could anyone else possibly have known? Certainly, no one close to the family knew. Much later on, Aunt Diana found out. But she's the only one. Mamma and Papa never told anyone. So how could this be a trick? How?'

Very slowly, she drew a long breath. Then, equally slowly, she exhaled it. What to do? By the sound of it, there was a chance this *wasn't* a hoax. On the other hand, it wouldn't be the first time a trickster had tried to dupe a grieving woman. 'So—'

'I know it's hard to believe,' Naomi said, staring down at the tiny baby's face. 'But I do believe that this child is related to me. If what Ada says is true, then Bertha was my half-sister, which makes this baby my flesh and blood. This dear little orphaned innocent is my half-niece.'

—

'Well, she was grateful for the clothes.'

Unable to help it, Kate raised her eyebrows. 'She was. And the hot meal.' *And the money I'm not supposed to know you slipped her*, she went on to think as she pictured Ada taking her leave of them barely half an hour previously. Quick enough to accept the offer of a paid ride home in a cab, too.

And now there was a further cab fare to pay, she thought as they awaited the arrival of a woman, produced as though by magic for them by Marjorie Randolph: a wet nurse by the name of Mrs Norris, whose expenses Naomi would also now have to bear.

'I do hope she's not much longer,' Naomi remarked in between trying to soothe the fractious infant. 'The poor thing is terribly distraught. Just hark at her. And I can't say I'm surprised, poor mite.'

The baby's cries doing little to help Kate win out against her exhaustion, she went to the window and twitched aside the curtain. It was almost midnight, and, at this rate, she would soon fall asleep standing up. 'Where did Miss Randolph say this woman is coming from?' she asked before yawning widely.

'Shush, shush. Not long now,' Naomi tried to comfort the infant. 'I don't remember. I was so relieved that she knew of someone, I barely heard what she said to me after that.'

Spotting a weak beam of light on the cobbles, she pulled the curtain wider. 'Here, this must be her,' she said, drawing the curtain back across and moving hastily towards the front door.

'Mrs Norris,' the woman announced herself. 'Miss Randolph came to wake me. You have a newborn?'

Standing aside, she beckoned the woman into the hallway. 'Yes,' she said. 'Please, let me take your things.'

Beneath her dark cloak, fashionable in style and trimmed with toning braid, Mrs Norris wore a plain dress of grey wool that buttoned all the way down the front. Her mousey-brown hair was pulled neatly to the back of her neck, and at her throat was a simple cross on a gold chain.

Somehow, although Kate was far too tired to know why, this young and straightforward woman was completely at odds with the sort of person she had been expecting.

'Is there somewhere private?' the woman asked, making to take the baby from Naomi as soon as she appeared in the hallway.

'Upstairs,' Naomi replied, her entire body seeming to soften with the relief of being able to hand over the child to someone who knew what they were doing. 'Please, follow me and I'll show you.'

As the baby's cries grew quieter and then ceased altogether, down in the hallway, Kate finally allowed herself to relax a little. When Naomi then eventually reappeared, she followed her into the drawing room.

'Ma'am, Naomi,' she began as Naomi sank onto one end of the sofa. 'I'm sorry to say this but this is… mazey.'

'Mazey?'

'Madness,' she clarified. 'We don't neither of us know how to care for such a tiny baby. What will we do in a couple of days, when this Mrs Norris has to leave? *Two days*, Miss Randolph said to you – this woman can only be here for two days. What about after that? What will we do then?'

'It is, I will concede,' Naomi said quietly, 'all rather unexpected. And yes, clearly, we are going to need help. And no, before you ask me what sort of help and how we are to go about finding it, I have no idea, truly, I don't. But, for now, we will at least be able to get some sleep. And then, in the morning, I have decided I shall speak to Miss Randolph again and see what she suggests. She's told us before that when a baby is abandoned at the vicarage she has to make arrangements for its care. And she did know how to find this Mrs Norris at short notice. So, it occurs to me that she can probably point us in the right direction. Get through these first few days and then I'm sure we will be able to sort out something – or someone – for the longer term.'

For the longer term? Naomi was planning to keep the child? Moments ago, when she had pronounced the thing mazey, she had meant that it was madness *now*, this instant. Seemingly, though, it was worse than that.

'But Naomi, please, you must know that you can't just keep a baby, least of all on the say-so of someone turning up on our doorstep, late at night, and with but a cutting from the newspaper in support of their claims.'

'Kate, all I can say to you is that I feel strongly that Ada's story is true. Either way, at this precise moment, it doesn't really matter, does it? We have taken in an infant and all I know for certain is that it must be cared for.' Watching Naomi get slowly to her feet, Kate shook her head in dismay. 'Now, I am going up to see how Mrs Norris is getting along. One assumes, from the lack of crying, that the child is feeding. Given the hour and our lack of any other choices, one can only hope so. After that, I intend trying to get some sleep because tomorrow, all manner of things will require thought and preparation.' Moving towards the door, she reached a hand to Kate's arm. 'Please,' she said wearily, 'do go on up to bed. There is nothing you can do for now. And I promise you that in the morning, I will keep an open mind about what happens next.'

When Naomi left the room and started up the stairs, Kate sighed heavily. Her limbs felt wooden and her eyes ached, everything that had happened since supper this evening beyond her to make sense of. As for going up to sleep, well, that felt beyond her, too. Her body might be crying out for her bed, but she just knew that no matter how hard she tried, the whirling of her thoughts would see to it that she was unable to nod off. An orphaned baby, of all things. And just when Naomi had been acting so much more like her old self, too.

—

'Mrs Lloyd, thank you for coming. I'm ever so grateful.'

Standing back from the open door, Kate bade Diana Lloyd step inside.

'Nonsense, my dear. When it comes to Naomi's well-being, I would never refuse to help. But how are *you*, young lady? All well?'

She smiled. Of all the members of Naomi's family, she liked Aunt Diana the best. Never judgemental and always chirpy, she was a joy to talk to.

'I'm fine, thank you,' she replied, noticing that today, apart from being an unusual burgundy colour, Diana Lloyd's outfit was surprisingly conventional. 'Although those fearful Zeppelins are the final straw.'

'Aren't they? But then I'm sure you remember my views on the whole matter of this war. Naomi not up yet?'

Glancing to the staircase, she shook her head. 'No, and I'm not going up to wake her yet, either. If she was anything like me last night, she probably spent hours wide awake and fretful.'

'And yet here *you* are.'

She laughed. 'Yes, here I am.'

'And your husband? I trust he is safe and well?'

247

Flushing hot, she thrust her hand into the pocket of her apron. How long ago had she stuffed his poor field postcard in there? Ages and ages. And she hadn't given it a single thought since. Until that very moment, it hadn't crossed her mind once. Nor had Luke, really. How awful was that?

'He is, yes,' she said, the slyness of her remark making her prickle. In truth, she had no idea how he was. Then, so as to draw attention away from her discomfort, she rushed on, 'Mrs Lloyd, would you mind if we went down to the kitchen? Only, down there, we're unlikely to disturb Naomi. Or the baby.'

'Not at all, my dear. I rather enjoy a homely kitchen – the heart of the house, I always think.'

'I always think so, too,' she replied, starting down the stairs, her mind now on her neglect of her husband.

'So, what's all this about then?' Diana Lloyd asked, settling onto one of the kitchen chairs. 'When you telephoned me and mentioned a baby, I thought we must have got a crossed line. But then I thought for you to have gone all the way down to the telegraph office in order to speak to me, it had to be true.'

And so, while making a pot of Earl Grey, Kate dragged her thoughts back from Luke to the momentarily more pressing matter of Naomi and the baby, relaying events from the previous evening and ending up by saying, 'I'm terrible sorry I disturbed you so early, but I couldn't think who else to ask for help. I suppose I was hoping you might know whether there could be any truth to the story as told by this Ada girl.'

The story relayed, she studied Diana Lloyd's face in the hope of gleaning something of her initial thoughts. That her expression hadn't changed wasn't really a surprise. Aunt Diana played things close to her chest; she knew that from past experience. Now that she was here, though, she felt even more certain that telephoning her had been the right thing to do. Yes, Naomi would be cross with her for involving anyone else at all, but, sometimes, Naomi still didn't seem to have fully recovered her ability to think clearly. In any event, on this occasion, she was too close to the matter to be able to view it dispassionately. Far too close. But, if anyone could get through to her, it would be Aunt Diana.

'Bit of a pickle, isn't it?'

Pouring a cup of the pale-coloured tea, Kate placed it in front of Mrs Lloyd, the citrusy scent of it rising up with the escaping steam. 'Being somehow sure that the story was the truth,' she said, 'or even that it wasn't, would be a start.'

'It rather seems there are two issues at play here,' Diana Lloyd observed. 'One is the veracity of the actual story and thus, the truth of the child's origins. The second is the appropriateness or otherwise of Naomi's response. For so very many reasons, one can't just take in a child.'

'I know,' she said, slipping onto a chair at the opposite side of the table. 'And I tried explaining that to her. But she wasn't willing to hear it.'

'Hardly surprising, I suppose, given what she has just been through. So, let us tackle one thing at a time. Upon the matter of the child's parentage, the story as told to you *would* match certain events from around twenty years ago.'

Listening carefully, Kate fought to keep her expression neutral; there was much about the Russells – Hugh and

Pamela in particular – that she wasn't supposed to know. 'It would?'

Diana Lloyd nodded. 'Hugh did stray from the marriage, although, as far as I know, beyond the immediate members of the family, no one would be aware of it. At the time, every care was taken to hush it up.'

Kate flushed. That was the other thing about Aunt Diana: once she took you into her confidence, she didn't beat about the bush.

Oblivious to her discomfort, Diana Lloyd swept on. 'I believe his dalliances started while Pamela was expecting Naomi and Ned. By itself, it didn't particularly come as a shock – at least, not to me, it didn't. Hugh had an eye for the ladies – made little effort to disguise the fact. None of the family were pleased that Pamela should be marrying him to start with but, on the other hand, she had well and truly blotted her copybook. She had made her bed and had to lie in it.'

On the other side of the table, Kate wriggled in her seat. This was fascinating – albeit in a prurient sort of a way. That said, knowing what had gone on might help her to understand, and to figure out what was to be done. Even so, the only way she could think to reply was to murmur a sort of agreement. 'Mm.'

'As to how many women he betrayed my sister with, I couldn't say,' Diana Lloyd continued. 'I should be surprised if it were just the one. In any case, such conjecture is rather beside the point. With regard to this current allegation, there was indeed a dancer. And she did indeed have a child. Of course, money, along with a document from a solicitor, ensured that a lid was kept tightly on the whole affair. And, as far as I know, that lid has remained upon it ever since. Indeed, until the matter of your own paternity came to light last summer, I don't recall even thinking of either the woman or the child since. Hugh did what Hugh does – he used his money. As far as he was concerned, that done, the inconvenience went away.'

'So,' Kate said, setting her cup of breakfast tea carefully back upon its saucer, 'this Bertha *could* have been half-sister to Naomi. Like me.'

Slowly, Diana Lloyd nodded. 'It is certainly possible – likely, even, yes, because no one outside of the immediate family would know enough of the details to affect a pretence, especially since the record of the girl's birth would make no mention of the father. The question is, if this new baby is indeed related to the family, and if she is indeed an orphan, what do we do now?'

'Aunt Diana! Whatever are you doing here?'

Cross that she hadn't heard Naomi approaching, Kate winced, and then tried to look casual as she glanced over her shoulder, leaving it to Diana Lloyd to reply.

'Come to see *you*, of course, darling.'

'At this hour?'

Diana Lloyd got to her feet. 'It's almost ten. And you know what an early riser I am.'

While the two women embraced, Kate gathered the cups and saucers and slipped through to the scullery.

'Hm,' she heard Naomi remark. 'I suppose Kate has told you all about the events of last night?'

Hearing Naomi settle at the table, Kate proceeded to fill the kettle for fresh tea.

'She has, yes. What a turn up. Where's the little mite now?'

'I've just looked in on her. Mrs Norris – the wet nurse – is just about to feed her again. The trouble is, she can only stay with us until tomorrow night.'

'Then we must waste no time working out what we're to do, must we? And not solely about how to feed the poor little thing, either, wouldn't you say?'

In the scullery, kettle in hand, Kate heaved a sigh of relief. Fetching Aunt Diana had been precisely the right thing to do. She was level-headed. She would help them to sort this out. However things ultimately worked out – something she didn't have room in her head to think about at that precise moment – she knew that Aunt Diana would neither judge nor desert them. She would remain on hand to see Naomi through it. And, given Naomi's recent experience, that seemed to be about the best for which any of them could reasonably hope.

Chapter Nine

Dilemmas

Somehow, she could see what Naomi meant. Holding the baby for the first time, Kate, too, had a strong feeling of kinship. There was something in those tiny dark eyes. If pressed, she would be unable to offer a sensible explanation other than to say that she could feel a connection. Yes, it sounded taffety – even to *her* ears – but to deny it would be to ignore the strength of her conviction.

It was the day after Aunt Diana's visit – the day that she and Naomi should have been travelling to Woodicombe. As it was, late yesterday afternoon, they had hastily cancelled their arrangements, Naomi sending a telegram to Mabel and Edith to explain that owing to unforeseen circumstances, they would have to postpone their visit, at Kate's insistence going on to add that nothing was amiss and that they were both well.

For Kate, it had then turned into a truly upside-down sort of a day, one that required her involvement in many new things. In the knowledge that Mrs Norris was unable to stay for long, both Aunt Diana and Marjorie Randolph had contacted people they knew to try to find a replacement wet nurse. While all of *that* had been happening, she, Kate, had been despatched to Selfridges with a list of the items deemed necessary to care for a newborn. At first daunted by the task, she had soon warmed to it, quickly coming to understand the different quality shawls, the advantages of nainsook slips over plain cotton ones, the different weights of blankets, and how many lengths of towelling cloth would be required for stitching into nappies. Then, at the suggestion of the incurious but efficient store assistant, she had acquired an enamel pail, a steel boiling pan, and a box of soap flakes – all for the laundering of the nappies once soiled. The items tallied up and charged to Mr Lawrence's household account, delivery had been arranged for later that afternoon.

Journeying to and from Oxford Street on her own, she'd had time to mull over what she now knew about Hugh Russell, the man who was, in essence at least, her father. What sort of man must he have been to have behaved with such flagrant disregard for the consequences of his actions, she wondered? With Edith, he had got away scot-free – had escaped all responsibility. This dancer woman, though, had clearly been more savvy. It was a realization that made her wonder where she, Kate, would have been now had Mabel and Thomas Bratton enlisted the help of the Latimers and made Hugh Russell do right by Edith. While he might still have been unlikely to marry her, her own start in life might have been very different. She might have grown up to be something other than a domestic servant. *Might* have. By contrast, this nameless little baby girl – Hugh Russell's first grandchild – looked as though she was going to get a different start in life, certainly if Naomi had anything to do with it.

Later that same afternoon, she had once again been despatched for supplies, this time to Mr Herschel, the chemist, where, according to Mrs Norris, a feeding device could be obtained, the contents for which she would show them how to make up from condensed milk and water. It would suffice, she had explained, until proper arrangements could be made.

The other momentous thing to have happened that day was when Naomi had decided to act upon Aunt Diana's suggestion that they make proper investigations into the supposed parentage of the baby, as told to them by Ada.

'I am of the opinion that you will need to enlist the help of a professional,' Aunt Diana had said. And, when Naomi had queried what sort of professional she had in mind, she had replied, 'A private investigator, I suppose. Although how one goes about the engaging of one, I'm afraid I have no idea.'

To Kate's surprise, Naomi knew precisely how to go about it.

'The reporter who came to write about the dinner we held for St. Ursula's,' she said, stirring from the sofa and going to fetch her address book from the side table in the hall, 'would seem to be the very man. That evening, the *Telegraph*'s own reporter for the social pages was unable to attend, there already being another function elsewhere requiring his presence. In his place, was this fellow, yes, here, I kept a note of his details.' Bringing her finger to rest upon a page in her book, she went on, 'Mr Donald Scott. When he had finished recording the names of the guests attending the dinner, he gave me his business card, explaining that reporting for the *Telegraph* is purely the means by which he supplements his earnings as a private investigator. He seemed most respectable and not at all... grubby.'

'Perhaps you should telephone him,' Aunt Diana had remarked, a suggestion Naomi had later gone out to pursue.

And now, here they were, sitting in the drawing room with Donald Scott himself, the essence of Ada's story having just been relayed to him.

'So, let me see if I have understood you correctly,' he paused from listening to say. 'The girl who brought the baby to you claimed her name was Ada.'

Kate and Naomi nodded. 'Yes,' they answered in unison.

While Donald Scott then wrote something in his note-book, Kate frowned. '*Claimed?*' she queried his remark. '*Claimed* her name was Ada?'

Donald Scott smiled. 'Mrs Channer, I discovered a long time ago that what people *say*, and the truth of the matter, can often be two very different things.'

'Oh. Oh, I see.'

'In my profession – indeed, if I am to do my job properly – it pays to keep an open mind. For instance, it would be wise not to discount the possibility that the young woman who arrived bearing this child might in fact have been its mother.'

When Naomi seemed visibly shocked, Kate reached for her hand.

'No,' Naomi said, leaning forward in her seat, her manner instantly agitated, 'no, her figure wasn't that of someone who had only the day previously given birth to a baby. There was nothing of her.'

'That's true,' Kate agreed. 'Rasher of wind, she was.'

'Besides, for her to be Bertha Jones, she would need to be older by several years,' Naomi went on. 'By now, she would be at least twenty years of age – more probably twenty-one – whereas this Ada was no more than... what would you say, Kate? Sixteen? Seventeen?'

For a moment, she struggled to recall the girl's face; she had certainly looked quite young. 'About that, I would say,' she replied. 'For certain no more.'

Donald Scott scribbled frantically. 'That's good,' he said. 'Information like this, no matter how seemingly incidental, helps me to build up a picture and work out what I need to look for. Now, what was Ada's surname?'

The two women shook their heads.

'She didn't volunteer it.'

'I didn't think to ask.'

'That's a shame,' Donald Scott said before appearing to draw a question mark alongside the place in his notebook where he had written the name Ada.

'Will the lack of a surname hamper your investigation?'

To Naomi's question, he gave a slight shrug. 'If the story you were told is true, then Ada would seem to be our only link to this child and her family. If both the baby's mother and father are indeed dead, and the birth has gone unregistered, then without Ada, it might take me longer to establish the facts. That said, it is by no means a lost cause. Do either of you happen to recall where she lived?'

Kate turned to Naomi. How foolish it seemed now to have asked the girl so little about herself.

'I'm afraid I don't, no,' Naomi admitted.

'Me neither,' Kate agreed. 'Although, no, wait. When we put her in a cab to go home, I heard her speak to the driver. Oh, dear Lord, what did she say?'

'May I give you a tip to help you remember,' Donald Scott ventured, 'something I myself find helpful?'

Regarding him warily, she nodded. 'Instead of concentrating so fiercely, try to relax a little. Picture yourself standing on the pavement, seeing the young lady off.' To his instruction, she frowned, but, nonetheless, followed his advice. 'And now, listen to her speaking. What is she saying?'

To her surprise, the scene started to rerun itself through her mind. It was dark. The cab's motor was running. With Ada having climbed cautiously inside, she had closed the door behind her. 'White-something,' she said as Ada's voice came back to her.

'Whitehall?' Naomi suggested.

Donald Scott pressed his lips together. To Kate, it seemed as though he was trying not laugh. 'While not altogether impossible,' he said, 'I do think it rather unlikely.'

'Is there a place called White*church*?' she asked.

'White*chapel*?' Donald Scott prompted.

'Yes! Yes, that's it! Whitechapel.'

'Good. Well, it's a sprawling area – and not the sort where people will readily talk to someone like me – but it's a start. A clue, if you will. Since Ernest Ward and Bertha Jones appear not to have been married for long, if I begin with the parish records in Whitechapel, I believe I stand a chance of learning something. Who knows, this Ada might even have been a witness to their marriage. If I can verify her account of events, at the same time uncovering some of the actual facts, I should be able to work from there towards the truth. I certainly believe that I will be able to help you, Mrs Colborne, which is, I am sure, what you were hoping to hear when you telephoned me.'

'Thank goodness,' Naomi remarked, rising eagerly to her feet. 'And yes, you are quite right. That was precisely what I was hoping to hear.'

'And you understand my terms of engagement—'

'Yes, yes,' Naomi said, starting to usher him towards the door with what felt to Kate like indecent haste. 'I understand your fees perfectly.'

'—and that they apply irrespective of whatever I may go on to discover.'

'Yes, Mr Scott. You have been most diligent in that respect. I understand I am paying for your labours, not necessarily for the results.'

'Good.'

'Now, how long do you think it will be before you have something to report?'

Donald Scott smiled. To Kate, he seemed to do so with great sympathy.

'My dear Mrs Colborne, to respond to that, I must quote the favoured expression of an American friend of mine by saying *how long is a piece of string?*'

'But that's ridiculous,' Naomi rounded on him.

Catching Kate's eye, Donald Scott winked. 'Ridiculous, you say?'

'Of course it is, for a piece of string could be of whatever length one cares to make it. Without seeing it, one simply cannot offer an accurate answer.'

'And that,' Donald Scott said, swiping his hat from the hall stand and thus denying Kate the chance to reach for it, 'is what makes it such an appropriate expression in this case.'

Standing alongside her, Kate squeezed Naomi's arm.

'Oh. Oh, yes, I see.'

'But, given the delicate nature of the matter, I promise you that I shall give it my earliest and fullest attention. If nothing else, it will make a change from trailing about behind errant husbands. Or from trying to trace the long-lost beneficiaries of old ladies' wills.'

With that pronouncement, he trotted to the bottom of the steps and turned to head away along the pavement, his departure leaving the two women standing in the hallway, looking at one another in amusement.

'How on earth I shall manage to sleep until he brings news, I don't know,' Naomi eventually said to her.

Noticing the way in which she was wringing her hands, Kate shrugged her shoulders. She felt the same. 'Me neither,' she said quietly.

'Nor do I know what I shall do if he finds Ada's story to be anything other than the truth.'

'Me neither,' she again agreed, the picture of the baby's dark eyes so clear in her mind. 'Me neither.'

—

'Well, my dear, all we can do now is wait and see what transpires.'

With Donald Scott having just left and Naomi, claiming nervous exhaustion, having gone to lie down, Kate was left in the drawing room with Aunt Diana.

'Yes,' she agreed with a long sigh. 'Though I don't know how we shall manage it. Waiting about is something neither of us is much good at.'

Diana Lloyd smiled. 'No,' she said. 'I must say I don't envy you. Patience never was one of my niece's virtues.' Lowering herself to the sofa, she gestured to Kate to join her. 'Tell me, have you had word from Luke recently?'

Instinctively, Kate's hand went to the pocket of her apron and his field postcard. She *still* hadn't written to him – hadn't even thought about it. 'Not these last couple of weeks, no. But happen he's waiting for *me* to write to *him*,' she said. 'It *is* my turn. And I have meant to, honestly.' She glanced to Diana Lloyd's face. If she was casting judgement about her remiss ways, she gave no outward sign.

'You must be finding it hard, having been so long without him.'

When Kate sighed, her whole body seemed to collapse in upon itself, her chest sagging and her shoulders caving forwards. 'Truth be told,' she said, 'I don't know how I'm finding it – other than different to how I did back at the beginning.'

'I'm sure you're not alone in that, my dear. Who among us could possibly have foreseen how this war was going to drag on? I doubt even our own government knew.'

As usual, Diana Lloyd's tone was so kindly that Kate felt drawn to explain herself. 'For certain *I* didn't know. If someone had told me, back when Luke joined up, that after knowing him like I have all these years, a mere eight or nine months on from getting wed to him I'd be struggling to remember what he's like, well, I would have called them mazed. But then I think to myself, well, if *I* don't remember *him* all that well, what will *he* remember of *me*? And then I think, if he's changed even only half as much as I have in that time, what will he be like when he comes back? See, I can't help but think that 'though he was already full-grown when he went away, being at war must surely have turned him into a proper man now – with a proper man's ways and a proper man's views.

I mean, look at *me* – sometimes I don't recognize my own self, I've changed that much – and all *I* did was leave Woodicombe.'

Her concerns aired, she glanced up. Whenever Aunt Diana saw fit to impart advice, it was always worth listening to. And so, in anticipation of her reply, she straightened up.

'These last few months in particular,' Diana Lloyd indeed began, 'since Christmas time, I suppose, I've watched you and my niece turn into capable young women. In Naomi's case, having to take on her own household – no matter how small – has completed her transformation into the woman she was always destined to be. But you, my dear, have changed beyond all recognition. I've watched you become someone quite different. You have blossomed – found yourself, I suppose.'

On the point of decrying Diana Lloyd's observation, she stopped herself. 'I have, haven't I?' she said, realizing it to be true.

'You have become your own person. And you should feel proud, growing into such a selfless and caring woman in so short a space of time and with so little guidance.'

She *was* proud. She liked the way her life was turning out. But therein lay her problem.

She glanced to Diana Lloyd's face. All around them, the house was silent; with Naomi having – presumably – gone to sleep, she found herself with the rare luxury of a moment to stop and sit and reflect. She also had Aunt Diana's undivided attention.

'I *am* proud,' she said. 'By chancing upon St. Ursula's, it would seem I have stumbled upon something I enjoy doing. Not only that, but my labours there serve a purpose – a real purpose. 'Tis just a shame it can't last.'

'Can it not? Why do you say so?'

'Because, like Marjorie Randolph remarked to me not so long back, once Luke comes home, I'll have to give it all up to be a proper wife.'

'And that isn't what you want.'

Slowly, she shook her head. 'I could claim to not having given it any thought – say to you that I don't know. But, see, I *do* know. And, truth be told, I never did want to be just somebody's wife, up to my neck in drudgery and at the beck and call of a man every hour of the day and night. But, for a girl like me, it's all there was – a husband and children and be grateful for it. But now, see, since coming to London, and especially since volunteering my time at St. Ursula's, I've had a taste of summat else. And it's greatly to my liking. I see now how it's what I was looking for all along.'

Beside her, Diana Lloyd remained still. 'I see.'

'And then, I think to myself, well, what if the same thing has been happening to Luke? What if, away in France, learning new things and meeting new folk, he's having a high old time and feeling the same way – you know, that perhaps us getting wed in such a rush was a mistake?'

'You believe it was a mistake to get married?'

This time, she shook her head less certainly. 'No. Well, maybe. Oh, I don't know. Truly Mrs Lloyd, the inside of my head – if you could but see it – feels like a mat of dodder on top of a gorse bush, all my thoughts tangled one with the other and no end in sight. All I know with any faith is that back at the beginning, when Luke was first gone away, I thought of him all the time and worried what ills might befall him. But, more lately, I've come to realize just how little I still think about him. Worse than that, I do fear now that were he never to come back, I shouldn't fret overly much for my loss. How poor a wife must that make me?'

'Well—'

'To think in such a way must surely mean I've fallen out of love with him, mustn't it? Either that, or I wasn't ever proper in love with him to start with.'

'Well, what you must—'

'Sometimes, I even get to wondering whether the only reason I got wed to him in the first place was so as to be able to come to London and work for Naomi – it being Mr Lawrence's preferring that me an' Luke be husband and wife. But that was when we all thought to soon be living under the same roof. Turns out, maybe there was no rush at all. And, see, it always *was* my dream to get away from Woodicombe and do summat different. So, who knows, perhaps in my haste not to let the chance slip through my fingers, I would have agreed to anything.'

'Oh, no, my dear, I don't think that's—'

''Course, without this war, I wouldn't be in this caddle, would I? Luke wouldn't ever have gone away, I wouldn't have got to go off and do all these things by myself… and by now I'd be proper fettered, with a child to curb my wandering thoughts and ways…'

'Kate, my dear girl, please, do stop for a moment and draw a breath! I can hardly keep up with you.'

Jerking upright, she looked about the room. Heavens, she'd been going at it nineteen to the dozen. 'Forgive me,' she said, blushing. 'Seems I got carried away.'

'There is no need to apologize,' Aunt Diana remarked. 'I merely wanted you to stop for a moment to breathe. I was starting to fear that in your agitation, you might keel over from a lack of air to your brain!'

Unable to help it, she laughed. 'Sorry.'

'All I was going to say, my dear, were you to give me the chance, was that contrary to what you might think, with all you've gone through, I do believe it's only natural that you find yourself questioning the direction of your life. Of course you wonder what it will be like when Luke comes home – you've been without each other almost since the day you were married. And yes, I'm certain that he *will* be wondering the same as you. But I also think you will find – at least, after a while, and given the chance to settle down – that you will each be delighted by how the other has grown. You will both have come to know your own minds and yet, at the same time, will surely have become more tolerant and accepting.'

Without meaning to, Kate scoffed. More tolerant? Her? That *would* surprise Luke. 'But what if that's *not* the case?' she said. 'What if he sees how I've changed and don't like who I've become? What if he's cross I'm not the person he's been thinking to come back to all this time? What if, after all he's been through, what he wants most is to come home to a meek and obedient little wife?'

'A natural enough concern. But, as you say, both of you have seen something of life now – in different ways, yes, but I do believe that, rather than work against you, you will find it is to your advantage. After all, it is not only the two of *you* who are changing – the entire country is. One only has to look to the swell of support for women's

265

suffrage to appreciate how times are changing – especially for us women.'

'Hm.' Aunt Diana did have a point. There was very little this war hadn't changed – and wouldn't continue to. Women went out to work now. They did the jobs their menfolk had once done. Some of them even wore overalls. And, like her, the experience had to be changing them, didn't it?

'No matter how it might feel, we none of us change in isolation.'

'So, it's not horrible of me to have a husband away at war but like my life the way it is?'

Diana Lloyd laughed. 'Oh, no, my dear, you are simply making the most of the way things are. You might be a war wife – in the parlance of the newspapers – but keeping the home fires burning is rather easier for them to urge than it is for you to do, isn't it? No longer a single woman, but not truly a married one either, you rather have the worst of all worlds. But trust me, I do believe everything will work out just fine.'

'Hm.' How could anyone – even Aunt Diana, with all of *her* wisdom – possibly know that?

By her side, Diana Lloyd got to her feet. 'But now, I'm afraid I really must take my leave of you. I shan't go up and look in on Naomi in case I disturb her, but perhaps you would tell her that I shall call in a day or two.'

'Yes, ma'am.'

'Excellent.'

'Thank you for listening to me with such patience. I hadn't intended going on so.'

'Kate, sometimes, in order to make sense of a thing, we must speak of it out loud. For you, this was one of those occasions. Try not to fret too much. Try to keep your chin up, as our American cousins would say!'

Having seen Diana Lloyd out, Kate went to the top of the stairs and listened for any movement from Naomi's room. Hearing none, she went back down and wandered out into the garden. She could take no issue with the bones of Aunt Diana's advice. Every word she had said made sense – it always did. The problem was that on this particular occasion, she had been offering her counsel while not privy to the whole story. It wasn't Aunt Diana's fault: she, Kate, just hadn't been entirely truthful with her. Yes, perhaps one of the reasons she didn't feel married was indeed because so far, she'd been denied the chance to be a wife. And, clearly, once Luke came home, that would change. But what she had failed to tell Aunt Diana was that the more she thought about it, the more she became convinced that being just a wife was no longer what she wanted at all.

–

'Ma'am, can you wake up?' Expecting Naomi to be grumpy at being awakened, Kate gave her arm only the most timid of shakes. 'Ma'am?' she urged softly. 'Please, do wake up.'

It was the following morning, the day after the visit by Donald Scott, and Kate rued having to rouse Naomi so early – especially after the disrupted nights they'd had of late – but, on this occasion, she had no choice.

Slowly, Naomi stirred. 'Kate?' she mumbled, lifting her head to look at her. 'What is it? Is it Baby? Is she all right?'

'Baby's fine, ma'am. Mrs Norris has just changed her and fed her again. It's... well, I need you to get up and put on your robe and come downstairs with me—'

'Come downstairs? Why? What time is it?'

'A little after six-thirty—'

'On Saturday?'

'Yes, ma'am. It's just that there's someone in the drawing room—'

'Mr Scott? He's come back already?' Instinctively, Naomi ran a hand through her hair while with her other, she pushed back the bedclothes.

'No, ma'am,' she said, her tone apologetic, 'it's not Mr Scott.' *If only it were.* 'Truth to tell, I don't know *who* it is. He's asleep on the sofa in the drawing room. He's in evening dress – sort of – and I can only imagine he must have come home with Mr Aubrey.'

'*What?* A stranger? Asleep in my house?' Her expression turning to one of displeasure, Naomi got smartly out of bed and thrust her arms into her robe. 'Is Aubrey *up*? Is he even *in*?'

Reaching to tie the belt about Naomi's waist, she shook her head. 'I don't know, ma'am,' she said, it not having occurred to her to check. 'I went into the drawing room to open up the curtains, and there was this man. Not liking to confront him, I came straight up to fetch you.'

'Come on, then, let's go down and see who he is and what he's got to say for himself. And then we'll wake Aubrey and ask him the same thing.'

'Yes, ma'am.'

In the drawing room, just as she had described, a man in dress shirt and trousers lay asleep, his jacket cast over the back of one of the easy chairs, his shoes kicked off nearby. Beneath his head were a couple of cushions. He was snoring softly.

'Wake him up,' Naomi said, gesturing her towards him. 'Wake him as rudely as you can.'

Kate exhaled heavily. Why did *she* have to be the one to do it? Naomi was mistress of the house.

'Sir?' she ventured all the same, stepping as close as her discomfort would allow. 'Sir? Please wake up.'

'Oh, for heaven's sake,' Naomi said crossly. 'You!' she shouted. 'Wake up and get off my sofa.' When she then pushed at the man's shoulder, he rocked away from her before falling back again. With a sharp snort and a quick wriggle, he continued to sleep on regardless. 'I say, you, wake up!'

In response to being prodded fiercely, the man did at least open an eye. A couple of seconds later, he opened the other one. 'Well, hello,' he said. To Kate, he sounded even more plummy than Aubrey. 'I say, where the deuce am I?'

'Get up,' Naomi ordered, pulling at his arm. 'Now! Get up from my sofa this minute or I shall telephone for the police.'

Taking a small step backwards, it was on the tip of Kate's tongue to point out that they didn't have a telephone. But then she realized the intruder didn't know that.

'All right, all right,' the man said, levering himself upright. 'No need for the histrionics, woman. My name is Poundsby, and I am a guest of a fellow I met last night. He said I could stop here. Mind you, I hadn't realized there wouldn't be a bed. Rotten stiff neck.' Evidently then spotting that Kate was in livery, he turned to her to say, 'Any chance of a coffee, dearie? Dashed thick head. Black, if you don't mind. Strong and sweet.' Returning his attention to Naomi, he went on, 'And whose totty might you be?'

'I,' Naomi said, grasping the man's jacket and throwing it at him, 'am the owner of this house. And you,' she added, almost spitting with rage, 'are trespassing upon my property. So, you have as long as it takes for me to go upstairs to the telephone to put on your shoes and leave.'

'Look, there's no need for all this… venom,' the fellow replied. 'The chap who invited me back here clearly misled me. He didn't say anything about having a landlady, let alone a shapely little one like *you*.'

'I'm going to telephone for the police,' Naomi turned to her to say, her look one that Kate immediately understood. 'The constabulary is close by, on the High Street, so I don't imagine it will take them more than three minutes at most to get here. I shall tell them that we have an intruder and that we are in distress. Here,' she added, stepping out into the hallway and pulling Mr Lawrence's umbrella from the stand, 'take this and, if he attempts to go anywhere except out through the front door, stab him with the end of it. Aim for somewhere… fleshy.'

The sound of Naomi trotting up the stairs seemed to prompt the stranger to struggle to his feet. Then he pushed his feet into his shoes, slung his jacket about his shoulders, and started towards the hall.

'You can go up and tell her I've gone,' he said as Kate stood back to bar him from heading any further into the house. 'No sense disturbing the boys in blue.' With that, he sauntered out through the front door, leaving her to scamper behind him and turn the key in the lock.

'Has he gone?' Naomi peered down from the landing to ask.

Breathing heavily, she nodded. 'Yes, ma'am. He's gone.'

'Right then, come with me.'

Dutifully, she climbed the stairs and turned to follow Naomi along the landing.

At the door to the bedroom occupied by Aubrey, Naomi pounded upon it with her fist. 'Aubrey!' she shouted, 'Wake up this instant! I want a word with you.' When there was no response, she pounded again. 'Aubrey, I'm warning you, open this door!'

Still there was no response.

'Is he even in there, do you think?' Kate whispered, growing uncomfortable at how this was turning out. Finding a stranger on the sofa had been alarming enough but Aubrey riled was something that frightened her far more.

'I've no idea. But if he's not downstairs, where else would he be?'

She shrugged her shoulders. 'For certain I don't know, ma'am.'

'Aubrey!' In the silence that followed this latest attempt to rouse him, Naomi bent to look through the keyhole.

Warily, Kate watched her. 'What can you see?' she asked in a whisper.

'Nothing. Either it's very dark in there or else the key is obscuring my view. Tell me,' Naomi said, standing upright and turning towards her, 'do we have a spare key to this room?'

She tried to picture the contents of the tin on the shelf above the range. From what she could remember, it contained about half a dozen keys, most of them much alike in appearance. 'I don't know,' she said. 'I'll go and check.'

On her way back up from the kitchen, she paused to draw back the curtain on the landing, and then pried the lid from the tin.

When each of the keys had been tried in turn – and all of them had failed to fit – Naomi sighed with frustration. 'I believe the key is in the other side of the lock,' she said. 'Pop down to the bureau and bring me a pencil and a sheet of paper. No, bring a sheet of newspaper if we have one – it will be larger.'

Not stopping to ask what Naomi had in mind to do, Kate did as she was told. Aubrey's continuing failure to answer the door was worrying – even someone with a heavy hangover ought to have awoken by now.

'What are you going to do?' she asked, returning with the items.

'Something Papa did one morning when no one could raise Ned. I'm going to try and poke the key out of the lock. The gap between the bottom of the door and the floorboards is quite large and so it *might* work. It's worth a try.'

'Do you think he's unwell?' she asked, watching Naomi slide the sheet of newspaper under the door.

'I don't know what to think. Until this morning, I thought Aubrey and I had developed a sort of under-standing – a friendship, even. I mean, he was a tremendous help with the whole business of the gala dinner. But then he does *this*? All I can think is that to have told a complete stranger he could spend the night here, he can't have been in his right mind. He *knows* I would never allow that.'

'I haven't seen hide nor hair of him for several days,' she observed, unsure why she was whispering when the whole point was to rouse him.

'Which, in itself, was starting to become odd,' Naomi agreed.

For a while, she said nothing further, watching while Naomi poked the end of the pencil gently through the keyhole. To the surprise of both women, there followed a dull clunk.

'Heavens,' she said, returning Naomi's surprised look.

'Hm. That was the easy bit,' Naomi replied. 'We're not there yet.' Within a few seconds, though, she had pulled the sheet of newspaper – complete with key – under the door and out onto the landing. Picking it up, and with a look that conveyed uncertainty, she slotted it into the lock. 'I'll try raising him once more, just in case,' she said before knocking on the door and calling loudly. 'Aubrey? Aubrey, I'm coming in.'

With the lock clicking undone, Naomi turned the knob and gently opened back the door. On the other side, there was just enough light coming through the fabric of the curtains for the two women to make out the fully clothed form of Aubrey lying face down on the bed.

Crossing to the window, Kate drew aside the curtains and pushed up the lower half of the sash. With rather more trepidation, she turned back into the room. 'Is he... all right?'

'He is breathing,' Naomi replied. Reaching to his shoulder and giving his inert form a sharp shake, she shouted, 'Aubrey!'

When, finally, he stirred, Kate exhaled heavily. 'Thank goodness,' she muttered.

'Aubrey, wake up!'

In response to being shaken further, Aubrey put out a hand and turned onto his side. 'Ugh,' he groaned.

'Aubrey, get up. Now.'

Watching from a few feet away, Kate saw him raise his head a fraction and strain to look back over his shoulder. His hair was dishevelled and his complexion grey. One of his eyes was bloodshot. 'What... the... devil?'

'Sit up,' Naomi ordered him. 'Now.'

'Why? What the devil's going on?' he wanted to know, bringing a hand to his face to shield his eyes. 'What time is it? And why are you in my room?'

'I said, sit up.'

It was, Kate realized, the first time she had seen Naomi so angry, and it made her uncomfortable.

'All right, all right. But you haven't answered my question—'

'Forget how I got in here,' Naomi said, bringing her hands to her hips. 'Where were you last night?'

Aubrey frowned. 'Out...'

'Patently. With whom?'

'What?'

'I asked: with whom were you out?'

'I... look, what's going on? Why the inquisition? I went out. I met some friends. What business is that of yours?'

'It became my business when you brought home a stranger to sleep on my sofa.'

'I did?'

'Into my home, you brought a man I do not know – and have no wish to.'

'Poundsby came back here with me?'

'You don't remember?'

'I…'

'Aubrey, I have to say I find your behaviour disappointing in the extreme. Twice now, I have opened my home to you – willingly, I might add. But, this last week in particular, I feel as though you've been treating it as little more than a… than a *dosshouse*—'

'Don't be vulgar, Naomi, it doesn't become you.'

'For several days now, I have been keeping a look out for you in order to tell you that we were to depart for Devon—'

'Devon? When?'

Glancing about, Naomi stooped to pick up something from the floor. 'In the end, on account of your continued absence without word, I was forced to write you a note and push it under your door. See? It is still here. It's dated Tuesday. Fortunately for you, we were forced to change our plans. So, where have you been?'

Slowly, Aubrey rose to his feet. Without his shoes, Kate noticed that he only just about matched Naomi for height. 'I don't think that's any of your business.'

'I disagree. You are staying in my home. And, while I harboured no desire to keep watch over your movements, I do think it would have been common courtesy to tell me that you were going to be away – and to give me some indication as to how long.'

'I hadn't planned to *be* away,' Aubrey said, squinting, and then, crossing to the window, re-drawing one half of the curtain. 'Circumstances… overtook me. But I'm back now. And I promise that in future, I shall be a more considerate house guest.'

'In the future, you won't be here,' Naomi said. 'I'm asking you to leave. We *will* be returning to Devon, our recent postponement merely short-term. I *shall* be locking up the house. Until the events of this morning, I *would* have extended your invitation to stay until we depart but now, I no longer wish to have you here at all.'

'What if I say it doesn't suit me to leave.'

'It doesn't *what*?'

Remaining completely still, Kate winced. She didn't like this at all. Beginning to feel panicked, she started to edge carefully back towards the door.

'Affairs I have here in town require my ongoing attention and so, since this isn't your house at all, but my brother's, I shall remain for as long as it suits me to. The only person who can ask me to leave is Lawrence. And oh, look,' he said, making an odd gesture with his arm, 'he isn't here.'

'Aubrey—'.

'So hand me back the key to my room.'

'I shall do no such thing. In Lawrence's absence, the running of this house falls to me. So, you have until the end of today – until six o'clock, in fact, to leave.'

'Give me back the key to my room or you will force me to change the lock.'

'You have no right to do that.'

'Stop me.'

As their two faces came within inches of one another, from further along the landing the sound of crying started up.

Instinctively, Kate turned towards the door. But then she paused. What did she do? On the one hand, while Mrs Norris was bound to have things under control, the baby crying gave her an excuse to escape from the increasingly ugly hostilities. On the other hand, how could she even consider leaving Naomi alone with Mr Aubrey while he was in such a temper? Uneasily, recalling what a brute he could be, she stayed where she was.

'Who else do you have staying here?' he demanded of Naomi. 'Because *you* don't have a baby.'

'I think you will find that who I have – or don't have – staying in *my* home, has nothing whatsoever to do with *you.*'

Despite Aubrey's unforgiveable behaviour, Kate wished that instead of riling him further, Naomi would see sense and back down. It would be safer all round. But what could she do? It wasn't her place to intervene.

Along the landing, the baby's crying started up again. It gave her an idea.

'Ma'am,' she ventured uncertainly. Hm – having decided that she couldn't intervene, here she was, about to do just that. 'If you wish, I could go and see whether everything is all right with Mrs Norris. But it might be better were you the one to determine that…'

Naomi turned sharply, the look on her face fleetingly one of irritation. Yes, Kate thought, she should have kept quiet.

Unexpectedly, though, Naomi nodded. 'You're right. I should see that nothing is amiss. But,' she added, swivelling back to Aubrey, 'do not mistake this for me backing down. On the contrary. I still expect you to be gone from here

– and all of your possessions to have gone with you – by six o'clock this evening.'

Once out on the landing, Kate sighed with relief. 'I'm sorry, ma'am, for stepping in as I did,' she whispered as Naomi accompanied her away, 'only, I didn't think it wise to allow Mr Aubrey to become even more angry. Strikes me, he wouldn't be above raising his hand to you – and then claiming it his right to do so – saying that you somehow challenged or provoked him.'

By her side, Naomi looked pale. And her hands were trembling.

'No, well, *I* wouldn't put it past him, either. Don't apologize for intervening. You did quite the right thing.'

'Thank you, ma'am.'

In the bedroom along the corridor, entirely as she had expected, Mrs Norris was managing just fine, Naomi nevertheless suggesting that she take the baby until her next feed, thus allowing Mrs Norris to take a nap.

To that end, down in the kitchen a few moments later, with the baby in the rush basket loaned to them by Marjorie Randolph, Naomi sank onto one of the chairs at the table. 'He's right, though,' she said wearily.

'Right about what?' Kate asked, moving to sit on one of the other chairs. She could only assume Naomi to still be talking about Mr Aubrey.

'This is Lawrence's house. I don't really have the power to turn him out.'

'All due respect, ma'am, but Mr Lawrence didn't invite him in,' she said. 'You did. Both times. So, doesn't that entitle you to ask him to leave?'

'I did ask him to leave,' Naomi replied. 'You saw how he responded.'

278

'Hm.' To her mind, all wasn't right with Mr Aubrey, and hadn't been for some time. And now they had the well-being of the baby to think of, too. She glanced to the basket to see her tiny fists moving. It seemed, then, that there was only one thing for it.

She cleared her throat. ''Though I hadn't been in favour of the idea at first,' she said, 'with what's just happened, seems to me now we *might* be better off back at Woodicombe. First that Zeppelin setting fires with those bombs – who knows when *they* might come back again – and now Mr Aubrey acting odd, well, seems to me there's little question to it.'

'Ordinarily, I wouldn't take issue with you, Kate. But, Aubrey and his unforgivable behaviour aside, I really can't leave here now until Mr Scott returns with his findings. It would be most unhelpful to be all the way down in Devon only to learn that he has uncovered something important.'

'There's always the telephone.'

Naomi scoffed. 'Hardly an appropriate medium through which to learn that he's found a living relative. Or even that he hasn't. Don't you see, Kate? What Donald Scott finds out determines the very course of this poor child's entire life. Returned to a close relative, her start in life will be – at best – hazardous. Allowed to remain with me, she will want for nothing.'

Feeling her cheeks colouring, Kate hung her head: much the same as the difference between her and Naomi, then – not that returning to dwell on that would do anyone any good. Let sleeping dogs lie, Ma Channer had cautioned her on her wedding day.

Raising her head, she stared across the room. Should she continue to try to persuade Naomi to change her mind about remaining in Hartland Street? The way she felt at that moment, she would rather be well away from Mr Aubrey – and chance not being there to hear first-hand what Mr Scott turned up – than the other way about. That being her opinion, she would have one final attempt at convincing Naomi to see it that way too.

'If I may say, ma'am—'

'Actually, Kate, while I thank you for your concern, and indeed, your alertness and help this morning with Aubrey, I have decided that I would prefer to remain here until we hear at least *something* from Mr Scott. Then, all being well, we will depart. Who knows; by then, Aubrey might have left of his own accord. In the meantime, I have decided that I shall write to Lawrence about him. I know Aubrey asked me not to mention that I had seen him but, with the way he has behaved this morning, I think he has forfeited his right to my continued compliance in that regard. I shan't divulge all that much, merely write that his stay here has caused a by-no-means insignificant level of discomfort.'

'Very well, ma'am. As you wish,' Kate agreed. In her mind, she thought Naomi guilty of a grave misjudgement. Not that she could press her point any further. What she *could* do, though, was keep a very close eye on Mr Aubrey. Of late, something about his comings and goings didn't add up. And the sooner she found out why that was, the easier it might be to persuade Naomi to change her mind.

–

Heavens, it was dark; she could barely see a hand in front of her face. Whatever could be down such a dark alley – other than something dubious, hidden away for good reason? And, if that was the case, what might she be about to let herself in for?

It was the evening on the day following the contretemps between Naomi and Mr Aubrey and, having watched the latter go out last night and then not heard him return until she had been giving the baby her six o'clock feed this morning, she had determined that today, she would watch and see whether he did the same again. Naomi, taking care of feeds throughout the night – Mrs Norris having now departed – had retired to bed at around ten o'clock. For her part, Kate had made to do the same, except that as soon as she had thought it safe to do so, she had crept back downstairs to the dining room to keep watch for Aubrey. Scarcely ten minutes later, she had heard him come down and let himself out, closing the front door carefully behind him, presumably so as not to alert anyone to his movements. And if that wasn't suspicious, she didn't know what was.

Not wasting a moment, she had set off after him. It was only when she had been walking along the deserted street, trying to skirt the pools of light cast by the electric lamps, that she realized that had Mr Aubrey taken a cab, her plan to follow him would have been scuppered from the off. As it was, she alternated between hanging back and then skipping lightly to keep him within her sights. To anyone watching from the windows of the houses she knew she would look suspicious, but it was a chance she had to take. For Aubrey to be on foot, she reasoned, he couldn't be going far. And all she wanted to do was see where he went.

At the end of Hartland Street, his route had taken him onto Marylebone High Street and then quickly left into a side street, the name of which she had been unable to spot. Not much further on, he had turned into an alleyway, at the corner of which she was now stood, watching covertly as his shadowy form ducked into a doorway, his movement illuminated from overhead by an electric light. Staring towards it, she was reminded of the stage door to a theatre.

For a moment, she simply remained where she was, trying to decide what to do. For early June, the evening was surprisingly humid, the general stickiness only worsening her feeling of discomfort. Dare she go along and see if there was a name above the entrance? She peered again around the corner of the wall. There was no footpath, just a cobbled drang, as she would have called it at home, the single bulb above the doorway the only source of light along its entire length. What harm could it do to go and look? If anyone challenged her, she could always claim that she was lost. Besides, she hadn't walked what had to be the best part of a mile only to miss finding out where he had gone.

Glancing over her shoulder, she drew a breath and set off. The closer she came to the entrance, though, the more her feet seemed inclined to drag. Eventually, drawing near enough to get the measure of the place, she was able to make out that down two or three steps was a door, recessed into the wall. She edged closer.

'You lost, love?'

Startled, she took a half step backwards, her heart hammering in her chest. From the darkness of the over-hang at the bottom of the short flight of steps a woman appeared. Despite the harsh shadows cast across her face by the overhead light, she looked quite young, maybe not much older than her own two-and-twenty years.

'Um…'

'Only, we don't get many of your type down here.' *Your type?* What did she mean by that? 'And by that,' the woman went on, as though reading her puzzlement, 'I means respectable. Clean.'

She swallowed hard. Respectable was by far and away preferable to being mistaken for a… well, for a *lady of the night.* 'Um… well…'

'It's all right, dearie, I won't bite you.'

Trying to be discreet – while minded that this woman was clearly used to being stared at – she took in her appearance. Her costume was that of a performer of some sort: garments she would ordinarily consider underclothes – albeit of garish scarlet and black satin – worn with shiny lace-up ankle boots, and a headdress and collar studded with what she presumed to be paste stones. They could hardly be real diamonds.

'I'm looking for someone,' she finally chose to reply.

'Aren't we all, love?'

'Um…' Oh, dear Lord what was she doing? Perhaps she should just go home.

'Sorry. Your fella, is he?'

But then she spotted her opportunity. Drawing her hands behind her back to conceal the narrow band of her wedding ring, she said, 'My… fiancé, yes. I saw him come along here but then he disappeared.' She couldn't believe her own gall; that she could tell lies with such ease really ought to worry her.

The woman took a step closer. 'What is it you're worried about, love – that he's with another woman, or that he's gamblin' away 'is pay?'

'I'm worried he's in some sort of trouble,' she said, deciding not to commit either way and, in any event, comforted by the fact that her response wasn't too great a leap from the truth. Presumably, this woman would eventually have to return indoors and if, before that happened, she could find it within herself to be bolder still, she might find out what she had come all this way to discover. And so, reminding herself that she was doing this for Naomi, she cleared her throat and said, 'What is this place, then?'

While she stood anxiously, her blood pounding in her ears, the woman gave a weary sigh.

'Fella what owns it would 'ave it be thought a *gentleman's club*. Truth of it is, it's a gamblin' den with the odd bit of whorin' on the side. Ordinary punters for the most part, though we do get the odd toff from time to time, down on his luck, his welcome elsewhere worn through. Regular here, is he, your fella?'

This was getting tricky: too many lies and she'd forget the tale she'd already spun. Perhaps it was time to leave. After all, she was almost certain this was where Aubrey had come. And gambling *would* explain his shifty nature of late. And the hours he'd taken to keeping.

But something wouldn't let her give in. 'No,' she answered, truthfully. 'I think this habit is new-found.'

'Brought 'ere first time by a pal, I shouldn't wonder.'

She nodded. 'Most likely.'

'Minded to go in and take a look around for him? Catch him at it? Best grounds for being done with a fella are always to catch him red-handed. Look, love,' the woman said, tugging the top of her corset higher, her ample chest rippling as she did so, 'I'm on any minute now – Tanzy Rose, that's me stage name – but I *could* forget to latch the door proper – leave it ajar for you to slip in behind me. Can't look out for you once you're inside, mind. Any rate, if he's through in the back room – where the big money goes – you won't clap eyes on him like you were hoping to. Won't get past the fellas on the door. But, if you don't see him at any of the tables, pound to a penny, that's where he'll be.'

'It's possible he'll not be in there at all,' she said, her observation a further but lukewarm attempt to justify simply turning about and going home. After all, she'd seen enough to be fairly certain what he was up to.

'Suit yourself, love,' the woman said, turning back towards the door. 'But take it from one who knows, if he's in 'ere, you're best off finding out about it now. And by that, I mean *before* he wedges a ring on your finger and then, no time at all after, rips it off again to pop.'

When the woman went back down the steps and in through the door, Kate exhaled heavily. Then she spotted the tell-tale strip of yellowy light against the frame: the woman had left it open for her anyway.

Before she could change her mind, and without stopping to look about, she stole down the steps and eased open the door. Ahead of her stretched a corridor, its walls painted the colour of cocoa powder, the light – such as it was – coming from a couple of gas lamps hissing overhead. The place looked grubby and gave off an unidentifiable smell; not unlike Tanzy Rose, she thought, giggling as her nerves started to get the better of her. This was foolish in the extreme, she chided herself, sheer bloody-mindedness the only thing preventing her from turning back. But, if she was to be certain of what Aubrey had been doing, she *had* to witness him doing it. She couldn't go back to Naomi with accusations based on nothing more than supposition; she had to be able to state, truthfully, that she had seen Aubrey gambling in an illegal club.

Even more warily, she continued along the corridor. From beyond the doorway ahead of her loud music suddenly blared. With the sound of either a trumpet or a saxophone, along with a piano and a drum, it was almost as deafening as the bawdy cheering that followed. Tanzy Rose – what an absurd name! – must have gone on stage. With any luck, then, most of the people beyond this door would be looking at *her*, and she, Kate, would be able to slip in unnoticed.

Folding her fingers around the door handle, she felt suddenly light-headed. Dare she do this? Turning the knob anyway, she edged open the door and peered beyond it. As fortune would have it, she seemed to be standing at the rear of the room. A larger affair than she had been expecting, at the far side was a brightly lit stage. Below that was a dozen or more tables, around which were sitting any number of men, some of them in uniform. On the walls were gas lamps, their light insufficient to do much other than illuminate a small patch of the crimson damask wallpaper, while above the tables, blue-grey smoke hung like a modesty veil over the antics of Tanzy Rose on the stage. Closing her eyes against the sight of her provocative cavorting, she shuddered. What sort of way was that to make a living? A desperate one, presumably.

Remembering why she was there, she scanned the men at the tables, fewer than half of them seated such that she could see their faces. Despite that, and even in the murky light, she could tell that none of them was Aubrey.

She glanced about. Away to her left, a man bearing a tray of drinks slipped behind a curtained opening in the wall. Was that the way to the room at the back to which Tanzy Rose had referred? The private one? Thankful to be wearing dark-coloured clothing, she edged along the wall towards it. At that precise moment, an immense roll of the drum coincided with a burst of bawdy laughter from the audience. Preferring not to see what had given rise to such mirth, she seized the opportunity presented by the momentary distraction to edge further towards the curtain, halting less than ten feet short of it. From beyond it, the man who had been carrying the drinks reappeared, his tray now stacked with empty glasses. As the curtain swung back behind him, she realized that it didn't lead into a room at all but into another corridor, this one wallpapered and more brightly lit than the one earlier. This, then, had to be it. This was the location of the private room – and, unless she had misjudged his reasons for coming here, the whereabouts of Aubrey, too.

Staring down at her feet in order to avoid accidentally witnessing the display on the stage, she wondered what to do for the best. She was unlikely to be granted access to the room itself. And she couldn't really afford to get caught trying to sneak along the corridor. On the other hand, nor could she wait where she was on the off chance that Aubrey would leave any time soon. Even then, she wouldn't have seen him actually gambling. So, what to do?

Mulling the possibilities, she heard raised voices behind the curtain. Hastily, she turned to face in the opposite direction, leaning against the wall and tucking her chin down against her chest to conceal her face. Behind her, she heard the curtain being swiped aside, and what sounded to be a scuffle breaking out.

'You was warned before,' a voice barked. The reply, to Kate's ears at least, was less audible, consisting largely of moaning. 'Clear off. And don't show your face round here again. You ain't welcome no more. Mr Vince has had enough of you.'

It was then Kate realized that barely three feet behind her, someone lay sprawled on the floor. Without turning around, she glanced to her side; it was a man in dark clothing, his arms stretched out in front of him.

'I'll have you for this,' he shouted, starting to get to his feet.

Aubrey? It was. It was Aubrey!

'You won't do nothin' of the kind,' the voice replied. 'I know your sort – can't afford the scandal. Now clear off before I throws you onto the street.'

Perilously close to Aubrey's scrabbling form, Kate stood, shaking. As though ready to defend herself, she drew her hands up to her chest and clenched them into fists. She must *not* let him see her. She must not.

Behind her, she heard Aubrey groan. Then she saw him stagger past, heading towards the exit. Watching the door close behind him, she exhaled heavily. He was gone.

Then she tensed all over again: what if he was going back to Hartland Street? If he was, there was every chance he would go in and lock and bolt the door behind him. And, while she did have her door key, she could do nothing about the bolt if he drew it across. She had to beat him home!

Keeping her face turned to the wall, and with raucous applause ringing out from the wider room, she scuttled towards the door, eased it open and, taking in that the corridor was empty, sped along it. At the far end, the door to the street hung wide open and so she scampered straight up the short flight of steps to the street. Away to her left, where the alley gave back onto the road, she saw the silhouette of Aubrey, standing as though trying to decide which way to go. *Don't turn right*, she willed him, *please don't turn right*. If he headed directly home, she would be unable to get there ahead of him.

To her utter disbelief, she saw him turn to the left. Nevertheless, unwilling to risk him changing his mind, she grabbed a handful of her skirt, pressed her hat to her head, and ran the length of the alley. Reaching the far end, she paused, drawing great gasps of the warm night air. Standing at the curb, thirty yards or so distant, Aubrey was hailing a passing cab. No! If he took a cab home, he would definitely arrive there ahead of her. The cab, though, turned in the street so as to face in the opposite direction.

Feeling less need now to run, and already prickling with perspiration, she strode back towards Marylebone High Street, where she kept up a brisk pace until coming upon Hartland Street. There, she slowed her pace and tried to gather her thoughts, this being her first chance to reflect upon what she had discovered. Mr Aubrey had been gambling: not in one of the more respectable gentlemen's clubs, but in a seedy – and most likely illegal – dive. Clearly, Naomi needed to know this. But was it something she should wake her up to tell her tonight, or could it wait until the morning? Looking up ahead and spotting the porch to number twelve, she glanced quickly over her shoulder and then slowed her pace even further. Naomi could do nothing with the information at this hour, especially since Aubrey didn't seem to be heading home anyway. Moreover, she was already getting up at least twice during the night to attend to Baby.

Yes, her news would keep until morning – when they would both have clear heads and be in a better position to decide how to proceed. Aubrey could do them no harm tonight – especially since she intended bolting the front door behind her.

Goodness, she reflected, finally stepping quietly inside and glancing about the shadowy hallway: she had never expected life in London to be quite *this* full of intrigue. How exhilarated she felt! How alive! That said, she would only rest easy once Aubrey had left for good, and all this concern about what he was up to – and all of the ill feelings between him and Naomi – became a distant memory.

Chapter Ten

Truths

'And you are absolutely certain it was him?'

In the few hours since she had followed Aubrey, Kate had been barely able to sleep, her mind going over and over what she had witnessed, listening for Aubrey's return. Dogged by worries of what Naomi would make of it all, she had risen with the lark. And now, with Baby cleaned, fed, and put back down again, she was sitting with Naomi in her bedroom, recounting what she had seen.

'No doubt in my mind whatsoever, ma'am,' she replied to her question. 'I recognized his voice. Know it anywhere, I would.'

'And where did you say this place was? This... club?'

'Not so far very off Marylebone High Street.'

'A gambling club.'

She nodded. 'A seedy one, ma'am. Not the sort of place a gentleman might frequent. There were Tommies and rough sorts – not that I'm saying Tommies are rough,' she hastened to clarify.

For a moment, she watched Naomi slowly shaking her head.

'What I find hard to understand, Kate, is what on earth possessed you to go somewhere like *that* in the first place? How did you even get in? Do they ordinarily allow unaccompanied women onto such premises?'

Feeling her cheeks colour, she shrugged her shoulders. 'I couldn't say,' she replied, determined that she wasn't going to start making excuses or apologising for what she had done. It had been for Naomi's benefit that she had taken such a risk. 'Save for what I gleaned while I was there, I know nothing of the place at all. If it had a name, I didn't see it.' Despite her resolve, she glanced to Naomi's face; she did hope she wasn't going to be cross. From her expression, she couldn't decide whether she was truly annoyed or merely bemused. From the tone of her voice, she thought perhaps it was a bit of both.

'You should know, Kate, that while I must confess to admiring your courage, I am also rather displeased with you. What if some terrible thing had befallen you? How would we ever have found you when I didn't even know you had gone out?'

Getting up from the end of the bed, Kate went towards the window and stood for a moment, looking down onto the street. At the time, she hadn't given a moment's thought to how Naomi would react upon learning of what she had done, her mind given only to finding out what Mr Aubrey had been up to. 'Well, you see, ma'am,' she said, 'even before you had that… confrontation with him, Mr Aubrey's behaviour had begun to concern me. For a military man, he's been proper woolly about his plans. And a mite too cagey about his movements, too. Secretive, I thought he was. Furtive – even that first time he came back. Catch his eye and he was always real quick to look away, too. Sign of a fellow who's hiding something, that is.'

292

'I must admit, I *was* beginning to have concerns about him. Though don't think that excuses your rash behaviour.' Again, Kate blushed. But still she didn't apologise. 'Anyway,' Naomi continued, 'you followed him into this gambling club. And then, a while later, you saw him forcibly removed.'

Slowly, she looked up. 'I did, ma'am. Thrown out on his ear, he was, and warned not to come back.'

'And then *he* threatened *them*.'

She nodded. 'Half-heartedly, truth be told. I can't think he truly meant to do harm.' *They were a lot bigger and burlier than him*, she thought but didn't say, her glance to the man ejecting him having been, of necessity, a brief one.

'I would have thought,' Naomi began, the look on her face still pensive, 'that to have been thrown out of an establishment like that, he can only have been cheating.'

'Either that,' she surmised, her confidence slowly returning, 'or else he owes them money.'

'If he owes them money,' Naomi replied, 'I don't think they would have let him just walk out of the door.'

She gave a long sigh. This morning, she wasn't really sure what to think. Mainly, she was just relieved that Naomi now knew enough to insist that he leave.

'Anyway, when I came in, I made good an' sure to bolt the door,' she said, recalling how, at first, the bolt had refused to budge, before then shooting across with a crack loud enough to awaken the dead. 'At least this morning he can't sneak back in without us knowing.'

'No. And you're right to say I shall now demand that he leaves. I shall tell him that if he departs quietly, and without a fuss, I shall refrain from reporting him to his regiment. That ought to ensure his compliance.'

'Good idea, ma'am,' she said, relieved with the way things were turning out. 'I can't think he'll want to court *more* trouble.' It was then that she remembered something – specifically, the sight of him scrabbling to get up from the floor. 'Last night,' she said, unsure as to the significance of what she was only now recalling, 'I'm minded his wrist wasn't in its sling. And, though I wouldn't swear to it on the Bible, I don't remember seeing even so much as a bandage upon it.'

'Well, it must be any day now that he's due before this medical assessment board he keeps talking about. So perhaps, after all of these weeks, his injury has finally healed. Perhaps he no longer has need of a sling.'

She wished she shared Naomi's generosity of spirit. She didn't, though, not for one second. 'Happen that's so,' she nonetheless agreed.

'Not that it matters because once he returns, this time, I shall *insist* that he leaves.'

'Yes, ma'am.' And thank goodness for that! Now, on Naomi's account as well as her own, she would be able to truly relax, her efforts – and the risks she had taken – having been worth it. 'Well, then,' she said lightly, 'how about for a change for breakfast this morning, I make us a couple of omelettes? There's some of that nice Norfolk ham, and a few mushrooms left over from the beef pie.'

Taking Naomi's agreement as read, she turned to leave the room only to be pulled up by a crashing sound – the sort of tinny clashing noise that her stack of baking tins would make were they to be knocked to the scullery floor.

Beside her, Naomi stiffened. 'You did say you bolted the front door?'

'Locked and bolted it, ma'am. I remember distinctly.'

'Only, that noise seemed to come from down in the kitchen.'

'Happen I left something poorly stacked,' she said, trying to picture what it might be. 'Or happen that cat from number sixteen has found its way in through the scullery window again. I'm going down now anyway, so I'll see to it.'

'And I'll put on my robe and bring Baby. She can sleep on in her basket while we have breakfast.'

'All right. See you down there dreckly.'

Heading down the stairs, Kate's thoughts turned to the private investigator, Mr Scott. Perhaps, today, he might have news for them. She hoped so. The waiting about to hear from him was becoming unbearable. They needed to know where they stood, being left in limbo doing neither of them any good. As it was, she couldn't bring herself to contemplate what would happen if he arrived to say he had found a living relative, and that Naomi had to hand the poor thing back. The only consolation was that Baby herself was too young to know what was going on around her – was too young to sense how jangled their nerves were.

Arriving in the hallway, she looked towards the front door – bolted, just as she had known it would be. And for now, that's how she was going to leave it. She felt safer knowing that Mr Aubrey couldn't come wandering in, especially since when he did, he would probably be the worse for wear.

Starting down the second staircase, she turned her mind to the matters of the day ahead. Having expected to be back in Devon by now, she hadn't placed the usual week's order with Mr Boucher for their meat – hadn't given it a thought. Same went for Monk's the fishmonger. She would need to shop for vegetables and fruit, as well. By now, there might be some cherries to be had. If there were, she would make a cherry pie for dessert and serve it with custard. One thing at a time, though; first, there was the matter of breakfast to see to.

'Ah, finally, there you are!'

Rounding the doorframe into the kitchen, she stopped dead. Mr Aubrey? In the kitchen? How could that be? With her heart pounding from shock, she shot a hand to the wall for support. Then, pointlessly – given that she was now one floor down from it – she glanced over her shoulder as though to recheck the front door. No, it had been bolted. She would swear to it. So, how on earth…?

'What—'

'Looks as though we're in for another fine one, wouldn't you agree?'

'Um…' *How could this be?*

'I was hoping you'd be down soon,' Aubrey continued ordinarily. 'Only, I don't seem to have the knack with this range. Can't get the thing hot and I'm desperate for a decent cup of coffee and a proper breakfast.'

'M-Mr Aubrey,' she finally stammered. 'How did you get in here?'

When he made to fish about inside his jacket, she watched, his face so plainly written with mock surprise that she wanted to march across the room and slap it.

From within one of his pockets he eventually produced a key, going on to hold it out for her to see. 'Took the precaution of getting one cut for the back door,' he explained. 'You know, on the off-chance you should retire one night and draw the bolt, unaware that I had yet to come in. It would be a simple enough oversight. We're each of us only human after all.'

With that, her eye was caught by movement in the scullery. Turning sharply, she saw a young woman, glancing about as though taking everything in. Attired in a simple woollen skirt that stopped just short of her ankles and a closely buttoned jacket of dark checked cloth, her face reminded her of Ada in that she appeared only just beyond adolescence. The difference, though, was that poor Ada had looked altogether more trustworthy.

'Posh lav, Archie.'

'Ah, Kate,' Aubrey said, entirely unconcerned, 'this is Nancy. Nancy, this is Kate.'

'Pleased to meet yer, I'm sure,' the new arrival said with a nod in Kate's direction. 'You the one what's going to give us breakfast? Only, I'm partial to a bit of fried bread wiv mine – *if you'd be so kind.*'

With so many thoughts pressing to be made sense of, Kate simply stood, looking from Aubrey to the girl and back again, lost to understand what was going on. At least her fear that Aubrey had seen her at the club seemed unfounded because surely, if he thought he'd been discovered, he wouldn't have come back. If only he *hadn't* come back! As for bringing yet another stranger into the house, how had it not occurred to him that Naomi would be livid?

'Mrs Colborne is just rising,' she said, regretting that she didn't have the nerve of this girl Nancy. 'So, it might be better were your… *friend* here… to be gone before she comes down.' Turning to the girl, now leaning against the corner of the range, she added, 'And no, miss, I'm not going to give you breakfast. I shall not be preparing food nor drink of any kind until after you have left.'

'Ooh! Rather a lot of sauce for a kitchen maid, wouldn't you say, Archie?'

Archie? That was the second time she'd called him that. Who *was* this girl? And why was Aubrey letting her get away with such impudence?

'Kate, whatever is all the noise? Baby has awoken and is refusing to—'

In the doorway stood Naomi, clad in her dressing gown, in her arms the rush basket containing Baby. Quickly, Kate moved to take it from her and place it on the low table, brought for the purpose from one of the bedrooms. In the basket, Baby was snuffling.

'Naomi,' Aubrey greeted her arrival unperturbed. 'I was just enquiring about the chance of some breakfast. 'Nancy and I are absolutely ravenous.'

Satisfied that Baby was all right, Kate turned back to see Naomi's face rigid with displeasure.

'Aubrey, I thought I made myself plain. You are no longer welcome in my home. And your friend here most certainly isn't. There will be no *breakfast* for either of you. Young lady, please leave my house this minute. Aubrey, I shall accompany *you* upstairs, where I shall wait on the landing while you collect your things. Then I shall see you out.'

'You gonna let *this* 'oity-toity bit talk to you like that?' the girl turned sharply to Aubrey to ask. 'Cheeky madam.' In an apparent show of support, she then sidled along the range and slipped her arm through his. To Kate's mild amusement, he withdrew it and handed it back to her.

'I shall not,' he replied evenly, his face showing no hint of irritation nonetheless. 'If you recall, my dear Naomi,' he said instead, 'in response to your previous ultimatum, I advised *you* that at this precise moment in time, it does not suit me to leave here. I also reminded you that in any event, since the lease on this house belongs to my brother, you do not have the authority to remove me. And so, since there has been no alteration to that state of affairs, I intend remaining here for as long as it suits me to. Now, would someone please make me a cup of coffee and some breakfast?'

'No, Aubrey,' Naomi replied, a faint tremor discernible in her voice. 'I have already made plain that there will be neither coffee nor breakfast.'

'My dear,' Aubrey said, making as though to take a step towards Naomi and then scoffing when she recoiled, 'I have no wish for us to fall out, none whatsoever. You have been more than kind to me during these last few weeks and, for that, I am indebted to you. However, the fact remains that for a day or two longer – a week at most – it is imperative that I do not depart London. Soon enough, my business here will be done. After that, I shall make no further call upon your hospitality. In the meantime, please, both of you, do as I ask and prepare some breakfast.'

By Naomi's side, Kate squirmed. She couldn't see how this was going to end, only that it was likely to grow more ugly before it did. And she could think of no easy way to summon help from anyone else, either. If she thought May Davis' son, Albie, would be next door, she would make a dash up the stairs and run out to fetch him. Albie was a great lump of a man, who didn't look as though he would think twice about using his fists.

Naomi, though, interrupted her thoughts.

'I should have thought *your* only *business* should be the rejoining of your regiment.'

She had to hand it to Naomi, she was remaining remarkably calm – at least, outwardly she was.

'And it will be, dear lady. Very soon now, it will be.'

'Look, Aubrey, I'm warning you, do not push me. If there's one thing this war has done, it has been to teach me how to get on with things and stand up for myself. You should know that I am no longer someone you can dominate or bully.'

'Bully? Good heavens! Do you truly think so little of me? Good Lord. Nancy, tell me, do I strike you as the sort of man to bully a woman? A member of my own family, at that?'

'Lord, sir, no, sir, you do not. I've met some bullies in my time, I can tell you, and they weren't nothin' like you, sir.'

Naomi scoffed. 'Push me, Aubrey, and you won't like what I do next.'

'My dear sister-in-law, push *me*, and neither will *you*.'

'Why, is it your intention to press me up against the wall again? Is that your plan?'

A bystander to this exchange, Kate wished Naomi wouldn't provoke Aubrey in this way. Once he was riled there could be no predicting what he might do.

'Of course not. Don't be so vulgar. No,' he said, 'but I shall write two letters.' Kate frowned. Two letters? Now what was he talking about? 'The first,' he went on, 'which it will give me no pleasure whatsoever to write, will be to my brother, informing him that just this last week, you gave birth to a child, a daughter, and that she is mine, from our little dalliance at Woodicombe last summer.'

While Kate gasped, beside her, Naomi stiffened. 'Don't be ridiculous, Aubrey. There *was* no dalliance.'

'Terribly difficult thing to try to prove now, though, wouldn't you say? Especially, I think, given the age of the child in question.'

'The baby's not even mine!'

'But just think, far away, on a battlefield somewhere in France, having not been home these last five months or so, there will be no way for Lawrence to know that, will there? Just imagine the agony and the torment such news would cause him. Oh, the pain. The humiliation!'

In the corner, her hands curled into fists by her side, it was as much as Kate could do not to cross the room and strike the repulsive man. 'Mr Lawrence wouldn't believe you!' she exclaimed, the nails of her fingers pressing into the palms of her hands.

'If that is a risk you are prepared to take, then you are bolder than I gave you credit for – both of you. You see, my dear Kate, the second letter I shall write – the early draft for which is already coming along nicely – will inform Private Channer that since his last period of leave, his wife has had her head turned by the bright lights, such that she now works as a dancer in what might politely be termed a gentleman's club.'

'You wouldn't dare!' she exploded, regretting that between her and Aubrey stood the kitchen table. 'And anyway, same as for Mr Lawrence, he wouldn't believe you!' How dare he think of upsetting Luke! How dare he!

'For two women with husbands so briefly gained and so little seen, you seem awfully sure of yourselves,' Aubrey replied.

'Of course we're sure!'

'Kate, ignore him,' Naomi cautioned, her arm held out as though to prevent her from lunging at him. 'His threats are empty ones. He is merely trying to sow seeds of doubt and create discord and disharmony between us. Ignore him. He is not worth stirring your breath over. As you rightly observe, neither Lawrence nor Luke would believe a word he wrote. Indeed, who is to say that a letter from him would even reach either of our husbands before one sent to them by either of us?'

Aubrey, though, gave a smug smile. 'You overlook, dear lady, the fact that you lack my means. I am in a position to expedite messages to the front. You are not. Desist from asking me to leave this house before I am ready, and there will be no need for either of us to put your conviction to the test.'

When, feeling as though she might boil over, Kate made to move towards him, Naomi once again held out her arm. 'Please, don't,' she said levelly. 'Assault him and he will consider it a victory.'

'But he shouldn't be allowed—' Her retort, though, was broken by a sudden and thunderous hammering at the front door. So forceful and unexpected was it that all four parties stiffened from shock. In the ensuing stillness, she glanced to Naomi. Wary of leaving her alone, she asked, 'Should I g-go and see who it is?'

'Please do,' Naomi answered calmly. 'But do not admit anyone you do not know and trust.'

Leaving the kitchen, she pounded up the stairs and along the hall, pausing just short of the front door to calm herself. Before she could draw so much as a further breath, though, the hammering came again. Startled by the volume of it, she leapt back. But then, steeling herself, she stretched up to draw back the bolt, turn the latch, and open the door.

On the other side stood a police sergeant and his constable.

'Apologies for disturbing you at this hour, miss,' the sergeant began. In her chest, her heart seemed to double its pace. This had to be bad news. But about whom? Mr Lawrence? Luke? The baby? Oh, dear Lord, had someone accused them of stealing the baby? 'Would this be the home of Lieutenant Lawrence Colborne?'

In that single moment, she felt her knees weaken beneath her. It was news of Mr Lawrence!

Somehow, she managed to nod. 'Yes,' she said. 'This is his home.'

'Then please, miss, stand aside.'

As the sergeant made to step across the threshold, she tightened her hold on the latch. 'Mr Lawrence isn't here,' she said. 'But, if you will tell me your business, I'll go an' fetch *Mrs* Colborne.'

'Very well. We have reason to believe that his brother, Second Lieutenant Aubrey Colborne of the Wiltshire Regiment, has been lodging here. We have been asked by the Military Police to apprehend him.'

Struggling in that instant to draw breath, she gestured in jerky fashion along the hallway. 'D-Down in the k-kitchen,' she stammered.

But, before either of the officers had even stepped inside, a woman's scream rang out, followed almost immediately by the shrill cry of a baby.

On the doorstep, the two police officers exchanged looks.

'Wait here, miss,' the sergeant commanded. 'Constable Woods, come with me.'

–

'Thank you for coming so quickly, Mrs Lloyd.'

With Naomi in a state of distress seemingly beyond consolation, and at a loss to know what else to do, Kate had run to the telegraph office to telephone Aunt Diana for help. And now, seeing her on the doorstep, she was relieved that she had.

'Nonsense, my dear. It was quite the right thing to do,' Diana Lloyd replied. 'But, before I go and see her, tell me, did Aubrey harm her?'

Kate shook her head. 'Thankfully, no, he didn't. She said that though he pressed her to the wall and held a knife to her throat, it seemed he did so only to enable the girl to grab Baby from her basket and make off with her. Once she'd gone, he dropped the knife and followed her out.'

'All right, my dear. Thank you for that. And the police have not yet returned with any word?'

Again, she shook her head. 'No, ma'am. Not yet.'

'No. Too soon, I suppose,' Diana Lloyd surmised.

'I did think of calling the doctor – you know, to see whether he might give her something to calm her. But I don't suppose she'd take it even if he did.'

'I doubt that she would.'

'But I did at least get her to agree to go up and lie down.'

Diana Lloyd glanced towards the stairs. 'And is she still up there?'

'Yes, ma'am.'

'Then I'll go up and see her, if I may.'

Grateful for Diana Lloyd's presence, Kate stepped aside. 'Yes, of course. I'll come up with you.'

At the top of the stairs, the door to Naomi's room stood partly open, meaning that from where she was sitting propped up against the headboard, she spotted their approach. 'Oh, Aunt, it's you,' she said flatly. 'I hoped it might be someone with news.'

Ignoring her observation, Diana Lloyd went to sit on the side of the bed. 'My poor dear girl. What an appalling thing to happen.'

Naomi sobbed. 'He's taken Baby. Aubrey's taken my baby.'

'Yes, dear. Kate told me.'

'And she's such a tiny little thing. That girl he had with him – that Nancy – she didn't look as though she'd have the first clue how to care for her. She didn't even take the blanket from her basket. She just snatched her up and ran out through the back door.'

'So I heard.'

'I begged her not to, but Aubrey put his hand across my mouth. What with that and the knife he was wielding, well, there was nothing I could do. But I should have found a way to do *something*.'

'Naomi, dear,' Diana said carefully. 'There was *nothing* you could have done. There were two of them and only one of you. And they clearly had a plan. It is the only possible explanation.'

'But *why*? What use to Aubrey is a baby? And who was that girl anyway? Where do you suppose she fits into all of this?'

'I don't know, dear,' Diana Lloyd said, lifting Naomi's hand and taking it in her own. 'But such an odd couple, especially with a newborn baby, will find it hard not to draw attention.'

'It's true,' Kate said, longing to believe it. She would pretend to, though, even if only to dissuade Naomi from continuing to blame herself.

With that, from down in the hallway came the sound of the door knocker. Although it made Naomi jump, Diana Lloyd kept tight hold of her hand. 'Stay there, my dear. Let Kate go down and answer it.'

When Kate arrived at the door and opened it, though, her heart sank. 'Mrs Russell, ma'am,' she greeted the woman on the doorstep, struggling to conceal her dismay; having her mother turn up was the last thing Naomi needed right now. 'Please, do come in.'

'Where is my daughter?' Pamela Russell immediately wanted to know, stepping straight past her, the furrow to her brow suggesting that the whole thing was an insufferable disruption to her day.

'She is upstairs,' Kate replied as evenly as she could. 'Please, follow me.' Fancy Mrs Russell looking so put out! Her daughter was in distress – you'd think she would show a little more concern.

Having shown Pamela Russell into Naomi's room, Kate decided to remain within earshot of the door.

'Naomi, dear,' she heard Mrs Russell greet her daughter, her tone rather cool.

'Mamma. I told Kate not to trouble you with this. She gave me her word she would only telephone for Aunt Diana.'

'And she did, dear,' Aunt Diana cut in. 'It was I who thought your mother should know.'

'Oh. I see.'

On the landing, Kate shifted her weight and continued to listen.

'Naomi, I'm sure this is all dreadfully upsetting for you and, in the circumstances, it grieves me to say this. But say it I must. *Whatever were you thinking?*'

'Pamela, I hardly think this is the time to—'

'No, Diana. When you telephoned to tell me about this... this child, you surely weren't expecting that I would keep my thoughts to myself. No, I'm sorry but I feel compelled to speak my mind—'

Out on the landing, Kate curled her hands into fists. *Why* did Pamela Russell feel compelled to speak her mind? Why couldn't she keep her tongue in her head and her opinions to herself just this once? Couldn't she *see* the state her daughter was in? Or did she simply not care – voicing her disapproval of far greater importance to her?

'I don't understand, Mamma,' she overheard Naomi reply. 'What was I thinking about what?'

'—taking in an abandoned baby—'

'She wasn't abandoned. She was orphaned.'

'—you might know that would spell disaster. Even if the baby's parentage *is* as claimed – which I *highly* doubt – what on earth possessed you to take it in? We know nothing whatsoever of its parents. The father could have been a common criminal or a... a—'

'He was a Tommie, killed at the front while fighting for his country.'

'—and the mother could have been a tuppenny harlot. Indeed, given the sort of people with whom your father was once involved, it's not hard to imagine how the whole story of the child being orphaned could be a complete fabrication – some sort of ruse to get yet more money out of this family.'

In the stiff silence that followed, Kate hardly dared to breathe. At least Mrs Russell's invective seemed to have run out of steam. Even so, what a nerve the woman had, casting aspersions about the characters of ordinary hard-working people.

'I am well aware, Mamma,' Naomi began, 'that people can be underhand and deceitful. One only has to look to Aubrey to see *that*. It's not as though I'm some giddy debutante—'

'But neither, just lately, have you been thinking clearly. I'm sure the baby's misfortune makes for a harrowing tale. But it doesn't fall to *you* to atone for your *father's* wrongdoings.'

'And how is Papa, Mamma?'

'That, you would have to ask *him*. From the little I see of him, I can only deduce that he is once again quite well.'

'I'm pleased to hear it.'

'At this precise moment, what I'm more interested in is you and your state of mind.'

'My *state of mind*?'

Unable to see into the room, Kate nevertheless pictured Naomi shooting sharply upright, the look on her face showing just how deeply she took exception to what her mother was implying.

'Darling,' she heard Pamela Russell say then, her tone patronizing though no doubt intended as sympathetic. 'You miscarried a child. Take it from me, a loss of that magnitude affects one more deeply and for far longer than one might think. Having to then discover the familial history of miscarrying, well, you could be forgiven for being unable to think clearly, let alone to make decisions. There you are, still in shock, when you are presented with a supposedly abandoned baby and a tale of woe. Of course you're going to want to take it in and care for it. It would be only natural.'

'Mamma, I accept that the whole business of miscarrying has had a profound effect upon me, as has discovering the unlikelihood that I shall fare any better in the future. Indeed, it would not be overstating the situation to describe it as numbing, and I won't belittle the plight of women similarly afflicted by denying it. I will even go so far as to concede that the timing of the arrival of an orphaned baby was, perhaps, regrettable. But, I assure you, the idea that I am somehow atoning for Papa's past is nothing short of ridiculous. *And*, for your information, at no stage have I been unable to think clearly. Indeed, that I sought counsel from Aunt Diana and was guided by her suggestion must surely be demonstration of that.'

'Words, words, words, Naomi. It's selfishness, that's what it is. I mean, have you even stopped to think about Lawrence? Have you considered what he will say when he finds out what you did behind his back? Do you even have a care how *he* will feel?'

'Lawrence?'

'Although quite why I should concern myself with what *he* thinks, I don't know. I mean, what sort of man puts his wife in a house like this and then leaves her with nothing more by way of staff than an illegitimate Cornish farm girl?'

'Mamma, Kate is neither Cornish nor a farm girl!'

Beyond the bedroom door, Kate clenched her fists more tightly still.

'Well, choose to ignore me. It is your entitlement to do so. But I'm telling you now, this whole thing will end badly. It has catastrophe written all over it.'

Why should it be a catastrophe, Kate wondered?

At least on the other side of the door, Naomi was finding the strength to stand her ground.

'If I remember rightly,' she said at that moment, 'it was *you*, Mamma, with that relentless will of yours, who pushed me towards the Colbornes in the first place, going on and on about what a good family they were and about their wealth.'

To Kate's ears, when Mrs Russell replied, she sounded exasperated.

'About *Aubrey*, yes! And I was right, wasn't I? Had you married *him*, none of this would have happened – to him *or* to you. You would both have been more settled. While he was away in the army, you would have been installed at Avingham with Ralph and Cicely, instead of living, apparently solely to spite me, in this… this *hovel!*'

Out on the landing, where she had been holding her breath, Kate was startled to hear the tinkling of Naomi's handbell – the one she had placed on her bedside table for her to summon help if she felt unwell.

'Kate?' Naomi called loudly. 'Kate! Please come in here.'

Hoping not to appear as though she had been hovering there throughout, Kate crept away to the top of the stairs, counted to five, and then walked normally back across the landing. Drawing a breath, she tapped at the partly open door. 'You called, ma'am?'

'Kate,' Naomi greeted her purposefully as she stepped into the room. 'Mrs Russell is leaving. Please show her out. And please convey to her as you do so that she is no longer welcome in my home. Please make it plain to her that if she calls, I shall not receive her.'

'But Naomi—' Pamela Russell began, getting to her feet nevertheless.

'Goodbye, Mamma. And when you have done that, Kate,' Naomi continued, looking across at her and smiling warmly, 'Aunt Diana and I should like to take tea.'

'Naomi, dear, I only have your best interests at heart.'

'Thank you, Kate. We shall come down and take it in the drawing room.'

She might not like Mrs Russell – indeed, at times she had despised here – but having to witness their exchange made Kate squirm. Her feelings aside, though, Naomi had charged her with a task and so, she would overcome discomfort to see it through.

'This way, please, Mrs Russell,' she said, sounding many times more purposeful than she felt. 'Please allow me to show you out.' There was, though, no need, she thought as she went ahead of Pamela Russell to the landing, to repeat Naomi's words about not receiving her in future; Mrs Russell couldn't have failed to hear that for herself. Moreover, if she couldn't see with her own eyes how unhelpful she had been in Naomi's hour of need – disparaging, even – then she wasn't really much of a mother at all.

After the events of the morning, to Kate, the rest of the day seemed to drag. Aunt Diana stayed to take luncheon with them and although afterwards Naomi had suggested that she return home, she had refused point blank.

'I shall do no such thing,' she had said. 'Leave poor Kate to try and cajole you into sleeping, or even eating or drinking? I think not, my dear. I shall wait with you. Indeed, if, by, shall we say, four thirty, there is still no news of the baby, then I shall go to the Marylebone constabulary and ask to see the chief inspector.'

'Aunt—'

'Learning what is going on will be the only way any of us are able to even *think* about getting some sleep tonight.'

And she was right. As the afternoon progressed, Naomi alternated between beating a path back and forth across the drawing-room window, her eyes permanently affixed to the empty street below, and slumping onto the sofa to sit with her head in her hands.

Finally, several hours later, the mournful silence was broken by a heavy rapping of the door knocker. Echoing down the hallway, it caused Naomi to leap to her feet and rush from the room to answer it.

'Yes?' Kate heard her say above the sound of the door being opened.

'Mrs Colborne, may we please come in?'

By now, Kate had also reached the door. Taking in the sight of two police officers but no baby, she was concerned that Naomi might faint. 'Here, ma'am,' she said, putting her hand under Naomi's elbow, 'let us bring these two gentlemen through to the drawing room.'

Seemingly almost unable to breathe, let alone speak, Naomi nodded and allowed Kate to lead her along the hall and towards the sofa where she had been sitting previously.

'I am afraid, Mrs Colborne,' the taller of the two officers began, 'that Second Lieutenant Colborne would appear to have given us the slip. He and the girl both. We have searched the neighbouring gardens and outbuildings. We have alerted our officers whose beats include the railway stations at Marylebone, Paddington, Euston, St. Pancras, and Kings Cross. We will continue to keep a look out—'

'But you *will* find her?' Naomi interrupted him to ask. 'You will find my baby?'

When Aunt Diana shot her a look, Kate knew what it meant; she, too, was becoming worried about Naomi's state of mind.

'Sergeant, you never did say what brought you in search of Aubrey in the first place,' Diana Lloyd said.

'Begging your pardon, ma'am, but events overtook us,' the officer replied. 'In any case, we wouldn't ordinarily disclose our reasons for pursuing an enquiry. However, bearing in mind the way things have turned out,' he went on, glancing to each of their faces in turn, 'I will say to you that we came in search of Second Lieutenant Colborne because for some time now, he has been absent without leave from his battalion.'

'No, he was wounded,' Naomi corrected him. 'He has been on medical leave.'

'It is my understanding that at some stage he was indeed wounded, ma'am, yes. But his wound was minor

– *superficial*, is the word the army used – and he was treated for it in France. He was never granted leave to travel back to England. From what I gather, he absconded from the field hospital where he was being patched up.'

'But he's been back to his regiment in Wiltshire,' Naomi pointed out. 'He went before a board for an assessment as to his fitness. *They* knew he was back here.'

'He might have told you that, ma'am, but, by all accounts, that's not true. No one from his regiment has seen him since he slipped away while being treated for his injury.'

For a moment, there was only silence, each of the women apparently trying to understand what they had just heard. Eventually, it fell to Naomi to say, 'Next you'll be telling me he wasn't shot by the enemy at all, but that he inflicted the wound upon himself.'

'I couldn't possibly comment upon that, ma'am, other than to say that he wouldn't be the first soldier to do so. But now, if you will forgive me, I must return to the constabulary. Please be assured that our search for your child will continue, and that the moment I learn anything new – anything at all – I shall come straight round to inform you.'

When the sergeant then excused himself and headed towards the door, Kate gently let go of Naomi's hand and followed him out.

'Sergeant,' she said, opening the door for him, her voice little more than a whisper, 'when you find Lieutenant Colborne, what will happen to him?'

'No need to concern yourself on that score, miss,' he said, moving out onto the doorstep and replacing his helmet, 'he'll have no chance to return to terrorise you again. Deserters are shot.'

–

The atmosphere that evening was excruciating. Naomi sobbed endlessly, and Kate could do nothing to banish an image of Mr Aubrey standing before a firing squad. Even Aunt Diana seemed to have exhausted her usual supply of warm words and comforting anecdotes. By way of a combined refusal to admit the unthinkable – that Baby might never be returned to them – what little conversation they did make was centred inevitably upon Aubrey and his web of deceit.

'Do you think *any* of what he told us was true?' Naomi asked.

It was something Kate, too, had been wondering. To Naomi's question, she raised her eyebrows and shook her head. 'I don't know what to believe no more,' she said.

'Do you think it was even true about the enemy having shot him?'

'Can't say as I know that, either,' she replied. 'Were it any other man, I'd struggle to think him capable of something as despicable as wounding himself.'

'If he did inflict the wound himself,' Aunt Diana chipped in, 'one almost has to admire him for his bravery. It must require enormous courage to fire a gun into one's own body.'

When Kate winced, she saw Naomi do the same. She did wish she could persuade her to go to bed. She wished she would take a nice soak in a warm bath, have a hot milky drink, and place one of her little sachets of lavender under her pillow. When she had tried to suggest it, though, Naomi had replied that she would do nothing of the sort: that while there was even one single minute of daylight left, she would sit up and wait for news.

'It's always possible he *was* shot by the enemy,' Naomi chose that moment to say, 'and then, without actual forethought, simply acted upon an impulse to flee the battlefield.'

'I see now why he was often so vague about his plans,' Kate remarked. 'He had to be vague because he was living on his wits.'

'It does explain the apparently haphazard nature of his travel arrangements,' Naomi agreed. 'And the fact that he didn't have any money. And, I suppose, when we were down at Woodicombe, it would also explain his sudden fondness for what we assumed to be walking but which was, more than likely, gambling.'

Across the room, and from where she had been perched upon the window seat, Diana Lloyd got to her feet. 'I think perhaps I should take my leave of you,' she said, rolling her head in circles as though to relieve stiffness from her neck. 'But I shall return first thing tomorrow morning.'

When, having kissed Naomi on the forehead and bid her goodnight, she went towards the door, Kate followed her. 'Would you like me to go to the end of the street and fetch you a cab?' she asked her.

'Thank you, my dear, but no. You remain here. I am more than capable. There is still enough light left in the day for me to see to walk. And in any event,' she said, lowering her voice and, taking her by the arm, guiding her further into the hallway, 'it is my intention to call upon an acquaintance who lives fairly close by – someone who knows the Colbornes of old. Without disclosing what has transpired, I'm minded to see whether I can find out anything that might help in the search for Aubrey. There have been rumours circulating for a couple of months now – rumours that, until today, one felt to be little more than just that. But, with the way things have transpired, I ought perhaps *try* to establish whether any of them have any substance.'

Rumours? That was worrying. In her experience, rarely was there smoke without fire. 'Rumours about Mr Aubrey, or about the Colbornes in general?' she risked asking.

'In this instance, my dear, I fear they are one and the same. Of course,' she said, noticing her reflection in the mirror and reaching to adjust the wide brim of her hat, 'my enquiries might yield nothing. The rumours as conveyed to me might prove entirely without foundation. And it's a long shot, anyway, to think that they might shed light upon where Aubrey could have gone. I shall try nevertheless. In the meantime, not a word to Naomi, please, dear.'

'Of course not, Mrs Lloyd.'

'Separately, should the police return with... bad news... ask them to send a man for me. Don't worry about the hour. I shall come regardless.'

'Thank you,' she said, submitting to a light embrace.

'Remain hopeful, my dear, for, until we hear otherwise, all is most definitely not lost. Having said that, you might wish to start thinking about taking Naomi back to Woodicombe. *If* things don't end well, she might be better off in Devon than here in town. Just a thought.'

She nodded. With things as they stood at the moment, she couldn't see herself managing to persuade Naomi of anything. 'All right,' she said, accompanying Diana Lloyd out through the front door and onto the top step. 'Though I'm not sure she'd go.'

'In which case, we might not give her any say in the matter,' Diana Lloyd replied. 'Regardless, it occurs to me that it might also be wise for me to try to get word to Lawrence. I feel he should know what has been going on. But not, in the first instance at least, by way of some jumbled and highly emotional tale from Naomi. If I do decide to write to him, I shall mention that you might be going to stay at Woodicombe, just so that he is aware.'

With a heavy sigh, she nodded her understanding. It all sounded eminently sensible. 'Please take care, Mrs Lloyd,' she said.

'You, too, my dear. And let us all pray that tomorrow, a new day brings better news.'

—

'Good morning, Mrs Channer.'

It was early the following morning and, trying to hide her panic at finding Donald Scott on the doorstep – his hat in his hand and a polite smile on his face – Kate tried to smile back. In the circumstances, it would have been better had it been the sergeant from the police station calling – better still had he been bringing good news. As it was, with the baby still missing, there was now a charade to be kept up – no matter the nature of the news Donald Scott had come to impart.

'Good morning, Mr Scott,' she replied.

'I do hope this isn't too early to call.'

'No, not at all. Please, do come in.'

'Only, I have uncovered some facts I thought Mrs Colborne would want to hear.'

Despite staring back at him, she could tell nothing from either his tone or his expression to indicate the nature of these facts – whether for good or for bad.

'Please,' she said, struggling to sound calm, 'do come through and I will go and fetch Mrs Colborne.'

Once Donald Scott was in the drawing room, she did her best to walk calmly back out into the hall. But then, reaching the bottom of the stairs, and ignoring the panic that seemed to be buckling her knees beneath her, she took them at full pelt, arriving, breathless, to tap on the door to Naomi's room.

Having arrived barely ten minutes earlier, it was Aunt Diana who opened it to her. Upon hearing the name of Donald Scott, though, Naomi sprang up from where she had been seated at her dressing table.

'My dear girl,' Aunt Diana said, trying to calm her jumpy niece, 'there is no cause for alarm. No matter how greatly you panic, the information Mr Scott brings us will not change.'

'I know that,' Naomi replied, her manner abrupt. 'But I couldn't feel more frightened were my life to depend upon what we are about to learn.'

'Come,' Aunt Diana said, extending her hand. 'Let us face this head on. For the sake of that little baby, let us be brave.'

While Kate stood helplessly in the doorway, Naomi continued to hesitate. 'Aunt, I don't think I have it in me to do this. Would you go and see him for me – hear what he has found out? It would have been hard enough to learn of his findings had Baby still been here in our care. But how can I listen to him tell me *anything* about Baby when I no longer have her? Indeed, how do I even avoid letting him know that she has been taken from us and that we don't know where she is – that we might never see her again?'

'We will manage perfectly well,' Diana said, taking Naomi's hand and rubbing it between her own. 'If Mr Scott even notices your jumpiness, he will put it down to your natural anxiety to learn what he has discovered.'

'He'll see through me,' Naomi said. 'Uncovering the truth is his job.'

'Then allow me to do most of the talking, my dear. He won't see through *me*.'

Exhaling a long breath, Naomi gave a nod of resignation. 'Very well. Then I suppose there is nothing for it but to go down and hear what he has turned up.'

When Kate trailed behind the two women into the drawing room, Donald Scott was standing at the window, from where he was looking out across the street.

'Mrs Colborne. Mrs Lloyd,' he turned back to greet them. 'Good morning to you both.'

Greetings exchanged, and seats offered and taken, Kate decided to withdraw to the hallway. It was bad enough that Naomi was struggling to maintain *her* composure, without she herself dissolving into tears. When she had first opened the door to Mr Scott, she had been struck by the realization that with Baby gone, she no longer knew which outcome she feared the most: learning that the poor little mite *was* related to them, or learning that she wasn't.

Lacking the wherewithal to simply walk away and get on with her work, she peered around the edge of the door. From a pocket inside his jacket, Donald Scott was withdrawing a notepad, through which he then proceeded to flick, evidently seeking the relevant page.

'As it turned out,' he said, setting his notepad on his knee, 'establishing the facts of your matter proved easier than I had anticipated.'

'That's good,' Aunt Diana observed lightly.

Seated next to her on the sofa, Naomi was staring into her lap, while out in the hallway, Kate had to remind herself to let go of the breath she was holding in her chest. If *she* felt *this* dreadful, how on earth must Naomi feel?

'I propose to start, if I may,' Donald Scott began again, 'with details of the most recent events pertaining to your enquiry and work from there.' This was it, then. They were about to learn the truth. 'Last summer,' he continued, 'in the district of Whitechapel, east London, Ernest William Ward married Bertha Jones. The records of their union show Ernest residing at an address in Whitechapel, his age as twenty-one, and his occupation as a platelayer – essentially, a railway labourer. His father, William Ward, was listed as deceased. Of course, how many of those facts are true, one can only speculate. You would be astounded by the number of grooms and their brides who have facts they wish to conceal – be it their age, or the existence of a parent whose consent to the union might not be forthcoming.'

From the hallway, Kate watched as both Naomi and her aunt nodded.

'And Ernest's mother?' Diana Lloyd asked. 'What do you know of her?'

'For the purposes of registering a marriage,' Donald Scott said to her, 'the mother's name is not required. Thus far, her identity is something I have been unable to establish. But, please, bear with me. The absence of information on that score does not alter the general facts.'

'Of course. I apologize. Please, do go on.'

'So, to the bride, Bertha Jones. She also gave an address in Whitechapel – a street adjacent to the one given by Ernest.'

'They were neighbours?' Naomi looked up to ask.

'They do seem to have been, yes. One might reasonably suppose that is how they came to know each other. Now, on the records of their marriage, in the column where the name of *her* father should have been written, a line had been drawn through it. To me, that signifies that in response to being asked about him, Bertha stated that she didn't know who he was. Had he been deceased, his name would have been recorded in the same manner as the details of Ernest's father. Unfortunately for us, in circumstances where there are no details for the father, the mother's name is not recorded *in lieu*, if you will. So, to learn of Bertha's mother, I was forced to look for the record of Bertha's birth.' Listening to him speaking, Kate found herself thinking it was like a mystery story unfolding. 'With her having given her age at marriage as twenty-one,' he said, 'which, incidentally, turned out to be more or less the truth, I was able to find the record of her birth, registered in the district of Paddington, to a woman called Fanny Jones. Unsurprisingly, given what we know from the record of Bertha's marriage, the space in the register of births for her father's name was empty. *But*, in highly unusual but magnificently fortuitous fashion

– for our purposes at least – in the margin, in pencil, someone had written the name Lou-Lou La Belle, alongside which they had also recorded the words "stage name" and "dancer".'

In the drawing room, Naomi gasped, while, in the hallway, Kate's hand flew to her mouth. Then the story was true! It had to be. Warily, she peered more fully into the room. Naomi seemed to be shaking; Aunt Diana, comforting her.

'So—'

'If you would bear with me a moment longer, Mrs Lloyd, I should prefer to finish recounting the facts. Then I will answer any questions you might have.'

'Yes, of course. Forgive me.'

'So, we have Ernest Ward, whose father is apparently deceased and whose mother's whereabouts, without further investigation, I am, for the moment, unable to determine. Then we have Bertha Jones, whose father is unnamed, but whose mother we now know to be Fanny Jones. Incidentally, for Fanny, I failed to find any record that she subsequently married. There was no shortage of women named Fanny Jones who *did* marry – as you might imagine, given the prevalence of those names – but none with circumstances that would match our particular young woman.'

'I see.'

'And so, next, I came forward in time and tried to find evidence of a baby born to Bertha Jones – or Ward, as she became. I checked with all of the appropriate lying-in hospitals but found nothing. So I went to the area where I thought Ernest and Bertha might have continued to reside. As luck would have it, and beyond my wildest hopes, I came across a midwife making her rounds. She told me that while she hadn't attended Bertha's delivery herself, she knew the woman who had. She was even able to point me to where I might locate her. And, when I *did* find her, she was happy to tell me all that she knew. By her account, Bertha had been recently widowed, in addition to which, she had been sickly for at least four or five weeks prior to the birth. The midwife hadn't been expecting either mother or baby to survive. So, when the little girl did somehow live, she handed her into the care of the only other person present – a friend of Bertha's by the name of Ada, who claimed to know where to find some of Bertha's distant family.'

'Us!' Naomi exclaimed. 'Aunt Diana, that's us!'

'Yes, my dear.'

'It would appear so,' Donald Scott concurred. 'Yes.'

Of all the cruel things in the world! Unable to bear it any longer, Kate rushed into the drawing room and straight to Naomi's side.

'She's ours,' Naomi whispered to her, her eyes filled with tears.

'Yes,' she whispered back, grasping Naomi's hand, 'she is.'

'I told you she was, didn't I?'

'Yes,' she said, entirely unable now to hold back her own tears. 'You did.'

'I knew it all along – from that very first moment!'

'Yes,' she said again, reaching to hug Naomi tightly. 'And so did I.'

Chapter Eleven

Esme

Numb. To Kate, that was how her mind had come to feel.

More than an hour after Mr Scott had departed, neither she nor Naomi seemed able to put their minds to anything. Briefly, she had pleaded with her to go and lie down, but here she was, still on the sofa where she had sat listening to Donald Scott informing them of his findings. From the way she had wept almost incessantly since, anyone would think the news he had brought them had been bad.

'Please, Naomi,' she had begged, at a loss to know how to help her. 'Won't you go upstairs and lie down? You'll feel far less uncomfortable than sitting here, all a-fret.' It was feeble reasoning, she knew that. But, overwhelmed by a feeling of helplessness, she could summon no better nor more persuasive argument.

Naomi, though, was determined to remain where she was for as long as it took Aunt Diana to return from the constabulary. 'How much longer before she's back, do you think?' she chose that moment to ask, her manner listless.

From her vigil at the window, Kate turned back into the room. 'I wish I knew.' Although gladdened by Aunt Diana's resolve to do something to help, in her heart she felt it unlikely she would return bearing good news. After all, if the police had found any trace of the baby, or of Aubrey or the woman, then surely by now they would have been to tell them. As it was, there had been only silence.

Continuing to stare out through the window pane, she found herself noticing for the first time the drooping clusters of pale creamy blossom on the lime trees. Until arriving in London, she'd never seen a lime tree; as far as she knew, they didn't grow in Devon. Over the months, she had come to quite like the way their statuesque presence brought life to an otherwise rather austere street. It had been May Davis next door who, in response to her question, had told her the name of them, going on to mention with a knowing laugh how folklore had it they brought good fertility. Fortunate, she had said with a wink, that two newly wed couples should have one growing right outside the window of their new home. Fertility. Huh. There was irony.

Drawing her eyes away from the heart-shaped leaves fidgeting in the breeze, she cast her mind back to earlier. Once Donald Scott had learned of Hugh Russell's relationship with a dancer – a piece of information Naomi had specifically withheld until that precise moment – he had agreed with her assessment: there seemed little doubt that Bertha had been her half-sister, meaning that the orphaned baby was indeed her niece. His belief declared, he had gone on to tell them that, notwithstanding the unknown whereabouts of Ernest Ward's mother – the baby's grandmother – the child appeared to have no immediate family. Enquiries to the authorities, he had also told them, suggested they would look favourably upon any relative offering to take her in. It was then that Naomi had collapsed into floods of tears, leaving it to Aunt Diana to lead Mr Scott into the hallway, politely explain away Naomi's singular reaction, and show him out. If he had thought Naomi's response overly emotional, he'd had the grace not to comment.

Even now, Naomi was still beyond being consoled. 'I can't lose this baby, I can't,' she repeated over and over. 'Don't you see? Not only is she my flesh and blood, she might be my only chance of motherhood. Aubrey *has* to bring her back. He *has* to!'

'Ma'am—'

'What I *still* don't understand,' Naomi went on, ignoring Kate's attempt to say something, 'is why he took her in the *first* place. *Why?* Was it that girl's idea, do you think? Was *she* behind it?'

'I couldn't say,' she replied. She had certainly thought the girl shifty-looking, not that it would serve any purpose to say so now.

'No doubt he met her at that club you saw him go into.'

'He might have,' she surmised. 'Though when I saw him leave there he was alone. And, if you'd seen how he was thrown to the floor, you'd think he wouldn't ever want to go back there again.'

'I suppose it doesn't matter, now,' Naomi said bitterly. 'It doesn't matter whose idea it was. One of them, if not both of them, has Baby. *My* baby.'

It was then that Kate spotted an elegant form coming along the pavement. 'Oh! Here comes Aunt Diana.'

Despite her pronouncement, seated on the sofa, Naomi didn't move.

Already waiting by the front door before Diana Lloyd had even reached the top step, Kate stood back to let her in. Although bursting to know what had happened at the constabulary, she knew it wasn't her place to ask. Instead, she helped Aunt Diana out of her jacket and then stood, watching her unbutton her gloves, tug them off, and then unpin her hat. That done, Diana Lloyd glanced along the hallway and, in a lowered voice, asked, 'Is she still in the drawing room?'

'Wouldn't go nowhere else, ma'am,' she replied, accepting Diana Lloyd's things from her. 'Wouldn't budge.'

'Then I think you had better accompany me in, my dear.'

In that split of a second, it felt to Kate as though her heart stopped beating. Clearly, then, the news wasn't good.

'They haven't found her, have they?' Naomi stirred herself to ask as they went in, her voice flat and resigned.

Crossing to sit next to her, Diana Lloyd beckoned Kate around to the far end of the sofa. 'No, my dear,' she said gently. 'I'm afraid they haven't. As yet, there is no further news at all.'

'I knew it.'

'When I made a point of stressing the tender age of the child and made known our increasing concerns for her well-being, the chief inspector assured me that every constable and every sergeant remains on the lookout. Likewise, the officers at each of the railway stations. But, as he also explained to me, all they can do is remain vigilant. That we have been unable to provide them with even a single address where Aubrey might be hiding out – such as the home of a friend or acquaintance – doesn't help, doesn't give them an area upon which to base their search.'

'If we knew where Aubrey might be,' Naomi said flatly, 'we would have told them. Or gone there ourselves to look.'

Ignoring her niece's snippiness, Diana Lloyd continued. 'He asked me why I thought Aubrey might have taken her.'

'And what did you say?' Naomi asked.

'I said that while I couldn't speak as to his motives with any certainty, a couple of thoughts have more recently occurred to me.'

At this, Naomi showed greater interest. 'And those are?'

Money. Kate found herself thinking. And revenge. Although revenge for what, she was less certain. Despite his improved behaviour of late – until recently, at least – she still thought him the sort of man to harbour grudges.

'Firstly,' Aunt Diana replied to Naomi's question, 'it strikes me that his decision to take her could have been spur-of-the-moment. Finding himself in a scrape, and all too aware of the consequences of being apprehended while absent without leave from his regiment, it could be that he saw the snatching of the child as a sort of insurance should he subsequently become cornered. The chief inspector said he's seen such instances before – an escapee bargaining with the life of an innocent party in the hope of being allowed to go free. In this instance, it doesn't strike me as beyond the bounds of possibilities. Aubrey always has tended towards hot-headed.'

'More likely he did it out of spite,' Naomi said, 'because I asked him to leave.'

Slowly, Kate nodded her agreement; while Aunt Diana's suggestion could be true, Naomi's supposition was just as plausible.

'But the idea that he panicked – that it was spur of the moment – wouldn't explain the presence of the girl,' Aunt Diana went on. 'To my mind, *her* being there makes it feel as though he *had* given it some thought beforehand – that he did have a plan. *Premeditated* was the word the chief inspector used.'

'But why even *plan* to take her? What could he possibly stand to gain from such an evil act?' Naomi wanted to know.

'Well, with payment of his salary having been suspended – and to evade capture in the longer term – Aubrey's first thought would surely be to obtain some money, and more than just the odd few guineas. Hence, one might deduce, his frequenting of gambling clubs. But then, with that particular avenue apparently closing down to him, he presumably had to resort to other means.'

'Yes!' Naomi suddenly exclaimed, recognition on her face as she turned to Kate. 'Yes, that explains something else, too. You see, that day he presented me with the banker's cheque for the money we raised at the gala dinner, I was surprised that the amount wasn't greater. Of course, it didn't for a single moment occur to me that he might have taken some of it. I mean, why would it? But now, listening to you talking, I do believe he helped himself to some of the donations. In fact, I think it could even have been his plan all along. After all, he was so dreadfully keen to help out. In particular, he was so very eager to take charge of the money.'

'Wasn't the dinner his idea from the outset?' Kate asked, trying to think back to the evening when the plan had first been mooted. She was sure Naomi had said that *Aubrey* had had an idea. The notion that he could so coolly dream up such an evil scheme – to take money from people in despair – was enough to make her blood boil.

'I dare say so. I don't really recall now. Either way, he was terribly clever. He knew I would be able to work out how much we had collected from the sales of the tickets – so he couldn't take any of *that*. He also knew I would see the account from the Royal Gardens. But what he *also* knew, was that I would have no way of accounting for any additional donations he might solicit on the night. And *that* is why he made a point of telling me he would take care of them. Oh, what a fool I've been! So taken in was I by his reformed ways, I simply fell into line with his suggestions as to the arrangements – just as he knew I would.'

'Don't blame yourself, dear,' Aunt Diana said. 'Someone that cunning – someone prepared to bide that much time to see a scheme come to fruition – would fool anyone.'

By Naomi's side, Kate nodded her agreement. 'Mrs Lloyd is right,' she said. 'It's no more your fault than mine. It's as you said: what reason would either of us have had for suspecting him? Even Mrs Russell didn't see through him.' *And she distrusts everyone*, was the thought that went through her mind.

'That's true,' Diana Lloyd agreed.

Naomi, though, gave a long sigh. 'Perhaps,' she admitted. 'But I still feel a fool.'

'Anyway,' Diana Lloyd said, exhaling heavily. 'I fervently believe that what lies behind Aubrey's actions is his need for money. And so, rather than believe that he took the baby in a moment of blind panic, I'm beginning to think he did so with a view to extorting money from you.'

'*Kidnap* Baby? Is that what you mean?'

Kidnap? Mr Aubrey would kidnap his own sister-in-law's child? To Kate, it beggared belief, even for Aubrey Colborne. Such a thing was beyond evil.

'I might be wrong,' Diana Lloyd admitted. 'And I said as much to the chief inspector. After all, not only has there been no demand for a ransom but the whole idea would have necessitated considerable planning in advance. As the chief inspector pointed out, if Aubrey desperately needed money, he would have been quicker served simply demanding it from you. That said, to me, a kidnap, in part thought out in advance – hence the presence of the girl – still feels the more likely.'

'No,' Naomi said. 'Despite everything, I fail to believe he would use an innocent baby just to get money from me. It is just too evil.'

'You can't believe it of him at this moment, no,' Aunt Diana replied. 'But what you wouldn't know, my dear, is that when it comes to money, Aubrey is no stranger to trouble.' Listening intently, Kate frowned. *Now* what were they about to find out? 'And that is why I wanted to talk to the chief inspector.'

She turned to study Naomi's reaction. She looked thoughtful.

'When we were down at Woodicombe last summer, I remember you told me you'd got wind of some scandal or other. What was it now? That the Colborne fortune wasn't quite what Mamma imagined it to be? Was that it? But surely that was just Ralph struggling to keep up with the rising costs of running an estate, wasn't it?'

For a moment, Diana Lloyd hesitated. But then she said, 'That was the gist of the story doing the rounds at the time, yes. But, just yesterday, in response to my making enquiries of someone close to the family – someone whose reliability and honesty is beyond question – I have come by certain facts that would have it otherwise.'

'Go on then,' Naomi said. 'Apart from desert the army, steal from a charitable fund, gamble in an illegal club, and kidnap a defenceless infant, what else has the man done? And please, whatever it is, tell me that Lawrence had no part in it.'

Steeling herself, Kate watched Diana Lloyd squeeze her niece's hand.

'My dear girl, Lawrence is entirely without a stain upon his character. On that, you have my word. And, so well concealed has the whole thing been that, as far as I can tell, to this day, he remains ignorant of the whole business.'

'Truly?' Naomi said. 'It would seem hard to believe – they're a small family.'

'I'm certain of it.'

'So, go on then, what has Aubrey done?'

Hardly daring to breathe, Kate felt as though every sinew in her body had pulled itself taut.

'Well… I'm still not sure…'

'Aunt! If it has to do with Baby, you have to tell me. I need to know!'

'Very well. He has gambled away the family fortune.'

In her incredulity, Kate felt her eyes widen.

'N-Not *all* of it, surely?' Naomi eventually stammered.

'More or less all of it, I'm afraid.'

'Aunt! And you know for certain, without a shadow of a doubt, that it's true?'

Very slowly, Diana Lloyd nodded her head. 'Sadly, yes, I do.'

'But how? How could he do such a thing? How could Ralph and Cicely even allow it to happen?'

'Well, it all started quite a while back when Aubrey was first up at university. There, he fell in with a couple of young men – cousins, I believe – who had almost limitless wealth but very little idea of how to behave. That much is widely known because one of them got sent down for his behaviour. I'm referring, of course, to their penchant for gambling – and gambling on a scale that is hard for most of us to comprehend. Anyway, in order to avoid a scandal, Ralph settled Aubrey's debts and, for a while at least, things returned to normal. Sometime later, though, Aubrey was once again in trouble. This time, his debts were rather larger and the creditors less savoury. But, again, Ralph bailed him out, nearly bankrupting himself in the process. Then, for a long time unbeknown to anyone—'

'Don't tell me,' Naomi interrupted her aunt, 'he did it again.'

'He did. This time, though, the debts he ran up were here, in town. In addition, he also… well, let us just say that he *became involved* with a man—'

'A man? What man? I don't under— Oh, good God!'

'—a junior minister of His Majesty's government, as it turned out. And, since *that* little piece of information came to me through a trusted acquaintance, I know it to be utterly reliable.'

'When you say became involved—'

'Yes, I'm afraid it's as bad as you fear.'

By Naomi's side, Kate frowned. But then, when Diana Lloyd continued where she had left off, she felt a nasty taste rising up in the back of her throat. Aubrey, whose shameful secrets were only now coming to light, had invited himself into their home, when all the while... ugh! *And* he'd had the gall to bring back that stranger – that fellow Poundsby, too.

'Dear God. But you say Lawrence knows nothing of this?'

'I have every reason to believe he is entirely ignorant of the whole thing. But I'm afraid that's not even the worst of it.'

'There's *worse*?' Realizing she had just blurted out her disbelief, Kate blushed violently. 'Sorry,' she said. 'Forgive me. I'll take my leave.'

'Nonsense,' Aunt Diana and Naomi said in unison as she made to get up from the sofa.

'My dear, you are part of this family, with all that entails.'

'Yes, do stay,' Naomi urged her. 'Not only are you family but you are my friend – my confidante. Do stay. *Please.*'

Forcing herself to swallow her discomfort, Kate replied with a single nod. She would stay for Naomi. But she would try not to dwell on any nastiness she might be about to hear.

'So, where was I? Oh, yes. By chance or otherwise, it would seem that Aubrey, once again up to his neck in gambling debts, saw an opportunity to get his hands on the sort of money he needed to settle them – by black-mailing the man with whom he had become involved.' At this, Kate felt Naomi's grip on her fingers tighten. 'The problem for Aubrey,' Diana Lloyd continued, 'was that he didn't realize just how well connected the man – his victim – was. And the next thing he knew, Ralph Colborne arrived in town, having been contacted by the fellow's own father.'

'Then what happened?' Naomi asked.

Forgetting her earlier distaste, Kate found that she, too, was desperate to know.

'Obviously, the matter of Aubrey's latest debts came to light. Except that this time the man who had been subject to the blackmail attempt made it clear that unless things were settled to his satisfaction, he would go to the police and have Aubrey arrested. Poor Cicely was beside herself. And, by all accounts, it was she who talked her husband into agreeing to the man's terms.'

'Which were…?'

'Which were that if Aubrey's debts were settled in full, no action would be taken over the matter of the blackmail.'

'Heavens.'

'But, to raise the sum required, Ralph had no choice but to sell Avingham.'

'*What?*' It was something Kate hadn't been expecting to hear, either. 'Are you telling me that the Colbornes no longer live at Avingham?' Naomi asked.

Even to Kate, this was an incredible thing to learn. Aubrey had even mentioned Avingham several times while staying with them.

'No – by virtue of the agreement reached, they still live there. But merely as tenants – they no longer own it. A deal was struck whereby, for a trifling amount, the property was transferred to the aggrieved party on the understanding that Ralph Colborne be permitted to see out his days there.'

'*Ralph* Colborne. Not Cicely?'

'As I understand it, when Ralph dies, the tenancy expires with him. So, no, Cicely would not be able to remain there on her own.'

'So,' Naomi said with a disbelieving shake of her head, 'after all the fuss from Mamma about Aubrey inheriting Avingham Park, he will do no such thing.'

'There is no longer anything to inherit,' Aunt Diana replied. 'To all intents and purposes, Aubrey has already had his inheritance and gambled it away.'

'Clearly, Mamma doesn't know that.'

'No one does, dear. Cicely keeps up a fine pretence, and Ralph is too humiliated to tear down the veil of deceit.'

Sensing that Naomi had just realized something, Kate felt her let go of her hand. 'What is it, ma'am?' she asked.

In response, Naomi made a little scoffing noise. 'As recently as last August, Cicely Colborne was attempting to marry me off to Aubrey, all the while knowing full well how things stood. She must have intended hoodwinking us – me and Mamma. Clearly, she's as evil as Aubrey. Indeed, perhaps that's where he gets it from.'

'I suspect,' Aunt Diana said with a long sigh, 'she thought you might be her way out of the disaster – in the longer term, I mean.'

'Her way out? How? I don't understand.'

'In your mother's desperation to see you marry well – at least, as she thought it at the time – I believe she rather exaggerated your own standing; you know, the scale of your trust. From one or two of the conversations I overheard, I certainly believe it to have been the case.'

'My trust?' Naomi said. 'But it's tiny. Well, in comparison to the Colbornes' woes it is.'

'Yes, I know that. But that's not how your mother saw fit to represent it, especially since *she* had her eyes fixed firmly upon securing Avingham Park for you.'

'While, at the same time,' Naomi observed thoughtfully, 'Cicely Colborne had *her* eyes on my money to alleviate *her* problems. Goodness. I can only suppose she thought that if I married Aubrey, in the absence of any wealth on his part, we would still have some means and, that when Ralph died, and she became homeless, we would take her in. She must have thought the lure of Avingham would see me fall blindly into her trap. Goodness, she really is evil.'

'All rather ghastly, isn't it?'

'Ghastly?' Naomi almost barked. 'I must tell you, Aunt, that I am beside myself with rage.'

'And rightly so, my dear. The only thing is, you can never repeat a word I have told you. Neither of you can. None of this must ever go further than this room.'

For a moment Kate thought she had misheard, Naomi evidently feeling the same.

'What? Why ever not? People should know what sort of family they are.'

'You cannot speak of it because the details were provided to me in confidence. They were disclosed to me purely as a favour on account of your present suffering at Aubrey's hands.'

'But Aunt—'

'I'm afraid I mean it, my dear. Were it not for what Aubrey has done here, I would know none of this myself. In any event, telling the story to others will bring you no advantage. After all, you didn't marry Aubrey—'

'But I might have,' Naomi said, 'especially had Mamma had her way.'

'But she didn't have her way, did she? You exercised your free will.'

'And you're certain that Lawrence knows nothing of this whatsoever?'

'I am. It's why, initially, I held off telling you. It seemed wrong that you should learn of it before he did – to speak of it to you behind his back, as it were.'

'Well, you can't *truly* expect me to keep this secret from him *now*.'

'No,' Diana Lloyd agreed, 'Lawrence will need to know. That said, I feel most strongly that it is not your story to tell. It is something that ought, by rights, to be explained to him by his father. Indeed, although dependent upon how this current matter with Aubrey turns out, I do not see any way that Ralph can now avoid telling him.'

'Hm.'

'Moreover, being party to this information does nothing to get the baby back.'

Falling to silence, the three women simply sat, each apparently reflecting upon the sad truth of Diana Lloyd's statement. For her own part, having been swept along by the unfolding of the tale, Kate realized with a jolt that until that precise moment, the plight of Baby had slipped from her mind. Worse still, the momentary disappearance of such a worry had been a blessed relief; for those few brief minutes, the leaden lump that had been sitting in her stomach had dissolved clean away. Now, though, it was back there, the dreadful burden sitting heavily inside her. Worse still, with no sign that Baby was about to be returned to them, she could see no way that the situation was about to change.

—

'But Naomi, dear, I do feel it would be for the best.'

'For the best? Aunt, there is no *best*. Even if there *were*, I highly doubt it is to be found at Woodicombe House.'

It was the following afternoon, a bright and warm day that, at any other moment in time, would have been suggestive of poplin dresses and picnics in the park, of children playing with pond yachts on the boating lake and ices purchased from gaily painted barrows and then consumed with much giggling and haste. But, in Hartland Street, the cornflower blue of the sky, and the sweet fragrance of the poet's jasmine trailing along the railings at number fourteen, went unnoticed. In this house, on this day, listlessness and gloom continued to prevail.

'My dear—' Aunt Diana began.

'What would I even *do* there?' Naomi wanted to know. 'Spend my mornings selecting flowers from Mr Channer's cutting borders and then poking them into arrangements that no one else would see? Pass the afternoons stitching a baby's smock or sewing a layette for a child I no longer have? Dress for a dinner to be eaten without company? Hm?'

'Whereas sitting here twitching the curtains, watching for movement in the street below and awaiting a knock at the door that might never come is preferable?'

Kneeling alongside the trunk where she was packing the linen bags that contained Naomi's shoes, Kate felt as though both of the viewpoints to-ing and fro-ing above her head held equal merit. As far as she could see, while Hartland Street meant that they were on hand should anything arise, Woodicombe offered the benefits of being distant from Hartland Street and the restorative powers of the fresh sea air.

'It would offer you respite,' Aunt Diana responded, leading Kate to feel a certain satisfaction with her own conclusion.

'The only thing that will bring respite is the return of my baby.'

'Of course, dear,' Diana said. 'And we would both of us move heaven and earth to bring her home to you.'

With that, Naomi turned back from the window. 'All right,' she said, 'so what if I get all the way down there – or indeed, I am still travelling on the train – and Baby is found? What then?'

'In that happy event, the moment you received word from me, you would turn around and come straight back again. It's not as though I'm proposing you travel all the way to the Pyrenees to partake of the curative waters there, splendidly beneficial an idea though that might be.'

'Aunt! Listen to me, I beg you! I'm not going *anywhere*. All the while there is even a chance Baby will be found and brought back to me, I intend staying put. *And*, should it turn out that at the hands of that… that *girl*, my baby has come to harm, then I shall dedicate the rest of my days to hunting her down and throttling the very last ounce of breath from her body.'

In an instant, Diana Lloyd was on her feet and crossing the room to enfold Naomi in her arms. 'There, there, my dear,' she soothed, Naomi's sudden wailing enough to bring tears to Kate's own eyes. 'This is a terrible strain upon all of us, but upon you especially. Thoughts of revenge, understandable although they are, will not ease your burden. They will simply eat away at your insides, poisoning your mind and making you feel even more unwell. And that's not the sort of state you want Lawrence to come home and find you in, is it?' In Diana Lloyd's embrace, Naomi continued to sob noisily. 'Which is why I say that we must get you away from here. Wherever you choose to wait for news, it will not be easy. Please, do not think I make light of your situation. One does not get to leave one's troubles behind solely through journeying to a different place. Trust me, I know that as well as anyone. But one *can* reap a certain solace by being removed from the scene of the crime, as it were.'

'No doubt for some people that's true,' Naomi seemed to pull herself together a little to say. Reaching into her cuff for her handkerchief, she blew her nose. 'But how can I even *think* of leaving here when, at any moment, a constable could arrive bearing news that they have found her?'

Wondering at the point of continuing to pack Naomi's wardrobe, Kate fell still. If Naomi was determined not to go, no one would be able to make her.

'Well, my dear, I shall not force you to do anything against your will,' Diana Lloyd said. Getting up from where she had been kneeling at the trunk, Kate frowned.

Coming from Aunt Diana, this seemed something of a turnabout. 'But I do think you should try to get some rest.' Then, catching Kate's eye, she went on, 'No sense the baby coming back and you being too worn out to care for her, is there? Take a nice warm bath and have an early night. It's what *I'm* going to go home and do. And then, in the morning, we'll all have fresh heads. Much more useful.'

When Diana Lloyd then headed out onto the landing, Kate followed her. 'Yes, ma'am?' she said, reading the look upon her face as one of frustration.

'I think, my dear, that for a while at least, we must let the matter of Woodicombe drop. Tomorrow morning, perhaps make as though to unpack the trunks. Rehang a few gowns, that sort of thing. Let her think she has won out. What is required here, I do believe, is stealth. Let her sleep on it and we'll see how she feels in the morning.'

Kate nodded her understanding. In the circumstances, the suggestion seemed sensible. 'Yes, Mrs Lloyd.' But then, unable to help herself, she lowered her voice further and asked, 'Do you think, ma'am, that the baby *is* going to be found?'

Diana Lloyd's first response was to shake her head. 'I'm afraid I have no idea. All I can do is make a nuisance of myself with the chief inspector to ensure that her plight is not forgotten.'

It wasn't the answer for which she had been hoping. But it was at least truthful. After all, in circumstances such as these, what use was false hope?

–

'I simply can't sleep.'

'No, ma'am, nor I,' Kate replied to Naomi's announcement.

'I woke ages ago.'

'So did I.'

Having eventually persuaded Naomi to take a bath and get into bed, Kate, too had tried to get some sleep. After what felt like hours of tossing and turning, she had eventually fallen into a fitful doze, awaking each time to find that the hour-hand on her alarm clock had barely moved. Then, from the floor below her had come the creak of floorboards and the sound of Naomi drawing back the curtains at her window. The disturbance had come as a relief, giving her reason to get up, put on her robe, and see whether there was anything Naomi wanted.

'I had hoped it would be lighter than this,' Naomi said then, apparently unsurprised to find that Kate was also awake.

'It will be soon, ma'am,' she said, taking in the state of Naomi's bed. 'But how about, in the meantime, I tidy your sheets and plump up these pillows, and then you get back in? We can't be up at this hour.'

'I shan't sleep. I haven't all night.'

'No, I know. But get back into bed and I'll sit with you.' As ploys went, she knew it was as good as transparent, but she was loath to go and brew tea and make a proper start on the morning at such an early hour; it would make the rest of the day stretch endlessly – especially if there was still no news.

Surprised when Naomi dutifully climbed back into bed, Kate crossed the room and reached to draw the curtains back together. Away to the right, she glimpsed the tiniest streak of dawn just showing above the rooftops.

Returning to Naomi's bedside, she sank into the easy chair, still standing where it had when Diana Lloyd had occupied it yesterday afternoon. Thank goodness for Aunt Diana, she found herself thinking as she wrapped her robe over her nightgown: Pamela Russell's presence wouldn't have been – *hadn't* been – anywhere near as helpful or as calming. Even faced with what they had gone on to learn, she couldn't imagine Mrs Russell seeing fit to accept that she had been wrong about Aubrey and the Colbornes.

With Naomi then falling still, and the room feeling warm and dark about her, she let out a little sigh. Wearily, she closed her eyes. She wouldn't go back to sleep, but she would just rest a moment. Just for a moment…

–

Rap-a-tap tap. Rap-a-tap tap.

Reaching to pull herself upright, Kate felt her hand strike something that turned out to be the arm of a chair. Disoriented, she strained to make sense of where she was. Naomi's room? She had fallen asleep in Naomi's room? Rolling her eyes, she took in her surroundings. Beyond the fabric of the curtains she could see daylight. Whatever was the hour? She wriggled her shoulders, trying to rid herself of a crick to her neck and a woolliness to her thoughts.

Tap tap tap.

And was that someone at the door? Was that what had woken her? Lord alive – had she even remembered to bolt it?

Blearily, she got to her feet, turning an ankle beneath her and cursing at the pain.

From the bed, Naomi stirred. 'Kate?' she asked. 'What is it?'

'Nothing, ma'am. Seems I fell asleep in the chair. Try an' go back to sleep.' Above the rustling of starched linens, she heard Naomi mumble incoherently.

Pulling the door swiftly shut behind her, Kate hurried down the stairs, pale sunlight through the arch of glazed panes above the front door illuminating the otherwise shadowy hallway. She just had to hope that whoever had been knocking was still there. She tried to think who it might be. Aunt Diana? Unlikely at this hour; the hall clock showed it was barely six. And it hadn't sounded like the urgent summoning of the police; they pounded away as though needing to awaken the dead. No, the knocking, unless she had dreamt it, had sounded almost apologetic.

Arriving at the door, she drew a breath, slid back the bolt, and turned the latch. Warily, and thinking to smooth a hand over her hair, she opened it just a crack, movement at her feet causing her to look sharply down. Crouched on the doorstep was someone in dark clothing, fussing with what looked to be a bundle of rags.

Before she could fashion her puzzlement into words, the form shot up to full height. 'Jeez, Missus. *You* took your time. Thought you wasn't going to answer at all.'

'Nancy?' she ventured, willing her eyes to make sense of the sight before her.

'That toad Aubrey lied to me,' the girl announced matter-of-factly. Bending back down and picking up the bundle, she thrust it towards Kate's middle. 'So I brought 'er back. She didn't come to no 'arm. Swear to God. I saw to it.'

From behind her in the hallway came the sound of slippers shuffling across the tiled floor and, when she turned to look over her shoulder, it was to see Naomi coming towards her, tying the sash of her robe about her waist.

'Kate? Who is it? Is that oh… oh…' Almost snatching the child from Kate's arms, Naomi cradled it to her chest. 'Baby, oh, Baby! You're home.'

In that moment distracted, Kate turned back to see Nancy tiptoeing down the steps to the street. 'Wait!' she called, setting off after her, no regard to the state of her undress.

'What – so you can call the rozzers? Not bloomin' likely.'

'No, please,' she called, catching up to the girl and reaching for her arm. 'We're not minded to get you into trouble. We just wanted the baby back. It's Mr Aubrey we want to see caught. Please, come back inside a moment and tell us what you know. *Please. You* mightn't have meant her harm but for certain *he* did.'

Snatching back her sleeve, the young woman stared back at her. To Kate, she still looked like a slightly less destitute version of some of the women at St. Ursula's.

'Two minutes. I'll stay two minutes to tell you what I know but then I'm off. I ain't waiting around on the off-chance.'

'No, all right,' she said, belatedly wondering as to the wisdom of bringing the woman back into the house anyway. She was, though, their only real chance of finding out what Aubrey had intended. More importantly, she was their only chance to establish where he might be and thus have him apprehended.

When the two women returned, Naomi looked up, her expression one of alarm. 'What's *she* doing back here?' she demanded, edging back along the hallway.

'She's come back to tell us what happened,' Kate explained, beckoning Nancy inside.

'No funny stuff, mind,' the girl warned. 'One whiff you've sent for the bill and I'm off. Then you'll never catch 'im.'

'We shan't summon the police,' she said, beckoning with her arm. 'I promise you that. Please come in off the doorstep.'

Uneasily, the girl stepped inside. 'Leave the door wide,' she instructed. 'Or I won't stay.'

'Yes, I can do that,' she reassured the fidgety young woman, trying to sound less fearful than she felt. 'We'll leave it wide and you can stay right where you are. Then, if you want to, you can check both ways along the street, see?'

With that, the girl glanced sharply in both directions. 'I come across your Aubrey on a street corner in Mayfair,' she announced without further ado. 'Tells me 'is name is Archibald Cole and that he's looking for someone to 'elp 'im out of a scrape. It's only when I get here and hear you call 'im Aubrey, I realize he's lied to me about who 'e is. Not that it matters to *me*. *My* real name's not Nancy.'

Kate felt Naomi come to stand close behind her. Over her shoulder, she could hear her shallow breathing.

'Did he say what sort of scrape?' Naomi asked.

'He didn't say, and where trouble's concerned, I know better than to ask.'

'I see.'

'Any road, he tells me he's about to leave for New York on a steam ship but that he's owed money. Lots of it. If I'll help him get it, he says he'll pay my passage, too.'

'To New York?' Naomi queried.

'That's what 'e said. New York. Couple of days' time. Some fancy great vessel.'

'And where did he have to go for this money he was owed?' Naomi enquired, moving to stand directly alongside Kate. 'Or didn't he tell you that, either?'

Nancy shook her head. 'Nah. Didn't say.'

'And you weren't in the least bit curious?'

The woman shrugged. 'Look, I got me own troubles – my *light-fingered* ways, if you know what I mean, have seen me up before the beak once too often for comfort. One more brush with them and they'll put me in clink. Chance of getting away to New York, no questions asked, suited me just fine. So, when I asked 'im what I'd 'ave to do, he said go wiv 'im to an 'ouse in Marylebone an' get a child. Then all I 'ad to do was look after it for day or two while he got the money he was owed. Once he got it, he'd buy me a ticket and we'd be away. Told me if I didn't ask too many questions while I was about it, he'd give me a bit extra on top. Me lips are sealed, says I. 'Course, didn't know the child was going to be such a tiny mite. Nor did 'e say anyfink about stealing it away from its Ma... or whatever. But, in my shoes, New York's New York, right?'

'Indeed,' Naomi answered encouragingly.

'An' then, when we got 'ere, an' he let himself in wiv a key, ordinary as you like, I thinks to meself, must be he's fallen out with his wife. And what's that to me, right?'

'So then what happened?' Kate asked. As evil plans went, everything the woman had outlined thus far did seem to bear Aubrey's hallmark.

'Once we've got the baby, he takes me to this place a few miles over. Never been round those parts before—'

'A house?'

The girl shrugged. 'Empty one. Well, full of posh fings but no folk in it – that sort of empty. He tells me to wait there. Well, I already seen him hold that knife to your throat, so I do as he says. Hour or so later, 'e comes back with food and some stuff for the baby. Tells me to take care of it best way I can. Won't be for long, 'e says to me. Then off 'e goes again. Gone to fetch the money, I thinks to meself. So, I waits. But then 'e don't come back. But I've got the baby, right, so I reckon he'll need to come back sooner or later, and so, I wait some more. Next day, though, it dawns on me – I've been had. He's got his money and legged it without paying up. Either that, or he's been nicked. Not much I can do about it either way – *he's* gone but *I'm* left with the baby.'

'And when was this?' Naomi asked.

'Last night. So, since it was already nigh-on dark, and seein' as I didn't know where we was, I stayed on there a bit. I did think about just running off – you know, leave the baby an' hope it'd be found. But I couldn't do it. Couldn't leave it. Besides, I thought of you. Thought you'd be going near out of your mind with worry. So, while it was still dark, and thinking the bill might be on the lookout by now, I set off to find me way back here again. Bloody hours it's taken me, Missus. Bloody hours. You try finding some street in Marylebone when you only went there the once and don't know where you are to start with. *And* before it's barely light.'

'Kate,' Naomi said, suddenly decisive.

'Ma'am?'

'Please go and fetch my purse.'

'Ma'am?'

'My purse, Kate. Please go and get it. On account of the behaviour of my brother-in-law, this young lady has been to put to a good deal of inconvenience. The least I can do is make sure she isn't out of pocket.'

She stared down at the floor. For so many reasons, this seemed entirely wrong. 'Your purse. Yes, ma'am.'

Naomi was going to give the girl money? For bringing back a baby she'd *stolen*? Resigned to the fact, she trudged up the stairs. While she didn't think the girl deserved to be thrown into gaol – after all, they'd all of them fallen prey to Aubrey's charade – neither did she think she deserved to be rewarded. But Naomi was free to do with her own money as she wanted.

When, with a long sigh, she returned to the hallway, it was to see Naomi standing where she had left her, with Nancy – or whatever her real name was – extending one of her fingers towards the baby.

'Pretty little thing, ain't she?' the girl observed.

'Ma'am,' she said, wary of the way the woman seemed so friendly all of a sudden; she still wouldn't be surprised to find that this was yet part of Aubrey's ruse.

'Take Baby, please,' Naomi said, handing her the child and accepting her purse from her as she did so. 'Thank you, Nancy, for doing the right thing.' Opening the clasp, she took out a couple of coins and pressed them into the girl's hand. With no wish to know the sum involved, Kate looked away. 'You have a good heart,' she heard Naomi add. 'Please, heed your conscience as you have done today and try to stay out of trouble.'

'Do me best, Missus. But you know how it is.'

When, without further ado, Nancy went out through the front door and down the steps to the pavement, Kate went to stand under the porch, watching until the girl had walked all the way to the end of the street. Only when she had seen her turn the corner and disappear from view did she heave a sigh and close the door behind her. Then, just in case, she turned the key in the lock and shot the bolt across at the top.

'Well then,' Naomi said as though what had just happened required no further consideration. 'All's well that ends well.'

Completely overwhelmed – and far too exhausted to invite any sort of argument with her – she nodded. 'It would seem so, ma'am, yes.'

'Now, though, this little girl needs feeding. And she needs getting out of this tatty piece of blanket and into something nice and clean and snuggly and warm. Don't you, Baby? Yes, you do. That's right. And then, once I've done all of that and put her down, I might go back to bed and try to get some proper sleep.'

'Proper sleep,' she echoed Naomi's remark. 'Won't that be lovely.'

–

'Kate, for goodness' sake, do hurry along. I have no wish to cut it fine for our train.'

From where she was standing on the pavement, Kate peered in through the window of the cab. Despite sounding impatient, the expression on Naomi's face as she cradled Baby was one of utter contentment.

Unable to help smiling, she turned back to Aunt Diana, waiting to see them off. 'Thank you, ma'am,' she said, 'for being of such help to me these last weeks – what with Aubrey, and the baby, and, well, my own... quandary.'

'Think nothing of it, my dear,' Diana Lloyd replied, bringing a hand to rest upon the sleeve of Kate's jacket. 'It is I who should thank *you*.'

''Tis kind of you to say so,' she said, but then, lowering her voice went on, 'Truly, I am most grateful to you for listening to me speak of my turmoil about... well, you know, things regarding Luke. This last day or so, I've thought a great deal about what you advised. And, well, I think the time has come to be honest with him.'

'Eminently sensible, my dear. Rarely is it wrong to be true to your heart.'

'Yes. That's what I've come to see.'

'Good. Now, that aside for a moment, please do promise me that once you get to Devon, you will try to have a bit of a rest.'

Somewhat doubtfully, she nodded. 'I do promise I'll *try* to.'

Peering into the cab, Diana Lloyd then called across to her niece, 'Enjoy your break, my dear. And give my love to Lawrence when he arrives.'

She smiled. 'Thank you for that, as well. Without your letter, I doubt the army would be letting him come home on leave.'

'Well, if having one's wife miscarry a baby and then be subjected to the unbalanced behaviour of one's absent-without-leave brother doesn't qualify one for a short spell of compassionate leave, I don't know what does!'

'Kate!' Naomi called again. 'Aunt Diana! Do stop being such windbags, the pair of you. We're in danger of missing our train!'

Kate returned Aunt Diana's grin. 'And this new nurse will be waiting for us on the platform?'

'Miss Maylis, yes, she will be.'

'Thank heavens.' Reaching to kiss Aunt Diana on the cheek, she climbed into the cab. 'Goodbye, then.'

'Telephone me when you get there.'

'We will. I promise.'

With the cab then beginning to draw away, and Aunt Diana waving to them from the kerb, she let out a long sigh. Finally, they were on their way. At last, she could relax.

Seated next to her, Naomi also gave a little sigh. 'Well then,' she said. 'Here we go, my dearest little Esme, off to get you your first breaths of fresh Devon air. And then, in just a few short days' time, to introduce you to your new Papa.'

Having barely got herself comfortable, Kate blinked several times in quick succession. Which of those two revelations did she tackle first? '*Papa?*' she opted for, it seeming the more momentous of the two. Was Naomi really proposing that this little girl grow up thinking of her and Lawrence as her parents? Had she learned nothing from the fallout of the deceit spun by Mabel and Edith?

'Oh, please don't look at me like that!' Naomi admonished her. 'For now, while she is too young to understand otherwise, I am going to suggest to Lawrence that she calls us Mamma and Papa. And that she calls you Aunt

Kate – because, to her, that's what you are. For heaven's sake, I mean it – do stop looking at me so aghast! I shan't conceal the truth about her *real* parents. Truly, I give you my word that the moment she is able to understand what happened to them, I shall explain everything to her. And then, should she no longer wish to think of us in those terms, I shall abide by her decision.'

She tried to smile. Fine words, but would Naomi be able to stand by them? Would she not find it easier to let the child grow up as *she* had done, never suspecting for one moment that her entire life was a lie, the moment never quite right to disabuse her?

'I'm minded Mr Lawrence will be astonished to discover he now has a baby in his household,' she said, trying to ignore her concerns about Naomi's decision.

'And delighted, too, I should hope. Once the shock subsides.'

'And *Esme*?' she asked, it being the other surprise.

'Yes,' Naomi replied, raising her voice in order to make herself heard over the commotion of the traffic as they headed away towards Waterloo. 'I've decided upon Esme because it means *loved*. And love is something this little girl is never going to want for.'

Smiling more genuinely this time, Kate dabbed at the corner of her eyes. 'Just so long as she's loved and not spoiled.'

'On that front, Aunt Kate, I'm afraid I make you no promises.'

'No, ma'am.'

'*Naomi*. Please, Kate, I truly believe the time has come for you to stop calling me *ma'am*. I know I said I would leave it up to you but, after all that has happened, matters between us have come to feel very different. In my hour of need, you put yourself out for me. Without a single moment's complaint, not only did you care for me but you were so endlessly patient. To my mind, that is less the behaviour of a housekeeper and more that of a devoted sister. And, since this war has taught me that one should take nothing for granted and leave nothing unsaid, from now on, that is how I should like to think of you – as my sister.'

Her emotions already close to spilling over, the smile Kate managed was a wobbly one. 'Thank you, Naomi. That means a lot to me.'

'Right. Well, then, though by some standards we might be an unconventional little family, it's onwards we go. To Woodicombe and happier times!'

Only by *some* standards? Unable to help it, she smiled. 'Yes,' she replied, her eyes brimming with tears. 'To happier times.'

My Dear Husband.

Settled into her seat on the train – the very capable-seeming Miss Maylis taking care of Esme, Naomi smiling serenely, and the lush Surrey countryside hurtling past the window – Kate put down her pen and tried to decide how to go about setting down her thoughts to Luke. The only thing she knew for certain was that she had to be honest with him. Unfortunately, recognizing that didn't make the composing of her letter any more straightforward! What was it Aunt Diana had said to her? Rarely is it wrong to be true to your heart? Then true to it, she would try to be.

Resting somewhat awkwardly on the writing case Naomi had bought her, she picked up her pen and examined its nib. And then she started to write.

You won't never believe some of the things that have been happening hereabouts. I can scarce take it all in myself. But more of that by the by. First off, I want to tell you that I am well. I also want to say that I am sorry I have not written to you in a while but, as you will soon gather, much has been happening. She had been going to add 'to prevent me' – but, as it wasn't strictly true, she decided against it.

Now that I have time, she began again, *I want to tell you of some of the things that have become important to me, and to tell you of my hopes for how they might continue to be a part of my days once you come home. After you have read of them, happen you will write back and tell me what you think. That way, we will each know how the other feels. After so long apart, there will surely be things upon which we no longer see to eye to eye, but I do believe it is best to be honest with each other and not let differences of opinion go unsaid, only for them to one day come as a surprise or cause resentment. In this way, perhaps neither of us will be left expecting different things of each other or be disappointed by what we find come the day we are back together for good. So, let me start by telling you more about what I do at St. Ursula's…*

Beyond the window of their compartment, towns and villages flicked past and, when those gradually thinned out, farmland and rolling countryside did the same. Later, with those giving way to the dusty chalk plains of Wiltshire with their deep valleys and almost hidden hamlets, she continued to write, oblivious to all of it until, finally, her fingers cramping from the effort, she sat back and looked up. Across from her, Naomi was holding Esme, her face a picture of contentment. Unable to overlook the familiar feeling of envy it brought on, she hastily looked down again. *Honesty.* Having chosen it as her watchword, she knew she must apply it to everything – the innermost workings of her heart and mind included. And so, once again picking up her pen, she wrote, *Quite unexpectedly, I find I do envy Naomi with baby Esme. So, let us hope that one day, we shall know the joy of children of our own.* There. If expressing such deeply buried thoughts didn't count as honesty, then she didn't know what did.

Staring back down, she finished by writing, *Please do keep yourself safe and well, and come back to me real soon, your loving wife Kate.*

With great care, she turned the final page of her letter onto her small square of blotting paper and gently smoothed across it with her hand. Having finally admitted to her feelings, she was surprised by just how different she felt. Lighter. Gladdened. At peace.

The only thing left for her to do now, she thought as she stared out through the window, was pray for this wretched war to be over, for Luke to come home unscathed, and for the two of them to be finally able to get on with making a proper start to being wed.

'Would Aunt Kate like to take a turn at holding Esme for a while?' Naomi chose that moment to look across at her and ask. 'Now that she has finished scribbling away like a demon?'

Setting aside her writing box, she smiled and held out her arms. 'Of course I would,' she replied. 'After all, who in their right mind wouldn't want to coo and cuddle with such a beautiful little baby, eh?'

Acknowledgements

To Kiran Kataria, I say thank you for your invaluable support and advice. To Laura McCallen, I say thank you for coaxing the best from me. And, to my long-suffering husband, I say thank you for the way you always manage to lift my spirits, no matter the depth of my frustration or doubt.

The Woodicombe House Sagas